PRAISE FOR *NO BEAST SO FIERCE*

'. . . The most compelling quality of *No Beast So Fierce* is that, solidly rooted in his own experiences, it explores the nature of the criminal mind with almost blinding authenticity. Bunker is obviously a man of unusual gifts honed under circumstances that would destroy most men . . .'

Los Angeles Times

'. . . A gripping and harrowing read . . .'

Daily Mail

'. . . The best first person crime novel I have ever read . . .'

Quentin Tarantino

'. . . Quite simply, one of the great crime novels of the past 30 years . . .'

James Ellroy

PRAISE FOR *THE ANIMAL FACTORY*

'*The Animal Factory* joins Solzhenitsyn's *One Day in the Life of Ivan Denisovich* and George Jackosn's *Soledad Brother* in the front rank of prison literature . . . a stone classic.'

Time Out

PRAISE FOR *LITTLE BOY BLUE*

'A scalding experience – and a literary triumph in the tradition of Dreiser, Farrell and James Jones. This is an important book . . .'

Roderick Thorp

Also by the same author

Death Row Breakout Stories

The Animal Factory

Little Boy Blue

Dog Eat Dog

Mr Blue

Stark

EDWARD BUNKER

no beast so fierce

no exit press

This edition published in 2008, reprinted 2013, by No Exit Press,
P.O.Box 394, Harpenden, Herts, AL5 1XJ
www.noexit.co.uk

A CIP catalogue record for this book is available from the British Library.

EAN 978-1-84243-266-2

6 8 10 9 7 5

Typeset by Ellipsis Books Limited, Glasgow
Printed in the UK by Clays Ltd., St Ives plc

To Louise Fazenda Wallis,
who gave an eighteen-year-old convict,
a typewriter and friendship

"No beast so fierce but knows some touch of pity"
—*Richard III*, Act 1, Scene 2

Introduction

by William Styron
1988

Edward Bunker is one of a small handful of American writers who have created authentic literature out of their experiences as criminals and prisoners. Now fifty-five years old, Bunker has been out of prison since 1975, but before that time he spent nearly all of the years of his life, except those of his earliest childhood, behind bars. That is to say, until his early forties Bunker was far better acquainted with incarceration as a way of life than he was with even limited freedom. That this career, so practically devoid of any of the normal inducements toward education and self-realization, could have produced writing of any kind is most unusual; that it yielded not only *No Beast So Fierce* but two other novels of genuine literary achievement (so far) is astonishing, placing Edward Bunker among the tiny band of American prisoner-writers whose work possesses integrity, craftsmanship, and moral passion in sufficient measure to claim our serious attention. In order to understand the nature of Bunker's extraordinary accomplishments, it is necessary to recount some of the details of his life, which was one of deprivation and violence, indeed, an existence so close to nihilism—at least in the mind of the bourgeois reader—as to make almost totally implausible any idea of creativity or the eventual blossoming of a literary career.

Bunker was born and reared in, of all places, Hollywood, California. Unlike the majority of American criminals, he was born white. His father was a stagehand in legitimate theaters around Los Angeles and occasionally found employment in the movie studios—he once worked for the Hal Roach organization during the filming of the famous *Our Gang* comedies. His mother was a professional dancer, and performed as a chorus girl in Busby Berkeley movies. Alcoholism drove Bunker's father into a state hospital and the couple were divorced when Eddie was four. Exacerbated by the hard times of the Great Depression, the boy's life followed the pattern of so many others that are the product of alcoholism and broken families. He was in and out of foster homes and military schools, from which he began to run away with determination augmented by an obstinate anti-authoritarian streak well developed even at that early age. At eleven he was committed briefly to Camarillo State Hospital for observation, and a year later he was sent to the juvenile reform school at Whittier. He made his escape, and when caught was sent to a much tougher school designed for unruly boys four or five years older. Here he spent a year or so and at fourteen was paroled. Twenty-nine days into freedom he was caught trying to rob a liquor store and was shot (though not seriously wounded) by the owner. This crime gained Bunker a sentence to the youth prison at Lancaster, even though he was considerably younger than the legally mandated age of eighteen to twenty-five. Throughout this period, Bunker was consistently thrown into an environment with older criminals. After having stabbed a guard at Lancaster, he was taken to the Los Angeles County Jail, where at fifteen he was placed in the tank reserved for notorious cases. His companions included several murderers awaiting the death penalty. Because of his age, and because his lawyer, the celebrated Al Matthews, who took the case pro bono, was able to show that correctional officers had abused Bunker on prior occasions, the judge deemed him too young for San Quentin and gave him a county jail sentence with probation. Proceedings were suspended. He was set free.

It was while he was briefly at large that Eddie was befriended by Mrs Hal Wallis, wife of the renowned film producer (*Casablanca*,

Becket, and many others) and herself a onetime comedienne in Mack Sennett's *Keystone Comedies*. Louise Fazenda Wallis made efforts to steer Eddie in the direction of probity and worthiness, but her concern came to naught. His friends, except for Louise Wallis, were reform school graduates and confirmed professional criminals. Bunker, now sixteen, began selling marijuana and was enthusiastically engaged in boosting (professional shoplifting) and learning to play short con games such as The Match and The Strap and Laying The Note. He was delivering some marijuana when a pair of detectives flagged him down. A wild chase ensued through Los Angeles streets; the automobile he was driving caromed off three cars and hit a mail truck head-on before he was captured. The judge was still unwilling to send a sixteen-year-old to San Quentin and gave him a year in the county jail and more probation. He promptly escaped.

At this point Bunker's luck ran out. Rather, the calendar said he was seventeen—still not eighteen, but old enough. For the escape and the assault on the Lancaster guard, he was sentenced to two concurrent six-month-to-ten-year terms, and he was sent to San Quentin.

It was during the four-and-a-half-year stay at San Quentin that Bunker discovered books and began to read and write. Louise Wallis sent him a Royal portable typewriter and a subscription to the *New York Times* Sunday edition and *Book Review*. In his excited exploration of literature, he became a voracious reader, absorbing four or five books a week, ranging from a two-volume *Military History of the Western World* to collections of short stories from *The New Yorker* to novels by Thomas Wolfe, Faulkner, Dreiser, Hemingway, and Dostoevsky—and others equally or less celebrated. He also wrote a novel, which he later regarded as very bad, and many short stories, all unpublished.

When released on parole, he returned to the outside world with serious intentions of going straight, and once again he was taken under the wing of Louise Wallis, who obtained a job for her protégé at a nearby boys' home, where she was the foremost benefactress;

there he was employed as a combination chauffeur of boys, pool supervisor, study hall tutor, and counselor. Unfortunately, his protector began suffering severe depression and became dysfunctional, and Bunker lost his only anchor in a precarious world. Now twenty-three, he tried to obtain such legitimate jobs as story analyst or reader at various movie studios, but because of his criminal record he had no luck. Realizing that he had been not only locked up, but locked out of society, he resolved, as he has said, "to get by on my wits," which at first meant selling used sports cars as a front while planning crimes in the back. He conceived schemes for robberies that were executed by others. "These guys were heisting liquor stores on impulse," he recalls. "I laid things out so they could make some money." He also planned to organize Hollywood call girls by extorting the pimps and madams to pay him protection. He lived this way for four years. By then he had drifted away from his relationship with Louise Wallis. Finally, caught in a forgery and check passing scheme, he was sentenced once again to San Quentin for an indeterminate term of six months to fourteen years. This was Bunker's longest imprisonment, and one that did not terminate until he had served seven years. During this period he continued to read widely and to write with passion and amazing industry, producing four unpublished novels and many short stories. Lacking the money for postage, he often sold his blood to make up the needed amounts to send the stories to magazines. He recalls this interlude as one of near madness—so long was the sentence in terms of the crime, forgery usually being considered a minor felony. Worst of all, the sentence was meted out a year at a time, so he never knew whether he would be paroled in six months or six years, or anything in between.

No Beast So Fierce deals largely with the rage and frustration which the book's protagonist, like Bunker, feels when, on release from prison, he faces at best the indifference—and at worst the hatred and hostility—of the outside world. One of the sharpest memories Bunker retains of that time is how, after years of wearing the ample prison brogans, his new dressout shoes caused severe blistering of his feet. He wrote over two hundred letters in application for legitimate jobs—but received not a single answer, his prison record acting effectively as his curse. Such is the fate of most ex-convicts in America, for whom the expiation of sin through incarceration does not usually serve, in the eyes of society, as meaningful redemption. A true outcast, Bunker fell once again into crime. One night, after having burglarized a floor safe in a bar, he was arrested following a high-speed automobile chase.

At the moment of arrest, he feigned insanity, claiming he was born in 1884 and that he had warned Roosevelt about the Japanese attack on Pearl Harbor. During the arraignment, he told the judge that the Catholic Church was trying to put a radio in his brain. Proceedings were suspended pending a psychiatric hearing. The psychiatrists who examined Bunker found him to be an "acute, chronic schizophrenic paranoid with auditory hallucinations and delusions of persecution." So successful was this ruse that he was sent to the prison at Vacaville, where he was deemed a high security risk, a threat Bunker was at pains to exploit by taking every opportunity he could to loudly babble at the walls.

Eventually returned to Los Angeles for trial on the safe burglary charge, he made bail and remained free for a year. While on the streets, he shuttled back and forth between Los Angeles and San Francisco, managing what he now refers to as a "little drug empire." At this point, to augment his income, he decided to rob a prosperous little Beverly Hills bank. The ensuing series of coincidences might have possessed comic overtones had the outcome not been so dire. Unknown to him, Bunker's car, at the time he set out to rob the bank, had been secretly wired with a radio device by narcotics agents, who expected the "beeper" to allow them to trail their dupe to a drug transaction. Bunker, however, armed and prepared to commit a robbery, and now followed in his car not only by motorized agents but also by a helicopter, led the officers to the very door of the bank, where pandemonium ensued as the thwarted robber was suddenly recognized, pursued, and, after a long chase by car, caught at gunpoint and severely beaten. This time the outlook was truly grim. He tried suicide. A three-time loser, Bunker was sentenced to five years for the bank robbery and six years for drug conspiracy, the terms to run concurrently.

There our story might have ended—that of another wretched misfit swallowed up in the living death of institutional retribution—were it not for the saving grace of art. For it must be remembered that even during his life of crime Bunker had toiled at being a writer. His first novel, *No Beast So Fierce*, was accepted for publication while he was awaiting trial.

He was now in the federal penal system because of the bank robbery and narcotics charges, and found himself packed off to serve his time at the McNeil Island federal penitentiary in Puget Sound, Washington. While there, he once again displayed his anti-authoritarian rage and refused to let himself be housed in a ten-man cell. For this revolt he was transported to the most fearsome prison in America, the hulking lockup at Marion, Illinois, which supplanted Alcatraz as the fortress where the nation confines its worst felons, a place in which six hundred guards oversee three hundred inmates. Still, while imprisoned in this place, Bunker continued to write. His second novel, *The Animal Factory*, was completed there. (A third novel, *Little Boy Blue*, appeared in 1982.) Meanwhile, and most importantly in terms of his writing career and his eventual fate, the year 1973 saw the publication of *No Beast So Fierce*; it was received with excellent reviews and considerable attention. It should be pointed out, however, that by this time Bunker was already a prison legend and his fame had extended to the outside world. He had written angry articles for *The Nation*. A searing essay he had penned concerning the racial crisis in American prisons had been featured in *Harper's Magazine* and announced prominently on its cover; its thesis—that the irreconcilable enmity between blacks and whites in prison would certainly lead to catastrophe— was a warning that evoked wide concern. This article and the publication of No *Beast So Fierce* were instrumental in gaining his parole in 1975. He has serenely remained outside the walls in the years since.

Bunker presently lives with his wife in Los Angeles, where he continues to write fiction and where he has obtained notable success as a screenwriter. In 1978, No *Beast So Fierce* was made into a film entitled *Straight Time*, starring Dustin Hoffman. The film was not a commercial success and suffered critical neglect, rather mysteriously, since it is a taut and exceedingly well made work which explores the themes of crime and punishment with great insight. In 1985, Bunker was co-author of the screenplay of *The Runaway Train*, a gripping drama about escaped felons from an Alaska prison; it was a critical and commercial hit and gained Oscar nominations for its stars, Jon Voight and Eric Roberts. Bunker has adapted well to civilian life after his many years of violence and desperation. His attitude and demeanor bespeak the composure of a man who is at peace with himself after a lifetime of existential dread such as the average law-abiding citizen can only distantly imagine. Of medium height, compact and muscular, he still has a tough and streetwise expression, the face of a man who has known cruelty and suffering; but his eyes twinkle; the initial appearance of ferocity is softened by a quality both wise and benign. Reserved, almost shy in manner, he can become animated and powerfully articulate; his intellectual ability, which possesses scope as well as nimbleness, is all the more impressive for being the product of passionate self-education. The letters he writes—and he writes dozens out of the habit formed in the loneliness of prison cells—are splendid models of the epistolary art, shrewd, discursive, witty, beautifully expressed, and often profound. Edward Bunker was dealt a rotten hand at the beginning of his life, and his days thereafter were largely those of a victim in society's brutalizing institutions. That he emerged from these dungeons not a brute but an artist with a unique and compelling voice is a tribute to his own invincible will, besides being a sweet victory by the artist himself over society and its contempt for the outcast. In *No Beast So Fierce* readers will be able to discover urgent truths about crime and punishment—and therefore about our ultimate concern with freedom—set down by a vigorous and important writer.

Part One

In every cry of every man
In every infant's cry of fear,
In every voice, in every ban,
The mind forg'd manacles I hear.
                              William Blake

1

I SAT on the lidless toilet at the rear of the cell, shining the hideous, bulb-toed shoes that were issued to those being released. Through my mind ran an exultant chant, "I'll be a free man in the morning." But for all the exultation, the joy of leaving after eight calendars in prison was not unalloyed. My goal in buffing the ugly shoes was not so much to improve their appearance as to relieve tension. I was more nervous in facing release on parole than I had been on entering so long ago. It helped slightly to know that such apprehensiveness was common, though often denied, by men to whom the world outside was increasingly vague as the years passed away. Enough years in prison and a man would be as ill-equipped to handle the demands of freedom as a Trappist monk thrown into the maelstrom of New York City. At least the monk would have his faith to sustain him, while the former prisoner would possess memory of previous failure, of prison—and the incandescent awareness of being an "ex-convict", a social outcast.

I finished with the shoes, set them beneath the bunk and stood up. The cell was small, less than five feet wide. The bunk occupied so much space that my shoulder brushed against the wall as I passed by the bunk toward the front. How many hours had I spent in this cell? From four in the afternoon until seven in the morning, for eight long years. It was beyond computing in my mind. Now the cell was especially barren. I'd given away my small collection of books, the braided throw rug, the soap, shaving cream and toothpaste—everything. "Aw fuck it," I muttered meaninglessly, without object in mind. I looked out through the bars—thirteen of them, set so close together that only a hand and wrist would pass through. Around this cell were five hundred others, most of them containing two prisoners (I'd angled a single cell after five years) locked down for the night. A typewriter clattered nearby: a letter home or a petition for habeas corpus. Live steam in a pipe thunked and clanked. But the loudest sound was several convicts entertaining themselves with a game of the dozens. It had been going on for half an hour but only now caught my attention.

"Say, motherfucker!" one called.

"What the fuck do you want, asshole?"

"There's a flick of your mama in today's *Chronicle*."

"I didn't know you read the society page."

"It's in the sports section. She's wearin' boxin' gloves and a head-guard, gonna fight Liston for the title. She wrote a poem, too. Wanna dig it?"

"Fuck your mother, punk!"

"Man, cough up the poem," someone else yelled.

"Here we go," the poet said. "'I'm the Lady White Hope / My pussy's so long I use it for a jump rope / I'll beat that spook into a fit / I've got dynamite in my dukes and muscles in my shit / I'll wipe that chimp like a chump / When I finish with him, his face is gonna be one big bump / I'm the Lady White Hope / I'm so bad I wipe my ass on pictures of the pope.' How's that sound, brother?" the poet finished—amid laughter.

"Look, dick breath motherfucker. Get off my mama's back or I'm gonna put your pedigree on the tier."

"I'm your daddy, punk."

"My ass. You're the result of a few drops of syphilis from a bulldog's dick rammed in your transvestite father's ass. You shot shit out and hatched on a hot rock."

A Negro voice full of anger interrupted. "You honkies better ease up on them 'spooks' an' things."

I'd been expecting this response, and my stomach went tight though I was uninvolved and leaving in the morning.

"Fuck you, nigger!" someone else yelled.

"Where you live an' we'll see in the mawnin'?"

"Yeah, honky redneck motherfucker!" another Negro yelled. "What's your cell number?"

The cell block was silent. Murders had come from less than this.

"It's my *room*, for your information. And if you're inquiring about my address, my dear mother warned me against having anything to do with ghetto riff-raff."

The reply, so unusual for prison, brought a blast of laughter— but afterward there was silence except for the typewriters. The thoughtless, vulgar repartee could have ignited another prison race war. There'd been several during my stay, each resulting in several deaths and dozens of wounded. And there were no uninvolved inmates. Those who tried to stay uninvolved were the most likely to be ambushed; they made the best targets because they were unprepared. It'd be a bitch, I thought wryly, to have some dumb nigger run a shiv in me the morning I'm blowing this jail.

Attention went out through the cell house's barred windows to where the prison property fell into San Francisco Bay. The banked floodlights illuminated everything except the black water. The massive concrete and steel buildings gleamed; so did the gun towers set in shallow water on stilts. Two miles away, across the black pond, were rolling hillsides. Only their lights, cast like handfuls of jewels on black velvet, suggested their outline. A highway curved along the base of the hillsides. Headlights and ruby taillights streamed endlessly. Further marking the highway was red, silver, green, blue neon. I didn't know what signs the neons represented, for I'd only seen them in the distance. And when I'd come to this cell the highway had been dark except for a handful of automobiles, and the hillsides had been empty. The landscape had changed. The question was, had the world changed too much for me? Had the mental and emotional tools necessary for life outside—different tools than

21

those necessary for life in prison—gone rusty in eight years? Again I was back into my anxieties. The churning caused me to grab the cell bars and shake with all my strength. They gave not a millionth of an inch.

Leroy Robinson appeared on the tier outside, carrying a water bucket with a long spout that would go through the bars. The cells had only cold water. The inside of the bucket gave off steam. He caught me wrestling with the unyielding bars. "Say, motherfucker, what're you doin'? Dynamic tension?"

"I'm breakin' out, damn fool. Can't you see!" Leroy made me smile; he always made me smile, both through friendship and because he transmitted, perhaps by osmosis, his outlook of absurd humor. Leroy would make jokes on the way to the gas chamber. He used wit both to diminish confrontation with his own failures (he was a four-time loser) and to put the world in perspective.

"I know what you're tryin' break out from," he said. "You're up tight as a Thanksgiving turkey the second week in November. I brought you something for your nerves." He put the water bucket down and put his palm through the bars. Wrapped in the cellophane from a cigarette package were two yellow nembutals. They were worth a carton of cigarettes, a considerable sum when ten cartons could get someone stabbed, and twenty cartons would buy a killing.

I unwrapped the capsules and put them on the bunk while he poured hot water into a peanut butter jar and I mixed my last dab of instant coffee into it. The coffee washed down the pills.

"Don't forget to call my sister and tell her I'm okay."

"Man, you ought to write yourself. She wants to hear from you."

"Look, she's married; they've got kids growing up in suburbia. They live in a different world."

I shook my head. Leroy pulled the walls around him like a cloak.

"I used to get full of anxiety," he said. "That was when I was going out with some crazy ass idea of straightening up."

"Well, that's my idea. I'm tired of this shit." I hesitated to express my fears. It would be shameful to whine when he would give anything to change places. And he'd probably make jokes of my worries. Yet, after hesitation, they bubbled out—my fears, vague except for not having a job: "I wrote two hundred letters and didn't get an answer," I said.

"Damn, motherfucker, you don't expect anyone to hire an ex-convict sight unseen, do you?"

"No, but somebody should have at least said to come see them."

"I don't have that problem. I start stealin' from the gate."

"That's what I don't want to do. Man, I can root in some fool's cash register—but I want to hang it up. Eight years in this stinkin' fuckin' place is enough."

"Look here, Max," he said, "I went through the same shit you're going through—in your mind—until I decided not to fight destiny, and my destiny was to be a criminal and spend three-fourths of my life in prison. Maybe your destiny is different. But someday, maybe tomorrow, maybe twenty years from now when you're fifty, you're gonna realize that whatever you are and whatever you've done, it couldn't have been very different. You'll see that you're required to do *this* in life, and when you're at the end and everything's totalled, you'll have been *that*, whatever it is. Hope is still ahead of you— but someday it'll be behind you. That's really the point of children, to have someone to pin hope to. I have no children, that's why I have so much feeling for you."

It was the most serious statement I'd ever heard from Leroy. I might have argued with his pronouncements, but preferred to keep the moment of rapport. "Well," I said, "I just hope I last longer than you did. I hope I can handle it out there."

"Shit, I didn't get busted because I couldn't handle it. It was just the way the cookie crumbles. Besides, I'd just as soon be in this concrete cunt as be out there without having anything. I'm like a fool in a poker game who's lost all his dough except a few cents. Ain't no way to quit. Maybe I'll win next time, get me a four- or five-year run. After that they can bury me. Fuck it."

"I don't want to come back, next year or twenty years from now. I just want to live like everybody else lives."

"More power to you—if that's for you. It ain't for me, and I accept it."

"I'm burned out."

"If you can handle the lunchbucket routine . . ."

"I'm gonna try. I'm scared, though. I'm trying their game. That's something new. Besides, I don't even know if I remember how to fuck a broad anymore. I've been down so long I might want young boy butt."

"Just get one of them hookers to put a carrot on her stomach until you get used to things."

We stood a few more minutes. The conversation was broken with long silences. My departure upset the chemistry of our relationship. Friendship remained the same, but the paths of our lives were separating, and between us would be the prison walls—and on each side of those walls was a different universe.

A bell rang, bouncing off the walls. The public address system blared, "Final lockup for count. Final lockup."

"Later on, brother," Leroy said, sticking his hand through the bars to shake goodbye.

Music came from the earphones until midnight. The nembutal relaxed me, but failed to drive me to sleep. My thoughts turned, sometimes to the music, to the squeak of footsteps as a guard prowled the gunrail, to the hollow gasp of a flushing toilet, or a muttered curse torn from an anguished dream. Mainly, I thought of freedom, of how tired I was of crime and punishment. Having something different would require my being something different. Was that possible? I was articulate, fairly intelligent, very well read (in eight years a cretin would become well read), but what could I do? My only previous job had been selling used cars in New Orleans, and I'd taken that job for cover because of a federal fugitive warrant. I was thirty years old and I'd never filed an income tax return, or used my social security card.

A job was important. Even more than money it would be an anchor holding me stable until I made the transition to a new life. The lack of even a single reply to my letters worried me. Was it prophecy? Would it be different when I was there? Could I hide my background?

My letters seeking a job, though truthful, diminished the full truth. Faces would blanch if the facts had been complete: "Dear Sir," I thought. "Do you have a position for a journeyman burglar, con man, forger and car thief; also with experience as armed robber, pimp, card cheat, and several other things. I smoked marijuana at twelve (in the '40s) and shot heroin at sixteen. I have no experience with LSD and methedrine. They came to popularity since my imprisonment. I've buggered pretty young boys and feminine homosexuals (but only when locked up away from women). In the idiom of jails, prisons, and gutters (some plush gutters) I'm a motherfucker! Not literally, for I don't remember my mother. In my world the term, used as I used it, is a boast of being hell on wheels, outrageously unpredictable, a virtuoso of crime. Of course by being a motherfucker in that world I'm a piece of garbage in yours. Do you have a job?"

The mental letter contained too much ugly truth for the humor I'd intended—not the whole truth, but that which was important for the world to judge me. I could not tell them the truth of myself; perhaps nobody can tell the world the truth. Maybe truth is something with dripping organs, gears, unfilled holes, a background of nothingness on a field of melting and shattered time. Maybe I could tell them my memories of being thrown into a pitch black cell, naked, without even a mattress, me and the concrete and darkness—when I was nine years old. Or of being handcuffed to a hot steam radiator in juvenile hall and having a grown man kick my ribs in—I was eleven years old. (But to give the man justice, I had spit on him.)

Whatever the truth, I wanted peace. Tomorrow would be a new beginning, the phoenix rising from the ashes.

It was dawn. The sparrows that nested in high corners of the cell house were unbelievably noisy. The convict keyman was turning the locks on each cell door; but the doors wouldn't open until the security bar on each tier was raised. As the keyman worked, the unbroken rhythm of steel striking steel—clack, clack, clack—rose and fell. It was loud when he was overhead or below, receding as he reached the end of each tier. I was dressed and shaved long before he reached my cell.

Once released, I passed through the mess hall without getting a tray and stepped into the main yard. It was jammed with men from other cell houses. In minutes the yard gate would open and the convicts would flow out to the rest of the prison. The asphalt-topped yard, formed into a rough rectangle, was a concrete canyon surrounded by the giant cell houses. Their faded paint and rusted bars blotted out the morning sun and added to the gothic bleakness. Riflemen patrolled on catwalks overhead, ready to break up fights with bullets.

I'd said goodbye to most of my friends during the preceding two days, while making the rounds to check out. Half a dozen of my closest comrades were waiting just beyond the mess hall door. Most of them I'd known since reform school, a couple had been crime partners. They wanted to shake hands and wish me luck. There was nothing else to say. I was going and they were staying.

Aaron Billings, the person I really wanted to see, failed to appear. He was black and would avoid a group of whites, just as I would avoid a group of blacks. The races had become totally polarized during recent years. Because of this I'd talked with Aaron less and less, but our friendship remained. He'd stopped me at the dentist's office yesterday (he worked there) and mentioned that he might be transferred to camp and wanted me to help him escape. There'd been no time to talk, and he was going to meet me this morning.

I excused myself from my friends, for whom life in prison would continue unchanged by my absence, and began searching through the crowd. I was more conscious of my surroundings than I had been in several years. Two thousand voices collected into a roar as powerful as wind from the sea. The roar moved up the cell house walls toward the sky, failed the ascent and echoed back into the pit. To someone seeing the yard for the first time it would remind them of a teeming anthill, each man identical with every other.

A voice cut through the uproar: "Clear the way! Dead man coming!"

In seconds there was a path ten feet wide. Moses couldn't have parted the Red Sea any more cleanly. First came a guard, whose voice was calling out. Six feet behind him came the condemned man, a tall young Negro. He was followed by a second guard. Overhead, a rifleman covered them.

It was early for a Death Row procession. This one seemed to be going toward the inside administration building. The doomed men always wore new denim and soft slippers without laces. The man's slippers were still new, indicating that he'd just arrived. He was probably going for fingerprinting and a mug photo. He was a dozen feet away and I studied his face, seeking (as everyone did) an answer to the great mystery: as if someone sentenced to die at a specific hour by cyanide gas knows more—or is more doomed. The black face gave no message. I didn't know who he was or why he'd been sentenced to die. Eighty men were waiting on the row. A handful had made headlines; the others were anonymous. Several I knew personally. Sometimes a condemned man had been on the prison main line and waved to friends when he was brought through. Not the black. His eyes remained ahead, except for an occasional glance at the sky. Another detail that told me he'd just arrived was that he was thin; after a few months everyone on Death Row got fat from the special menu. Each time I saw one of them with swollen belly I thought of hogs being fattened for the slaughter.

The procession disappeared. The crowd closed in its wake. The work whistle sliced the air. The gate slid open and in minutes the yard had only a scattering of convicts.

Aaron was near the east cell house wall; he was alone, as usual.

His brown head, shaved and oiled, glistened in a vagrant sliver of sunlight. Tucked under his arm were three thick books, all on higher mathematics. His faint smile on seeing me was the equal of a gush of affection from most persons. His ambition was to face life with precise, scientific detachment, with as little emotion as possible. The only decoration in his cell was a charcoal sketch of Albert Einstein.

We shook hands. In prison, the gesture was more than empty ritual. It was the clasp of friendship.

"How do you feel?" he asked.

"Up tight."

"Are you ready?"

"I'm jack-ready for some freedom. How ready I am for a parole officer is another question."

"After eight years you're ready as you'll ever be."

"Yeah, if I'm not ready now I'll never be ready. I know I hope I'm ready."

"Let's walk a few minutes. I told the doc I'd be late for work."

We began to pace the now-empty yard. Though we were the same height—six feet—he outweighed me by thirty pounds, all of it in shoulder, chest, and arm. Years ago, before the racial climate brought too many ugly stares from both black and white, we used to pace the length of the yard for an hour or two at least once a week. The walking habit had developed because if we remained in one place our friends would walk up and intrude in the conversation. The occasional serious conversations we shared—about books and their content—had had a salutary effect on me. Prison conversations usually concern murder, mayhem, homosexuality, gambling, narcotics, stool pigeons, cops, and escape. The all-purpose word is "motherfucker", serving as noun, verb, adverb, and adjective—it's meaning depending on context and intonation. Remove this word from the convict vocabulary and prisons will fall silent. Neither the vulgarity nor the topics offended me; they were too close to my own existence. But an unrelieved diet of them left me hungry for something different. Aaron's intelligence stimulated me. In his eleven years of imprisonment he'd learned to speak Spanish, French, and Portuguese, had mastered computer programming and electronics, was a dental technician. His reading habits were less eclectic than mine, but he had a unique precision of mind.

This was our first walk in six months. I'd backed away from him. He knew the reason and had said nothing. We'd never have become friends if the foundation hadn't been placed before racial hate began erupting into wars. The atmosphere had changed in the last two years. The rifles kept things from erupting into wholesale massacre, but there were murderous skirmishes. If a black was stabbed by a white, whatever the reason, there would be retaliation: several blacks would suddenly rush down a tier and stab any white available. Whites would wait and reciprocate. Aaron viewed both sides as ignorant. This was not because he disclaimed his heritage or lacked pride— but he refused to make it a condition of shame or a rallying point of hatred. Quite simply, he found racists on either side to have unsustainable attitudes, lacking scientific foundation. And it was not white convicts who were the problem, assuming the blacks could change the world with violence. The blacks disliked him, too, because he disdained their ignorance. If they tried to force their opinions on him, he could make them back up, for his calm was not fear or passivity. He could be dangerous. He met every person as an individual, and no amount of ignorance could dissuade him. This view created an unusual situation. Many militant white racists treated him as a person first, his negritude being secondary. In other words they reacted to him as he reacted to himself.

When I came to prison I had few prejudices, despite having been through racial gang fights in reform schools.

Now I hate most blacks—because of their paranoia. Suspicion on their part may be justified, but paranoia is a disease. If they hate my whiteness, I hate their blackness. They hate whitey; they want revenge, not equality. They consider themselves unbound by white laws and moral codes. They pose a direct and immediate threat to me, and to meet it a loathing and hatred has grown—so when I look into their amber eyes glowing with hate, my blue eyes glow with a mirrored hate.

I was ashamed of this attitude where Aaron was concerned, but the prison's racial situation was something we seldom talked about, having agreed that there were no universally acceptable answers. But the situation had driven us apart—not our friendship—and so we talked infrequently. And this would be the last time.

"I've only got a couple minutes," I said. "You want me to help you escape from camp—if you go to camp."

"Here's the situation, precisely. I've got eleven years served and I've been eligible for parole for four. I go to the board again next month. Yesterday I saw my counselor, and if the board denies me again he's going to recommend to the classification committee that I go to camp. You already have my mother's address and I hope you'll keep in touch with her. I'll write you there and tell you what to do. All I really want is to have you give me a ride."

"*If* you get denied at the board, *if* you go to camp, *if* you send for me, I'll come for you. But I want you to know something, you're putting weight on friendship. I wouldn't give a shit if I was going out to do wrong, but I plan to straighten up. Even before I get there I'm being put in a cross between friendship and breaking the law. I'll be a dirty motherfucker if it isn't a drag to promise to commit a felony before I even get out."

Aaron grinned and squeezed my shoulder. "I thought it over a long time before I asked. If it was anything less than freedom I wouldn't ask. And it's no risk. You know that. Drive up to the Sierras, pick me up, and drive back."

"I hope you get parole. You goddam sure got one coming."

"What one has coming and what one gets is often quite different."

"You're a cinch next year."

"I could say 'next year' to doomsday. I'm no mule chasing a carrot."

I understood his view—and agreed with it. We walked another lap in silence. I wanted to go. The sooner I reached the front gate the sooner I would be outside the walls. My mind had left him. He understood what was happening. When we reached the end of the yard he stopped and stuck out a brown paw. "Later on, brother. Good luck."

"All right." I grinned. "I'll be seeing you."

It was time to report to Receiving and Release.

2

I RODE off the prison property with sixty-five dollars, a cheap suit (ten years out of style), a set of khakis and change of underwear in a brown parcel, and a bus ticket to Los Angeles. A uniformed guard drove me to the depot and waited until I was on board.

I hurried onto the bus, glad to escape the eyes of the citizens in the depot, eyes attracted to me by the guard. Through the tinted window I watched him depart. An almost electric awareness went through me. I was free. Free!

Other passengers filtered aboard, heaved bundles onto overhead racks. The idling motor made the vehicle tremble. A sense of unreality, so intense as to make me dizzy, swelled up. Everything was weird. The tinkling resonance of women's voices, which I hadn't heard in eight years, was as alien as Chinese to my ears. The variety and color of clothes—the reds and yellows of summer print—crashed against my sensibilities with blinding force. I sat in a trance.

The driver came down the aisle, a stocky man. His belly rolled over his belt buckle; his hat was off and his hair was damp with perspiration. He joked with each passenger as he checked tickets. On reaching me, his smile disappeared. He grunted, wouldn't meet my eyes. Shame and anger made me want to retch—but then I wondered if it was just my imagination. Yet the driver resumed his banter at the next passenger. "Fuck it," I muttered. In a few hours I'd blend into the swarm and nobody would know.

Brakes whooshed, the diesel motor churned. My freedom journey began. All other feelings were eclipsed in the excitement of seeing the world beyond the walls. While we inched through the town's back streets, I soaked up every sight. Commercial garages, body and fender shops, beer joints, and ramshackle grocery stores were pitifully ugly in the unrelenting sunlight—but to me they were beautiful beyond description.

Soon the bus was in the country. The black asphalt sliced through mile after mile of alfalfa, the emerald growth polished by water from revolving sprinklers. I watched the fields with the fascination of a child at his first kaleidoscope.

Wheels and hours turned. The bus passed through rolling scrubland—it was beautiful—and small towns where gas stations bustled, farm workers in Stetsons loitered, and children played in the streets. There were more fields, rippling voluptuously beneath fingers of a breeze. I felt as if I could ride the bus through eternity and be happy.

Two teen-age girls got off in a small town near an airbase. I watched them walk away. They wore stretch pants that clearly outlined thigh and butt. I stared at them hungrily, fantasy rising with swift intensity. Years without a woman sharpens a prisoner's ability for imagery—one has to have imagination to use a stubble-bearded, plucked-eyebrow fairy. Close your eyes and imagine someone else— perhaps the exotic movie star you saw at the weekend movie. Imagination is necessary where a hand slippery with pomade serves for a woman. Pomade, closed eyes, and imagination. When the two girls disappeared I was worked up with imagining.

For an hour the bus ground a slow ascent up a canyon between slabbed rock walls spotted with scrub. There was no view. I used the interlude to examine an envelope of papers handed me at the prison gate. Three parole report forms. One was to be filled out and sent in the first week of the month. Name and prison number, address, place of employment, income, savings, description and license of automobile. There was a copy of the parole agreement I'd signed, and its conditions. They were standard—maintain suitable employment (what's "suitable"?), make no address change and drive no automobile without written permission, no drinking, make no contract, borrow no money, avoid ex-felons and persons of ill repute, and heed the advice and counsel of the parole officer. Failure to comply with any condition was grounds for return to prison without notice or hearing.

A form letter told me the parole officer's name was Joseph Rosenthal. I was to contact him and report as soon as I arrived. I liked the idea of having a Jew: Jews had suffered so much that he should have some empathy for my problems.

The bus stopped for twenty minutes in Santa Barbara. I hurried to the sidewalk, wanting to just walk around until it was time to go. The tangle of movement and color dizzied me. Everything was strange, a different world than I was accustomed to. Impulsively, I ducked into a liquor store for a twenty-five-cent cigar and a half pint of vodka. The desire wasn't so much to get drunk (I was drunk with freedom already) as to exercise some choice, buy something.

But drunk I was as the bus swept along the seacoast on the last leg of the Journey. I watched the surf weave lace patterns along the beach and the sea glaze with the molten hues of early summer twilight.

I forgot the proximity of Los Angeles until the bus turned up a ramp into Santa Monica. Then awareness of being home crashed with complete surprise and some disbelief. As avidly as a child, I pressed my nose against the tinted window and stared out. Each block was familiar, yet each was renewed surprise.

In West Hollywood we changed boulevards. To the left was the Sunset Strip, and I could see the green hills dotted with white apartments. Memories jumped to mind with almost physical force. This was my territory the year before prison—the only good year in my memory. Not good in any moral sense, quite the contrary, but money had been easy and I'd spent it on easy living, an expensive apartment, sports car, silk suits, good liquor, and food. However meaningless and unfulfilling such a life had been, it was a constant intoxicant. With so much hedonism there was no time to think of "meaning". That year had cost me eight of nightmare, an unfair bargain.

The bus entered Hollywood. I recalled dreary stucco bungalows of yellow and pink, already going to seed after their heyday in the '30s. Now there were high-rise apartments and skyscrapers.

Suddenly the bus was pulling into a depot. My ticket was for downtown Los Angeles. I hadn't thought about stopping in Hollywood. Now I grabbed my parcel and hurried off, my stomach churning.

The depot was small, uncrowded. The time was 5:20. It was late for the parole office to be open, yet I decided to telephone and see.

A woman answered. Her "please" and "sir" sounded strange. I was more accustomed to "asshole" and "motherfucker". Rosenthal was still in his office.

"Hi there, Max," he said. "I'm surprised that you called. Your bus wasn't due 'til six and I'd be gone by then."

"I got off in Hollywood."

"That's where you are now?"

"They said I was to contact you on arrival. That's what I'm doing."

"Good. Good. How do you feel?"

I told him I was a little drunk. Though the statement seemed naive, and it was in a way, there was a test in it. If he accused me of doing wrong, I knew I had a prick and could act accordingly, lying to him forever after. If he passed over it with humor or understanding, I would know that I could manipulate him. But he did neither. He just said, "Oh," and I blushed, cursed myself as a fool—for not having learned the lesson to keep my mouth shut to authority. He asked where the deport was located. And the bizarre thing was that I didn't know. I'd been born in Hollywood but remembered no bus depot. Leaving the receiver to hang, I walked outdoors.

The street sign said Vine Street; the cross sign said DeLonpre Avenue. I must have passed the bus depot hundreds of times without noticing it.

I froze, looked around in fascinated wonder. To the left was the downtown Hollywood skyline, familiar to me since childhood—now both known and new as birth. Beyond were the low, hazed hills with a giant sign, Hollywood, perched on top. To the right, a block away, was the Ranch Market. It was old and huge, open-stalled in the style of another era. The sight of it brought a rash of memories. In the postmidnight hours the market—its hot dog stand and magazine rack—catered to weirdos and geeks, freaks and tipsy whores and their pimps. One had to pass the hot dog stand to reach the parking lot, and here at darkness gathered the strange people, watching with predatory eyes those who shopped at 3:30 A.M., cocktail waitresses and musicians red-eyed from smoky bars and marijuana, pills, booze, inadequate sleep. In my teens, too young for bars, with nowhere to go, I'd come to the market on the prowl for a drunk or a fairy to lure somewhere and knock in the head—for fifteen or twenty dollars.

During daylight it may have been just another market. I'd only seen it in the middle of the night.

Remembering Rosenthal, I hurried back, gave him directions, and promised to wait on the corner; he was going to stop on his way home from work.

Before going outside, I bought a handful of picture postcards and addressed them to friends left behind in the cage. I had appreciated the gesture from others in the past and was certain my friends would do the same.

The shadows were lengthening and a wind was rising. It was the first twilight I'd seen in eight years, for the prison was locked up at four in the afternoon. Leroy, Aaron, all the numbered men, were now settled with earphones, books, thoughts.

Rosenthal arrived in a plain, compact automobile, pulling up to double-park and beckon me. I got in quickly and he pulled around the corner, parking on a residential street of small bungalows. My first impression was of a fat, merry little pig in rimless glasses. Bristles of a heavy beard contributed to this impression; so did his suit, which was far too tight on the pudgy frame. This was exaggerated by a moon face squirting from a tight collar. Perched on his head was a ridiculous porkpie hat with a green feather. His appearance was more absurd than threatening.

The advantage I had of appraising him while he drove was more than offset by his having a large file on me. He eyed me with frank curiosity while we shook hands.

"I imagine you feel pretty good," he said. "You were busted a long time."

"Yeah, I'm kind of dizzy, freedom drunk." I was trying to place a trace of doubt in his mind about what I'd said over the telephone. His eyes narrowed; he had joined the statements. He said nothing about it.

"You don't look so tough," he said, smiling affably, getting to what he knew from the file. I grinned back with a candor I didn't feel. There was no forgetting that our relationship was essentially that of a knife held to a throat. He could order me jailed whenever he felt like it. I sensed that his affability hinged on my agreeing with him.

"Think you can do this parole?" he asked.

"I don't see why not. It's just a matter of living like millions of other people. I've got problems, but they're inside me and I should be able to handle what's in myself."

"Good, positive attitude. But sometimes it seems harder than that for men who've been in prison. They need help. That's what I'm here for. I've seen both good and bad in your jacket. Most parole officers have eighty or ninety cases. I've only got thirteen—special cases."

"I'm a special case . . . I only had a forgery."

"A forgery, yes. But the record goes back so many years, and there's been episodes of violence. That's why you're a special case."

"I need more watching," I said bitterly.

"They think so, and it's my job." He paused, then went on, "You don't have a job, so to get my supervisor to approve your release on schedule I had to submit something. I've got you a place in a halfway house on Twenty-fourth and Vermont."

"Halfway house!" The idea of going to a rescue mission for ex-convicts, which halfway houses are, made me sick. And the address was in what had been the ghetto border eight years before; now the area was 95 percent black, I knew.

Seeing my feelings, he explained that halfway houses were made for such men as me, those without home or family or assets. "It's just a refuge until you get settled."

Perhaps he was right, but it seemed like welfare and it was still under authority. I wanted freedom, not a change of cells. He sensed by attitude and changed subjects: "What about a job? Anything in mind?"

"They always need car salesmen. I talk pretty well and I did it once."

"I've gotta say no to that. Too much temptation to bilk someone."

"Well, do you have any ideas?"

"We'll talk about it tomorrow. My supper's waiting and my wife will chew me out. What about the halfway house? Try it for a night or two."

"Let me decide that tomorrow, too."

"Where're you staying tonight?" I saw the thought behind his suspicious eyes: was I going to disappear, hang up the parole?

"I'll be at your office early. Keep my bundle in your car. And I've got thirty dollars gate money. I won't lam and leave that behind."

"I don't care if you run. It's no skin off my ass." He reached for the ignition key. "I'm going past Hollywood Boulevard. Want a ride to there?"

"That's fine."

Hollywood Boulevard seemed as good a place as any, though I'd had no thought whatsoever beyond Rosenthal.

When I stood on the curb and Rosenthal drove away, freedom's full impact landed. Until that moment I'd been carried along by the thought of reaching the city, the necessity of seeing Rosenthal. Now my freedom was absolute, of a kind few persons experience. If I went north or south, east or west, up or down the sidewalk, it made absolutely no difference. It was freedom to the point of being in a void.

A faceless crowd hurried by me with destinations born of choice and linked with past choice. Everyone had somewhere to go, and they were happier in their invisible fetters than if confronted by freedom. I was dizzy and overawed and somewhat frightened.

A neon forest was coming alive. The aureole of brilliance around each tube grew as it ate the night. Colors flashed spasms, bubbled illustrations, whorled and exploded, gleamed on the waxed metal of automobiles. I began walking toward the west simply because the brighter lights were there. I had to make some choice, some movement.

"Now what the fuck should I do?" The question should have been absurd, for I'd been born less than two miles from where I stood, had lived my whole life (when free) in Los Angeles. Yet among the city's millions I could think of nobody to telephone. Among the multitude were hundreds of criminals and ex-convicts whom I knew, who were more or less friends. They'd be in cocktail lounges on the Sunset Strip, or in dingy bars downtown, or beer joints and cantinas on the east side. They lived furtively, deliberately made themselves hard to find. A tour of the hangouts would put me in contact with a few. Through them I would find the others. In a few days I could be returned to the underworld milieu. It would be easy—and it was precisely what I wanted to avoid. Suddenly the neon burned my eyes; it was like the sensation on the bus except more intense. The crowd scurrying by might as well have been insects, so alien to them did I feel. I struggled for mental equilibrium.

The odor of food and awareness of hunger brought me back to reality. A greasy hamburger in a crowded coffee shop tasted delicious after so many years in a place where Velveeta cheese was a delicacy. I was finishing a cup of coffee and studying people (men wore their hair longer now) when I flashed on who to telephone. Willy Darin, the dope fiend. He'd been on parole from the Narcotic Rehabilitation Center for two months, according to the grapevine. His father-in-law's telephone number was in the directory, and someone there would know how to contact Willy.

My hand sweated on the receiver. I knew the entire family and anticipated knowing whoever answered; but the man's voice on the other end was unfamiliar.

"Is this the Pavan residence?" I asked.

"Yeah. Who do you want?"

"Who's speaking?"

"Man, you called here."

The game of mutual suspicions was ridiculous. "My name's Max Dembo," I said, "and . . ."

"You're jivin'!"

"I'm not jiving."

"Goddamn, man! This is Willy. When did you raise?"

"This morning. Damn, brother, I didn't recognize your voice. Say, I'm stranded out here in Hollywood. Have you got some wheels?"

"Yeah, sort of. It might get there. But it'll be a while, say an hour. You're lucky you caught me here. I just stopped on my way home from work. I've gotta go home and shower."

"How's Selma?"

"Same old shit. We'll cut it up when I get there. We'll get loaded."

"Not on junk."

"Some pot or something."

"Don't hang me up. You know how fuckin' undependable you are."

"Don't sweat it. Where'll you be?"

"Hollywood and Vine. Where else, motherfucker?"

"I'll be there in an hour."

When I went outside to kill an hour wandering, the tumultuous uncertainties were gone. The ache of being alone was also gone.

Prison atrophies many emotional needs, but it increases others, among them the need for companionship. The twenty-four-hour crowding grates the nerves, but insidiously it addicts.

I walked the boulevard, window-shopped—and saw that my dressout suit, with cuffed and pleated trousers, was an anachronism. I loved clothes—perhaps through some insecurity—but forced down a rising hunger with the thought that they would come with work and patience. Those who had the things I desired had been striving for them while I vegetated in prison. Only crime would allow me to catch up overnight, and that was out of the question. In many ways I'd never catch up. I accepted that reality.

3

THE automobile that double-parked and honked aroused stares of disapproval from several pedestrians, but made me grin. Willy hadn't changed. He bought wrecks for fifty dollars, tinkered until they moved, and when they gave out he abandoned them. This one had a dead headlight, an asthmatic motor, and a broken muffler.

Willy's wife and two sons were in the car. I'd known Selma since she was eleven and I was fourteen. I'd met Willy at her house; her sister was my first girl friend. The boys had been babies when I last saw them. It was odd that Willy brought the family. It was as if they were a shield. He had no reason to fear me, but in the criminal world (Willy was more drug addict than criminal) there are many guilts and fears. Constant suspicion is good for survival. Willy had a reason—and all I could think of was that his brother had turned stool pigeon three years before. He might have fears that someone would use him as a surrogate for revenge.

"I didn't believe it was you," he said when I was beside Selma. She was carrying a baby in her arms. Considering that Willy had been imprisoned for two years, either the baby was not Selma's or she'd been stupid.

"How're Joe and Mary?" I asked.

"He's back in Folsom on a parole violation."

"When was that?"

"Two, three months ago."

"He and Mary broke up anyway," Selma said.

Joe had been out a year. Word should have come from Folsom but had obviously missed me. Willy explained that Joe had been doing "good", which was a criminal euphemism for making "good" money illegally. "He beat a possession," Willy continued, "and by rights it wasn't his shit. He had a dude in his car and the heat gave them the red light. The other dude threw a bag out the window. He got on the stand and cut Joe loose, but the fuckin' narks didn't go for it. They made sure he was violated."

"Joe had a new car and everything," Selma said. "Mary could've had it, but she couldn't make the payments."

Joe's fall was bad luck for me, too. I now remembered the word that he was making a bundle of money. He would have helped me get on my feet. We'd been teen-age crime partners, smoking mari-juana, drinking wine, and riding in stolen cars with rhythm and blues honking from the dashboard radio. We'd burglarized together, committing strong armed robberies, and we'd snatched purses. Over the years he'd been incarcerated when I was out, and vice versa. Our styles had also gone separate ways. Where I'd become an active thief—burglar, bandit, forger—he'd become a drug peddler and sometimes pimp. Yet he would have helped me, as I would have helped him.

Willy turned onto the freeway but crawled along the slow lane. At fifty miles an hour the automobile shook violently.

In the quick, flicking shadows I looked at the couple beside me. Willy, as usual, radiated seediness; the best suit became wrinkled and sloppy the moment he put it on. In the odd light it was hard to see Selma clearly, but I did see gauntness and hardness. She'd never been pretty, but in her youth there had been a sensual bloom. That had withered with her arid life.

Beyond downtown, Willy got off the freeway, following boule-vards and side streets east through the seamy core of the city. He'd gotten a ticket on the freeway for the missing headlight a few nights earlier and wanted to avoid meeting the same highway patrolman.

One of the boys in the back seat complained to Selma that he was hungry. I'd forgotten them. Now I was ashamed of our casual talk about crime and prison.

"We'll be home soon," Selma said.

"Where you living?"

"El Monte."

"With your parents?"

"God, no!" she said. "Mom isn't there anyway . . . and the house is as bad as on Court Avenue."

"Grandma's in the nuthouse," one of the boys piped from the rear, causing Willy to glance back and admonish him not to say it that way. "That's the way *you* said it, dad," the boy said, feelings hurt.

"Where's Mary?" I asked.

"She lives a couple miles from us."

"I suppose your father's still wrestling with lettuce and carrots."

"Sure . . . and hoarding his money."

The family lived on Court Avenue in Lincoln Heights when I had met them, in a big, gray frame house. I'd run away from nearby juvenile hall with their older brother, Gino. Even then the house was run-down. Ten years later it had a stench that made one nauseous. The walls were coated with grease and grime, garbage rotted for weeks in the kitchen, trash littered the floors. An exterminator was brought in and removed two barrels of cockroaches. The deterioration had come after the children moved out, the girls to their sorry marriages, Gino to the gutter of dope and jail.

The tragic aspect was that their father was wealthy. An uneducated, dull-witted immigrant, he'd gotten a two thousand dollar insurance settlement in 1932 for losing a thumb and two fingers. He'd bought a four-unit slum dwelling, meanwhile working the fresh produce stand of a market. Property values climbed; he borrowed on what he owned and bought more slum property and kept working. After the severe housing shortage during the war and the postwar boom in Southern California property, he owned three dozen slum buildings, duplexes, triplexes, storefronts.

As he was lucky with money through no virtue (unless miserliness and tenacious drudgery are virtues), he was unlucky with his family through no fault, beginning with his wife, Jessica. Once pretty, she was already fading when I met her. Her husband refused to buy her anything—and she knew he could afford it. She took to barbiturates, then booze, and became a screaming, slovenly shrew, and sometimes withdrew into the private world of schizophrenia.

Gino, the oldest son, had been prettyboy handsome, with a powerful physique and curly hair that fell over his forehead. He became a sneak thief junky who stole from friends and family. He once served a prison term for writing checks on his father. The old man had been given the choice of prosecuting his son or accepting the monetary loss. He prosecuted.

Mary was next ... my first girl friend and my favorite in the family—though my taste in women had changed since childhood. She had a tranquil, sweet disposition miraculously untainted by the sordid milieu. Narcotics and crime affected her life but not her basic sweetness. Her naiveté was also her curse, for she lacked the toughness to break clear of the morass. "Nice boys" had never come into the zone occupied by such violent delinquents as her brother, Joe Gambesi, and myself—and our friends. She'd married Joe when she was seventeen. At that time Joe wanted something else from life than crime—but he quickly became what destiny ordained: a dope peddler. It was the sole path he could see to get the material things he craved. His background, too, was bleak. He'd been raised on a pittance of county welfare by a religious-fanatic mother. They'd lived in a single windowless room. Rats sometimes scurried across the floor. The room was rancid from the candles always burning in his mother's private altar. Joe escaped to the streets and never went to school; he could see no reason to. We met when we were fifteen and I was escaped from reform school.

Selma had become pregnant by Willy, married him, and escaped from one pit of misery to another. Willy became a junky, as had his brother, and Gino, and Joe Gambesi, and myself for a while.

One other Pavan child, Georgie, was a shadow in the background. He still lived at home. He was severely retarded and nobody knew what went through his vacant mind. He'd been arrested just once—for being a peeping tom.

A year before I went to prison the old man had bought a modern, ranch-style house on a large lot in El Monte, complete with orange trees in the back yard. Now, according to Selma, it was in the same condition as the house on Court Avenue. I wondered what the neighbors thought.

And the house on Court Avenue was the only place I'd known to call. I wondered if it said something about me.

"Want to stop and see Mary?" Willy asked as we neared El Monte.

"Take us home first," Selma said. "The boys haven't eaten and I have a headache."

I silently approved. I wanted to talk to Willy alone, get loaded, and possibly find a woman.

The Darin home was a tiny, cheap bungalow with a dirt driveway. It was on a semi-rural, semi-industrial road where the few ramshackle houses were separated by gravel pits and construction yards.

We waited in the automobile until Selma and the boys were inside.

"Mary?" Willy asked, backing out.

"I'd rather smoke some pot and rip off some cunt."

"Pot is a cinch and I know a couple hustlin' broads we can call. But that'll take some bread."

"My bankroll's too light for buying pussy. Can I get some credit?"

Willy laughed. "Man you know how dope fiend hookers are . . . 100 percent business."

"Fuck it. How about you. Are you using stuff?"

"I fix once a week, the day after nalline. They can't test you two days in a row."

"You're working, too. Never thought I'd see it."

"It's a bitch, riveting aluminum walls on trailers eight fuckin' hours a day." Grinding monotony was hard on Willy, yet he had no ability to offer for other employment.

"Can you get me a spot there?"

"You're jiving. Man, I know you. You're gonna rip off everything in town."

"No, I'm hanging up the gloves. I'm going to get a job and settle down." I wanted to explain more fully—and then saw how burlesque the situation was: a man explaining why he wasn't going to be a criminal. Willy's respect for me, however, was based on my being a criminal, on my ability to steal money, some of which trickled to him. He respected me as the jackal respects the lion, and profited in the same way.

In East Los Angeles he parked outside a cantina on a dark street of frame houses and machine shops. The rhythm of a mariachi issued from an unseen jukebox. He told me to wait in the car and was gone less than five minutes, returning to throw a small matchbox of marijuana in my lap. "It's free," he said. "The dude wants me to deal heroin for him. There's a lot of dope fiends in El Monte."

"Yeah, you'll make a ten-dollar sale and get a ten-year sentence."

"Yeah, the jivin' motherfuckers give you more time for a cap of heroin than murder."

We stopped to buy two cans of beer and a package of cigarette papers; then parked under a street light and rolled the dark green flakes into half a dozen skinny cigarettes. We shared one, sucking the fumes deep, occasionally sipping beer. I'd smoked marijuana since my early teens—every day for a long time—but it came into prison so infrequently that this was like the first time, and I've always gotten higher than most persons from marijuana. It was always as if a partially opaque veil—the one of everyday reality—was lifted so I could see things more clearly: the same thing, but as it really was. Color was especially brighter, as if a dirty window had been washed clean. The neon had already entranced me; now it transfixed me as if supernaturally brilliant. Willy turned on a dashboard radio and the music, intricate piano jazz, was so simple to my perceptions that I could pick each note from the air—and almost see it. For no reason except that it bubbled in me, I began to giggle. The world was crystal clear.

"Man, you're stoned," Willy said.

"Goddam sure am . . ." but kept laughing. "It's been a long time. This is like cherry kicks."

"What gets me is this—we've been smokin' pot in the ghetto all our lives, and it used to be the most terrible crime. You never got a break in court if you got busted. Now that all those sons and daughters of senators and shit are smokin' grass and gettin' busted they're changin' the laws. They didn't give a fuck when it was us poor suckers."

"That's saying something—but we were out of step with the time."

Willy started the motor and we cruised aimlessly, recalling other days. Soon his brother was mentioned, and Willy cursed him as a "dirty stool pigeon motherfucker—not my brother". I doubted that Willy's feelings were anywhere near so intense as his words (he was probably saddened), but he knew my feelings about stool pigeons and wanted to disassociate himself from his brother.

A lighted clock in a dry cleaner's window gave the time as 11:40. Sleep was the farthest thing from my mind (fuck sleeping the first night out), yet tomorrow I had to see Rosenthal, find lodging, look for a job. I needed a chemical substitute for sleep.

"Where can we get some bennies?" I asked.

"L&L Red is the only one I know who fucks with them, but he won't be at his pad yet."

"Is that old freak still around?"

"Worse than ever."

"Let's make one of those fruiter bars downtown. They drop stimulants like chickens peckin' corn."

Willy started to protest that we were too likely to get stopped by the police downtown, but finally deferred to me—and I knew it was because it was my first night. I remembered when he'd jump at the chance to go wherever I wanted—when I had a pocketful of money and picked up the tabs.

Main Street was as bright as Hollywood Boulevard. Willy drove slowly while I scanned the teeming sidewalks. Only ground floor businesses were open, pawn shops, hot dog stands, penny arcades, movie theatres showing porno films twenty-four hours a day. Mainly there were the bars, Western, Mexican, Rock and Roll, each with its front door flung wide and the particular style of music cascading forth. I suddenly remembered how the all-night theatres smelled of piss.

Vice here was bargain basement and wore no masks. A whore was liable to grab a sucker through his pants and drag him by his tool into a bust-out hotel. Clots of seedy blacks were on the sidewalks. They viewed themselves as con men and pimps, but with beaver hats, pointed shoes, and zircon rings looked so hip they scared all but the stupidest suckers, which were young servicemen.

But homosexuality was the reigning vice here. Young male prostitutes outnumbered female whores, posturing so masculinely as to be a parody. And the feminine "queens" were everywhere, roaming up and down, alone or in groups, congregated most thickly around certain gay bars, posing and swishing, each fluttering hand gesture or thrown shoulder a caricature of womanhood. Their loud gaiety was defiant, if not hysterical.

Pairs of uniformed police with nightsticks patrolled each block, looking for a cripple—the drunks, brawlers, or those who otherwise disturbed peaceful order. A paddy wagon journeyed constantly between Main Street and the city jail. Plainclothes police also prowled around in search of whatever luck and someone's stupidity might bring them: a fugitive, a dope addict with contraband, an AWOL serviceman.

Everything was familiar. Even the rich stench of frying grease and onions from hot dog stands recalled when I'd been hungry on this street. While on the escape from reform school I'd survived eight months by preying on the street. Gambesi had been my partner. Many nights we'd spent in the twenty-four-hour movie theatres, one napping while the other watched for police. One would buy a ticket, go inside, and open the rear exit for the other. Once Joe was waiting for me to open the door, became impatient, and began knocking. Instead of me (it was why I hadn't opened it) a policeman stepped out, splitting Joe's head open with a nightstick. Because of Joe's youth, the cop was afraid to arrest him. We spent other nights in flop-house hotel lobbies, or in a truck parked behind a bakery. Sometimes Mary Pavan let us into the house after her father had gone to bed. We slept on the floor of her room and crept out into the city's dawn before her father got up for work. Joe sometimes went home to see his mother and get us clean clothes. Mainly, we lived by robbing queers. One of us would entice a homosexual into an isolated spot, or even into their residence, and the other would rush in. We'd beat them up and rob them. The word went around and we were unable to find victims. The interlude ended after a high-speed chase in a stolen automobile. It smashed into the rear of a parked truck. Joe got away in a fusillade of bullets, but the door jammed on my side and I was caught. I'd never hung around Main Street since then, but from time to time, as now, I'd gone there to buy amphetamines. It was the easiest spot in the city to get them; the queens were great consumers because their use stimulated sexual pleasure.

I had no doubt that one of us would see a familiar face—an ex-con, a Junky, a queen—on this street. But we saw nobody on the sidewalk that we recognized. We parked in a dark lot, threw the matchbox of marijuana near a wheel where it could be retrieved, and began walking along Main Street, stepping into bars and scanning the faces. We both wore business suits and the denizens eyed us with suspicious fear, thinking we were policemen.

One bar was in a cellar and was jammed. Colored lights spun through filters and hurled grotesque silhouettes. Voices challenged the throb and pulse of electrically amplified guitars from the jukebox. My senses had been opened by the marijuana and now I was immersed in the naked heart of sensual chaos. The music penetrated, drowning me. Once such sensuality would have thrilled me. Life had consisted of sensation, of *now*, without moderation or meaning. But after years in the state's monastery it was too rich. I struggled against losing myself in the vortex.

Someone appeared on my right from the crowd. It was a queen I'd seen in prison, but didn't know his name. There he'd worn skin tight pants and plucked eyebrows. Now he was conservative, though the bar was swarming with flaming faggots. He found out what we wanted, took two dollars, and returned ten minutes later with two rolls of pills wrapped in aluminum foil.

Willy wanted to have a drink; he was eyeing a young blonde queen who was expertly frugging with another boy.

"Let's blow," I said. "I'm not against buggering a boy, but I'll be a dirty motherfucker if it's the first sex I'm gonna have after eight years of nothing but fairies and jacking off."

We drove toward Chinatown and stopped for coffee to wash down the pills, and hasten their effect. Back in the car the stimulant spread through me, eradicating a sense of depression. It was great to merely ride the decrepit car through empty streets. I was free.

"Let's go check L&L Red," Willy said. "He should be at his pad now. It ain't very far."

"So he finally moved away from his folks, huh?"

"They died about three years ago, a month apart. He sold the pad and was broke in two months. Horses, whores, and getting high. All he's got left is a M.G. roadster that's falling apart.

"You should've seen the old fool with twenty grand," Willy continued. "Every night he had a hooker or two on his arm and his chest stuck out. I'll say one thing, he enjoyed himself while it lasted. He'd have killed himself in a couple more months if he hadn't run out of bread."

"What's he doing for a living now?"

"Same shit. Works until he's eligible for unemployment, then he folds. He still smokes pot, drops pills, and drinks tokay wine, and his mind is still on his prick." Willy kept talking about Red's spree, which was really an extension of the spree he'd been on for a dozen years that I'd known him, and a dozen more before that. He seemed to thrive on self-abuse. Still large and powerful, he'd once been hand-some. Too afraid of jail to steal, his constant cut-rate bacchanalia brought him in contact with many persons who straddled the line into the underworld—scrap dealers, bartenders, bar owners. He also knew many thieves. The straddlers were willing to purchase bargains even if they were stolen. Red wasn't actually a "fence", but he acted as middle man when opportunity presented itself. I'd once noticed a meat truck with a driver who habitually left it unguarded while he stopped for coffee. I knew where to sell cigarettes, liquor, television and sound equipment, business machines, cameras, furs, jewelry in small amounts, clothes, and even spark plugs. Three tons of raw meat was something else. Red knew a man who owned three restaurants and who liked the price we offered. I stole the truck before the driver had stirred the cream in his coffee.

Red also served as thief's guide for celebrations after a successful score. Some thieves have been imprisoned so much that they don't know where to go or what to do even when they have a pocketful of money. Red knew and adored showing others.

While I thought of Red, Willy had been driving through the streets of a rundown, hilly neighborhood. It was within sight of the downtown area. He turned into a narrow road that turned to dirt as we began ascending a hill. The automobile bounced, its headlights spraying over bare earth and clumps of dry weeds. This part of the city had been built up when flatland was still cheap and the builders had bypassed the hills to avoid construction costs. The buildings at the bottoms were now falling apart and the hills were still bare, while bulldozers erased orange groves fifty miles away.

On the hilltop I saw a clapboard cabin's lights through holes in a window shade. I recalled another of Red's quirks: he never prepared for bed. He slept on sofas, chairs, the floor, whatever was available and appeared most comfortable when he was fully dressed. He undressed and got under the sheets only for sex. Sleep was a waste of precious life as far as he was concerned.

L&L Red heard the car and came outside. He stood framed in the doorway with a half gallon wine jug dangling beside his hip.

"Hey, Big Red, what's to it, baby?" Willy said.

"Nothin' happenin'. Who's that with you?"

"Come check for yourself."

Red leaned his huge head through the driver's window and peered into the gloom. "I'll be a mother—! Max Dembo!"

"What's to it?"

"When did you spring?"

"Just this morning."

"Glad to see you. Ain't many like you left anymore." I couldn't see Red's face, but in the hot night I could smell him, the sour stench of the elderly.

"Come on inside," he said.

On the way indoors, he shook hands, and immediately began raving about his recent sexual conquests. "Same old shit. You know me . . . chasin' cunt, stayin' high, havin' a ball."

"That sure is you," Willy said.

The cabin was three rooms connected by doorless arches. Only the small bathroom had a door. Bare wood could be seen through worn linoleum. The furniture was junk except for a portable color television on a chair. A cardboard trash box was in the corner, but empty wine bottles and such had spilled over. Half of one wall was covered with photographs of naked women with their legs spread open. It was both sad and ludicrous.

"Red's washed up," Willy said, taking the wine jug from Red's hand and flopping on the sofa. "He can't even buy pussy no more."

"I can still get it up," Red said. "You stick that shit in your arm and your dick won't get hard."

Willy laughed. "I'm just jivin' you, Big Red. You're the greatest freak of all."

I looked at Red's vice-ravaged face, the sallow complexion, the once powerful body sagging in wrinkles. He sat on a chair, belly sagging over the unbuttoned top of his pants. I felt disdain, yet I also compared us and knew that on a scale balancing good and evil, I was worse than Red. He was harmless, for all his depravity. He'd never harmed anyone, except those with sexual inhibitions, whereas

I'd beaten and maimed and stolen from everyone. And one thing could be said for him: he lived fully according to his desires, and there might be something to be said for someone whose interests were sex and staying high.

We smoked the last three joints, L&L Red sucking so greedily that one would have thought that he had been away from it for eight years. He gobbled half a dozen benny tablets, too. Soon he was recounting episodes of the spree that Willy had mentioned earlier. As Red recited, an entranced glassiness came to his eyes. Drool ran from his mouth. His voice was an impassioned liturgical song. The memory of those few months was obviously his most precious possession, and he polished the stories and lived them over and over. He finally ran down, tilted the wine jug, and his Adam's apple bobbed as he swigged the last drop. "We'll have to party together," he said to me. "I know some new spots you haven't seen. I know where it's at, don't I, Willy?"

"Damn sure do," Willy said.

Red suddenly jumped to his feet and began popping his fingers. I thought he'd gone crazy. "Jesus, Max, oh Jesus. I just remembered. Goddam you're lucky!"

"What're you talking about?"

"A caper . . . a boss caper. A guy's been hittin' on me to find a good heist man. You're here. It's a fuckin' miracle . . . and it's bread, man, like fifteen or twenty grand. It's beautiful for you, beautiful."

"What is it?" I asked the question without thinking, but as my words hung in the air I wanted to bite off my tongue.

"A crap game—old Wops and Armenians."

I told him to forget it and refused any further explanation. I felt ridiculous, as I had with Willy earlier, to be in a position where it seemed necessary to explain why I wasn't going to commit a crime. Men used volumes to justify their evil, but I was faced with justifying not doing evil. Red stared at me in disbelief.

"It's a cinch," Red said. "Why, they won't even call the heat."

"Then why don't you take it off? You can use twenty grand."

Red's mouth worked like a guppy's. Fear was what held him back, but he wouldn't admit it. "Some of the players know me," he said. "Man, let me tell you about it. It's beautiful."

"I don't want to hear it."

"Just listen."

It was easier to let him talk and ignore him than make him be quiet. "Go ahead . . . but remember I'm not interested."

"You will be. I shouldn't mention names, but I know you're both solid. When you know who's fingering the score you'll know I'm not bull-shitting about how good it is. Johnny Taormina is the guy. He's dead broke, flat on his ass and in debt. He needs bread."

"He's supposed to be a mafioso," Willy said. "What happened?"

The question mirrored my own. "Big Johnny T" was a name I'd heard since I was fifteen years old. He was supposed to be a Mafia, Cosa Nostra, Syndicate (whatever it's called this week) semi big shot. He'd controlled the bookmaking and loan sharking in the Lincoln Heights District, and it was said that he'd made a couple of hundred thousand dollars in the black market during World War II. It was a shocking surprise to learn that he was soliciting armed robbers to rip his associates.

"He blew everything gambling," Red said. "Half a million scoots in five years. He ain't got a dime, but he still knows things . . . a dozen soft scores, crap games like this one, layoff bookies that carry big bankrolls, money drops."

"Yeah," I said, "and after three get heisted they'll figure out who's the finger man and string him up by his nuts."

"That's no sweat off your balls."

"I don't give a fuck about the Mafia anyway . . . but fuck it. I don't want any of the action."

Red blinked. "Man, they didn't break you, did they?"

My face reddened. "Call it what you like—but like you told Willy, it's better to be a has been than a never was. And fuck Big Johnny T. He's probably a stool pigeon like the rest of those racketeers."

Willy said: "You could use the bread to get on your feet, Man, I know what you think now, but I know you. You've been a criminal since you were born."

"I changed."

Red was silent, confused. He struggled through rotgut wine, marijuana, and benzedrine to understand my refusal. I wondered how he'd become Johnny Taormina's solicitor. I'd never met the racketeer, but on the face of it Red appeared an unlikely choice. On reflection, however, it seemed more reasonable. They were from the same neighborhood and generation. Red was a drunken lecher, but he did keep his mouth closed and knew criminals outside the rackets, persons Johnny didn't know. Nor could Johnny run a classified advertisement for a bandit. Racket and thief underworld touch borders and sometimes overlap, but they are different. My few dealings with racketeers had made me simultaneously respect and despise them. They were successful, organized, cunning; they used money to make money. Only a small percentage ever went to jail, and then it was for a short vacation. On the other hand, most of them were, by my standards, traveling under false colors, more businessman than criminal. They pander to society's prohibited desires during business hours and live as paradigms of morality . . . And by comparison to the heavy criminal, who is the world's most independent predator, they are weaklings. Many will inform to the police on the heavy criminal. Society talks about police being corrupted by racketeers, but police also corrupt racketeers. The bookie stools on the robber quite often.

The folly of my thoughts rushed into awareness. I was thinking from the criminal view, with attitudes alien to my new goals. Decent citizens don't speculate even momentarily on robberies and stool pigeons and the ethics of crime.

It was 3:00 A.M. when we departed. L&L Red walked us outdoors and offered to chauffeur me around in his car until I got one of my own, providing (he laughed) that I bought the gas. He wasn't working. The cabin lacked a phone, but he wrote the number of a pool hall where he could usually be reached during the day.

*   *   *

As Willy drove toward El Monte my mood vacillated between exhilaration and depression. It was a joy to ride through the night and look up at stars thrown like powder across black velvet. Yet I was enmeshed with the same kinds of persons, the same sordidness, that accompanied all the wasted years. Willy and Red were friends—but their lives were so circumscribed, so hopeless. Entwined, such people trap each other. I wanted to break clear, find other kinds of persons and another life. Yet I'd called Willy. It had been my free choice against the alternatives of the halfway house or wandering alone my first night of freedom. I felt no wrong in making the choice under the circumstances—what was wrong was the circumstances. I hoped I'd meet other kinds of persons I could like where I worked—wherever that was going to be.

"Are we going to your pad?" I asked.

"We could, but Selma's gonna be in my ass for being gone so long. I've gotta go to work in about three or four hours. I missed two days last week she doesn't know about. They're gonna fire me if I miss another one."

"What kind of parole officer have you got?"

"A hope-to-die asshole. Man, he's so square—one of those educated fools. Got book learnin' up the ass, but doesn't know a fuckin' thing about life or people. He's one of those guys that lived in a neat white house with a picket fence and pretty lawn and went to Sunday school every day until he was sixteen. He never stole anything in his life—never had to steal anything. Him and his wife both teach Sunday school. I know he doesn't give her any head . . . probably didn't ball the broad until they were married. He acts like his job is some kind of missionary among the heathen parolees."

The crude description was funny in a way, yet Willy's difficulties were vivid. There'd be no communication between someone like Willy and the personality he described.

"He should be happy you're not hooked and stealing," I said.

"He wants everyone to be like him. People are different. I know that, and I'm just an illiterate dope fiend. I'll show you what an asshole he is. If he knew I was driving a car he'd throw me in jail and write a report to the parole board. He'd feel bad, but to him it would be his responsibility. Can't he understand that being without a car in L.A. is like being in Death Valley without water? It'd take me four hours to ride a bus to work."

Willy went on to recount how he'd already lost two jobs because the parole officer had told the employers that Willy was a felon-addict on parole. The regulations required an employer knowing, but not many parole officers pushed it. A man running a business wasn't interested in ex-convict problems; he was more worried about something being stolen. So Willy was fired after a couple weeks, the employer giving some lame excuse and the parole officer never realizing the truth of what had happened.

"How're you getting along with Selma?"

"It was pretty shaky when I got out. I didn't go with her right away. You saw the new baby, huh?"

"Hers—but not yours?"

"Right. I was down two years. I didn't expect her to watch television. Shit, I didn't even leave the television. I sold it and shot up the bread the month before I got busted. But a baby! It's so stupid. Nobody has unplanned babies anymore, not with pills and shit. Even an abortion. And she didn't even tell me until I was ready to get out. The baby was four months old. Right then I didn't want to see her anymore, and when I got out I stayed at Mary's for a week until I got a paycheck. Joe was already busted. Anyway, Selma came over, one thing led to another, and we made up. Who am I to throw rocks at anybody? And the broad's treated me pretty good considering everything. She's a pain in the ass sometimes, but I'm used to her. We're all right, I guess."

Willy stopped talking. He made me smile—so phlegmatic, unruffled by poverty and frustration. His dream was the permanent euphoria of narcotics and to be left alone. He would stumble along, accept the parole officer's indignities, incarceration being worse, live with his shrewish wife in patience, and he might finish five years parole.

"Let's stop and see Mary," he said. "She'll groove on seeing you."

"It's 3:30 in the morning."

"She won't give a fuck if we wake her up. She's used to it."

Mary Gambesi lived two miles from her sister and brother-in-law. Willy turned down an alley in the lower middle-class suburb and switched off the headlights. "She lives in the back."

Willy cut the motor and glided to a halt. Tiptoeing, our shoes nonetheless scrunching on gravel, we moved through extreme darkness to a darker bungalow. Willy knew his way. He rapped his knuckles against a window. A dog yipped nearby, aroused by the sound. A dozen canine voices instantly joined in chorus.

"Now some fool will call the police about a prowler. Sonofabitch." Willy rapped harder.

The windowshade fluttered; a pale, featureless face appeared. "Is that you, Willy?"

"Yeah, it's me . . . your old faithful brother-in-law."

"Is that Max with you?"

"That's him." Willy turned to me. "Selma must've called."

We trampled through a flower bed and around the corner of the building. Willy muttered curses at the yelping dogs. Mary waited until the door was closed before turning on the lights. She held a flannel housecoat tight around her throat with one hand. She put the other to her mouth at sight of me. The gesture was so dramatic that it had to be spontaneous. "Selma called and told me, but I can't believe it."

"Lazarus risen," I said. "Everybody gets out some day, parole or pine box." I could see that time had been gentle with her. Even barefoot, hair in curlers, she looked no more than eighteen. She waited for my appraisal, smiling softly. We shared a bond of affection.

"You haven't aged a day," I said.

She made a deprecatory gesture; she was unaccustomed to compliments. "Sit down," she said. "I'll be right back." She wanted to put on slippers and close the doors to the children's room. She asked us to be quiet.

"You two got somethin' goin'," Willy said. "Why don't you pull her? She's a thoroughbred and she's free. Joe and her are all over."

"She's still Joe's old lady as far as I'm concerned. And I dig her in a different way, anyway."

"If you really want to straighten up, she's perfect for you. I know you dig them stallion blondes, but you've gotta be on top for that. For someone to stick with you, ain't none better'n Mary. She's almost too fuckin' sweet to be real."

"Maybe she's too sweet for me."

Mary returned at that moment, hair brushed out. The vast black mane tumbled over her shoulders. Again I was struck with how young she looked. "Don't you ever age?" I asked.

"I pluck out the gray hair," She laughed, coloring.

"If I did that I'd be bald."

"I noticed . . . but you look distinguished."

"You still know how to make a fella feel good."

She blurted suddenly: "Oh, Max, I'm so glad you're free. I just hope you can stay out and enjoy life for a change." The gust of emotion made her blush. She turned to Willy. "Do you have any cigarettes? I know Max doesn't smoke."

"Just cigars," I said.

"Smelly cigars if I remember right." She asked if we were hungry, but the amphetamine in our systems left no appetite. Coffee was another matter. She began heating water and getting cups. I tilted the chair back against a wall and relaxed, tranquility spreading through me. I bathed in the warmth of friendship in the room. Watching Mary, I wondered what would happen to her now that Joe was gone. Would she find some working stiff? Yet she was so accustomed to criminals. I could remember her in the background when addicts came to buy from Joe. They'd fix in the bathroom and lie in stupors around the living room, dropping lighted cigarettes onto the furniture.

I wondered, too, about their children. Lisa was six and Joey Junior three when I went away. How had they turned out? What effect was the bizarre world of their parents and in-laws having on them? I asked Mary about them. Lisa, it seemed, was boy crazy and presently worried because her breasts weren't filling out as quickly as her friends'. Joe was a devil—but a delightful devil.

Mary mentioned that Selma was worried about Willy being with me, that I'd lead him into trouble. Willy shook his head in disgust, finished his coffee, and went into the living room to nap a while.

I didn't tell Mary, but Selma's fears were unfounded. If I was going back into crime, Willy would never be a participant. Beyond getting equipment and menial chores I'd never be able to trust him. I'd gone on one score with him—rather I'd taken him with me—and it would be the last time. The score was easy (as scores go): a bookmaker who carried at least two thousand dollars on him. The bookie weighed about two hundred and thirty pounds. The plan was to break into his apartment and wait for him. Willy would wait outside and follow him in and help me tie him up.

I made entry by cutting a screen in a bathroom, and waited in a Halloween mask. The bookie arrived twenty minutes later. I faced him, got the money, and sat him down on the sofa. He wanted to jump me. I could see it in his eyes. Willy never came. It was impossible to tie him up with one hand while holding a pistol with the other—and getting that close to him would be dangerous. I waited half an hour, finally backed out of the apartment. I knew the victim was leaping for a telephone the moment I closed the door behind me. I'd planned to have time to get away by tying him up. That was gone.

So was Willy. There was only a vacant space at the curb where Willy had parked. I sprinted through back yards and alleys to get away.

Willy was waiting at my apartment. He was trembling. He claimed that a prowl car had cruised by and doubled back, the policemen eyeing him. That's why he'd fled. I disbelieved him—but accepted the story without argument. Friendship was more important. But it was the last time I considered Willy for a caper. He lacked the necessary courage.

"Do you hear from Joe?" I asked Mary.

She sipped coffee and kept her eyes down. "Once in a while he writes, claims it's going to be different next time. But it's over, Max, all over. I've waited years for him to change. He won't. I don't think any of you will. I'd stay if it was just me, but I've got the children to think of."

"You should wait until he's on the streets, not quit when he's down. You know how that looks."

"I don't care how it looks. I've waited half a dozen times. I never even go on dates. When he's behind bars he always promises that things are going to be different. Maybe he believes it . . . I don't. All of you have some kind of sickness. This time he moved out before they got him. He'd come here and start fights and"—tears shone in her eyes—"he was living with a whore and selling heroin again. When he came to see the kids he brought her along."

"Was he giving you any money?"

"He wasn't supporting us if that's what you mean. He'd buy things for Joey and Lisa and they thought he was wonderful, but he wasn't putting beans in the pot. We get more from welfare now that he's back in prison. It's strange to realize it's easier to raise my children—and feed them—if my husband's in prison."

She poured fresh coffee and we talked until she was stifling yawns. I chased her back to bed, promising to drop by in a few days to see the children. Dawn was only an hour away. Willy and I could stop for coffee and pastry. He could then drop me downtown and go to work. I'd look for a job until it was time to report to Rosenthal's office.

My first night of freedom was over. It had not been accompanied by rockets, brass bands, and flying banners.

4

THE classified section of the *Los Angeles Times* had pages of job listings. A tiny fraction might suit me, and of these only half a dozen were downtown where I could answer them before seeing Rosenthal.

I answered four that morning. One was filled. Another was a giant firm that required employees to be bonded and I walked out without making an application. Two others needed salesmen—but needed a man with an automobile, and neither of them had a guarantee or advances while the salesman learned. I had neither car nor money to tide me over.

I'd walked three miles from office to office. My feet, after so many years of prison brogans, were unaccustomed to low-cut shoes. Blisters the size of half dollars, puffed with fluid, had formed on each Achilles tendon. When I reached the branch parole office on West Olympic Boulevard I was limping severely. Adding to my discomfort was ferocious heat beginning to press its fist on the Los Angeles basin.

The building housing the parole office was inconspicuous. Only the lettering on the tinted glass door—Department of Corrections, Community Services Division—set it off from being a small medical building. The waiting room had bare, hard benches, and was empty. A receptionist announced me and pressed a button. The door to the office area buzzed as the electrically operated door was freed. The sound made me wince inwardly. Beyond the door I would be in custody.

Rosenthal stood in a short corridor beyond, framed in a doorway with a pool of sunlight spilling around his legs. He was coatless and his short-sleeved shirt exposed a carpet of coarse black hair on his forearms. "Come on in," he said. "I was worried you'd run. You were pretty nervous last night."

"If I'd known about your electric doors I might've skipped. Something like that is frightening. I feel like I'm in a police station."

"Oh, those . . . not my idea. Have a seat."

"I can use that gate money."

Rosenthal shuffled through papers on his desk. "Here we are," he said, handing over the check.

I held it up. "Thirty dollars for eight years. Not much per annum."

"Society doesn't even owe you that."

"It isn't much to start a new life with."

"Try feeling more penitent and less the martyr."

"I'm sorry, I don't feel anything but a little bitter . . . and I'm trying to suppress that."

"So, what'd you do last night?"

I had a lie waiting in ambush for the question. "Visited friends, saw a girl."

"You stay with her?"

"No, in a hotel."

"That's pretty expensive for someone in your position."

"Not this hotel."

Rosenthal tilted his chair and propped his feet on the desk. He laced stubby fingers into a web behind his neck and watched me with candid intensity. He chomped gum placidly. Tension grew with the silence.

"I'm less than satisfied with your attitude," he said, "and about how you're starting out. First you don't want the halfway house, next you run around all night. It isn't a good start, not at all. It's your attitude, your outlook."

I flushed, wanting to protest, but snipped off the hot words. Confrontation with authority was a game I'd played often, and I knew its unfairness. If I argued, Rosenthal could put me in jail (unless I knocked him down and escaped), write a report saying whatever he wanted, and I'd be riding a bus with barred windows back to prison. There would be no hearing, no appeal, and I wouldn't even see what he wrote. So I checked myself, and decided that a plea for reason might get through.

"I'm sorry, if you think that," I said. "I'm trying to be forthright and sincere. Tell me what I've done wrong."

"It's your attitude. I keep telling you that. You act like you're free, can do what you damn well please. You're not free. You're still in *custodia legis*, a legal prisoner being allowed to serve part of your term outside on parole. Besides that, you've got a long, long record of mismanaging your life. And you should feel some remorse for what you've done."

"Eight years for bad checks should clean the slate." I saw the flippancy in the words after they were out. Rosenthal's face soured. He was obviously a moralist and outraged by my file. He knew more about me than anyone should know about another. Yet the words in the file were less than the whole of me. Nothing there showed that I was human.

"Look, I'm thirty-one years old. I've got more gray hair than you. I hope I'm old enough to make some decisions, at least where to sleep. If I didn't learn that much in prison it was a waste."

"It protected society. That's my job, too, my first job."

"They let me out. I want to stay out. You don't have to be on my back. You're doing a better job if you help me, aren't you? I want to be a decent human being. I might not understand what it means exactly the way most people do."

I paused, struggling to channel the tumult into words, sweat on my forehead and under my arms. "You've got to realize I'm not like you. I'm too warped and tangled by too many yesterdays to be like you. This doesn't mean I'm fated to be a menace to society. If I believed my future had to be like my past, I'd kill myself. I'm tired. I can bend enough to stay within the law, but I'm never going to be the guy who goes home to San Fernando Valley to a wife and kids. I wish I was that guy, but I'm not. And your threats aren't going to hold me. Threats instill fury, not fear."

"Nobody is threatening you," Rosenthal said. "I'm just telling you the realities of the situation, what you must adjust to."

"It sounds like threats."

"I'm here to help you with your problems."

"By giving me 'thou shalt' and 'thou shalt not.'"

"I don't make the parole conditions. I just enforce them. I can't give you a license to break the rules even if I wanted to. I wouldn't have a job very long if I did."

"Bend a little and I'll bend a little. Just ask that I don't commit any crimes, not that I live by your moral standards. If society demands that, society shouldn't have put me in foster homes and reform schools and twisted me. And these last eight years. Shit, after that, nobody would be normal. Just understand my predicament. I don't know anyone but ex-convicts, hustlers, and prostitutes. I don't even feel comfortable around squarejohns. I like call girls instead of nice girls. I don't need a Freudian explanation, which wouldn't change the fact anyway. But because I prefer going to bed with a prostitute doesn't mean I'm going to use an acetylene torch on a safe."

"It means you want permission to be a pimp."

"No! No! I just want you to understand that you can't reduce persons to formulas." I stopped to gather breath and select intelligible words from the bewildering thoughts rotating through my mind. "In essence, I'm asking you not to make this parole a leash that chokes me."

"In essence, you want to do what you want to do, right?"

My stomach sank. Rosenthal was unmoved. I'd tried. Rivulets of sweat trickled down my torso. An awful thought geysered up. What if Rosenthal was right? What if blindly following the rules was the path to happiness and inner peace? Could a person alone, even if certain, be right? Maybe Rosenthal had sight of me while I was blinding myself with words. To think thus was placing a foot over the abyss. I drew back to the firm ground of hidden indignation.

I'd tried to be honest and the motherfucker wasn't to be trusted. Now I'd use deceit.

Rosenthal watched me, a Giaconda smile on his fat lips, eyes gleaming, jaws working the gum. "Let's quit the bullshit and get down to cases," he said. "I'm going to tell you what I expect of you."

I nodded acceptance.

"I'm not putting you in a halfway house," he said, "simply because they're full. I think it'd be best, but I can't do anything. You've got a narcotic history so I'm putting you on nalline testing. Here's a form for you to sign." He reached toward a drawer.

"I haven't taken a shot of heroin since I was nineteen."

"If there is any history of narcotics of any kind—marijuana, pills, whatever, the subject goes on nalline testing." He slid the form and a ballpoint pen across the table. The form declared that I volunteered to participate in the nalline antinarcotic testing program. I signed the form, but I seethed. He told me that I was to report to the nalline center between noon and six-thirty on Friday, and gave me a slip of paper with the address.

"Now," he said, "what about a job?"

"I'm looking," I said.

"Someone in authority where you work must be informed that you're on parole."

The words make me sick to my stomach. I'd counted on being able to hide my past, be different by having others think me different. The enormity of the order stunned me. "How can I get a decent job under those circumstances?"

"It's the rules. This is the day you start doing your parole." He glanced at his wristwatch. "We have to break this off. I'm due in court this afternoon. When you find a place to live, leave the address with the girl outside." Rosenthal reached for his coat and ushered me outside. On the way he told me why he was going to court. He'd gone to pick up a parolee who'd missed nalline testing. On the way to the nalline center the parolee had reached into his pocket and surrendered a ten-dollar balloon of heroin. It was sad, Rosenthal said, because the man had two prior narcotic convictions and would mandatorily not be eligible for parole for fifteen years. The man was forty-six years old now.

I said nothing. I felt no sorrow for the man who'd played the fool so grossly. Nor was I angry at Rosenthal, who'd done precisely what I'd expected of him. He was more blind than me. I could see me through his eyes, but the empathy was unreciprocated. If I succeeded it would be in spite of him.

On the sidewalk, I felt pressed down by the heat. I had to find a room and sleep. The pills were wearing off and the delayed exhaustion was doubly intense. And the weight of the parole was growing into an albatross around my neck. And I had to comply with it or go back to prison. "Bastard," I muttered, "cocksuckin', motherfuckin', bastard."

5

I RENTED a room in a third-rate resident hotel near Seventh and Alvarado Streets, a neighborhood of decaying brick apartment buildings and Victorian mansions turned into boarding houses. This was an area of transient poor and near poor, alcoholics (not quite winos), pensioners, ten-dollar whores, junkies, and hustlers down on their luck. All were abundantly served by pawn shops, bars, and strip joints. I chose the neighborhood not because of the atmosphere, nor the cheap rents, though that was considered, but because it was easier to get around town from here than anywhere else. Downtown Los Angeles was twenty minutes away, and Hollywood half an hour by bus; these were the likely places to find a job.

I selected the particular small hotel because it had no desk clerk. Rosenthal would be unable to question my hours. A lifetime of furtiveness, plus my distrust of the parole officer, made this a prime consideration. The room had a sink, but the bathroom was down a hallway. The carpet was threadbare, but compared to bare concrete it felt luxurious. The window opened to a passage between the hotel and the brick wall of a garage. Leaning from the window, I examined the ten-foot drop as a possible escape route—then laughed at what I was doing.

My feet were throbbing. The blisters were swelling. I took off the ugly shoes and went downstairs barefoot to call the parole office and leave my address. Then I went upstairs. The day sizzled outside, a heat so intense it befuddled the mind. When I slept, sweating, I dreamed of drowning in the Sargasso Sea, pulled down by greenish-yellow seaweed. When I woke up the sweat had been chilled by the breeze. It was twilight and I was hungry. I was also refreshed from the sleep, so that after eating the special at a neighborhood café I decided to go for a walk and stop to buy toiletries.

The blisters kept it from being a long walk. After two blocks I decided to go back, but by a different route. On Eighth Street I started for a liquor store to buy a cigar. An old man came out. He wore the uniform of lost old men: baggy khaki pants and drab olive sweater. He walked stooped and crablike, but too firmly to be a wino. Yet a paper bag was in his hand, gripped by the neck of the bottle within. The bottle was answer to a lonely furnished room, to meals eaten alone at a fountain counter or cafeteria. Such old men gravitated to these neighborhoods, survived on company pensions, social security, insurance—but they were all alone, and lonely.

The old man brought memories of my father. He'd been fifty-two years old when my mother died bearing me. Four years later he was invalided with the first of many heart attacks. Ours was a family without relatives or close friends, so at the age of four I was taken before my first court, declared to be a needy child, and made a ward of the county. The county placed me in a foster home, and my father began the slow process of dying in convalescent homes and furnished rooms. From the very outset, I was a troublemaker—runaway, prone to tantrums, thief. If this behavior had any purpose, I was too young to articulate it, nor do I remember what I felt. Later my feelings were mingled—hatred for authority, loneliness, yearning to love. By then the state—or society—was committed to breaking the rebelliousness. By the time I was ten years old the circle was welded closed.

My father was never an important figure in my childhood, just an old, stooped man in khakis and sweater who visited the foster homes and juvenile hall. I remember begging him to take me home and was unable to understand how someone could be "too sick" if they were on their feet. Sick meant in bed. While on the runaway from juvenile hall with Gino, I went to his furnished room after spending three nights sleeping in a gutted automobile in a wrecking yard. He wanted to turn me in and I ran away from him and hated him. It was the last time I turned to him for help. Now I understand that he had sacrificed to give me clothes better than those the county provided and books when I developed the urge to read. But he was never a strong influence in my life. I grew up alone.

As I grew stronger, he grew weaker. He lingered, semi-invalid, for thirteen years. I became the visitor, stopping by the drab room or park for a few minutes, wishing I felt more. My feeling was more pity than love. While I was in reform school he had another coronary and was placed in a home for the aged to wait for death. The carpenter's union and social security paid for it, I guess. He was in this home the last time I saw him. It was while I escaped from reform school, prowling the streets with Joe Gambesi. The home was near where I now stood, a gabled Victorian building with large grounds. Tiny bungalows had been built in the back yard. A cleaning woman directed me to one of these. The interior was dark and gloomy, shades drawn to deny the sun and the flowers outdoors. A stench of human decay pervaded the bungalow. Half a dozen old men were in pajamas. Their faces were sagging, wrinkled flesh and stubbled beard. Their eyes all had a vacant glaze.

The visit was an agony. My father did not recognize me, and when I reminded him who I was it registered dimly. He began a whining harangue about the food, the other old men, and the people who ran the place. Someone had stolen the few dollars in change he had for cigarettes and he wanted some. They'd taken his watch, too, but he didn't seem to care about that. It was a big, gold pocket watch, the only valuable thing he'd ever owned, and he'd carried it for forty years. I gave him cigarettes and the few dollars I had. He begged me to take him away, reversing the role of half a dozen years before when I'd begged him. I was helpless as he had been. I was fifteen years old, escaped from reform school, and had five dollars in my pocket. I was crying enraged tears of frustration when I left. My father had become a baby, helpless, mindless, and alone. At fifteen the concept of death was unreal, but I understood loneliness with vivid clarity. And in the brief episode I saw human destiny starkly illuminated. This was the human condition, far from the glory of books and histories. I came away enraged at the universal indifference.

It was the last visit, the last time I saw him. On the way out I met a nurse. Her eyes widened, she blurted that the police had been there looking for me. She started for the telephone and I started running.

Two years later I was back in reform school when the chaplain showed me a telegram. My father had died. The chaplain glanced at his wristwatch, told me that he had to leave in fifteen minutes, but I could sit in his office and cry for that long if I wished.

Occasionally, when I saw an old man in khakis, such as the one coming from the liquor store, these memories were stirred. But nobody will remember my father when I die. He might just as well have never lived for all the meaning it had. I don't even know where he's buried.

Before returning to the furnished room, I telephoned Leroy's sister. A babysitter answered. I left no message. Through the glass booth I could see the city's lights beginning to go on. To spend the night in my barren room was too much like a prison cell. I tried the pool hall number L&L Red had given me, planning to have him come for me. A Mexican girl answered. Red had left an hour before.

I thought of walking downtown to the hangouts of ex-convicts, but walking was impossible because of my blistered feet. I bought two frayed paperbacks at a secondhand bookstore, picked up a newspaper, a can of beer, and cigar at a liquor store, and went back to the room.

6

MERELY looking for a job was agonizing, in several ways. The blistered feet made every step a limping torment. The heat wave, unrelenting and ferocious, sucked away strength and held down the polluted air so that my eyes watered constantly. Yet the worst part was psychological—the asking for work. No matter how often I told myself that uncounted millions of men had asked for work, it was new to me. Each office was frightening because it would expose the hollow desperation of need. I was, beneath whatever exterior I displayed, begging for a job. Only the trickle of money from my pocket—a dollar for lunch, two dollars for a second shirt, forty cents for carfare—kept me going, for I was terrified of going broke, of what I would do. I resented being thus driven, and perhaps it showed. I was ashamed of having to tell each prospective employer that I was an ex-convict, and perhaps I hid that shame with a note of defiance.

For three days I searched downtown, limping, full of self-doubt, torn from every personal tie that had ever bound me, trying to find the bedrock on which to commence building a new life. As the nickels and dimes trickled away, I felt the inexorable pressure of time. Nowhere could I find work. Being an ex-convict eliminated job after job, even menial ones such as delivery driver and janitor, because those jobs offered a chance to steal something, and nobody wanted to risk giving me that chance. I sat in stifling offices and air-conditioned offices, filled out forms, left my address. A giant insurance company gave competitive examinations. Knowing it was useless, nevertheless I took the examination and passed with the highest score in a group of thirty applicants. But when I told the interviewer that I'd been in prison, he said frankly that no company would bond me, and the job required bonding.

Back to the hot sidewalks and cramped buses—and to the crummy furnished room to count the dollars that remained.

Rosenthal came by on the third evening. He disliked the hotel's location: the neighborhood "smelled" of heroin. I wanted to talk to him about a job, ask him to let me be quiet about my record, but he was concerned only that I would appear at the nalline testing center on Friday.

Finally, a corporation that had a string of parking lots said they'd give me a job (the personnel manager had served time), but I would have to wait a month until they opened a new location. I was down to thirty-three dollars.

The temporary office help agency was on Wilshire Boulevard, on the eleventh floor of a blue skyscraper. It was the lunch hour and nobody was visible except a young woman at a rear desk. She flashed an impersonal, business smile and came forward to meet me. She was in her mid-twenties, and though not naturally pretty made excellent use of makeup. She had nice legs. They showed advantageously in a high, tight skirt. She made me ill at ease. After so long in an all masculine world, a sexually attractive woman made me nervous.

Efficiency personified, she ascertained my purpose, found that I could type, and had me at a typewriter for a test. She set a timer and went back to her desk. I pressed too hard for typing speed, made errors, cursed myself. The skill had served me well in prison, for I'd supplied my need for toiletries, coffee, and tobacco by typing football pools, petitions for habeas corpus, and letters for other convicts. Now I was doing less than my best work, yet reached the last line when the timer sounded. The girl came over, checked the copy and commented that I'd done very well. She was explaining that it would be easier to keep me working if I had other skills or would take other work. I only half listened. My jaws were tight. I felt shame for having a skill so trivial that thousands of halfwitted stenographers could do it.

She gave me an application form. Irritation smoldered as I filled it out. Where questions were asked about past work experience, I left the spaces blank. When I returned the form, a frown marred her smooth forehead. "There's something you left out," she said. "Where you worked."

"I haven't worked."

"Well, if you were self-employed, or in the armed services."

I shook my head.

"What did you do?"

"I was in prison."

She was looking down. Her eyes flashed up in surprise. Her pink lips formed an astonished O, and her eyes looked at me rather than through me. I stared into them and she blushed. They were dark blue eyes, with tiny coronas of gray around the iris. She averted them quickly. She pursed her mouth. Her long fingernails tapped a rhythm on the form.

"I need a job pretty bad," I said, gratified that I'd become a person to her. Superficially I'd told her the truth in order to comply with Rosenthal's rules, but a deeper need was to elicit precisely this response—this acknowledgment of some identity.

"Well, I guess we can leave it blank," she said, looking up with a sincerely warm smile. "We'll get you some work, don't worry. Do you have a telephone?"

"Yes, but I don't have the number with me."

"Call in and leave it with me. I'll call you a day in advance and tell you where to go. What about transportation?"

"I have a car I can borrow," I lied, sensing that it would open more jobs to have transportation.

"That does help," she said, marking the form. "Well, this is

Thursday. Tomorrow and Saturday we usually get calls for the following week. I'll keep your name right here on top of my desk and you should hear from me over the weekend." She went on, "I don't mean to be personal, but . . . what, why were you? . . ."

What crime might sound other than a crime? Now she saw me as a sufferer, but if I aroused the wrong image she would see me as a perpetrator. Compassion would turn to horror if the truth were known.

"I . . . had some marijuana."

"*That long* for that?" She was incredulous.

"This is California. There was a public panic about marijuana." My lie could have been the truth. A jazz musician I knew had served ten years for possessing a speck of marijuana so small that it had to be placed in a jar of clear oil and floated so the jury could see it.

"I'm sorry," she said. "I didn't mean to pry."

I muttered something unintelligible, ducking conversation. Other employees were beginning to filter back from lunch. The girl gave me her business card. Her name was Olga Sorenson.

While riding down the elevator, I felt as if an actual physical weight had been diminished. The work would be too trivial sooner or later, but for now it was a lifesaver.

Wilshire Boulevard shimmered in heat bounding off glass and concrete. The asphalt radiated heat waves, and the sidewalk burned through the soles of my shoes. My eyes ached in the harsh glare. A clock read 12:20. At 2:00 another possible employer was holding interviews for salesmen on the sixth floor of a Hollywood hotel. It was half an hour away by bus, which left me an hour to kill.

Hancock Park was nearby. I decided to rest on the grass for a few minutes and tour the county art museum, which was in the park. Sweat was running down my back as I found a shady spot beneath a tree and sat down. My shirt collar was wet and limp. The cheap suit had gone shapeless and would have to be cleaned and pressed during the weekend. My feet throbbed. Removing my shoes,

I found that the heel blisters had burst. The flesh was raw. New blisters had formed along the ball and big toe. It was ironic. I'd anticipated all kinds of problems on getting out, but not blistered feet. And they were crippling me. The art museum was out of the question. Art can hardly be appreciated with pulsing blisters.

In the distance I could see the hills above the Sunset Strip, a short bus ride away. The idea came that I could go there, look up someone I knew, and get some money from them. They would feel obliged, if not on their own initiative, then on urgings with implied threats from me.

I sat a few more minutes, watching three girls eat lunch and giggle. Then I moved on.

Across from the bus stop on Wilshire Boulevard was a men's shop. I remembered buying a sixty-dollar sweater there, mainly because it had cost so much. It was long ago, shortly after my graduation from delinquency to crime—before I was accustomed to expensive clothes and high living.

While riding the bus, I thought back to the two years before prison, to the Sunset Strip and, especially, to its vice underworld. The Strip underworld, with call girls that looked like ingenues and pimps that looked like young movie executives, was buffered from the savage underworld of the slums by location and money. My first awareness of it came from a downtown junky streetwalker. She had a notebook with several hundred telephone numbers, many of them well-known celebrities. Heroin had stolen her youth prematurely, and when she was beaten and thrown out for hiding money from her pimp, nobody else would take her. She told me how the top girls made seventy thousand dollars a year. The streetwalkers I knew made enough to buy dope and pay the rent. I was making good money with merchandise burglary, but there was risk involved, and certainly less money than what she talked about. She loved to tell stories and while I listened I sensed weakness in those who ran the racket. Nobody was organized—but the hint of possible weakness lay in their success. She told me they owned cocktail lounges, cigarette vending routes, and one had an eighty-foot yacht he chartered out.

I began frequenting their hangouts. Soon I decided that I was going to organize the call girl prostitution and take a percentage. The plan was to gather information about them, bring in some henchmen and show them that resistance would destroy everything. Force and fear would be necessary, but more important was the psychology of force and fear. They had to be confronted with something outside their experience, a knife-wielding maniac who raved about cutting their hearts out, who put a shotgun barrel in their girls' mouths and left no doubt that it was not bluff—let them know that their bars and businesses would be bombed, and the girls' tricks would be hassled over the phone, ruining the business. And the other part of the psychology was to show them that they weren't being ripped off, but were joining an organization that was beneficial. Floating whores and pimps would be kept from the territory, and if anyone gave them trouble they had muscle.

The main problem was getting help. The pimps, though un-organized, had money and could hire someone to eliminate one man. And getting help proved a stumbling block. Ragamuffins dragged from the slums would be ludicrous, especially if they were young, as were most of my friends. Junkies' horizons were too short—shoplift half a case of cigarettes to buy a spoon of heroin *now*. Older criminals wouldn't listen to someone my age. Some others I passed over as being inadequately violent. Others were too violent to direct themselves to a goal. They'd want to rape the girls, who were much more desirable than the faded creatures to whom they were accustomed.

Before I got ready to move, I made a mistake—I talked too much. I'd kept stealing, and during the weekend of celebration after selling the truckload of stolen meat, I took L&L Red to see the whore who'd given me the original idea. She cursed the pimps, and I drunkenly boasted about what was going to happen to them. The prostitute, from fear or maliciousness (who knows what goes through the mind of a dope fiend whore?), telephoned her former pimp.

The pimp and two goons caught me in a parking lot and bounced me around. It was a pretty fair ass-kicking, but I was able to drive away. That was the pimp's mistake.

A week later he walked into his apartment and I was waiting, pistol in one fist and brass knuckles on the other. I told him, "You didn't think this shit was over, did you?" Five minutes later his teeth were stubs, his jaw fractured, his ribs broken. He didn't walk away.

Leaving him alive was my mistake. Because I lived by the criminal code, I'd assumed that he did, too. He told the police what had happened and who I was. It surprised me at that time, though with more experience I would have expected it.

It took forty-eight hours to post bail, so the story preceded my return to the vice scene. The pimp was in the hospital, but the eyes of others were averted.

A week later he testified at the preliminary hearing, claiming he didn't know why I'd attacked him. Afterward, I couldn't find him. I wanted to persuade him to keep quiet. If persuasion failed, I'd be faced with the choice of fleeing California or murdering him.

Fate relieved me of the choice. He was killed by a hit and run driver. I expected to be arrested forthwith, punched around a substation for several hours until my lawyer got a writ. Nothing happened. Nobody came to see me. On the day of trial the charges were dropped because the prosecution's main witness was "missing". Incredible as it seemed, the police investigating the assault somehow didn't know about the accident, and those investigating the accident didn't know the deceased was a crucial witness in an assault trial.

The Sunset Strip underworld assumed that I'd killed him. Nobody knew the source of our quarrel, but rumors spread—the most generally accepted story was that he'd owed money to the Syndicate (or Vegas) and I was a "hit" man.

Fear had been indelibly printed in the Strip's underworld. Pimps turned their eyes away when I stared too hard. Bartenders became oily sycophants; seldom did I pay for a drink. It was funny to me, but I played it seriously.

The reason I never went through with the organization plan (besides still lacking henchmen) was that I got my own high-priced call girl, giving me nearly a thousand dollars a week, tax free. Twenty years old, from Texas, turned out in a New Orleans brothel, she called herself "Sandy Storm". It pays to advertise in whoredom like everywhere else.

Eight months later Sandy grabbed the brass ring, departed for Australia as wife of a man who owned a sheep ranch half the size of Texas. Her departure left me with twenty-two grand in a safety deposit box, a new Cadillac, and a good wardrobe. Instead of getting another whore to support me, I began using my leisure and money (criminals will listen to a man with a "front") to prepare scores, casing and planning and financing, for others to rip off. Most criminals live on desperation's brink, willing to act but lacking the wherewithal. They are quite willing to take the risk and give up a percentage if everything is arranged for them. One of my more lucrative operations was forgery. Twice a month I went to Tijuana and bought false identification and a book of checks printed on huge aerospace companies, Douglas, Boeing, Lockheed, or other giants such as Southern Pacific. Nobody questioned those kind of checks. Checks and three sets of identification costs $125, and finding thieves to hang such blue chip paper was easier than buying it. I took 30 percent. But this operation proved my downfall. A passer was caught, and in the police station had an attack of mouth diarrhea. Careless with success, I had checks, protector, and typewriter in the apartment when the door crashed in. The carelessness had cost me eight years.

By underworld standards (thief underworld), which consider how long the run of victories rather than the eventual fall, which is considered inevitable, I was a ringing success. Two years of silk suits, Cadillacs, and weekends in Palm Springs was the epitome of success, especially in the eyes of those with whom I'd been raised.

During the eight years in jail I realized that I hadn't been happy, and felt that what I'd had was a hollow triumph.

7

THE bus driver called out Sunset Boulevard, the brakes whooshed, and I got off—returned to the land of my success. I saw irony in what I was doing. Despite my sincere resolves for a new life, I was still trying to profit from the old one. I was hoping to find someone who knew me, who was afraid of me, and who would give me money because of that fear. Rosenthal would never understand, but he'd never been released from prison with the clothes on his back, no family, no job, and enough money for two frugal weeks.

Brassy sunlight dazzled me. Before I'd walked fifty feet down the boulevard the perspiration was stinging my eyes. The scenery was familiar—motels with giant signs, car washes, clothiers, towering palm trees. Yet it was different, too—time-yellowed. Motel paint was flaking, and streaks of red rust from leaky drainpipes marred building façades. Dust coated the palm trees, making them dull and lifeless rather than the bright green I remembered.

One thing was certain: my destination was more blocks away from the corner than my recollection. When I pushed through the padded door of the cocktail lounge my necktie was off, my coat was over my arm, and I was gritting my teeth to keep from limping. Confronted by the sudden dimness, wheels of coruscating light flashed before my eyes. Stretching a hand out, I eased forward and found a stool, feeling like a yokel, expecting gusts of laughter. Air conditioning washed coolly over my face, making me more conscious of my sweat-wetted body. A bartender—a dim figure in white shirt behind the plank—appeared. I ordered a Tom Collins and a glass of ice water.

While gulping the water and waiting for the drink, surroundings began to materialize as my eyes adjusted. The decor was a deep red trimmed with black. My memory was of gold and black. The dozen patrons made a good weekday crowd for any bar.

When I paid for the drink I was again uncomfortably aware of my dwindling funds. Who would the bartender most likely know? Rick DeLavelle came to mind. Rick was a coward; he'd throw an arm around my shoulder, profess undying friendship and offer help.

My glass was empty, drained faster than intended. The young bartender saw the empty glass and came over. He had long hair, his face was thin and sallow. I motioned to repeat the drink. "Say, I've been out of town. How can I get in touch with Rick DeLavelle?"

"You've been gone a long time, buddy. He died three years ago."

"Is that right? What happened?"

"I don't know." The bartender eyed me suspiciously, classifying me as a sucker or a policeman from the cheap suit and short hair.

When he brought the second drink, I asked, "What about Ernie Baker?"

"What about him?"

"Do you know him?"

"Seen him around."

"When does he come in?"

"I mix drinks and punch the cash register. I don't know when anybody comes in."

"Can I leave a note?"

"This isn't the post office, pal."

Anger had been smoldering because of frustration, everything; it suddenly geysered red to my brain. I stood up, leaning across the bar. "You dog ass cocksuckin' punk! I'll bust your head open and fuck you in your ass—punk! Say you don't believe, punk!" Saliva sprayed him. His eyes widened. Disdain was replaced by sudden fear. He shrank back until he bumped into the rear counter.

I trembled—but his face dissipated my fury. Only a vague, background recollection that a brawl would return me to prison had kept me from lunging across the bar and beating him senseless. And if furious words had not brought the proper response, I was ready to do it anyway. I was accustomed to men who were respectful of one another—not through etiquette but because each knew the other was dangerous and a slight could erupt in violence, possibly murder.

"Man, like cool it!" he said. "Please! I didn't mean—like when dudes come in here asking questions, what . . ." He spread his hands to explain confusion.

"Better learn how to talk to people or you'll get your ass brought to you, Jack," I said.

"Man, I'm sorry. I thought you might be fuzz."

"I might be, but talk to people with respect."

"No cop cusses like that." He tried to smile.

It was suddenly ridiculous.

"I'll cool it," I said. "Let me think a minute . . . Will you see Ernie?"

"He comes in now and then during the day. I go off at six—but I can leave word."

"I'll leave a note and call you tomorrow. What's your name?"

"Willy Epstein."

"Okay, Willy. Forget our little bullshit. How's Ernie doing?"

"Better'n me. He's got an old lady hustlin' and he's pushing a Caddy."

"You know where he's living?"

"I barely know him by sight."

"Then give me a pencil and paper."

Poised to write the note, thinking of the tone to establish, I suddenly saw how I was slipping toward the same old rut. I'd called Willy Darin and it had led me to L&L Red and the robbery proposition. Where would Ernie lead me? God knew I needed some money. I crumpled the blank paper and dropped it in an ashtray and started to walk out—then recalled that I hadn't paid for the second drink. "Fuck it," I thought, and kept going.

"Say," the bartender called. I ignored him.

Noonday's angry blaze swallowed me. Automobile traffic was a horde of shiny-backed beetles moving in jostling columns. Sweat was pouring down my body again and every step throbbed the blisters. It was time for the job interview in Hollywood, and my appearance would hardly be impressive.

A female voice called my name. A sleek new sedan was double-parked next to where I walked. Traffic was backing up. A blonde in the passenger seat was beckoning to me. I swerved off the curb and around the parked car. The blonde was too young for me to know, and whoever was behind the wheel was hidden by the windshield rejecting sunlight like a mirror. The blonde opened the door and moved aside to make room. "Get in."

I got in. The man behind the wheel was familiar, but memory failed to identify him. The car surged forward as those behind bleated their driver's irritation.

"Close the window, baby," the man said, "you're letting cool air out."

"Watch yourself," the blonde said to me, leaning across to push a button. Her breast rubbed negligently against my forearm. She sent electric shivers through my stomach. Whether from her blatant sensualness or my prolonged continence, the reaction was intense, and momentarily distracted me from trying to identify the driver. He was a big man going soft, belly spreading wide beneath a garish sportshirt. Full mouth, curly hair streaked with gray, olive complexion—Jew or Italian. The face of someone I knew fairly well, but long ago. No close friend.

"Introduce us, Abe," the blonde said, tugging his arm.

"Max, this is Angie Nichols—Max Dembo."

I acknowledged the introduction, but the blonde had clicked the tumblers. "Abe" was Abe Meyers, Bail Bonds. Only he hadn't been a bondsman when I met him, nor was he now if I remembered the newspapers correctly. His license had been taken for some shady deal. That was last year. When I met him, long ago, he'd owned a hot dog stand on the east side that catered to young hoodlums. He'd bought hot merchandise and sold pills. Later, he'd owned a down-town beer joint where bets could be placed. Someone else took the bets. Abe stayed in the background, always. Then Abe had moved to the Strip about the same time as myself. His action was different from mine and I didn't know what he was doing. But we were nodding acquaintances when our paths crossed, enough so that when I heard his name in prison it registered. He'd become a big time bail bondsman—but the main thing that rang in my mind was stool pigeon. There was a question mark involved. A pair of jewel thieves accused him of responsibility for their fall. I remembered that when I first heard the accusation I'd withheld judgment. The facts were flimsy. Yet there was enough to make me wary, avoid situations where a stool pigeon could harm me—and that would be easy considering that I was considering nothing illegal.

"We were at the light when you came out of Cheri's," Abe said. "Surprised hell out of me."

"It's me, in the flesh."

"Where you headed?"

I pointed down the boulevard.

"No car?"

"Not yet."

Abe frowned, caught my eye with a silent question. I looked meaningfully at Angie, also a question.

"She's all right," Abe answered. "She works for me."

"So?"

"So when did you get in town?"

"First of the week."

Abe whistled softly, "Been gone all that time?"

"Uh-huh."

Angie turned to me with wide blue eyes, accented by eye-shadow. "Where'd you go?" She expected names of places far away and strange sounding. Abe chuckled. The truth seeped through. "Oh," she said, blushing furiously. "I'm sorry."

"You didn't do anything to be sorry for." Her confusion eased my shyness.

We paused for a traffic light.

"I just opened a club down the way," Abe said. "Come on with us and have a drink, unless you're pushed for time."

"I'm for a cold drink. What happened to the bail bond business? I heard they folded you up?"

Abe gestured disparagement. "I'll be back in a couple months. I can always put the license in somebody else's name. I'll give you the whole story later."

"Later" indicated something beyond a drink. Abe wanted something. His friendship always had strings.

We were in Hollywood when he asked: "Say, do you know Lionel and Bulldog by any chance?"

"Yeah, I know 'em. They're saying things about you, too."

"It's pure fuckin' bullshit!"

His fervor was surprising. To genuine criminals such label was critical, but to a fringe criminal such as Abe the label figured to arouse as much fear as one feels listening to wild beasts raging in a zoo. Lionel and Bulldog were locked away for a long time, and gossip filtering from the faraway walls might irritate Abe, but it was nothing to get excited about. Abe's position was insulated by money, which always gains sycophants, and his position did not depend on the respect of thieves. Yet it was obvious that this was precisely why he'd stopped for me—for some reason.

Talk was cut off by Angie's presence. I settled back to enjoy her smell and speculate on her thigh brushing mine. I thought about the job interview in Hollywood, but I decided my clothes were too rumpled to give a decent impression.

The club, The Corral, was on a cross street between Sunset and Hollywood Boulevards, a narrow street. It occupied part of the bottom floor of a second-rate brick hotel. Abe's place had been given a façade of black tile so it appeared a separate establishment.

Abe pulled into an alley behind the hotel and parked in a narrow slot. "We don't open until seven," he said, "but people we know come in the back during the day."

A young man appeared in the doorway, drawn by the motor. He was good looking and dapper in trimmed slacks and loose sweater.

"Man, I'm glad you're back," he said. "The phone's been going crazy. Lloyd Johnson wants to know about that juke box deal and some broad keeps calling. Her old man is in the slammer and she wants him bailed out."

Angie sashayed ahead of us while Abe and the young man discussed the woman and bail. I watched Angie's butt wiggle against her stretch pants until she disappeared into the club. When the young man left us I said, "I thought you couldn't write bonds."

"I can't, but I do the work when someone asks and shoot 'em to Clyde Brooks. He gives me a kickback. I'll pick up a hundred or so on this one—for a couple of phone calls."

Rock and roll music coming from the interior suddenly stopped. When we reached the main room I saw the four-man band consulting over sheet music on a tiny stage cantilevered from one wall. Angie was climbing a short ladder to join them. The room was murky, chairs turned on tables. It was larger than it looked from outside. Two bars served the place. Tiny tables were raised on a dais at the front. Most of the floor had tables so close they almost touched each other. A miniscule dance floor was at the rear. The stage was ten feet high. The arrangement cunningly packed the maximum number of customers into the least space.

The young man joined us again. His name was Manny. He was manager and chief bartender.

"Have a drink while I make those calls," Abe said to me, gesturing to Manny to fix it. Abe went back into the short corridor to his office.

"Abe must love you," Manny said, placing a triple shot of gin and ice on the bar. "He'd rather give teeth than free drinks."

"I've known him for a long time," I said.

With unabashed curiosity Manny studied my outmoded clothes, the short haircut of another era. He wanted to ask questions, but years of conditioning in prison made me withdraw from his curiosity. Suddenly the band's twanging throb erupted and ended the necessity of conversation. Pulsing sound drowned out thought, much less talk. Angie was a dancer, prancing and gyrating in steps I later learned were frug, watusi, swim, and boogaloo. Whatever they were called, they were erotic. The gin was loosening me.

Abe returned and led me into the office, a cubbyhole holding a scarred desk, a chair and an ancient box safe that could be peeled open in thirty minutes, the kind that had made legends of safe-crackers four decades before.

Abe's girth seemed to spill over the desk as he flopped behind it. His fingers spasmodically squeezed a pencil and he perspired. He always perspired.

"They kept you a long time," he said. "What happened?"

"No juice with the parole board."

Abe's mouth worked in sympathy, but his eyes were calculating. "Got anything going for you yet?"

"I'm getting used to crossing streets again without getting run over."

"I'll bet it's a bitch adjusting." He paused, gathered himself. "You said you know Bulldog. What about Stan Bergman?"

"He's a friend of mine. What about him?"

"He's in jail waiting for trial on a robbery. I want you to go with me to visit him."

"Just visit him?"

"Well, there's more to it than that. Let me tell you the whole story. It's got to do with Stan, Bulldog, and Bulldog's kid brother." After vehemently denying that he'd finked on Lionel and Bulldog (but he could understand why they made the mistake), he told of how he'd been the middle man in peddling some hot diamonds—but he'd been unable to get the right price after they'd been delivered. Newspaper publicity was heating up the score and everybody was tense. Tempers got short. Bulldog wanted the diamonds back, but Abe had given them to a diamond wholesaler who was in New York. The two thieves had given him an "or else" deadline of twenty-four hours. That evening they were arrested with half the loot. They claimed Abe had sent the police through fear. He kept the diamonds he still possessed. According to Abe the value wasn't much, though I recalled Lionel mentioning twenty thousand dollars.

I interrupted: "That's a year ago. What's the trouble now?"

Bulldog's nineteen-year-old brother was the problem. Fresh from reform school, he was threatening Abe—he wanted ten thousand dollars for Bulldog's appeal. Stan Bergman was married to Bulldog's sister, making him the brother-in-law of the youngster. Stan could influence his wife, who could influence the youth. My role was to influence Stan. Abe had other blandishments, too, including a lawyer. If that failed—"Maybe you can help me with the kid."

"Why don't you come up with the ten grand? You were in on the play with those guys and made some change out of it."

"After all they said about me? Anyway, if I give in to some punk kid every two-bit hoodlum in town will try to muscle me."

The story disgusted me to a degree that only another thief can understand. He'd virtually admitted treachery about the diamonds—but that was insignificant to the possibility that he was a stool pigeon. If that was true he deserved to die. Yet his side of the story might be true. Stan Bergman could use help if he had a robbery charge. Abe wasn't going to cough up ten grand; that was certain.

Most important, I needed help, and going to talk to Stan was easy enough. If that was unsuccessful Abe would be on his own (I might even warn the youngster), but Abe didn't have to know that right now.

"I can talk to Stan. When do you want to visit him?"

"Soon as I arrange for a shyster to take us into the attorney room. The visiting room is probably bugged." Abe was looser now, savoring my acceptance and calculating what it would cost. He'd try to pay as little as possible. "I know you just got out. What can I do to help you get on your feet?"

"I need a job."

"A job! You?"

I explained the conditions of parole, that I had to work or go back, as if that was why I wanted a job. He'd been so incredulous that I couldn't tell him the truth—and the truth would have weakened my position with him anyway. "I'd like to get laid, too."

"You haven't got your ashes hauled yet. How long?"

"Eight semesters."

"Shit, there's plenty of swingers who'd take you home just for the cherry."

"Cut me into one."

"Come around here at night. The joint gets loaded with foxes. I'll fix you up."

"What about the job? That's the important thing."

"Are you serious?"

"Dead serious."

"Can you tend bar?"

"I can't do nothing but steal, talk shit and pull some slack."

"What about working as a doorman—just for a front. Check I.D. and pick up the cover tabs and keep the peace."

"That's cool."

"You've gotta show up. Twenty bucks a night. For you I throw in what you can drink. It'll give you a front until you get something going. You might catch a hooker, too. Enough of 'em come in here."

The job as bouncer would be ideal on a temporary basis. It would be an income and keep my days free to look for other things. I'd hold down the temporary office job, too. And I'd enjoy the night-club atmosphere.

Abe pushed away from the desk and apologized that he had pressing business. He told me to stick around if I wanted, slapped me on the shoulder, and reached for the telephone.

I sat in the club's dimness for the rest of the afternoon. It was too hot outdoors and I had nowhere to go. Manny got me drunk, Abe had told him that I was hired as doorman, so he was nominally my boss, but Abe had added that he wasn't to bother me. Manny sensed that I was something special. I wondered when the job started, wanted more details about Bulldog's kid brother so I could gauge the danger line of involvement. But Abe was too busy on the telephone to stop for conversation, and I was drunk enough to sit contentedly resting my feet.

Abe left to eat supper and change clothes for the evening's business. I lied about having business elsewhere and departed. I was feeling good. Temptation would be around this atmosphere, but it was comfortable for me, and I would make the decisions concerning temptations. Rosenthal would never appreciate the irony of the situation: I was getting a job solely on the basis of criminal reputation.

I got on the bus feeling satisfied.

After taking a bath and shaving, I walked from the room to a hamburger stand around the corner. The dusk crowd was a hurrying jumble. The hamburger stand had a patio beside it with an aluminum awning overhead. I sat watching the rush of pedestrians.

I was almost finished eating when a figure went by that I recognized. Augie Morales, reform school graduate, ex-convict, and childhood friend, was hurrying along the curb, passing pedestrians as if he was on the fast lane of the freeway. His clothes were rumpled, indicating his condition. Without thinking—and thought wouldn't have made any difference—I hurried after him. I caught up when he stepped into the gutter, bent over, and vomited. Some pedestrians glanced over. None stopped or said anything. The vomiting, I knew immediately, came either from too much heroin or withdrawal from lack of it. On arrival, I saw it was withdrawal. Sweat dripped from his cheeks, his shirt had damp circles around the armpits, and his eyes were wide, the pupils filling the complete iris.

I touched his arm and said his name. He jerked tense, like a cat

91

at a loud sound. He nodded recognition without surprise or warmth. It was understandable considering the supreme agony of his condition.

"You don't look good, brother," I said. "Got a runny nose."

"I'm one sick dog." He looked around at the traffic. "Got a car?"

"No."

"Let's keep moving. This neighborhood is full of narks."

"Where you headed?"

"The nearest fuckin' gas station to fix."

"You got some ghow?"

"Two grams in my mouth."

"What about a 'fit?"

"In my ass."

"My room's around the corner. You can fix there."

I led the way, limping. Augie wanted to go faster. He was having stomach spasms every twenty feet. His habit was obviously big.

I experienced a prickling of misgivings about my impulsive generosity. Offering my room was a fool's move. We might be stopped and arrested, and I'd go back to prison simply for being with him, especially if he had fresh marks on his arms. I should have turned back when I saw him vomit. Yet I'd known him for twenty years—we'd met in juvenile hall. He was there for stealing bicycles. Once in reform school, when I'd been fighting a Mexican, he'd kept others from ganging me. We were friends in prison, too, not intimate, but enough so we nodded and spoke whenever we passed. It might have been a fool's move to call him, but it would have been shameful to let a friend go by without speaking, or let him risk taking a fix in a gas station toilet.

All Augie said during the walk was "hurry up". A sick dope fiend has no thought beyond replacing misery with peace—or oblivion. Perhaps they are the same thing.

I locked the door and pulled the dresser in front of it. Augie spat out two red balloons, each the size of a tiny marble, each tied in a knot with the end snipped. Without embarrassment, he went to a corner and unfastened his pants. Crouching down, he poked a finger up his ass and prodded out a small, feces-speckled package. He rinsed it in the sink, unwrapped it and spread the contents on the dresser: the dish of a measuring spoon with a tiny wad of cotton stuck to its bottom, a shortened eyedropper with its tip wound in thread, glass fogged by previous use (men have been convicted of heroin possession by the scrapings from eyedroppers). The short needle was beneath the eyedropper's bulb, inserted in such a manner that the glass was a protective cover.

Though his body shook, his hands moved dextrously. "Get me a glass of water," he said.

As I drew it, a queasiness was in my stomach. Though microscopic when compared to what Augie felt, I had the same desire. Even after all the years my nervous system still craved the ecstasy that eradicates all pain—physical and psychological—and what it doesn't eradicate it makes unimportant. The difficulty in resisting the craving is something only the initiated can appreciate.

Augie's hands were deft and practiced. First he shot water through the needle to make sure it was clean, then broke a balloon and tapped the beige powder into the spoon. He added several drops of water and lighted three matches together, moving the spoon over the heat. The mixed odor of sulphur and heroin being cooked squeezed my entrails.

The powder became a semiclear liquid. Augie sucked it into the eyedropper through the dab of cotton. The needle fitted snugly over the threaded end. Holding the outfit delicately poised in one hand, he used the other to pull off his belt. Deftly, he wrapped his wrist and pumped his hand until the veins on the back became hard ridges. The veins were outlined by blackish-blue scar tissue from countless earlier needles. He tapped the needle's point into fresh scabs. A streamer of blood backed into the eyedropper, indicating he'd entered the vein. He squeezed the potion into his system.

Ten seconds—and Augie sighed blissfully. Torment was gone, so was worry. His swollen pupils contracted into tiny black points. The labored breathing slowed. His heartbeat had gone down, too.

Nothing had been said while he was fixing. There'd been no room for conversation. Now he gestured to the remaining balloon. It contained enough for five fixes for someone not hooked. "Take a taste," he said. "It's pretty good smack." His voice was slurred.

I'd been tempted, but finally decided. I shook my head. Augie's brow wrinkled in disbelief. "You use stuff."

"I quit."

"You're jiving. Are you sure?"

"I'm sure."

"I'll clean this mess up." He repackaged the outfit, slipped it in his pocket. He washed the spoon and rinsed his face in the sink, examining a stubble of a beard. "I need a shave."

"Shave here."

While he shaved he talked. Paroled a year ago, he'd worked as a punch press operator, happy to be free. Then the dreary treadmill had chafed him. He began taking a fix on payday—a few hours of well-being as great as anyone's. Then he added a second fix right after the weekly nalline test. His wife (he was married and had three children) began riding him about what he was spending for drugs. Each balloon cost ten dollars, the smallest buy he could make. Twice a week came to eighty a month, a substantial expense for a working stiff. Instead of stopping him, his wife's nagging drove him to peddle a few ten-dollar bags in the evening—just to pay for what he was shooting. With more heroin available, he used more. He began waking up needing a fix to go to work; he was hooked. He could no longer pass the nalline test, which meant he'd go to jail. So he disappeared into the city's swarm, a fugitive from parole. Fugitives cannot hold jobs, nor would any job pay enough to keep up his habit. He began peddling more ten-dollar bags. Every morning he'd spend fifty on a quarter of an ounce, package it into a dozen balloons, and go downtown, walking or sitting in coffee shops and bars. The addicts would find him. He'd sell enough to pay his rent and buy food and he'd shoot the rest. He carried two balloons in his mouth. The rest he stashed. A week ago he'd gone to visit his wife. Two detectives had been there—not for the parole violation but with a warrant charging him with sales of narcotics. He'd sold to an undercover agent.

"Wasn't your last beef for stuff?"

"All my beefs are stuff."

"Damn, brother, you're facing fifteen mandatory years. What the fuck are you doing wandering the streets?"

He shrugged; in heroin euphoria he was unable to experience fear or harsh reality. "What am I gonna do?"

"Blow this motherfucker! Get out of the country. Mexico. They'd never bring you back."

"I don't know anybody over there. I wouldn't know what to do."

His tacit surrender was horrifying. "Man, you're hooked like a mountain trout. They're gonna pick you up sooner or later. Get a biscuit and rip something off—a bank, anything! Get enough money to run for it. If you're gonna get busted, hold fuckin' court right on the street. You've got nothing to lose."

"Fuck it. If they bust me, I'm busted."

"For fifteen years."

"I've been locked up all my life anyway. The food's okay in the pen and I can play handball. I've got more fuckin' troubles when I'm out than when I'm in."

It was said in irony, but was too truthful to snicker about. His future was frighteningly clear. He'd stay as drugged as he could for as long as he could, continuing to make small heroin sales to exist. It would be a minor miracle if he lasted three months, especially when he existed in police-infested neighborhoods. They'd apprehend him and he'd spend fifteen years in the tomb of walking dead.

He patted shaving lotion on his haggard cheeks, combed his hair, and straightened his clothes. He sat down to rest a few minutes before plunging back into the maelstrom of the streets. He looked around the cheap room. "Not too bad. Most of these flops don't even have a carpet."

"A flop is a flop." I was angry because he allowed himself to be destroyed without anger. Whatever he was (and I didn't think it was bad, but tragic), and whatever society's right to protect itself, his survival right said he should struggle to the last gasp.

"When did you raise?" he asked. Before I could answer, his head drooped forward so his chin neared his chest. He jerked it erect. "Goddam! I'm nodding. What did you say?"

"Nothing."

He grunted and nodded again. I'd known him since he was a shiny-faced youth. Now the face had lines deeply etched. His shoulders, once thick and powerful, were bony—and his hair was riddled with gray. He jerked from the stupor again. "Hey, Max. I know you just got out, but can you let me have a few pesos?"

I'd planned to give him five dollars of my meager resources. Instead I gave him ten. "It isn't much. I'm on my ass too."

"It'll help. I've got that other balloon for tonight. I'll be sick in the morning but the connection is going to give me some stuff on consignment." He stood up and put on his shirt. "I gotta split. Are you gonna be staying here awhile?"

"A couple weeks."

"I might drop by."

I watched him depart down the hallway, moving with nonchalant swagger, one arm swinging exaggeratedly, shoulders rolling in a hipster's stroll. Affected in youth to show toughness, it had become habitual. Such a stride—like blue, hand-made tattoos—were a giveaway that a man had spent some of his youth in institutions.

I'd thought about going to a neighborhood movie, but that was before meeting Augie. The ten-dollar drain changed my mind. I read for an hour and dozed off. After midnight I woke up hungry and walked to a coffee shop on Alvarado. The sidewalks were still full, brassy music escaped from beer joints and cocktail lounges. The giddy laughter of couples coming out of these places aroused my envy. Everything magnified my yearning to be out on the Strip, or in Malibu—anywhere with good clothes and money in my pocket to enjoy life.

I settled for coffee and a piece of stale pie.

8

THE next morning, a Friday, I telephoned Olga Sorenson at the temporary employment agency. I wanted to hold down two jobs, if possible, and get money for clothes and some kind of automobile. She promised to keep me in mind, took the hotel's telephone number, and said that she would keep it on her desk. She'd be in the office over the weekend and wanted me to call again Saturday afternoon.

Then I called Abe. He, too, was glad to hear from me. A lawyer would be waiting for us at 5:00 P.M. in the parking lot of the Central Jail. He'd wasted no time in arranging the visit.

At 4:30, Abe picked me up on a Wilshire Boulevard intersection and headed toward the freeway. He was wearing a suit of light gray iridescent silk, elegantly tailored. On his little finger was a four-carat diamond pinky. It would buy me several suits—and an automobile. Taking it would be easy: wait in the alley behind the club and jam a pistol in his ribs. I could even walk him back inside and clean out the safe. I suddenly realized what I was thinking and stopped it.

He noticed my withdrawn mood, mistook its source. "Don't worry," he said. "There's no sweat with Stan. He's up the creek without a paddle. He helps us and we'll help him stay away from a habitual criminal sentence."

"Maybe the kid won't listen to him," I said.

"Oh, he'll get the message between Stan, Stan's wife, and you.

We might even put him onto something good, get him a whore. Anybody that young can be dazzled."

"For your sake, I hope you're right."

"Mmm, maybe for my sake, but probably for his. I'm not a sitting duck. I can throw a little muscle when I have to—better believe it! And I've got money. I'll hire what I can't put out."

I said nothing, but I silently modified my evaluation of Abe Meyers. He was riveted together with anxieties. Fear always sat on his shoulder. Yet it wasn't the kind of fear that paralyzes. Under pressure he could be dangerous. And he was cunning—probably too cunning for the youngster.

Leaving the freeway, we wound through ghetto streets, passed scrap yards. Suddenly we were on a dingy street where the sidewalks were lined with plywood bungalows, each with a sign: Bail Bonds, 24 Hours. The jail was nearby.

Moments later we could see the jail, across the street beyond a trimmed lawn and trees. The huge, beige concrete building was brand new, totally bland—yet it was the most modern and expensive structure in a square mile.

Word had come to prison that the new jail was worse than the old—that brutality was more freely dispensed—and I remembered being fifteen years old in the other one and having a fight with another juvenile. Three deputies handcuffed me to a drainpipe and took turns punching me in the body. After breaking three ribs they threw me in the hole, a steel box on wheels. It was utterly dark; I couldn't see my hand an inch from my face or know if it was noon or midnight. A quart of water and three slices of bread were the daily food ration. Every three days they brought a paper plate with a gruel of oatmeal sprinkled with raisins. Kneeling in the darkness, I lapped it up like a dog. Nineteen days later they took me back to the reform school (it was when I was captured on the escape) and I collapsed. I had pneumonia. And even if I'd now changed my life, I hadn't changed my loathing for such places and those who ran them.

Abe turned into the vast parking lot. "There he is," Abe said, indicating a man leaning on the fender of a brown Rolls Royce.

"Whose Rolls?"

"His . . . and the finance company. They've been trying to repossess it for nine months. Allen McArthur is the world's greatest deadbeat."

"That's Allen McArthur—the infamous motherfucker?"

"You know him?"

"Just about him. He took money for a friend of mine's appeal and let the time limit lapse. And he's done worse to others, so I hear."

"He's okay, for what he is."

"He's a piece of shit to me. Shyster lawyers are worse than stool pigeons."

"Hold it. We need him right now."

"Yeah, okay."

Abe parked in an empty space near the Rolls Royce. Allen McArthur came over and Abe introduced us. I took his handshake, but my lip was curled. The hand was delicately boned, and the face had a sunken chin, rheumy eyes, and acne-pitted visage. He saw my hostility and put Abe between us as we walked toward the building.

Entering the attorney room required passing through two electrically controlled gates ten feet apart, synchronized so that only one would open at a time. It kept anyone from rushing the gate. A deputy sat in a bulletproof control box between them. Allen McArthur showed his attorney credentials and filled-out forms. The deputy dropped them in a pneumatic tube for delivery to another part of the jail. The second gate opened and we went in to wait for Stan Bergman. The room was forty feet long; four lines of tables ran lengthwise. Along the center of each table a plexiglass partition was chin high to a seated person. A deputy stood at the end of each long table, able to watch down it and make certain nothing was passed over the divider without permission and examination.

It was the jail's supper hour and the room was only half-filled.

Usually the room was jammed with lawyers, bondsmen, parole and probation officers—everyone involved with criminal justice except judges. The prisoners sat on one side, jail-pallored (the blacks turned a sickly gray), haggard, reduced to urchins by wrinkled denim with County Jail blazoned in orange paint across knees and butt and chest and back.

Even half-filled the room babbled, each person in his own crisis, unaware of anyone else. Lawyers with calculating eyes drained every penny. They were selling hope, and the price goes high. Frequently they discarded the money-drained cadaver, or traded it to the district attorney's office for one who paid more: "I'll plead this one guilty. You give that child molester probation."

The room's clamor and my curtness to Allen McArthur stifled small talk. We sat in a row, Abe in the middle.

Stan Bergman appeared, stopping to check with a deputy at the door, his eyes meanwhile swinging over the room, seeking his visitor. I knew his worried thoughts. He wanted to be prepared for detectives.

Abe waved and beckoned. Stan came down the row between the tables. It had been years since I'd seen him. He'd aged two decades. He was stooped; his shirt seemed to be on a clothes hanger more than shoulders. His hair was gone and his eyes, sunk into cavernous hollows, burned with sick ferocity. In a single moment of utter and blinding clarity I was able to view existence through his eyes—a forty-year-old three-time loser waiting trial on armed robbery.

He recognized Abe from a distance and scowled—but when he got closer and saw me the scowl became a huge grin. We were friends, but hardly such good friends as to justify the radiant expression. It was his desperate predicament that added luster to his feelings. Abe had been right to bring me. I'd have influence.

Nodding terse acknowledgment to Abe and McArthur, Stan sat down directly across from me. The rules forbade handshakes. "Hot damn, Max! When did you spring?"

"A few days ago."

"Me and the Horse were cutting you up last night. He said you were short."

"Horse just got out last month. What happened?"

"Hot burglary. There's four ex-cons in our tank, all of us drove tight."

"Damn, baby, you're looking hard about the mug. You used to be a halfass pretty kid. You won't be able to catch yourself a man when you get back."

Stan laughed. Prison's ubiquitous homosexual banter gave a touch of humor to his grim situation. "Shit," he said, "I might turn jocker if I can't get a man to take care of me."

"They say all jockers are punks lookin' for revenge."

"Are you coppin' out?"

"Man, we're not discussing my sophisticated sexual habits."

Laughter flashed color to his sallowness.

"How you doin' otherwise?" I asked. "How's the jail?"

"About jails, I'm Duncan Hines—and this is the shittiest fuckin' jail in the world."

"I heard it was a motherfucker."

"These deputies must've been trained in Auschwitz. Even without the head thumpin', the place is a nightmare. Just going to court. They roust you up at 3:30, run you down to the bullpens, and put you in chairs, six dudes to a set. Each bullpen is eight by twelve, and each one is for a different court. So if there's fifty dudes going to Pasadena or Long Beach, there's fifty men in an eight-by-twelve cage, in chains—and they leave you like that until eight or nine in the morning. If you gotta piss, you drag five dudes with you. If you don't like it, they'll rattle your head. If I wasn't facing a life sentence I'd plead guilty just to get back to the pen away from this stinkin' motherfucker."

"You'll make it."

"I'll make it—but goddam! I ain't been convicted yet."

"Quit arguin' ethics. You know white folks don't care about that shit. What's your beef look like?"

"Routine supermarket heist."

Routine heist, I thought, but with two prior convictions it meant the habitual criminal sentence. And a supermarket! So many had been robbed in the early '50s (when supermarkets became abundant) that most of them now had elaborate security.

Stan gave the details. He'd used a stolen car, and someone had taken the license number, which didn't matter except that when the police found it they also found a single fingerprint on the rear view mirror. A single print was insufficient to pick him from the FBI fingerprint file (which is classified by ten fingers), but if there is a particular suspect the single print is positive identification. Eight months later someone had whispered his name to the police. His prints on file compared with the one from the car got him arrested. In a line-up one witness was "pretty sure" it was Stan who had the gun. "Might beat it with a good mouthpiece," he said. "But with the public defender . . ." He shook his head and turned a thumb down. "I can get some alibi witnesses, but with my record I can't get on the stand."

Stan was right about public defenders. He had no hope if that was his representation. Most were callow youths, totally inexperienced, or incompetents, and even if there was a budding Clarence Darrow among them, his hands would be tied by having sixty or seventy cases. No attorney can keep track of that many cases, much less represent each one individually. All a public defender could do was go through the ritual of "so stipulated . . . waive reading of the information," and try to keep the mill turning. And if most criminals' lawyers were equally incompetent, they could at least stall. From what Stan said, he wouldn't be acquitted without a miracle. But a decent lawyer might intimidate the prosecution, not to the point that Stan would win, but to the extent that he would stall for months, draw things out, jam up courtrooms, and cost money. The prosecution might well deal for a guilty plea to a lesser charge, or drop the habitual criminal complaint. What remained of Stan's life was in the balance. No wonder he'd aged. I felt sorry for him.

Woven into my compassion was disgust at Stan's incompetence. A squarejohn watching Dragnet would avoid Stan's blunders. Without a witness able to say, "That's the man," it was virtually impossible to get a robbery conviction. Yet Stan had gone bare-faced and he'd left a fingerprint.

Abe came into the momentary silence. Stan looked at him, the grin he'd worn talking to me was now turned cold. The outstanding accusations against Abe were enough to justify coldness. "How're things going?" Stan asked.

"Pretty good. Been planning to get down to see you—find out what I could do. When I ran into Max I figured you'd like to see him too."

Stan nodded, but he was scarcely listening. His mind had returned to viewing the gray hopelessness of his position. He sagged within himself.

"And I wanted to talk to you about Bulldog, get that business straight."

"That's none of my business," Stan said, again cold. "It's between you and him."

"The 'Dog's kid brother, your brother-in-law, is trying to put weight on me. Maybe you can talk to him."

"I haven't seen him since he was thirteen." Stan wasn't really listening. He was hardened against Abe.

"Maybe your wife knows where to get in touch with him."

"What!" Stan flushed. "I'm not gonna help set him up for you." Stan's eyes burned me—accused me of being Abe's hatchet man.

"Nobody's gonna hurt him," I said. "We just want him to lighten up. If you can help, it's to everybody's benefit, including yours."

"How's it to my benefit?"

I raised a hand to quiet Abe. "Look, homeboy, talk to him, or have him get in touch with me. I won't cross you. But put yourself in Abe's shoes. What would you do if some gunsel was talking about blowing you up? You'd get him first. Abe's trying to be sensible."

"What if it's true? What Bulldog says?"

"You know what. He's got it coming. But the thing is—" I purred like a used car salesman, and was ashamed of myself—"we don't know if it's true. You've been in the game long enough to know how quick dudes cry stool pigeon when somebody's fucked 'em out of some bread. I heard the story and I'm not sure. I wouldn't call 'em liars, but I wouldn't judge it on the evidence I have. You don't know anything more than I do. The kid knows less than either of us. Anyway, it's 'Dog's business. Say the kid gets hurt—or gets busted for hurting Abe. How will 'Dog feel about that? Now Abe wants to help you—get you a lip—but how can he do that when your kid brother is threatening to blow him up?" I stopped, looked into Stan's eyes and winked, and his eyes narrowed as he understood the situation.

"I guess I could have him visit me and get him to cool it. He used to listen to me. Why don't you guys come back next week?"

"What day?" Abe asked.

"Wednesday or Thursday. I won't see my old lady until Monday."

"Are you sure you can handle him?"

"He respects me. He'll listen."

"That's appreciated," Abe said. "Now you need a lawyer. I'll loan you the money. You can pay me back when you get out."

"If I get out. I'll be happy to squeeze from under the life jolt."

"What about Allen here?"

"Thanks, but no thanks." Stan started to elucidate; it was unnecessary.

"Fine lawyer," Allen said, and nobody gave him any notice.

"Who've you got in mind?"

"Richard Barton."

"Barton's expensive," Abe said.

I interrupted: "If you're gonna do something, do it. Don't fake."

Momentarily, Abe looked hostile, then nodded acquiescence.

"I talked to Barton already," Stan said, "and the tab isn't all that heavy. Fifteen hundred, maybe less if it doesn't go to trial. He already knows I'll plead guilty to a second degree. I'm going back as a parole violator if a jury said I was Jesus on the cross. With a second degree I'll have a chance for another parole in six or seven. Barton won't fight it like a murder beef for fifteen hundred, but he'll do what he can—and I think he can make a deal. I'm just another case, nothing special."

"Okay," Abe said, "you can get Barton. But we can have Allen here check on the prosecution's attitude toward a deal. That won't hurt."

Allen McArthur had mysteriously produced a note pad and silver ballpoint. "I'll call the first thing Monday," he said. "What's your case number and what department are you in?"

Stan hesitated, then apparently decided that what he said now wasn't a commitment to Allen McArthur as his attorney. "I don't remember the case number. It's up in the tank. But I'm still in Master Calendar, Department 100. I've been getting postponements for three months on the basis that I want to get my own lawyer. Judge Keene is getting pretty shitty about it. He's about ready to jam the public defender down my throat."

"I know the deputy district attorney assigned to that court," Allen said. "We get along okay. If he'll deal with anyone, he'll deal with me. If not—Barton can get it transferred to another court when they set a trial date. You can dicker when you get there."

"Maybe this'll be better," Abe said. "Why put out fifteen hundred if we don't have to?"

I asked Stan: "Have you got any money on the books?"

"Not a sou. I keep up my candy and cigarette habit by trimming suckers playing poker. You know how that goes."

"I'll leave fifty for you," Abe said.

"Who's gonna let me know what happens Monday with the D.A.?"

"Max can tell you Wednesday when he comes about the other," Abe said.

"I might be working next week," I said, thinking of the office job.

"Well, somebody'll be here."

"Man, not that long!" Stan said. "Put yourself in my jock strap. You'd wanna know what's being decided about your life."

Abe paused, obviously pondering what a premature disclosure of the legal situation would do to his lever on Stan. It was playing games with misery. I spoke up: "I'll let you know Monday afternoon, in person or by telegram."

"I doubt if the prosecution will make a definite commitment by then," Allen McArthur said. "They'll want to check the matter first."

"You'll know what their attitude is," Stan said. "Send me any kind of word. Shit, send word about the weather. When they bury you in here you can't even see if it's raining outside."

We agreed. Once the matter was decided, a chasm opened between the two sides of the table. One side was going into the city's twilight and night's myriad possibilities. I was going to the club with Abe, gulp down good Scotch, and try to pull a sweet-smelling broad into bed. Stan was going back to the jail tank where the fluorescent glare endlessly burned the eyes and where he had the choice of playing poker for nickels or reading lurid paperbacks—or he could stare at the ceiling, thinking of fifteen years served in prison with life to go.

Abe glanced at his wristwatch. "We've gotta go, Stan." He stood up and slapped me on the shoulder. "I'll keep Max out of trouble."

Stan wished me good luck and told me to have a drink for him. The waste and defeat of his life sorrowed me. I asked if he wanted me to call anyone.

"Everybody I know is in jail. The bitch I had blew me off in the sub-station. Just be cool." He got up and went up the aisle toward the deputy. We went toward the exit gate. I turned to watch Stan. He paused in the door and gave me a clenched fist salute.

The electric gate buzzed, unlocked. I turned to follow Abe.

And saw Rosenthal three feet away. The parole officer was at the deputy's booth, profile toward me, jowls drooping over wilted collar. He had obviously come to visit a jailed parolee, a routine trek for parole officers. His presence was against the odds, but far from incredible.

My heart pounded. I moved right and forward, squeezed in behind Abe's bulk. His shoulder was inches from the wall. If I could ease him between myself and Rosenthal and pass around his right while he turned left . . .

I grabbed Abe's arm. "Cool it," I said, moving him from the wall. Abe was startled. He stepped to the left to give me room, and bumped into Rosenthal. The parole officer reflexively turned. And we stared into each other's face. I flushed. His eyes widened slightly. The jowls changed color, first paling with blotches of red, then flaming but speckled with blotches of white. It was quite a display.

"What, pray tell, are you doing here?" he asked in too calm a voice.

My mind burned with awareness of the locked gate. I was in custody. "These men were visiting someone and I came with them," I said. "Mr Meyers here is giving me a job. He's a bondsman. This other gentleman is an attorney."

"So you came in rather than wait in the parking lot." His voice had an edge of shrillness. He glared at Abe and Allen McAthur, jerked his thumb toward the latter. "I've seen you before. Are you on parole?"

"I said he was a lawyer." The direness of the situation was spreading through my stomach.

"Here's my bar membership card," Allen said, bringing out his ascot. He started to offer it, then pulled it back. "You'd better show me your credentials, too."

Rosenthal colored again.

"Who is this guy?" Abe asked me.

"My parole officer."

"Oh."

"And who is he?" Rosenthal demanded, not to be outdone.

"He's giving me a job."

"What kind of job?"

"In a nightclub in Hollywood."

"Who'd you visit?"

Nobody answered. Rosenthal glared at me. Allen McArthur interrupted in his best courtroom baritone. "I came to interview a client. Mr Meyers is considering taking him out on bail. This gentleman—I don't recall his name—was with us, as it was rather warm outdoors." Allen smiled, shrugged, and conveyed that everything was natural and above suspicion.

The deputy sheriff in the booth buzzed the lock into the attorney room. People were waiting on both sides of the gates. Rosenthal had to decide now whether or not to arrest me. "Wait outside," he said. "I'll see you when I'm through here."

"These men have to go."

"I don't care what they do. You wait." He hurried through the gate. It clicked shut and the gate going out buzzed open. It was as if the gates of heaven opened.

Fury rose in me as we walked down the corridor. I was tempted to keep going, walk out and get in the car with Abe. But maybe it was what Rosenthal wanted. Once I jumped parole he'd have me dead to rights. It would mean three or four more years in prison—and another parole afterward.

"Goddam," Abe said, "how do you put up with that bullshit?"

"It's better than staying in prison. Not much, but some."

In the lobby, Abe asked what I was going to do.

"Wait to see this prick. What else can I do?"

"I'll wait with you if it's not too long."

"That'd just aggravate him."

"You're not in real trouble, are you?"

"I don't think so. I'll cool him out."

Allen McArthur coughed to get our attention. "Excuse me. I've got a dinner engagement."

"Okay, Allen. Get on that Monday and give me a call," Abe said.

Allen MacArthur went through the glass doors into the beginning twilight.

Abe pulled a roll of money and peeled off twenty bucks. "That'll take care of cab fare. Are you coming by the club tonight?"

"Yeah, if I'm not busted."

"I'll introduce you to some foxes."

He patted me on the shoulder and went through the doors. A minute later I remembered that he'd forgotten to put the money on Stan's books. That, too, Rosenthal had caused.

When Rosenthal returned twenty minutes later, I was outside smoking a cigar and watching the grimy shapes of the industrial neighborhood become less harsh in the deepening twilight.

"Living high on the hog, aren't you?" he asked.

"How's that?"

"Big cigars."

"It's a ten-center." I started to ask him if smoking cigars violated the parole conditions—but the bitter indignation was submerged in a mixed salad of emotional exhaustion, loneliness, depression, and a longing for peace. I was tired of conflict and wondered why a Jew, who had thousands of years of experience with oppression, could not see what he was doing. He was my *bête noir*, but not through deliberate malevolence. No, it was fear of being conned that kept him from listening. In rigidity he found safety.

"What really brought you here?" he asked.

"Just what I told you," I said quietly. "Look, Mr Rosenthal, try to get at least one foot off my neck. I'm not playing games on you, and I try to be sincere. One of those men owns a night club. Check on it. He's giving me a job. He might not be a booster in the Rotary Club, but he's got a job. I don't know the president of General Motors, and he wouldn't hire an ex-con anyway. Not many people will."

The weary lament got through, and Rosenthal's adamant manner lessened. "Max, you know a parolee shouldn't be visiting jails. If you're going to be a decent citizen you've got to get away from the criminal atmosphere. Bondsmen and night clubs and jails are the same rut, the same pattern. They're no good for you."

"I don't know where else to go, or anyone else to go to. I'm not going to someplace called the Sisters of Mercy Salvation House."

"Who was the man they came to see?"

The question landed heavily. A whole life conditioned me to never give information, any information, but especially a name, to authority. It was a holy commandment. Rosenthal's question clogged my circuits. It took a lengthy hesitation before I decided that he could find out simply by asking the deputy in the booth, if he had not done so already. A refusal or a lie would be dangerous. I told him.

"Why'd you take so long? It shows you still think like a criminal." Rosenthal didn't press for more details. He asked what kind of job Abe was giving me. When I told him what the job consisted of, he wanted to know what stopped me from pocketing the money.

"The guy trusts me."

"So he must. But it creates a bad image for the parole department when parolees steal from their employers. Makes it hard for someone else to get a job."

"He knows my record. If he trusts me what business is it of yours? You said I had to tell any employer I was on parole. That should be enough."

"We won't make a final decision now. What about the other job, the one you phoned in about?"

When I started to answer, Rosenthal gestured toward the parking lot. We walked together while I talked. He told me that he'd drive me to the hotel; it was on his path. While we rode, I kept talking. Without showing agreement, he was listening without the puckered expression of having sucked a sour lemon. This was good, for if he became even slightly flexible, if he would take a "wait and see" view, my problems would decrease. I would show him.

At the hotel, he cut the ignition, indicating a wish to talk more. I had to urinate and my feet were throbbing. I told him and invited him up. He agreed—and he was seriously concerned about the blisters. If they worsened he'd arrange an appointment at the General Hospital. Bad as the blisters were, I wished that he'd show less concern for them and more for my other problems. They were more urgent than my feet.

"Pretty dreary," was his comment on the room.

"Better than a cell. Even if it's not, I can walk outside."

I sat on the bed and took off my shoes and socks.

In the same way that my yesterdays trained me to peer from windows for possible escape routes, Rosenthal was conditioned to certain behavior. He examined rooms, especially parolee's, for signs of wrongdoing. He looked from the habit of looking.

"What's this?" he demanded, turning from the dresser. Pinched between thumb and forefinger, held before his eyes, were three burnt matches. They were fastened together where they'd been torn from the matchbook, and their burned tops were fused. Rosenthal had picked them from the ashtray where they'd been torn from the matchbook, and their burned tops were fused. Rosenthal had picked them from the ashtray where Augie left them. It was the way matches were used to cook heroin—and Rosenthal knew it.

The dipping sickness churned in my stomach.

"What's what?" I asked lamely; what else could I say?

"Already shooting junk," he said.

"Where'd you get that idea?" What a weak defense, playing lame—but any defense was weak in this predicament.

Rosenthal, still beside the dresser, rubbed a forefinger over a spot on the enamel and turned back, holding the forefinger up like a prosecutor presenting evidence. He displayed a smudge of black. "The bottom of a burned spoon left this," he said.

What he'd found was far more damning evidence of misdeed than my being at the jail. He knew someone had fixed in the room. To prove it wasn't me would force me to confess other misdeeds. I searched for words—yet I was unafraid. As I'd been starkly aware of the bars at the jail, I was now aware that we were alone. No deputy sheriffs could come to his aid if he decided to arrest me—and he could never do it by himself.

"You're crazy! I haven't shot any dope."

"I wasn't born yesterday. I know what this means." He waved the matches.

"You're accusing me on three burned matches in an ashtray. That's insane."

His eyes narrowed. He was considering whether or not he had enough evidence to send me back to prison. He needed very little to justify it, but three burned matches in an ashtray would appear silly in a written report. Even his superiors might think so. And he knew it. He demanded to see my arms. I showed them to him. Any glee I might have felt at this frustration was dampened by the knowledge that all hope of rapport was now forever destroyed. In his mind I was guilty, and if he couldn't prove it his hostility would be exacerbated.

He scrutinized my arms and the backs of my hands. His manner was arrogant, as if he were in a jail with help all around rather than a fat little pig alone. I submitted—but felt like laughing. Maybe he had delusions of grandeur, or maybe he'd handled too many passive parolees.

Next he searched my pockets; then the room, checking the hollow under the sink basin and the small ledges at the rear of the dresser behind the drawers. Both were routine places of concealment for addicts.

When he finished, sweating and breathing heavily, he wiped his hands and turned to me. I sat on the bed, and I'd anticipated his next move.

"Get your shoes on. I'm taking you down for a nalline test."

I'd been waiting for that, and decided that if he punctuated the order by reaching for his handcuffs I was going to put my fist down his throat—or whatever was necessary to get away. Handcuffs would show a decision to put me in jail. Without them it was more likely that he intended to wait for the test's result. Going with him at all was risking imprisonment, but if I assaulted him and got away, when I was caught it was certain imprisonment. I had to choose between lesser evils. I put on the shoes.

9

THE concrete building that housed the parole department's nalline testing center could have been designed by the same architect who devised the jail. It had the same neo-Orwellian blankness. And it stood in a rundown neighborhood.

Rosenthal parked in a lot beside the building. As we got out, I noticed the neighborhood's empty silence. The streets of the city's poor usually teem with motion and noise. This was deserted, as if the malignity in its midst was alien to life. Dusk's light had ceased to peer over the roof tops and now sneaked between the buildings and lighted the shapes into unreality.

The dozen automobiles in this lot were new or nearly so. Most were compacts—economical luxury, bucket seats, white sidewalls, gleaming chrome. This was for "personnel only".

We walked to the sidewalk and turned toward the front door. Another parking lot was on the other side of the building. It was much larger, but unpaved, a vacant lot. Automobiles were scattered at random, sagging from rutted earth and their own arthritic suspensions. They were a spectrum of yesteryear's models—each one looked as if Willy Darin belonged behind the wheel. But women occupied most of them, and some of the women held babies, or watched them skitter about in search of games, as if this was a park. Each woman was waiting for her man to run the gauntlet, and each was necessarily in fear that her man would disappear into the maw—to be next heard from back in prison.

I knew the women had worn faces, for they had to reflect the lives of their men.

The front door was frosted, opaque glass. As Rosenthal ushered me inside, a black face appeared above a suit collar. The room was very dim; the purpose was to get eyes adjusted to the gloom preparatory to the nalline test.

"What've we got here, Bill?" the Negro asked.

"One of mine. I think he's been using."

The Negro looked at me. "Naughty boy."

The levity grated my nerves. I was not a child—nor were these my parent surrogates—nor was the situation funny.

The Negro was huge enough to be a wrestler, and size was probably a factor of his assignment, whatever his other civil service qualifications. Most addicts shrug and ask what's for chow when it's time to go to jail, yet someone might rebel and the Negro's presence was to restore order. He was a good house nigger.

The Negro gave me a log to sign—name and prison number. I wondered if they'd engrave the number on my headstone. Rosenthal had me stand aside with him while my eyes adjusted to the gloom. The room had three rows of wooden benches. About fifteen figures sat quietly waiting in the shadows. I studied the faces of the waiting men. Most were Mexican, some blacks, a small number of whites.

Rosenthal beckoned me. I followed him, mind shivering on unreality's brink, and found myself in another room, seated in a chair before a doctor—a tall man with an ophthalmoscope casting a searing light. He chanted questions—medical history—and held up a strange instrument to measure the size of my pupils. A moment later a needle stabbed into my arm.

The nalline added cramps to my nausea. I waited in another dark room. Figures sat around me, were called one by one. My name was called. The doctor measured again. The pupils had gone down, grown smaller, and this meant I was clean. He shook his head and told Rosenthal I'd passed.

Rosenthal was unsatisfied and wanted a urinalysis; it would show up things other than opiates. "He's been shooting something," Rosenthal said.

Bottle in hand, he escorted me down a hallway. It had red signs indicating this was the exit for those who had passed the test. At the hallway's end was an electrically controlled grill gate. It was opened for those who passed, but not for those who failed. To the left of the gate was a short corridor into a cell. Those who failed had no choice but to enter the cell. It was also where urine specimens were taken.

A young Mexican was lying on a bench, head propped against a wall, hands folded on his chest. He opened his eyes when Rosenthal led me in, but otherwise remained motionless.

Recessed fluorescent light gave a sheen to the enameled concrete walls. Suddenly, words of fury boiled from me, frenzied and somewhat incoherent, an attempt to make Rosenthal understand that he shouldn't worry about me using heroin—that he should worry about driving me to much worse things. The confusion of my outburst kept him from understanding exactly what I said. It was just as well that he didn't understand.

Before the tirade finished, the burly Negro charged into the room, summoned by the noise. He was as ready as a trained dog to control any rebelliousness. His arrival checked me, for I verged on saying things that could bury me if quoted on paper. The hammering pulse in my head continued even though I was silent.

Rosenthal handed me the bottle. I pissed in it, fastened the white cardboard lid, and handed it back.

They walked out—and locked the door. Only those who have been caged can understand the horror of a key closing in a lock. Rosenthal had done it unconcernedly, without a word of explanation. And he'd been cunning, had completely tricked me.

I stood spread-legged in the cell's center, a dumb beast utterly helpless. An exquisite agony inundated me—yet a part of my mind was detached, calm, viewing the scene as if it was on a motion picture screen.

"Got any smokes?" the Mexican asked.

I shook my head, afraid to speak. Nor could I think. I was encapsulated in a form of mental shock. Things had gone beyond where thinking mattered, or so it seemed.

I sat down and waited without consciousness of time. Some time later the Negro entered, accompanied by another parole officer, who carried a set of chains, crashing and rattling as they dropped to the floor. The Negro slipped handcuffs on the Mexican. The chains were for me.

I was seated on the toilet and hadn't moved at their appearance. The other parole officer motioned me to stand up for chaining. I considered punching him in the mouth—but that would be a momentary satisfaction with prolonged regrets. As it stood, I was sure to be released when the test came back negative.

Silently, trying to show contempt in my posture, I submitted. Steel bracelets clicked around my wrists. A chain was run through them and circled around my waist—to hold my hands close to my body. Shackles were placed around my ankles. A length of chain dangled from my waist at the rear—to lead me.

"Like a Christmas package," the parole officer said.

"Not so tough after all," the Negro said.

I stared at the wall, ignoring them, until the Negro tugged the leash and led me, hobbling, to a station wagon outside. The Mexican was already in the back seat.

The Negro drove the vehicle, which made a mesh screen dividing front and rear seats. It was dark in the city and lights played across the station wagon. Soon we were in the neighborhood of the bail bond offices.

It was 2:30 A.M. before the booking process was finished. I'd been fingerprinted, photographed, given a lukewarm shower, sprayed with DDT, given denims, a blood test, chest X-ray. I was one of thousands booked into the jail every night. Finally, escorted by a deputy, I was taken in a group of forty prisoners to the tanks.

Cell lights were out, but the walkway outside them was brightly illuminated, casting slices of light through the bars. I was surprised that they were one-man cells. The particular tank, I later learned, had been designed for prisoners facing capital offenses, hence entitled to a semblance of privacy. After the jail was constructed the high-power prisoners were kept elsewhere, so this tank served for mainline jailbirds. Several were still reading when I passed. Their heads were toward the bars to catch the light outside. In the shadows their faces were blurs.

A gate on remote control clanked open. The sound was awesome, steel grinding steel. Yet down the tier someone continued to snore without pause.

I stepped into the cell. Steel crashed against steel. I was locked in. The familiar sight of bunk, lidless toilet, push-button washbowl and graffiti carved into the paint ("If you can't do time, don't fuck with crime") combined into a blow that shattered my shell of detachment. Imagine the hurricane emotions of a man who has served eight years in prison, has been free less than a week, and who finds himself again imprisoned without having committed a crime. A swirl of loneliness, rage and despair washed me into a tearful, blinded madness. I pleaded silently, "Oh, please help me." The plea was to Fortune, Fate, God or a nameless power, a plea that is torn from every man sometime during a lifetime.

Glutted of torment, stupefied, I fell on the bunk and buried my face in the pillow so nobody would hear my enraged yielding to despondency, a pillow greasy from hundreds of other heads. For hours I tried to find reason to justify what was happening, and there was none—unless eight years was inadequate penance. Yet there had to be justification somewhere for such suffering. If there was none—no justice—my very sanity was threatened.

Rage in cycles, directed at Rosenthal, made me dizzy. Moments later I became a dishrag, and then experienced waves of despair so massive that I confronted suicide as an escape. Nor was it just the present misery, which was merely an example of my whole life. This was how it had always been, and how it would continue. Why should I suffer pointlessly? Logic decreed suicide—but logic is easier to articulate to the end than to act to the end, especially when death is concerned. The body rebels against oblivion. I withdrew from the brink of suicide.

The worst of my dilemma was inability to find a bulwark of faith to lessen the blows of existence, to make my condition bearable. I had no god upon whom to place my burdens. Pain without purpose is the most unendurable kind. Even my anguished thoughts were of no more significance than the whirrings of a brown moth against a windowpane.

In this fertile abyss, this void, an encompassing indignation bloomed. It was a fury beyond hatred. It embraced God and man. It grew from the corpse of my last hope to belong to mankind and what mankind professed as good. Not only had hope died, but desire too. Soon the laboratory report on the urine specimen would come back. I'd be on the streets again. And even if I was returned to prison for more years, my choice would be reinforced—if something absolute can be increased.

I was going to war with society, or perhaps I would only be renewing it. Now there were no misgivings. I declared myself free from all rules except those I wanted to accept—and I'd change those as I felt the whim. I would take whatever I wanted. I'd be what I was with a vengeance: a criminal. My choice of crime and complete abandonment of society's strictures (unless society could enforce them against me) was also my truth. Someone else might have chosen to gain as much power as possible. Crime was where I belonged, where I was comfortable and not torn apart inside. And though it was free choice, it was also destiny. Society had made me what I was (and ostracized me through fear of what it had created) and I gloried in what I was. If they refused to let me live in peace I didn't want to. I'd been miserable that week of struggling—miserable in my mind. Fuck society! Fuck their game! If the odds were vast, fuck that, too. At least I'd had the integrity of my own soul, being the boss of my own little patch of hell, no matter how small, even if confined to my own mind.

When morning came I was strong; I'd transcended indecision.

10

IT was three weeks before Rosenthal came to the jail. Nobody else visited me. Stan Bergman, on a different floor, sent a note. The deputy district attorney was willing to bargain for a plea to a lesser charge, and Stan had talked to his youthful brother-in-law and settled Abe's problems. Until I received the note, I half expected Abe to visit me—but as soon as I got the note I forgot it; Abe would never even think of visiting me unless he had something to gain. I felt no anger at this; he was no friend who owed loyalty. I started to write Willy Darin at Sal Pavan's address, but delayed because I expected to be in jail no more than a few days. I'd be free when the reply arrived.

By the first Wednesday I expected each morning that I would be released by nightfall; this phase lasted for the first ten days. After that I refused to anticipate. Anguish cannot rise from shattered expectations when there are no expectations.

Twenty-one days after the nalline test I was summoned to the attorney room. Rosenthal sat across the divider, an affable smile on his moon face. His cheeks and forehead were pink with sunburn. Dead flesh peeled from a scarlet nose. He explained that he'd have come sooner except that he'd been on vacation. He wanted to know if I'd used the time in jail for serious thinking. I proclaimed the error of my ways, that I'd recognized my attitude was wrong. He smiled in the way of a man who believes he's conquered another and can afford munificence. I grinned sheepishly in return. He said the urinalysis had cleared me, but he offered no apology for putting me in jail. Rather, he was giving me "one more chance", and had worked out a program. He'd gotten me a job in a hot dog stand and was taking me to a halfway house. I was on nalline twice a week and had to attend group counseling.

I nodded agreement with everything he said. He commented on my improved attitude and promised to come for me at 6:00 P.M. He'd drive me to the halfway house and introduce me.

In the automobile that evening (nearer 8:00 than 6:00), Rosenthal said, "Your basic problem is emotional immaturity. You want life to be like the movies, full of excitement. That's how a child's mind works, but the adult accepts regularity, tedium, frustration."

We were shooting up a ramp onto the freeway. Traffic was seventy miles an hour. He prattled on, explaining the fullness of his own life in suburbia—golf and bridge and attending football games were enough excitement for any normal person.

"That's good, Mr Rosenthal. I'm glad you're happy. You know what I really like?"

"I can imagine."

"Speed. Going fast. I've always wanted to be a *grand prix* driver—vroom, vroom. Ever thought about doing that?"

"Taking unnecessary risks with your life is immature."

"Didn't you like hot rods when you were young?"

"Not really."

"Man, you should see what it's like." I'd been sliding closer to him. Suddenly I stamped my left foot against his right toe, pressing the gas pedal to the floor. The automobile jerked and leaped forward. "Hey! What!"

I locked my leg straight out as he struggled to pull his foot away. The car was weaving—but gathering momentum. We were going eighty.

"You're through," he threatened.

"Maybe both of us are."

The speedometer rolled across ninety.

"Please," he said, face ashen.

"Fuck your mother."

He reached for the ignition key. I grabbed his thumb and viciously wrenched it back; then backhanded him across the nose. We swerved over a divider line. A horn bleated in protest, and there was a screech of brakes.

My heart pounded. I was afraid—but it was insignificant compared to his terror. We bore down on the rear of a bus. He swerved away just in time. He was whimpering. The sound delighted me.

Vehicles ahead covered every lane, left no room to squeeze through. The wild ride had lasted two minutes—though time is frozen in such situations. I took my foot away. He hit the brake so hard we almost skidded. He was white beneath the sunburn, pouring sweat, and both hands clutched the steering wheel so tightly that his knuckles were bloodless.

"You'll never get out again," he said, but his voice was hysterical.

"Shut your mouth." I backhanded him again. Blood trickled from his nose. "Get in the right lane and get off at the next ramp. You don't run a motherfuckin' thing now."

"What're you going to do?" The question pleaded. And the crotch of his pants, pressed tight against fat thighs, was dark. He'd pissed his britches.

"You almost killed us."

"It would do the world a favor. You're as useless as me—you live on misery."

Florence Avenue was ahead. Our speed had slackened to fifty. Rosenthal swung over to the right lane, sniffling to stop the flow of blood dripping on his shirt. While we went up the exit ramp, I considered having him park on a side street and kicking the shit out of him. It would be the most satisfying act of violence in my life—leaving me three weeks in jail while he was on vacation. What dissuaded me from whipping him was lack of privacy. There was nowhere in the area that assured lack of interference.

When we slowed for a stop sign at the top of the ramp, I grabbed his necktie to make sure he didn't jump out and run. I understood the transience of my power. I'd reduced him to the frailty of a single man, but in a few minutes he would sound the alarm and become the focus of the state's authority. The chase would begin.

I had to disappear. I decided against throwing him from the car and taking it with me. The crime would be robbery—kidnapping for robbery, seeing as how I'd moved him through fear. The risk and penalty were unworthy of the gain. I'd be safer in the night's protective darkness. With a few minutes' head start I'd surely get away—at least for tonight.

We were on a boulevard. My power was imperiled. If a police car came by he would scream for help because he knew I was unarmed.

"Turn right," I said as we approached a residential street. He followed orders, trembling with fear, blood still dripping from his nose. I had him park beside the mouth of an alley and took the car keys. He would have to look for a telephone. I'd have a minimum of ten minutes before help arrived. I might have twice that much.

"You should be locked up for the rest of your life," he said bitterly. "You're a menace."

I feinted a blow, and laughed as he threw up his arms and cowered down. "That's right. The mistake was making a menace and letting me out."

Still hiding behind his arms, he said, "I feel sorry for you, Max. I really do. You need help." The sincere pity in his voice was more infuriating than his usual superciliousness. Yet hitting him would change nothing. His form of blindness, founded on an unshakable sense of his righteousness, was impregnable. Nothing would make him see that if persons like me were the disease, persons like him were the carriers.

"I don't feel sorry for myself," I said, quite truthfully, wishing for something more perspicacious to say. I was not sorry for my choice, though I was for the conditions that necessitated it.

I ducked from the car and sprinted down the alley, looking for a gate. I decided to circle back to Florence and catch a taxi.

Part Two

In the loneliest desert the second metamorphosis occurs; the spirit here becomes a lion; it wants to capture freedom and be lord in its own desert ... The great dragon is called "Thou shalt," but the spirit of the lion says "I will."

Nietzsche

1

CARRYING a half-gallon jug of cheap wine, I trudged up the hill to L&L Red's cabin. I'd left a taxicab driver waiting outside a neighborhood bar a mile away, telling him I'd be a few minutes. I'd ducked out the back, saving eight dollars. The Yellow Cab Company had paid for Red's wine. Red was malleable as long as someone kept him drunk, which I intended to do. It wasn't gaming on him. It was the coin of his realm and he appreciated it.

The cabin was dark; 11:30 was too early for Red to have finished his nightly prowl through dingy bars. The door was unlocked. Red had nothing worth stealing or hiding.

I reached for the light switch and, simultaneously, kicked an empty bottle. It skidded across the room, bounced against a wall and was still spinning when the bare hundred-watt bulb illuminated the room. The scene disgusted me, the array of tawdry clutter, the sour stench pervading everything. I'd thought about staying with L&L Red for a few days, until I made a move, but now decided I'd prefer sleeping under a bridge to staying more than one night.

I opened a window for air and looked out. The cabin, for all its ugliness, sat upon a high throne over the endlessly sprawling city. A breeze had cleared the usual haze and the air was crystalline, the sky powdered with recklessly spilled stars. For all its brilliance, the sky was merely a bland proscenium for the glory of the bowl below—a bowl of jewels sparkling to the horizon. From here the earth as lighted by man was more lovely than the heavens. Streets that were dreary in day's harsh red light were now flowing rivers of diamonds and rubies from thousands of vehicles going one way or another. The panorama evoked mingled exultation and the bittersweet pain of loneliness. I was indeed God's lonely man.

"Alone against all humanity," I said, shivering, the hanging words magnifying the thought and sensation. It was both frightening and glorious to be aided by nobody, have no creed, and be whole and secure in myself. "Alone against humanity." The phrase was both boast and lament. I'd made my choice and wished to abide by it— yet the pang of lonely wonder aroused by the lights questioned the verities so adamantly selected in the jail. A hunger to belong and for meaning apparently is ineradicable. A man may accept truth without necessarily liking it.

Such arabesques of useless thought could only weaken my determination. I put them behind me. They were too late. By now police radios had already crackled my name and description, the photocopiers and teletypes were sending for the allpoints bulletin. No great manhunt would be inaugurated, but if I was picked up on a drunk charge, or stopped for a traffic ticket (until I had identification), or if someone tipped them off, they'd haul me in. Once I had identification, and as long as nobody tipped them off or I didn't get arrested for a new crime, I'd be safe.

I needed money—for the identification and to live. Money is the lifeblood of fugitives. I'd decided in jail on armed robbery as a livelihood, though I didn't foreclose anything else that seemed promising. Armed robbery's classic simplicity appealed to me. I would indeed "take" what I wanted. True, the penalties for capture were enormous, but danger could be reduced to the caper's frozen seconds. Unlike other crimes there was no need for an armed robber to be in a criminal milieu where the police were watching. For the crimes available to me as a fugitive, robbery offered the largest possible reward for the least risk and investment. I was wagering my life, but as it stood that was worthless. I didn't care about it if I couldn't live as I wanted.

My thoughts turned pragmatic. I needed firearms, tools of my trade, and a few dollars to live on until I could put something together. L&L Red might know where to get firearms, someone who would loan them as an investment. Johnny Taormina might have enough money to finance the crap game robbery.

It was 3:00 A.M. when Red came up the hill on foot. The dented roadster had run out of gas two miles from home. Red was still drunk despite the long hike. He'd spent the night cadging drinks (in return for his lecherous humor) in various bistros. He was unsurprised at my presence, and only slightly curious about my three-week absence. L&L Red was most interested in the bottle I'd brought. He hadn't seen Johnny Taormina lately and didn't know if the robbery proposition was still open, but we could find out in the morning.

Red's empty gas tank and the hour dictated where I'd spend the night. Red didn't ask how long I was going to be his guest; a night, a week, or a year, it was all the same to him. My attitude was different. I needed him for transportation until something fruitful happened, but this was my last night in the cabin. Something had to be arranged during the coming day.

We shared the half-gallon of wine. Added to what was already in his system, he was pole-axed. He fell asleep on the sofa in his clothes and snored gustily.

Hanging my cheap suit over a chair so it would not become even more rumpled, I stretched out on the floor. I was drunk enough to ignore the smell of the blanket in which I was wrapped. Yet a floor and dirty blanket and the choice to live and die as I pleased were better than clean sheets and domesticity in a halfway house under Rosenthal's tyranny.

My last thought before sleep was of a sawed-off shotgun.

2

THE man who got out of a twelve-year-old Chevrolet in the parking lot of a bar catering to gamblers was a frail, gray sixty. His suit had been expensive a decade before, but was worn and sadly out of fashion. I'd expected a burly Sicilian, a flashy dresser. Big John Taormina, the mafioso, looked like a sad, nervous bookkeeper. His eyes had cataracts, shifted nervously, and met mine only momentarily when L&L Red made the introductions.

"Glad to meet you," he said, looking around the parking lot. "Let's go inside."

"I'll drink to that," Red said grinning with his stained teeth.

While we walked toward the side door, Johnny asked what Red had told me.

"Just that you want a heist man to rip off a crap game."

"That's all he knew." Johnny was showing how closed-mouthed he himself was. "You a heist man?"

"Among other things."

"Junky?"

"No." I answered, but I was piqued. He was no longer a big-shot gangster. Even if he was, I disliked being questioned. I said nothing more; the time would come to jerk his reins.

The barmaid, elderly for such occupation, called Johnny by his first name and smiled. She knew L&L Red, too, but ignored him except for a perfunctory nod. He leered at her despite her dowdy fifty years.

When the drinks arrived, Johnny started for his wallet, changed his mind, and told the woman to put it on his tab. She paused just long enough for it to be perceptible, then nodded acquiescence and moved away.

Before going into details of the caper, Johnny began explaining why he was fingering the game. He was impelled by guilt to justify why he was being a traitor to his friends. He was in debt, had mortgaged his mother's house (which he justified by mentioning that he'd bought it for her in the first place), and had lost four hundred thousand dollars gambling in five years, most of it to these same "schmuck" friends we were going to have robbed. All of them owed him favors when he was on top. None would help him. He needed money to pick up a bar with a cheap down payment and to set up a bookmaking operation in the General Hospital. It had thousands of employees, countless patients, and "big action".

"What's the score worth?" I interrupted.

"Fifteen to twenty-five g's, counting the jewelry some of 'em wear. Mostly cash though."

"What kind of end do you want?"

"Thirty percent."

"Off the top or after the nut?"

"It's not gonna cost anything to finance it."

"Oh, it'll cost something." I had thought of asking him for "front" money for weapons, but if he knew I lacked firearms it would weaken my position. What kind of bandit is without firearms? "Thirty percent is pretty steep," I said.

"I'm giving you a gift."

"Yeah, maybe thirty is okay." I was lying. Once I had the money he'd get 10 percent, take it or leave it. He'd be safely watching television while I risked my life; 10 percent was all he deserved.

"If you do this right, I've got some other sweetheart scores." His voice was plaintive. He was trying to insure that I didn't doublecross him. If I did, he couldn't sue me for breach of contract. He couldn't really do much of anything. He could shoot me—if he had the nerve and if he could find me. I doubted both of these.

"Let's sweat one at a time. How many people at the game?"

"Anywhere from seven to a dozen."

"Any guns?"

Johnny shook his head emphatically. "They've been playing together for years without any trouble. They're scared of guns." He leaned closer, whispering urgently, his cataracted eyes beginning to water. The game was in a rear suite of a large San Fernando Valley motel. It played once or twice a week. He couldn't know the precise evening until a few hours before. A regular player would telephone him; then he'd let me know. I had to be ready. I'd be able to tell if they were there by looking outside for a yellow Cadillac convertible with a black top or a blue pickup truck with Acme Vending on its side. Regular players drove these vehicles.

"The guy that calls you ... does he know you're fingering a heist?"

"Christ no! He calls because I sometimes play—when I can get a stake."

Though the score seemed excellent, Mr Taormina might be using a salesman's license. His need for money might cause him to gloss over defects, particularly when he was taking no risk.

My manner was coldly tough, which he expected and respected. "Let me have the address. Red and me can look it over this afternoon."

"Good. How long before you can get it?"

"Next week—if I can find the right crime partner."

"Don't you have anybody?"

"Nobody like I want. This is going to take a two-hundred-and-fifty-pound wrestler. Somebody built like Red here."

L&L Red had been swiggling ice cubes and sucking the empty glass. At mention of his name, he looked up. "Huh?"

"Nothing." I explained to Johnny that I needed someone big enough to knock down anyone who hesitated. "This'll be a small area with men already excited from gambling. We'll knock on the door, claim to be police, which'll get 'em more excited—but they'll crack the door. When they do the bruiser crashes in. I come behind him with a sawed-off shotgun. I don't want to blow anybody in half if I don't have to. The gorilla can flatten anybody who flinches wrong."

Johnny nodded at the explanation, understanding the tactical situation, liking the professional ring. The casual reference to shotguns also intimidated him—as it was intended to.

His handshake was firmly enthusiastic when we separated in the parking lot.

With the first full tank of gas the M.G. roadster had had in six months, we headed northwest on the Hollywood Freeway outbound toward the San Fernando Valley. Traffic whizzed along. The wind breaking over the roadster's windshield and the sun on my neck made me feel good. Life can be delicious even for the outcast and criminal.

The white-on-black sign, Vine Street Right Lane, made me think of Abe Meyers. He might provide guns, financing, even the identification. Abe would be at the club now. The motel wasn't going anywhere in the next hour.

From a gas station five blocks away, I phoned ahead to find out if the police had been there. Abe was surprised at the call, claiming he'd learned yesterday that I was in jail. I withheld voicing my disbelief, though I was tempted to inquire where he thought I was when I failed to handle the situation with Stan Bergman. He said no police had inquired about me. "You didn't escape, did you?"

"No. I just hung up the parole. I'm comin' in for a drink."

"Yeah, okay." He sounded unenthusiastic.

Red circled the block and went once down the alley without stopping. No plain cars or inconspicuous men were seen. I hardly expected them. I was too small a fish for so expensive a net.

As we started down the alley a second time, another problem

came to mind: L&L Red. He looked too much like what he was: a drunken, lecherous bum. His loose-lipped face was the archetype of depravity. His pullover shirt was torn at the right armpit so that hairs jutted out. I was ashamed of being ashamed—for compared to Abe he was virtuous, or at least had those virtues I esteemed: forthrightness and loyalty. Under the circumstances I couldn't risk his unpredictability. Telling him a lookout was needed, I gave him enough money for a couple of short dogs of wine and told him to wait outside the club's front door. If the police showed up he was to start kicking it. The thought of wine mollified his disappointment, and he was unable to argue against the need for a lookout. He let me off next to the alley door.

Despite Abe's assurances, and my own examination, I walked through the door with an inner coil. Police used moments like these to spring traps.

Music came from the jukebox. The lights were out and the chairs were legs up on the tables. The dim cavern was almost empty. Abe was behind the bar, facing Manny and a large baldheaded man who were seated on the stools. Spread before them was an adding machine, green ledgers, and piles of receipts. Abe saw me, gave a brief wave of recognition, and returned to the ledger and machine. The offhanded greeting indicated how much my influence of three weeks ago had declined. Manny, however, came over.

"What's to it, Max?"

"I want to see Abe and I haven't got a lot of time."

"Man, he's hung up. That thing they're working on has to be in the afternoon mail. It means ten g's."

"Shit," I muttered.

"Maybe I can help," Manny said.

Could he be trusted? Not for a moment did I suspect that he would voluntarily go to the police, but if he knew too much he'd have bargaining power if he was arrested for something minor, pandering or possession of marijuana. On the other hand, if all he could tell them was that I wanted, or had, some firearms it would be a minimal threat. It might intensify their desire to capture me, but it wasn't evidence of a crime they could use in court. As long as Manny didn't know where, when, or if they'd been used . . .

"Guns? More than one?"

"Yeah, a couple large-caliber pistols and a twelve-gauge shotgun."

"You can cop a shotgun at a pawn shop."

"If I had the bread. What I'd really like is some kind of submachine gun, a Thompson or a Schmeiser."

"Somebody called Abe the other day and wanted to sell an M16."

"Motherfucker! That's just what I want."

"I don't remember who called Abe. I'll find out."

"How much did he want?"

"Three bills."

"Goddam! How long will he have it?"

"Who knows? I'll talk to him. I'd loan you the bread but I don't have it either."

"What about pistols? Got any ideas? If you know somebody who'll loan 'em to you—it'll pay off for both of you."

"I might be able to help there. I know a dude. Yeah, there's a revolver in the office. One of the bartenders kept it while he was working. He had a heart attack and won't be back for a couple more months. I think it's only a .32. Want it?"

"Damn right."

Manny started for the office. I followed.

The revolver was a snub-nosed .32 made by a company I'd never heard of. As pistols go it wasn't much, but the checkered butt felt good against my palm. "What about the others—that guy you know?"

"I'll see him tonight. I know he's got some. Call me tomorrow."

When I left the office, Abe was still with the man at the bar. He saw me starting to leave and waved goodbye.

The motel was immense and gleaming new. There was an Olympic-sized swimming pool and a putting green for golf fanatics. There was also a large coffee shop. To arrive at the rooms and suites, which were two stories high, all facing inward toward the pool (upstairs was a balcony running all the way around) it was necessary to pass down a drive between the coffee shop and office, both of which had large windows. Walking in to take the score this way would be easy, but leaving, especially if I were in a hurry, might attract risky attention.

Red parked a block away and we walked back, turned in, and sauntered around the pool. The day was hot and middle-aged, middle-class tourists were supine on canvas lounges, sunning fish-white flab and hiding their eyes behind dark glasses. Once again Red's presence discomfited me, but not because of embarrassment. He stood out and this would cause him to be remembered. If the caper blew up and someone was shot the investigation would include tracing and questioning the guests. I always tried to be inconspicuous, hide my criminality.

The suite where the game was held was the last one on the balcony. As we walked below it, I saw that the balcony ran around the corner and we (whoever went with me) could drop ten feet into a vacant lot outside the motel. We wouldn't have to go back down the drive between the windows. Good.

A possible problem, besides something going wrong inside the suite, was that some guest might be taking a night swim and see us charging through the door. I decided it was a calculated risk worth taking.

"Let's blow," I told Red.

"What about inside the room?"

"I can't afford to rent it. But how many mysteries can a motel have?"

We went back to the car.

The freeway through the San Fernando Valley was raised so that the view through the chain link fence—protection for dogs, cats and children—was panoramic. Smog shortened the horizon, but as far as it went I could see roofs of houses through lines of trees marking the avenues. Houses of soft pastel, TV antennas defacing the roof line. Frequently there came an instant of pale blue, a swimming pool. The skyline was flat except for an occasional cluster of a shopping center. This was the Mecca of the American Dream, the world that everyone wanted. A world of sleek young women (allied with Slenderella to be so) in shorts and halters, driving 400-horsepower station wagons to air-conditioned, music-serenaded supermarkets of baby-sitter corporations and culture condensed into Great Books discussion groups. A life of barbecues by the swimming pool and drive-in movies open all year. It didn't appeal to me. Fuck health insurance plans and life insurance. They wanted to live without leaving the womb. It made me more alive to play a game without rules against society, and I was prepared to play it to the end. A tremor almost sexual passed through me as I anticipated the coming robbery.

I decided to visit Willy and Selma and told Red to head toward El Monte. When the traffic thinned, he eagerly, almost plaintively, wanted an assurance that I liked the score. Such servile eagerness aroused a reflexive resistance. I answered monosyllabically, but when he pressed me I agreed that it was "pretty good". That agreement sent him on a circuitous tangent. He sketched over what good friends we were, the parties we'd had, the parties we would have. He wanted one more fling. He was getting old; his health was bad; he needed money.

"I always look after you when you're right."

"I don't want a couple hundred as a handout. I want a share."

"Nobody gets a share unless they share the risk."

"I know . . . I know. But damn, Max . . . Jesus, I need it bad. I'm old and I gotta buy pussy. My blood pressure is way up. I need one more ball . . . a decent car and a gray silk suit; then I'm gonna kill myself."

The voice was impassioned and he undoubtedly believed every word. When the time came for suicide, however, he'd want yet another "last" hedonistic gasp.

He began a new tactic. He'd use his automobile as a trail car on the heist, follow us close, and if anyone pursued he'd block them off, ram them if necessary. He swore he'd do it for two thousand dollars. I promised to think about the trail car, though I rejected the idea when he mentioned it. On a different kind of score a trail car was sometimes a good idea—a daylight bank robbery, for example, where immediate pursuit is highly possible. Here there was virtually no risk of pursuit and, even if someone came after us, I doubted that Red would act. It takes nerve to ram a police car when you know you're going to jail and get your head whipped soft. Seldom can charges (beyond a traffic violation) be filed for such an "accident", but the police know what's happened and knock all the curl out of the driver's hair.

I silently decided that if things went right I'd give him a grand. It was less than he wanted, but good wages for driving me around for a few days. No doubt Johnny Taormina would give him something, too.

3

WILLY was still at work and not expected for at least half an hour. I decided to wait. Red had to pick up his check at the employment office before it closed. Red wanted to come back and take me barhopping on the money (his real purpose was to bind me closer), but I declined, easing his worries with a pat on the back and a promise that "everything is going to be all right, don't worry. I'll call you at the pool hall tomorrow."

Selma was cooking supper. Quite pointedly she told me that Willy was taking her and the boys to a movie that evening. She was cold to the brink of rudeness. I went outside to wait.

The residence, with a long dirty driveway and weed-infested lawn, sat back from a semirural boulevard down which rolled cement and gravel trucks. I sat against the bole of a scrubby tree. The scene was banal and dreary, full of energy without beauty.

Three young boys came down the roadside, carrying sticks they used to whack at high weeds. Two of them were Willy's sons. The other, a year or two older, was fairer in color, slender, and with smooth complexion, quite a handsome boy. All were scuffed and smudged.

They approached me with the shy openness of children who have known enough love, whatever other deprivations they may have suffered. The third boy was addressed as "Joey". I recognized his resemblance to Joe Gambesi. He was Mary's son. He went inside the house to telephone his mother; he was going to eat here and go to the movie with his cousins.

Moments later, Willy pulled up the driveway. The Darin boys immediately forgot me. They rushed to the car and mobbed their father as he exited, grabbing him around the legs, jumping up and down. He grabbed them, one in each hand, by the belt, and raised them from the ground, then swung them around. They screamed in delicious fear. Setting them down and gently hugging their necks in the circle of his forearm, he sent them inside to wash for dinner.

"Don't shake hands," he said. "I'm greasy as a pig."

"That job ain't treating you too good."

"Yeah, what the fuck can I do with Selma on one side and the parole officer on the other? She doesn't dig you anymore, either. She says I'd better keep away from you."

"I caught her vibes. She just wants someone to blame if you get out of line."

"Where you been? I expected you to come around."

I told him about the jail sojourn and my fugitive condition.

"So you're gonna start rippin' again."

"That's my best game . . . along with doing time."

"I hate to see it."

"What else can I do?"

"Nothin', I guess. That reminds me. I saw somethin' the other day that might interest you. A market. It looks easy."

"Right now I'm working on that crap game heist L&L ran down. I even met the great Johnny T. He's a pipsqueak has-been."

"That's better'n a never-was, like me."

A shadow appeared against the screen door of the house. Selma called out to Willy that supper would be ready in a few minutes.

"Let's go around back," Willy said. "I need a fix."

"So you're hooked . . . back in your bag just like I am in mine."

"Just halfass hooked. I can clean up in two days."

"Yeah, okay, clean up in two days."

The garage had a storage room nestled to its side. Baskets of old clothes, a sofa and a broken refrigerator were stored in it. From beneath the refrigerator Willy brought a water glass, inside which was a polyethylene-wrapped outfit and a condom of heroin.

"Want a taste?" he asked, unfastening a knot capping the rubber prophylactic. It was a half ounce of heroin and Willy couldn't afford a hundred dollars on his wages. He had to be doing some slight peddling.

"Yeah, I'll go for a little taste."

A minute later I pulled out the needle and suppressed the trickle of blood with my thumb. It had been many years, and I momentarily reviled my weakness. That was swept away in the quick flowering glow. Tendrils of warmth (an indescribable warmth) reached through every crevice of my body and the deepest recesses of my brain. Even loneliness was obliterated. This was peace on earth. Yet my fury was too precious to lose permanently in the addict's somnolent twilight.

"Good smack," I said, voice slurred.

"Pretty good. Fuckin' shit's gonna be my death someday."

"How are you passing nalline?"

"I'm not going. I don't fix for two days and take steambaths. Last week I missed; this week I've got a codeine prescription from a dentist, so it don't matter. Are you hungry?"

"What about Selma? She won't dig feeding me."

"Man, fuck her. Let's go grease."

"Where can I stash this pistol until I leave?"

"Damn! You sure got one of those quick. Here." He took it and shoved it behind the sofa cushions. "Nobody'll come in here. That reminds me about that market. I was cashing my check and they sent me to the manager's office. It's upstairs just inside the parking lot door. Nobody can even see you go up. There's a fat Mosler safe in the office."

"How big a market?"

"Not a huge Safeway or anything, but not a corner grocery either."

"How many cash registers?"

"Three."

"It might be worth something. Where is it?"

"On Santee, right near the freeway off ramp."

"Speakin' of money, how are you fixed?" I saw his color rise with embarrassment. "Forget it. We'll be shittin' in tall cotton soon as I make a score."

Decision was postponed while we went indoors. The children had already finished and were in another room. My appetite was good despite the heroin. Willy was shirtless across from me, leaning over the table as he shoveled in his food. His brawny torso belonged more to the image of a stevedore than to a drug addict. Selma saw that we were on drugs and glared at me accusingly. She scarcely spoke, rattled pans as she washed them—but she'd set a place at the table for me.

It was decided they would drop me at Mary's on the way to the movie. Joey was going to stay the night with his cousins. During the short ride in the stuffy, crowded, rattletrap automobile, I decided that the situation of hitching rides and sleeping on floors and couches was unbearable. Tonight, after dark, I'd steal a car and take off a small robbery. There was a motel near Santa Anita racetrack that I'd robbed years before; it would be good for a couple hundred dollars. Mary would have an old nylon stocking I could use for a mask. Stealing a car would be easy. All I needed was a pistol and guts. I had both. It was less than the smartest move in the history of crime, but fuck all that, too.

Stealing an automobile was unnecessary. Mary owned an eleven-year-old Plymouth. After a moment's lip-biting hesitancy, she gave me the keys, exacting a promise that I'd return by morning so she could go shopping.

By 9:00 P.M. I was passing Santa Anita and saw a department store where the motel had been. I began driving the boulevards of the suburban towns, looking for something else to heist. Time was limited. As night deepened, lights turned off, money was put away, and cars would become so few that I would lack cover. I was looking for a business by itself with only a couple of persons inside, situated so pedestrians and passing vehicles would be unable to see what was going on. Several liquor stores fulfilled these requirements, but they were taboo. Liquor stores are to bandits as flypaper to a fly. Frequently robbed, it's usually by amateurs unaware that too many are owned by ex-fighters or ex-policemen or other pugnacious personalities. A pistol is often beneath the counter, or the proprietor's wife is in the back room with a shotgun. Invariably, the money (except for a few dollars) is hidden.

At 11:00 I found a small market. It was on a corner where everything else was closed and dark. Around the corner was a residential street. There were no pedestrians. I parked two hundred yards down the side street, checked the pistol, and walked back. My thoughts were forcibly locked into place. I'd learned that too many thoughts about the consequence dampens courage. Going to commit a crime is like going into battle, except the criminal can withdraw until the action commences; the soldier is under orders.

Even with a locked mind, my body wanted to rebel. My legs were as stiff and jerky as stilts and my stomach knotted. I realized I needed this petty robbery for practice nearly as much as I needed the money.

Mask balled in one hand, ready to be jerked over my head, revolver in a hip pocket, ready to be drawn, I stepped through the doorway into the light—and froze.

A youth in white apron was on a ladder, placing orange boxes of detergent on a shelf. An elderly man, also in apron, stood beside him, handing up the boxes. Neither had seen me.

They were Chinese.

My stomach sank. When I was fifteen, I'd strong-armed an elderly Chinese. Mary's brother, Gino, was with me. The man was in his fifties, frail, face seamed like old parchment. I had a three-foot length of two-by-four lumber. I demanded his money. I'll never know if he was refusing my demand or didn't understand. I swung the piece of wood and it glanced off his head and he grabbed it.

We struggled for it momentarily; then I loosened one hand and punched him in the mouth. A cigarette was dangling from his lips. It disappeared, and then, I'll never forget the sight, he spat out mashed tobacco, blood, and pieces of teeth. I demanded the money again and again, and he kept shaking his head, and I kept punching him. I could feel his facial bones breaking, and each blow drew the blood up through his flesh. I panted with frenzy. He shook his head and wouldn't fall down. Gino watched, horrified. Finally, I threw the man down and tore his wallet from his pants. When I washed my hands in a gas station, blood covered them to my wrists. I vomited. The wallet had twelve dollars.

I never forgot the episode. And as I went through jails I heard experienced thieves advise to never rob a Chinese; they won't give up the money.

Now, poised inside the market, I wanted to back out. But I wanted more money. I jerked the pistol and moved toward the cash register. They didn't have to give me the money. I only had to hold them at bay while I took it.

The old man heard my footsteps. I raised the pistol as he turned. "Don't move." The words came out embarrassingly shrill.

His eyes hooded; otherwise there was no response. I kept moving, meanwhile watching them. If necessary I'd shoot, first at the legs.

"Hey, man," the younger one said, stepping off the ladder. I raised the pistol to his stomach. The old man grabbed his wrist.

Neither said anything more. I opened the cash register, using a knuckle so as to leave no fingerprints. I then realized I'd forgotten the mask; it was still balled in my hand. They'd be able to identify me if I became a suspect. For one moment I thought of killing them, then recognized the absolute madness of the idea. I scooped bills and coins into my pockets, not bothering to count, though I knew it was meager. Facing them, I backed around the counter and out the door. Then ran for the car.

Ten minutes later—a world away from the crime in a city of millions—I counted the money: $185.00. It was so insignificant for a possible life sentence that I wanted to cry. What kind of a life was this? It hurt, too, because I'd robbed the downtrodden. What I'd taken in fury and violence was probably more than they profited in a week's hard work. My feelings were not exactly repentant, not remorseful—merely agonized at the whole tangle of human existence. I cursed especially a situation where crime was my only exit.

4

A CHANGING flicker of gray-white light around the edge of the window shade indicated that Mary was watching television. She was wearing a flannel housecoat with her hair in curlers. She pressed a forefinger to her lips to hush me and whispered that Lisa might be awake. We went into the kitchen.

I had two bags of groceries, both a gift of friendship and a tribute to Fate from crime. Most of what I'd bought—steak, lobster, and a huge canned ham—are too expensive for a welfare family.

When she emptied the bags, she stared at me, dubious and questioning. She wanted to know where I'd gotten the money.

"Well, would you believe . . ."

"No, I wouldn't."

"So don't look gift horses in the mouth, right?"

"Whatever you did, whatever you got, it isn't worth it. Selma told me you jumped parole. You didn't even try."

"Willy tells her too much, and she talks too much in general."

"Why didn't you even give it a try?"

"You don't have to try to swim the Pacific to know you can't do it."

"So now what happens?"

"It looks like I'm either going to get a pocketful of money or a booking slip. If I can't get the money, I don't give a fuck about the second."

"What kind of life is that?"

"None for you. It looks right for me. Just put the meat in the refrigerator; then you can preach."

"I'll save my breath. Thanks for all this."

While she moved around the kitchen, I learned that she had somewhat anticipated my return. Lisa was sleeping with her and, as Joey was with Willy and Selma, I could use the children's bedroom. "If you're hungry," she said, "I can make you a sandwich or something."

"Bed's better."

"Come on. Use either bed; they both have clean sheets."

The room was small, clean, Spartan. The walls were bare; no toys lay around.

"Come in for a while," I said, reaching for her arm as she started to go. My voice was hoarse. Her eyes looked into mine, widened. I was frightened both that she wouldn't understand and would turn me down.

"I'll be back," she said.

While I waited, naked under the sheets, I felt misgivings about Joe Gambesi. Whatever their relationship, she was a friend's wife. And, too, though she was attractive she was too familiar in a different relationship to stir intense passion. It was faintly incestuous. Into these waverings came a bizarre thought: the epitome of failure for a man released from prison was that "he came back so quick he didn't even get his dick wet". It was a threatening thought, a possibility, and this as much as anything reinforced my wavering lust.

Mary still wore the housecoat when she returned, but her hair was brushed out. It was black, fell below her shoulders, and was full-textured. The bedroom lights were out, but the door was slightly open so there was a sliver of light. As she came forward her legs flashed; she was naked beneath the housecoat. Her legs were strong and supple as a dancer's. The sight erased the last trace of hesitancy. I got hard immediately and was pulsing as soon as she dropped the housecoat to the floor, slipped under the sheets, and ran her fingers softly over my stomach. Her hair spilled over my shoulder and

145

cheek and the touch was electric. It had been eight years since I'd kissed a woman, and I'd practically forgotten the feel of a soft body scented with soap. Waves of sensation dizzied me.

We'd just started fucking when the doorway came fully open. The expanding light from the doorway made us turn our heads. "Mom, are you there? Oh . . . !"

The sheet was gone and Mary's legs were around me, the soles of her feet stroking the back of my thighs. She gasped and began struggling to throw me off. My eyes were transfixed by the aghast stare of the girl at the door. The glare from the hallway was like a spotlight.

"Get out of here," I said angrily, yet I felt absurd shame, as if we were doing something wrong. Behind that I wanted to laugh, too, for it seemed I was doomed to being celibate.

"Who are you?" the child demanded, near hysteria. I was moving toward her, my nakedness flopping. She shrank away. Mary had drawn a bedsheet around herself.

"I'll scream!" the girl said as I grabbed her arm. I could visualize the neighbors calling the police. "You'll do no such thing," I said, squeezing her arm until she winced.

"Leave her alone, Max," Mary said, her voice shrill. "Oh, Lisa go to my room. I'll be there in a minute."

The girl stared at us, the horror becoming venom. She whirled and disappeared, leaving the door open. Another door slammed.

Mary began rocking back and forth, the sheet still around her. I closed the door.

I put on my shorts and sat on the bed, personally wanting to finish—but Mary's sightless stare emphatically said No.

"That was a far out climax," I said, chuckling.

"It's not funny."

"In a way it is. And sometimes all you can do about things is joke. The saddest things are the funniest."

She ignored me. "What am I going to do?" she thought aloud. "This is the first time."

I wanted to tell her: "Then you're a fool." Instead I said, "Maybe I can talk to her."

"No. You'd better go. If you're gone I might be able to make her forgive me."

"Forgive you! For what?" I bit my tongue.

"We shouldn't have."

Words failed me. Mary really believed we'd done something immoral. It was fantastic, and sad, too. By begging forgiveness from her daughter she'd reinforced both their beliefs that it was wrong.

I dressed quickly. Mary waited modestly beneath the sheet until I departed.

It was 2:30 A.M. when I started the car, for I still had the keys. "I'm getting me some pussy," I thought, "even if I gotta jump out of the bushes." Twenty minutes later I was cruising slowly down Broadway in Downtown Los Angeles, looking for a whore. At the hour it was just a mite less risky than the rape, for every fourth automobile was black and white with a red light on top. I found a hooker standing in the light of the marquee from an all-night movie. She wore a mini-skirted dress of shiny yellow rayon. Twenty minutes later we were in a motel.

At dawn, when we left the motel, I stole the television set. Fuck it. A true criminal is a criminal all the time.

All the thief underworld hangouts would be virtually empty until night. I dropped the whore downtown, had some breakfast, and killed time until the stores opened. I went shopping, bought a decent pair of slacks and sweater and two sets of wash and wear clothes; also two pairs of shoes, one of them with crepe soles. Then I paid a week's rent in a motel near the Hollywood Bowl. The room was well-furnished, overlooked a swimming pool and sun-yellowed hillsides.

Though totally exhausted, I showered and shaved and prepared to throw the prison-issue clothes away. When I counted the grimy bills and loose change my wealth was eighty dollars—not much for having committed an armed robbery. However unlikely that I'd now be caught (they'd catch someone for a similar small robbery and display him to the victims of all recent small robberies), it could have meant a decade in prison. The gain for such risk was a few clothes, a piece of ass, and a week's rent. The most galling aspect was that if no "good" score came before I went broke, I'd make another fool move. It's disgusting to behave stupidly, but doubly so while knowing it's stupid in advance.

Yet when I went to sleep I was at peace with myself. During the week I'd tried to fulfill the parole I'd been torn and uncertain; now I was doing what I knew how to do.

That evening I journeyed through the city's criminal environs to make contacts and find a crime partner. I knew the last would be difficult despite my wide range of criminal acquaintances. I wanted an experienced heist man, someone physically large and tough who would balk at nothing. Finding thieves willing to cash bad checks or commit a small burglary was no problem; I could find half a dozen of these in a weekend. But they would stare at me as if I were insane if I mentioned ripping off a Mafia crap game and banks. Such criminals, however habitual, prefer crimes where to lose means short imprisonment and another chance, which has its points— except that the maximum profit is nickels and dimes. Criminals willing to gamble for big stakes, and whom I'd trust, were few and far between. The man I wanted had to give and arouse absolute trust where I was concerned. Only a fraction of the hundreds of criminals I knew by name fulfilled these qualifications, and those I could remember were all in prison.

The bars I visited were notorious: the Carioca on Temple Street, the Sunset near downtown, the Ebony on Brooklyn Avenue, Caballero's on North Broadway. It was dangerous just going to these places. The narcotics detectives were liable to stop you because they didn't know you. I slipped in through side doors, drank a beer, and studied faces. In each bar there were familiar faces, quite a few I could name. Most criminals in these places were in narcotics traffic, but that's who I wanted, for their business brings them into wide contact with criminals. I found two whom I trusted well enough to approach candidly. Both were Mexican, ex-convicts with "good" names in the underworld and prison yard. We mentioned names. They'd seen people here and there, at the parole office or nalline center, at a nightclub, at a ball game. None of the names we mentioned was the person I wanted. One of the Mexicans could buy phony drivers' licenses and draft cards. He promised to make arrangements for me. We drank beer and reminisced. Both were hooked and neither was rich: "I'd have some fool in here fronting for me if I was really swinging . . . wouldn't be dealing myself." Yet they pooled resources and loaned me fifty dollars, "until you get on your feet".

One sad piece of news was that Augie Morales had been picked up the night before—on the sidewalk outside this very bar.

My last stop was the Monticello. As I parked in the lot behind it my thief's eye caught on something. Two doors away, its back door on the parking lot, was a pawn shop. Pawn shops have firearms and easily sold merchandise. They also have burglar alarms. Next door in the same building, however, was a small barber shop—and it had no burglar alarm. Except for the Monticello, nothing within a hundred yards would be occupied at night. When I finished with my beer, I walked out the front and looked in the pawn shop window. The front room was lighted. I stood as if examining something in the window. Actually I was examining the walls for wires that would indicate they had an alarm. In this kind of building the construction company cannot install an alarm within the walls, so the later installer runs wires along wainscotting or in the juncture of wall and ceiling. None was visible. The pawn shop owner had limited his protection to windows and doors, routes no professional would consider. It would be easy to enter the barber shop and dig through the wall. I filed this knowledge away in case Manny January failed to get the weapons for the crap game robbery.

5

CONDITIONED by prison, I woke early. Already the heat beat down from a cloudless sky that was fuzzy with pollution. I debated between visiting L&L Red or driving to the beach. The latter won. It would be pleasant to walk in damp sand just beyond the surf's reach, soak color into jail pallor, and watch teen-age girls as they scrambled at volleyball or lay basking, bodies shiny from oil. I'd enjoy a respite from the struggle and tension. One of the best things in being a criminal is having no schedule.

Near UCLA I passed a black girl who was quite lovely, statuesque, hair fluffed into a giant natural. She reminded me of Aaron and, more pointedly, that I'd never contacted his mother. Walking the prison yard he would never know about the three weeks in jail. He'd merely know I'd forfeited on my promise.

At a large, bright coffee shop in Santa Monica I stopped for breakfast and made the call. From the little Aaron had said of his mother, mainly a mention of her Christian fervor, I expected the stereotyped "Mammy". She surprised me. Her voice was undoubtedly accented, but with the sibilance of culture and pride. She'd expected my call. Last week the parole board had postponed Aaron for two years and he'd sent a letter for me. She would forward it or hold it for me to pick up. The latter was best because my residence was unsettled.

I knew the letter was about the escape and I wondered how he had smuggled it out. Now I was more than willing. Aaron would be the ideal crime partner, yet I knew that it would be a few more weeks before he went to camp if he'd just gone before the parole board last week. I needed a crime partner before then.

As I walked back toward the counter, someone called my name. I turned, tense, conditioned to fear. A man was rising from a booth beside a window. He was big and he was grinning. Memory told me he was a friend, though not from where. He wore dark glasses, his hair was white and fell down his neck; he had long sideburns and a full mustache swirling down into a Mephistophelian beard. These embellishments and his loud sports clothes made me try to associate him with the Strip rather than jail.

We were shaking hands, and he was slapping me on the back, when the wheels clicked into place. Jerry Shue. We'd shared a cell in the county jail before I went to prison. He'd been acquitted on a burglary but had a warrant as a parole violator from a Rocky Mountain state. That was eight years ago. He'd been in his late thirties and had served eighteen years in one stretch, three of them on Death Row. At the age of sixteen he'd gone to prison for car theft. The next year he was one of eight convicts—all the others were older—who broke out. A guard was bludgeoned to death. After several days of a giant manhunt through blizzard and snowdrift, and after a gun battle at a farmhouse where they held a family hostage, the last four convicts were caught, Jerry Shue among them. Two had been caught within hours of the break and two others had been shot to death running a roadblock. All those taken alive were sentenced to death for the killing of the guard, Jerry among them. He sat under that shadow for three years, his hair turning prematurely white. The governor commuted five of the six sentences. Only the man who'd actually killed the guard was electrocuted. Jerry's commuted sentence was twenty years. After fifteen he was given a conditional release. He immediately fled to California. Two years later he'd been arrested on the burglaries.

At first I'd thought he was dull—"time-drunk"—but soon I realized it was the quiet stoicism of eighteen years behind bars. He occasionally said something so lucid and penetrating that it was amazing, twice so because of his placid demeanor. He was hardened to violence, too. Who wouldn't be after eighteen years in prison? We'd become close friends in the forced intimacy of the jail cell, talking sometimes until dawn and sleeping through the day. He was still waiting for a decision on the extradition when I was carted off to prison.

"It took a minute to recognize you in all that hair and sharp rags."

"I recognized you—but there's some miles on you since last time."

"The only miles I covered were running around the yard."

"That long?" He was incredulous. "For checks?"

"I just raised. What about you?"

"I went back for three summers. Topped out the twenty. No parole."

"You look successful."

"Get the waitress to bring your stuff over. I'll tell you about it."

While I ate, he sketched his situation. He'd "taken a couple" of scores when he first got out, but then he'd found a woman and she'd brought him the first happiness in his life. She, too, had been buffeted by life, a consort of eastern hoodlums in her youth. She was forty, "but looks ten years younger", and she'd been a barmaid when Jerry met her. (I assumed that she'd been a hooker at one time or another; anything else was unlikely.) They managed a plush apartment complex in Burbank and he worked as a housepainter and occasionally obtained subcontracts to paint from a small subdivider and hired a crew himself.

"From that outfit you've got on you're doing pretty good."

"I make twelve to fourteen g's a year. We got two cars, steak in the freezer, and Scotch in the liquor cabinet. I'm happy."

While he talked, I was thinking of how to inveigle him into coming out of retirement. He was less violently inclined than what I wanted, yet it was unlikely I'd find anyone more suitable. He was unperturbed by sight or threat of violence, but he lacked viciousness. Yet he could stand pressure and knew the game. If it rained shit he'd remain composed and put on a slicker. He would never gossip, a serious failing of many otherwise professional criminals; they want recognition in a world where there is no place for it. That he might pause before shooting someone in a critical situation (though, hopefully, not when our capture was in the balance) was the solitary drawback—outweighed by certainty that my back would be safe if we were alone counting twenty thousand dollars.

Over a second cup of coffee I told him of my situation. He was attentive and sympathetic until I reached toward the heist of the crap game and my need for a confederate; then his face took on the blankness of withdrawal, lips set, eyes bland. One could almost hear his thoughts asking me not to force him to hurt my feelings. Not discarding my hopes, I said nothing directly.

"What are you doing right now?" he asked.

"I've gotta pick up a letter."

"Come by the pad this evening for dinner. I want you to meet Carol."

"I might do that. Let me call you first."

"After five. She's got a doctor's appointment and we won't be back until then."

"What's wrong?"

"Iron deficiency. Some bullshit. If you need some bread I can lay a yard or so on you."

"Not right now—but hold on. I might take it in a day or two. You ain't got a submachine gun around the pad, do you?"

He grinned, sadly. "That heavy, huh?"

"All the way. I need money."

"Is it the money—or is it really because you want the fame, or to strike back at them?"

The question sliced cleanly as a surgeon's scalpel. "There's things mixed in," I said, "but if I had the money I wouldn't be doing this. What difference does the motive mean?"

"Plenty. The decisions you'll make, the way you'll do things, the risks you'll take—even the risks you'd see and not see. You might win—against bad odds—if it was just money. The other way . . ."

"Man, I don't need all that Freudian shit. Anybody who analyzes everything too much winds up short-circuiting himself. He gets so involved that he can't make a decisive move."

"I'm in your corner. I hope you will pull a million-dollar sting and get yourself a villa in Rio."

We left together. Jerry pulled from the parking lot in a European station wagon, a new economy car, waving goodbye as he went down the drive.

Aaron's mother lived in a small, yellow frame house on a quiet tree-lined street in the heart of the ghetto between Compton and Watts. As I drove down Avalon Boulevard I wished I'd brought the pistol along, for at every traffic light black faces made me aware that I was the invader of a hostile land. What really worried me was that Mary's clunker might conk out and I'd be on foot. The young blacks in knee-length jackets of imitation leather stared so malevolently (and a few yelled curses) that I knew it was risky to be white in this area.

I got the letter at the door and left quickly, conscious that several children had gathered on the sidewalk to stare at me. The only white faces they saw were social workers or police.

I'd correctly guessed the letter's contents. Written with the same spare precision as his speech, Aaron said the parole board had told him he must serve a minimum of two more years. He was being transferred from behind the walls to a road camp in the Sierras. The closest town, population fifteen thousand, was twenty miles away through mountain forest. A camping ground for tourists was a mile from the correctional camp. When I was ready to come for him, I was to send a telegram under his mother's name saying that he'd get a visit on the weekend. On the following night at 10:30, I was to be parked at the entrance to the public camp site with my parking lights on. He would arrive within half an hour and it would give us two more hours before he was missed, by which time we would be burning up U.S. Interstate 99, southbound.

The letter took for granted that I'd come through, rightfully so. There was no need of a maudlin plea for loyalty. For a moment I thought of sending the telegram and going tomorrow. Mary's car wouldn't be trustworthy enough for an eight-hundred-mile journey, but stealing one was easy. What decided me against the impulse was that Aaron needed more than a ride. That was all he asked for, but he would require lodging, clothes, other help. His escape could wait—not long, but for a while.

I mailed him a greeting card saying that I'd gotten his letter and would send a telegram before the visit. I signed his mother's name and return address.

It was too late for the beach and too early to get in touch with Jerry Shue. I drove to L&L Red's pool hall and found him there. He said Willy Darin had come by and said his sister-in-law wanted her car back. And Johnny Taormina wanted me to call him. Red had the number.

"How's it look?" Johnny asked. "Are you ready?"

"When're they gonna play?"

"They played the same night I talked to you, but I knew you weren't ready. In a couple days . . ."

"Give me your number and I'll check with you every afternoon."

"So you're ready."

"Man, I don't fuck around."

"Good, good. I didn't think you were a bullshitter. Where do we meet afterward?"

"Up on Red's hill. How's that?"

"That's okay with me."

When I hung up, Red asked, "Are you ready?"

"Fuck no! But if worst comes to worst I'll try to get the mother-fucker by myself. Nobody's got a gun so the worst I can do is

155

shoot somebody getting out. Help me find a fuckin' crime partner, Red."

"I'll look around."

I next dialed Abe's club and talked to Manny.

"I've been expecting you in," he said.

"I've been hung up on business. Maybe I'll drop in with a couple friends later tonight. Any word on that business we talked about?"

"Yeah, pretty good. I'll tell you tonight."

"Yeah, okay. Later."

"Later."

6

JERRY was setting a sprinkler on the front lawn when I walked down the sidewalk, having parked Mary's car out of sight around the corner. Jerry wore plaid walking shorts, short-sleeved turtleneck shirt, sandals and dark glasses—strange garb for gardening. His long white hair accented his suntan. He looked more like an executive fighting a waistline and trying to maintain the styles of youth than a man who'd spent two decades in prison. He looked at me incredulously; anyone arriving on foot in Los Angeles is a curiosity. "Where's your wheels?"

"Around the corner. It's one I borrowed—so old and raggedy I'd be ashamed for anyone to see it."

"Man, you didn't have to do that. I know how it is getting out of prison."

"Yeah, but your tenants might think it's odd for a bum to be visiting you."

"Man," he laughed, "fuck 'em. C'mon, let's have a drink. I've got a little pot, too. Good for the appetite. Carol's anxious to meet you, too."

"What'd the croaker say?"

"Prescribed some vitamins. Took some tests. She's just run down."

Jerry led me along a brick walk between high, solid hedges. We entered a plaza surrounded by several two-storey buildings of yellow brick. Huge, leaded bay windows (one above the other, indicating that each building had two apartments) overlooked the plaza where

157

paths fanned from a fish pond and fountain. The paths created borders for beds of roses, pansies, and dahlias—a riot of purple and yellow and orange and white. A patch of lawn beneath a wide shade tree had a picnic table, barbecue and benches. A bucolic scene, peaceful as a cloister. Someone gave it tender care.

"This is too much. Who keeps it up?"

"Me, mostly. Carol does some. I've got a green thumb . . . and I like it."

"What's the rent here?"

"Six hundred furnished. There's a waiting list. Most apartment houses in the valley are running 60 percent occupancy."

"I can see why you've got a waiting list. I wish I could afford it."

We went up the few steps to his bottom-floor apartment. I noticed that his face was marred with preoccupation; the look of someone who's worried over something besides what they're doing, the worry surfacing at every lapse of concentration.

Carol did look younger than her years. She was tall and slender and wore her blonde hair straight down. She had high cheekbones that chisel the face and hide age. She extended both hands to grasp mine, smiling warmly. "Jerry's been talking about you all afternoon." The trace of Brooklyn in her voice didn't match her gracious manner-isms and dress, and the good taste of the furnishings. I warmed toward her instantly, though there was a wry thought that all Jerry could have told her was that I was a jailhouse friend planning a one-man crime wave—a less than ideal recommendation.

After the effusive greeting and a moment's small talk, she went back to arranging the table. Jerry mixed us highballs and brought out half a dozen joints of marijuana.

High on marijuana, which made me ravenously hungry, we sat down to eat. Jerry and I talked, and as the minutes clicked away and Carol believed me engrossed, I saw her exuberance fade into a thin shadow of those first minutes.

When my fugitive status became a topic, her eyes took on a glimmer of concern, and though there was no hostility in Carol, she made me think of Selma Darin. Jerry missed the slender thread of tension. He glowed, half drunk, stoned on pot, and babbled about winning three hundred dollars on a daily double at Santa Anita.

"So what do you do now, Max?" Carol asked in a pause.

"The best I can, I guess."

"You have to live and you can't work. That leaves crime. Right?"

"Well, I could go to Montana and herd sheep, I guess—but I can't work where I need a social security number. When I get enough money I'll blow the country."

Carol nodded her understanding, yet her eyes transfixed mine. Wordlessly she managed to ask me to keep Jerry away from my crimes. I liked her and my resolve to corrupt him shivered to indecision and remained there. I'd try to find someone else.

Half an hour later, when Jerry was in the bedroom getting his coat before we left for Abe's, I told Carol: "Don't worry, I'm not going to get him in trouble. You two have a good thing going. It wouldn't be worth the risk for him."

"Thank you," she said, very softly. "Desperate people are often inconsiderate."

"Yeah, but I'm not that desperate."

"Somehow you're the most desperate person I ever met."

"You might be right at that."

The motel was on the way to Abe's club. We stopped there to leave Mary's automobile and go in Jerry's, and to smoke the last two joints. Ever since Carol had said she didn't feel like going with us, and especially since we'd left, Jerry had been pensive. He wanted to go home and apologized for his mood.

"Damn, I wish you weren't on the lam," he said. "We could build a paint-contracting business out of west hell. Your education is the thing I need. I've got connections but I can't handle the administrative end."

"That's milk that got spilled a long time ago. Besides, I like being a criminal. I know what I'm doing there."

"Yeah, if I didn't have Carol . . ."

"That's like the spilled milk. It's a fact. You'd be a fool. You've got the world by the nuts."

"I hope so. I'm scared. What if something goes wrong?"

I laughed and slapped him on the shoulder. "Do you know how insane that sounds? Here's an asshole worried 'cause he's happy. Would you rather be miserable and have nothing to lose? Man, you're too fuckin' much."

Jerry laughed, too, but when I walked him out to his car the preoccupation had returned. He slipped something into my pocket just before he got behind the wheel. I knew it was money but waited until he dropped me at the club before checking it: a hundred-dollar bill.

Abe's club was so jammed that the overflow spilled onto the sidewalk. Every table was full and customers were stacked three deep at the bar. The doorman—a hunk of beef on the hoof—said that Abe was gone and would be back in half an hour. Manny was working the rush behind the bar. It took ten minutes to edge close enough to him to talk. His shirtsleeves were rolled up, perspiration beaded his forehead, and he was mixing drinks as if he was a machine. He yelled over the bar that he'd made arrangements to pick up a .45 pistol and a police-model shotgun. The yell equaled a whisper in the room's uproar. He threw a drink in front of me and went back to work. I found a corner from which to watch the crowd work hard to have fun.

Minutes later the band climbed the ladder to start a set. Angie was with them; she wore a costume bikini. The group twanged and thumbed, gathered themselves, and suddenly the electronically mixed music throbbed forth. It assaulted the sensibilities while overhead colored lights spun madly and added to disorientation. Still high on pot, my whole being was a conduit of feeling, a circus of awareness. There were no thoughts unless awareness of sensation is a thought. My body yearned to twist and gyrate.

Angie writhed and twisted and shook her ass in a stylized version of the arm-waving bacchanalia on the crowded dance floor. Yet she was indifferent, lacked the joy that others more clumsy were feeling. She was an erotic experience nevertheless; so were the others thronging the room, their skirts high, flashing white legs—or in taut pants that stirred the imagination. The music, the pandemonium, the young women all combined to make it a pleasurable way to spend an evening.

Two A.M. The last drinks had been served, the doors were closed and patrons were heading toward coffee shops or home. Bartenders and cocktail waitresses were rushing to rinse glasses, wipe the bar, clean ashtrays. The tawdriness of the club filled the vacuum created by the departing throng. I stood aside, waiting for Manny January.

Abe Meyers came up beside me. "Come on to the office. There's somebody I want you to meet." It was the first time he'd given me any attention during the evening, although our eyes had met through the crowd several times.

"Yeah, who's that?" I was cold.

"Somebody who buys jewelry."

Instantly I remembered Bulldog. The earth had swallowed him when he became involved with Abe Meyers and hot jewelry. But just talking to someone was no risk. And diamonds interested me. A big jewelry score is easier than a comparable score in currency. The problem was getting rid of a big load. A couple thousand dollars worth was easy, but when the amount became big it was hard. A friend of mine once robbed a San Francisco jeweler for three hundred thousand dollars in diamonds. A week later he was caught with all of it. He was living in a ten-dollar-a-week furnished room and had sixty dollars in his pocket and every piece of jewelry was in a bureau drawer. Two weeks later he committed suicide by leaping from the courthouse window—on the eighth floor.

The man sat behind Abe's desk and started to rise when we came in, but Abe waved him to remain where he was. He was husky, going bald, wore a plain white shirt, open at the throat, and a

161

cardigan sweater. He didn't look rich, except for the fat green cigar between his teeth—and when he removed it a ring flashed on his little finger, a diamond solitaire so big it had to be real. A man who wore plain white shirts and sloppy sweaters wouldn't put five carats of paste on his finger. He eyed me speculatively and I stared back.

Abe introduced us. "Eric Warren, Max Dembo."

"Can we do any business?" the man asked.

"We can talk about it and see."

"I'm mainly interested in diamonds, but I'll handle other gems if the amount is worthwhile."

"How much can you handle?"

"Whatever you can bring."

"What about a hundred grandworth?"

"I can handle, I'd imagine, half-a-million dollars worth." He smiled.

I was dumbfounded, had expected him to hedge on the hundred thousand. Silence dangled, broken only by the sound of movement beyond the door.

He cleared his throat. "A clarification is in order. I can definitely handle half a million dollars worth, providing it isn't one or two stones—say half a million in stones up to three carats—but it would take a few days to get all your money for that much. I'd have to take everything out of the settings and fly to New York. The trip would take two, perhaps three days. I'd give you a substantial down payment on delivery."

"Eric's a diamond merchant," Abe said. "He's got an office downtown."

"Here's my card," Eric said.

"What's to stop you from taking a flight to Buenos Aires from New York?"

"That wouldn't be good business," he said.

"Eric's got a wife and family," Abe intervened. "He wouldn't run off under those circumstances."

"It's happened before. But fuck all that for now. What's the price?"

"I'll do better than you'll usually get. I'll give you two-thirds of the wholesale—about a third of the retail. On half-a-million it would be about a hundred and fifty grand."

The price was right. The standard rate was one-fifth of retail, or a third of wholesale.

"What do you think?" Abe asked.

"Sounds good—but offhand I don't know of any score. I'll think about it and check on Mr Warren here." I fingered the card and slipped it into a shirt pocket.

"Call me when you want to talk some more," Eric said. "We'll have lunch together. Or drop in to my office. You might find something there for yourself—cut-rate for business associates."

"I might do just that."

Manny January was waiting when I came out of the office. Manny was now dapper in jacket and muffler. "What was that?" he asked.

"Just some bullshit. What about those guns?"

"The guy will loan 'em if I keep 'em until they're used. He wants me to be responsible. When the score comes off he wants three hundred dollars. It's a Colt .45 and a Remington 12 gauge."

"He wants more than they cost."

"I know it—but what can I do?"

"Get 'em. If the score comes off it'll be worth it."

"You won't burn the guy, will you?"

"No, I'll pay him. Like I said, it'll be worth it."

Abe Meyers came out of the office and passed us. Angie Nichols was waiting for him. Over her brief costume was a dark mink coat that fell just above her knees.

"Angie's doing okay for herself," I said.

"Abe's present to her."

"I thought she was a square."

"Squares know a good thing when they see it."

"Glad to hear somebody can get something from him. I wanted to bone her down—but it doesn't look like I can pay the tariff."

"Abe's got to pay. He's fat as a pig and got a dick like a mosquito, so I hear."

"They say it doesn't matter to your lovemaking abilities."

"Bullshit! I never had to buy a broad a mink coat."

It made me laugh.

Later, as I sat in a cab going through the empty streets, I felt good—quietly exuberant. Things were beginning to move, the possibilities were growing. I had the joyous sensation of being in control of my world. I was doing what I knew how to do.

L&L Red saw me come into the pool hall and quickly finished his mug of beer. He was enthusiastic, and led me back to the sidewalk where he joyously declared that he'd found the crime partner I wanted, a two-hundred-and-forty-pounder, an ex-convict out of San Quentin who knew the game and was looking for a score. "Name's George Rimmer," Red said, "big guy about forty years old." The name brought no recollection, but San Quentin has thirty-eight hundred convicts (and I'd seen three times that many faces with the turnover of eight years) and there was no way to know all of them. George Rimmer might have been a loner, or run with an Okie clique.

We went to see the man. He was living in a room two blocks from where Joe Gambesi had grown up; it had been a terrible slum even then. The stairwell was unlighted, smelled of urine where winos had pissed on the wall, and graffiti had been painted in black paint. It was an unlikely place to find a journeyman criminal. The criminals I knew and respected would prefer being on the prison yard for trying to get something than living like this.

Red knocked on the door. The man who opened it, bearded and wild-haired, made me burst into laughter. "George Rimmer" rang no bells, but the man before me was "Gold-tooth George", a wretch who'd sold fellatio in prison for two packs of cigarettes a trick—three packs to blacks. He also habitually locked himself up in protective custody after getting too deep in debt. On sight of me, he flinched, and I laughed even harder.

Driving away, I explained the situation to Red. He didn't think it was funny. He'd even bought George several drinks the night before.

"C'mon, I'll buy 'em back for you," I said. "I've gotta pick up some bogus I.D. and see some people."

"When're we really gonna have a party, Max? I mean really fuckin' ball it up?"

"Soon as I tear off some money you line us up a couple freaky foxes."

It made him happy to think about it.

7

WHEN I pulled into the motel, I was thinking of Johnny Taormina, wondering if he was having second thoughts. An hour before he'd claimed to be unable to give a definite time that the game was going off. I'd growled at him and he'd whined that he was telling the truth, never knowing that my rent was due in the morning and that was what disturbed me. Yet there was still a chance that he was balking at the last moment.

I was thinking of this—and of getting Mary's car back to her— when I trudged up the steps. One foot was in midair and my door was five feet away when I saw that the light was on and someone was moving around. Heat! Like a cat with its tail stepped on, I leaped sideways and broke full tilt at the darkness beside the building, crashing like a fullback into high shrubbery and breaking through; then leaping down a fifteen-foot embankment into a brush-filled ditch. I lay silent and motionless where I landed, staring up at the brink of the ditch and listening for any sound. All I could see was the black border of clouds drifting across the face of a half moon. All I could hear was traffic in the distance. My racing heartbeat slowed after a few minutes. I felt the scratchy nettles of the weeds and the itch where the bushes had torn at my arms and face. It was obvious that nobody had seen me. That there'd been no outcry and chase calmed me; if I was unseen I was as safe as I'd been an hour ago.

I began to move along the ditch. The most reasonable thing, I thought, was that the maid had found the revolver. If so, O.K., I'd lost it and a few clothes. Maybe I could find a way to get Mary's junkheap. They obviously hadn't seen me drive up in it. Twenty feet along the ditch where there was a dark area, I scrambled up the embankment to the shrubbery and peered out.

Jerry Shue's station wagon was parked ten feet from Mary's car. It was Jerry in the room. "Bastard motherfucker," I cursed. If I'd been properly watchful I'd have seen the light and the parked automobile the moment I turned in from the street.

When I walked into the room I expected Jerry's eyes to widen at sight of the cockleburs in my hair and bedraggled appearance and to laugh with gusto at the story. Jerry neither noticed nor laughed. There was a redness in his eyes. His clothes were also unkempt; he needed a shave and his hair was messed.

"I slipped the lock," he said, "I didn't want to wait in the car."

"Man, you look bad. What's wrong?"

"Carol's got leukemia."

"No. Man, goddam . . ." The awful statement left me without words. With eyes closed for emphasis, I shook my head in mute sympathy. "Are you sure?" I asked. "Maybe it's a mistake."

"No, it's something they call malo fibrosis—leukemia is part of it or it's a part of leukemia. I'm going to need money. I already owe eight hundred and she's going to have everything there is. If you still want me on that caper . . ."

"Man, I don't want you to decide when your mind's all fucked up. You're on the edge of hysteria."

"I've thought about it and decided. I know what I'm doing."

"Decide tomorrow. I want you with me—but—you know what I mean."

"I don't want to go back to the apartment tonight."

"Where's Carol now?"

"In the hospital."

"Stay here, or get a hotel room."

"What time is it?"

"Got no watch, but it's about one-thirty."

"Let's get something to eat. I'm hungry and I feel guilty about it. If I'm moving around I feel better."

Outside, he handed me the ignition keys. Summer was dying and the night air was chill. He inhaled deeply. Minutes later, as the automobile surged onto the freeway, he seemed less overwrought.

"Where to?"

"Doesn't matter."

I headed toward Long Beach; it was good a place as any.

"She's taking it good," Jerry said. "Either she's got unbelievable courage or she doesn't accept it."

Over coffee we decided that I'd go with him to visit in the morning. We talked about what we were going to do. He believed he was returning to crime solely to assure that Carol had everything money could buy. It might have been true, but I'm inclined to think that somewhere in the psychological mosaic was a need to fight dilemma with blind aggression—to lash out blindly and get revenge. His best move would have been to bear witness and endure, for it was better for Carol to be in a charity ward of the county hospital than have him in jail or dead—and she'd then be in the charity ward anyway. None of these arguments persuaded him, and so as dawn neared and we turned back up the coast highway toward Los Angeles it was agreed that he'd go with me.

"When do we make the first score?" he asked.

"Whenever he gives the word. It could be tomorrow or the next day. There's another thing—I met some dude the other night who wants diamonds. I'm gonna check him out . . . see if he's for real."

"I'm game for anything. Eight or nine grand will help, but not for very long. We've got no insurance . . . nothing."

"We'll make money. If you've got enough guts there's money damn near lying on the ground."

"Yeah, but the real good heists are where you can cut off that silent alarm and root around for fifteen or twenty minutes."

"I know somebody who can do just that. He's up at a road camp and wants to duff. I'm going to pick him up pretty soon. He's black."

"I don't care if he's polka dot if he's solid and can hold up his end—and I trust your judgment."

When we turned in from the seacoast the eye of day was opening. Jerry had gone to sleep beside me.

Carol used a remote control switch to turn off a television set as the nurse ushered us into the room and faded away. Jerry had shaved and changed clothes.

Carol looked much better than at the apartment. I hadn't noticed her pallor then, but recognized it now from the change. Jerry looked more sickly than Carol.

"I thought you might like to see Max," he said.

"Sure. Hi," she said, wiggling her fingers to me and smiling. "Don't look so solemn."

Her brightness made me feel worse, but I managed to smile. "How do you feel?"

"So good I can't believe I'm sick. All I needed was some fresh blood. I'm ready to go home."

"Tomorrow, the doctor says," Jerry said.

We stood at the foot of the bed, feeling uncertain. Jerry walked around and kissed her. She smiled and patted his cheek. "That's a good boy. Settle down. I'm not dying tomorrow. When the time comes you'll be tired of me. Sit down—both of you."

Jerry pulled a chair beside the bed and sat down. I stood beside him, wanting to light a cigar and restraining myself.

"Mrs Johnson called me today," Carol said. "She went by the apartment twice and you were gone. The chlorine machine is goofing and the pool is like poison gas. She was upset. She wants to know how long I'll be here. I told her I'd be home in a day or two. She didn't even ask what was wrong."

"We'll start paying our rent," Jerry said. "Fuck all that work. We wasted too much time for fun already. We'll get somebody in to do the housework."

Carol's face, which had been radiant, almost joyful, turned to darkness. "The money. Where's the money coming from?"

"Don't worry about money," Jerry said.

Carol turned to me with baleful accusation.

"I had nothing to do with his decision. I tried to talk him out of it."

"You weren't sincere."

"Every person does what they really want to do."

"Jerry, don't," she said to him. "Don't risk what little we have left."

"I'm doing what I have to do. I might've done it anyway."

"What if something happens?"

"Nothing's going to happen. We're both pros."

"That's why you spent your life in prison—because you're a pro?"

"That's where I learned to be a pro. Carol, we owe a thousand in hospital bills right now. It's going to cost and cost. We need money and I'm going to get it."

"I don't care if I die in a flophouse or right now this minute! I'd rather do that than see you locked up or shot down in the gutter."

"None of that's going to happen."

"It could with him. He doesn't care."

The statement, made without anger, stirred a chord. Her words were close enough for me to blurt, "That's not true." I wanted to argue, but who can argue with a dying person?

"Don't get on Max's case," Jerry said. "Can't you see how I feel— what I've got to do to be a man in my own eyes?"

"We don't need it."

"Yes we do."

"Not that much. I'd rather stick my head in an oven."

"If you were that cruel I'd be right behind you."

They verged on tears and I did too. They stared at each other, both in anger and agony. "Do what you want," Carol said. "It doesn't matter. I won't be here very long." She spoke tonelessly, suddenly drained of fire. "Just don't tell me anything about what you're doing."

When we left fifteen minutes later, the episode of wounding had

170

been healed, covered with layers of small talk and tenderness. Both chose to withdraw rather than hurt the other. Jerry had held his ground, yet Carol's remonstrations hung in the background and the scars would be there. I was a detached bystander. Carol was friendly to me—and it was sincere. It was no modification of her opinion of me, but merely an acceptance despite that opinion. Maybe she really decided that because of death's proximity such intense concern was ludicrous.

Walking down the corridor, under the hard lights, Jerry sagged. All at once the powerful frame was gaunt (or I saw gauntness for the first time) and he reeled. His face was bloodless. The scene in the room had unnerved him, sapped the last reserves. He was like a man in a trance as we drove back toward the motel.

But the human mind, when it reaches the bottom of the abyss, must bounce back or disintegrate entirely. Filled with Scotch and seconal, Jerry collapsed on a chair. Hours later, though groggy and stiff, he'd bounced back. After splashing cold water on his face, he grinned. "Why don't you give that Wop gangster a call and see what's happening? If I'm thinking about action I won't really be thinking. That's the way I want it."

"I can dig it," I said—and I could.

8

THE next day, Saturday, in late afternoon Jerry was going to bring Carol from the hospital. It was better that she didn't see me, but I spent the morning with him at the apartment, doing chores that had been ignored. Full of cold beer and marijuana, we watered flowers, cleaned the swimming pool, raked leaves, and dusted the apartment. Jerry had risen out of his despondency. He seemed more the easygoing man I knew; it was not diminishment of loss of love, it was the resilience of someone accustomed to loss.

In the afternoon I went back to the motel, sat basking beside the swimming pool and watching college football on a portable television set that two middle-aged men brought out. It was a yellow-warm day, the sun gentle, though in late afternoon the air turned chill.

I drove into Hollywood to eat. When I returned at dusk a note was scotch-taped to the door: "Mr Johnny T. called and left message that the game is for 8:00 tonight."

I'd been waiting with almost angry anticipation for this message. Now, holding it, the butterflies of imminent danger—a not totally unpleasant sensation—came to life in my stomach. I walked down to the motel office and used the pay telephone to call Jerry.

"It's tonight," I said. "I'll call the guy about the guns."

"We've just been here ten minutes. What'll I tell Carol?"

"She told you not to tell her anything. Just say you've got to go somewhere for a couple hours. You can't balk now."

"What time is the move?"

"They're starting at 8:00. Give 'em an hour to get comfortable."

"I'll be there in twenty minutes."

Next, I dropped a dime in the slot and dialed Abe's club. He answered and said that Manny had taken the evening off. Abe thought he might be shacked up with a broad he'd met the night before. I hung up and dialed Manny's apartment in West Hollywood. I listened to the unanswered ringing for five minutes and hung up, cursing in frustration. I went back to my room and stood at the window, waiting for Jerry and watching the hillsides turn from orange to purple. When Jerry arrived, I went back to the telephone. Still no answer from Manny's apartment.

So instead of charging through a door and robbing a dozen semi-racketeers (later joyfully counting fifteen or twenty thousand dollars on a bed) we spent the evening parked on a tree-lined street of apartment buildings in West Hollywood, waiting for Manny to come home. At 11:00 we realized the heist was a dead issue. Jerry laughed. I, too, saw the humor—but I also felt the burden of being a fool.

"Let's go home," Jerry said. "I'm hungry."

"We can kiss this one off for good. That dago isn't going to help us anymore. I suppose we could wait every night—but I can't wait very long."

"Neither can I. Is anything else pending? I need to make a couple grand in the next week or two."

"Just that jewel move and it's gonna take time to put together."

"We could start looking for a jewel score. Make a list of all the first-class jewelers and start looking 'em over. You check Pasadena and the east side. I'll get Beverly Hills."

"Yeah, but that's still a future thing. It'd take a month at least. Meanwhile you need a couple grand—and I've barely got gas money. What we should do is look at some banks. We can get that together in a week or two."

Jerry was turning the key in the ignition when headlights sprayed through the back window. It was Manny's automobile. He got out, his movements indicating that he was slightly drunk. I stepped to the sidewalk and called him. He came over, grinned, and leaned over to see who was in the car. He didn't know Jerry. His grin sandpapered my irritation.

"Where the fuck were you?" I snapped, not intending such anger to show; it was just a goof. He wasn't supposed to spend his life waiting for my call.

"I been balling some freaky debutante at her pad at Laguna. What's up?"

"Nothing now. We wanted those guns—but it's too late. We fucked off a score because you weren't here."

"It wouldn't have mattered. The dude picked up those guns yesterday afternoon. I was going to call you last night but I lost your number."

What he'd said registered several seconds later. When it did, I looked at his flap-jawed grin and punched him without warning. The left hook landed on his eye, split the flesh open, and dumped him flat on his back. The follow-up right hand punch sailed over his head because he was on the way down.

"Hey! Goddam!" he yelped. "What's that for?" He was more frightened than groggy or hurt. He raised himself on an elbow and wiped the blood away from his vision.

"You asshole!" I said.

"Man, what'd I do?"

"Never mind." The whole fiasco was aggravated beyond endurance by his casual failure to tell me about something so important as the man taking back the firearms. "Shitass, you were off sucking some broad's cunt when you should've been taking care of business. If we had known in time, Jerry could've brought a shotgun, and I still had the small revolver." I drew back to kick him and he wriggled to get away. He stayed prone, believing himself safer on the ground than on his feet.

Jerry had run around the car; he was holding my arm and pulling me back. "You crazy motherfucker! Cool it. Somebody's gonna call the heat and we'll be busted for a chickenshit street brawl. There's no money in that."

Jerry eased me into the car and we drove away. On Sunset Boulevard, amid the exploding neon, passing the sidewalks filled with women in high skirts and men in expensive clothes, I cursed, "Cocksuckin' motherfuckin' punk bastards. We're fuckin' snakebit."

"We'll get it together. Don't sweat it. This is just one of those things. Fuck it. Tomorrow we'll start working on something else."

No sooner was I back in the motel than two ideas burst almost simultaneously into mind: The market Willy Darin had spoken of, and the pawn shop beside the Monticello cocktail lounge. The pawn shop would provide the arsenal and a few hundred dollars (L&L Red could sell the merchandise); the market would be worth the two thousand Jerry needed—and my end would get me an automobile, clothes, a month's rent.

I was already keyed up to commit a crime. I'd go tonight, alone, to take the pawn shop with a burglary. The trunk of Mary's car had a tire iron and a long screwdriver, all I needed to use on the wall. At 1:10 I was on my way to commit the burglary, stopping in Hollywood to buy rubber gloves at an all-night drugstore.

The parking space directly behind the barber shop's back door was empty when I pulled into the lot, lessening the distance I'd be exposed while carying the loot. I backed in, cut the motor, and finished the last of a cigar, meanwhile watching the rear entrance of the cocktail lounge. The night was quiet. Business was slow. Half-a-dozen automobiles were in the lot. Nobody came or went. Nothing stirred signals of warning.

Extinguishing the cigar butt with deliberation, I slipped on the gloves, hefted the tire iron and slipped through the shadows to the barber shop's door. A tinkle of glass—and ten seconds later I was inside, pausing motionless to see if there was any reaction to the breaking glass. All remained silent, unstirring.

It was precisely as it had looked during my earlier examination. The pawn shop's flank was soft and unprotected. I stabbed into the wall with the tire iron. The plaster was dry and soft; it fell away, pattering lightly to the floor. The sound would not escape the building. From outside came flashes of light and motor noise as automobiles went past. Every sense was keyed to anything erratic in the night's pulsations, the slightest variation, the crunch of footsteps, an automobile that sounded wrong, an unusual silence. Any of these would make me freeze and turn like a predatory animal caught in a beam of light.

I kept working. Plaster piled on the floor, scrunching underfoot. I used the screwdriver and tire iron together to snap the wooden slats behind the plaster. In fifteen minutes there was a hole large enough to crawl through. The pawn shop's storeroom was beyond and it was lighted enough to see without a flashlight. Valuables in pawn-filled bins along the wall and floor. They were gathered by item, guns together, typewriters together, and each was tagged with the name of the person who'd pawned it.

I widened the hole with my hands, breaking off sharp edges, and squeezed through head first, coming down on my hands and dropping into a crouch. Motionless, I listened for the space of a minute. The possibility always existed that there was an alarm I'd missed— or that someone (perhaps drunk) was sleeping inside.

Both the pawn shop and surrounding night remained undisturbed. My fear-stimulated heartbeat now throbbed with the pace of success. For a moment I felt misgivings, for into my thoughts came visions of the persons who owned these things. Perhaps a sentimental value was attached to something they'd been forced to pawn. It was the reason I'd never burglarized homes. Taking money, or what had monetary value alone, was impersonal, especially if it was from a source that could withstand the loss. To cause someone emotional pain was something else.

This pang quickly disappeared. The middle of a crime is no place for throbbing conscience or meditation.

My first move was to the back door, looking for hidden alarms. I found none, nor did I expect to; such things were expensive. Yet facing years of prison I could ill afford to take things for granted.

Now I unfastened the lock on the back door for an escape route, although I would remove what I was stealing through the hole in the wall. If I opened the door the alarm would ring—but if I needed to flee the ringing would make no difference. Using the hole foreclosed taking large articles, but all I really wanted was firearms. Whatever else I got would be frosting.

The light was from the pawn shop's front room, making it unnecessary to use a flashlight. I was grateful. Once I'd made entry through the roof of a liquor warehouse with the aid of a hand drill and keyhole saw. I used a flashlight and saw a twelve-foot drop into an office. I hung down and let go—and crashed through a glass roof over the office that I'd missed with the flashlight. Miraculously, only my hand was slashed, but it could just as easily have been my throat. Contrary to the advertising by the electric company, as a burglar I preferred that lights be left burning.

Now I moved to the side of the archway into the front room, kneeled beside the arch and peered around, keeping my head near the floor so no silhouette would be visible from outside the windows. Automobiles flashed by occasionally. A vintage safe stood near the front window under the light. It would have taken me thirty minutes to open it with a sledge hammer and chisels—even less with an acetylene torch. It was too heavy to move and I couldn't work in front of the window even if I had the tools. I felt like a cat staring at a canary protected by a cage.

The pistols were in the display case. I stepped back into the storeroom, dumped trash from a cardboard crate and filled it with cameras and small business machines that would fit through the hole. Half a dozen rifles and two shotguns stood together, each with a tag around the trigger guard. All the rifles were .22s, which didn't interest me except to sell—but one shotgun was a double-barrelled .12 gauge.

I pushed everything through the hole into the barber shop, then crawled through to put it in the car and return for what was in the front room. The most dangerous moment would be when I rushed out and began stripping the display case. By loading the car now I'd be able to leave immediately after the second trip—time enough to get away if someone saw me and made a telephone call.

Plaster crunched beneath my shoes. Shadows in the barber shop writhed as automobiles passed. A door slammed, followed by footsteps and the resonance of a woman's laughter. A couple was moving from the cocktail lounge to an automobile, passing me ten feet away. The man's hand stroked her rump suggestively. When they drove away, taillights blazing momentarily as they paused at the street, I slipped out through the door with an armload of rifles. In thirty seconds I was putting the box of cameras in the back seat.

Back in the barber shop's darkness, I waited to see if I'd aroused anyone. The night remained undisturbed.

Sweat dripped from my forehead and chin and I was breathing heavily as I wriggled through the hole. I'd been working hard and moving fast under pressure. Pausing to pick up the tire iron, I peered through the arch just long enough to make sure nobody was on the sidewalk in front. I moved quickly to the display case—it had a lock—and bashed in the glass, the sound exploding in the silence. In thirty seconds I'd scooped out four pistols, one a Browning .380 automatic, my favorite handgun. Pistols in hand, I remained kneeling behind the case. The front window had several musical instruments; they'd sell easily but would be too bulky, especially with the ungainly load I already had.

A row of pegs on a wall contained wristwatches, each with a tag. They were a bonus. I loaded my pockets.

Three minutes later I turned the old Plymouth through dark streets toward L&L Red's hilltop cabin. Behind me was the pillaged shop, a hole ripped in its side. Suddenly, I envisioned the pain and anger on the owner's face as he examined the crime; each moment would make him find something else missing. Remorse swelled through me—not exactly remorse but a hope that he was insured.

178

Instantly, deliberately, I hardened myself against such feelings. I needed no justification for what I'd done, and even if I did it was easy to imagine him as a vile, penurious Shylock, a man lacking in both compassion and courage. I was able to make myself despise the man without ever seeing him. He was a squarejohn citizen, a believer in the death penalty, a coward, a dog. It was a blanket condemnation, irrational—the same as his kind had been giving me all my life.

Jerry Shue had a tool room and workshop. He locked the shotgun in a vise and sawed off both the barrel and stock, smoothed the former with a file and the latter with sandpaper. The shotgun now resembled an eighteenth-century handgun. Jerry wrapped the middle of the barrel with electrician's tape so it could be held from the top while being fired. He tacked a long thong in a loop from the handle so it could be hung from the shoulder inside a coat.

Leaving the guns behind, we drove to look at the market. Everything was like Willy said. I went up the stairs and walked into the manager's office. He looked up, startled, and I offered to sell him some shopping carts. He wasn't interested. I saw what I wanted to see: the safe was beside the door.

"How is it?" Jerry asked when I got back in the car.

"It's bear meat. If we brought the cannons we'd get him right now."

"That good, huh?"

"Does a bear shit in the woods?"

The getaway would be more difficult than the robbery itself. The market sat on an intersection. The street to its right side was one way, becoming a freeway on-ramp. The parking lot had wide access to this street and was the logical route. It would also be the first one covered when the alarm went out. A narrow driveway ran along the other side of the market toward the street in front, but if we went that way and turned left away from the market's face we'd be in a shopping mall two blocks away, a maze of one-way streets and streets where automobiles were not allowed. If we came down the driveway and turned right, we'd pass right before the market's front window—and we'd have to pause for a stop sign outside the main entrance; then we'd pass beneath the freeway to another stop sign. Yet just beyond the second stop was a residential street to the right (easier to turn into than a left turn, which was important on a getaway) and half a mile later we would turn onto Mary Gambesi's street a block from her driveway. We'd disappear down the driveway. We'd use Mary's car with stolen license plates taped over those that belonged to the car. Jerry's station wagon could be at the curb in front. We'd visit Mary, return her car, count the money, and stay out of sight until the noon rush.

We drove the route, pausing for both stop signs, obeying all traffic laws. It would take four minutes to be at our destination. With the manager bound and gagged we'd undoubtedly be drinking coffee in Mary's kitchen before the call went over the police radios.

"How's tomorrow?" Jerry asked.

"I'm ready."

We were speeding back toward Los Angeles. We detoured to see L&L Red, but the cabin was unoccupied. He was probably off selling the pawn shop loot.

"Leave me at the motel," I said.

"Don't worry about Carol. She digs you."

"Naw, fuck it. Let's not rub salt in the wound. It's better if I keep away from her for a few days."

"I'll pick you up about 9:00 tomorrow. It's better if we rip when the traffic's lightest."

"Get some extra ammunition."

"We can get it on the way out there."

Sunday afternoon and evening were a blank canvas to be painted with whatever design attracted me. Every previous moment since leaping from Rosenthal's automobile—even those drinking with Red or in Abe's club—I'd been under a storm of pressure. Today the sea was calm, the eye of the storm. Until tomorrow morning there was nothing to do but wait. Staying alone in the motel was a distasteful prospect, and so was the idea of finding some criminals. They'd soothe my lone-liness, but I wanted something restful.

I drove to a gas station near Hollywood Boulevard and left the car for an oil change and checkup. It would never get us away in a chase, but I wanted to be sure it didn't conk out as we drove away from the parking lot.

For lack of anything else to do, I spent an hour roaming along the boulevard, watching the youths in their bizarre costumes— sandals and long hair and feathered hats and beads. Abe's club was a few blocks away, but I preferred to stroll in the yellow sunlight. When I reached the end of tall buildings and crowds, I hailed a taxi and went to the new art museum, a serene place to spend an autumn afternoon. I looked at the people as much as I looked at the paintings, deriving pleasure from their intense seriousness about culture. I was not cynical. My general feeling was benign, even tender. It was unusual for me to be compassionate, except to individuals close to me. My usual view is a search for their weakness, for prey, as enemies, though not necessarily hated enemies; the lion doesn't hate the gazelle; he is indifferent to him. Today I liked them because of their foibles, and my gentle mood was comfortable.

In late afternoon I took another taxi, this time to a Wilshire Boulevard restaurant in Beverly Hills. Frascati's is acclaimed for its Belgian cuisine, but that isn't why I selected it (after being raised in prison my qualifications as a gourmet are restricted to beans). This restaurant had a tree-shaded patio separated from the boule-vard by a low wall, but one could sit and eat and look out. It was something I'd always enjoyed.

Next I went for a leisurely trek through the Beverly Hills busi-ness and shopping district. I would have liked to walk through the palatial residential streets, but pedestrians are unheard of in such environs, and they are routinely stopped and questioned by the police. All drifters, much less those with a criminal background, are summarily arrested and given thirty days for vagrancy.

On Wilshire and Beverly Drive, in the business section, I was at the hub of Southern California's jewelry business—good jewelry, I mean. The immediate area had several exclusive jeweler's: Van Cleef & Arpels, Tiffany & Co., Raymond & Co., among others. Raymond had been ripped, I remembered, for $250,000 in a daring robbery. I walked south from Wilshire on Beverly Drive, looking in the windows. They were empty, so were the display cases, but through the glass could be seen the plush carpets, the elegant cut-glass chandeliers, the cases with special locks, and the vault doors of shining steel.

A robbery in the immediate vicinity was impractical. Today the streets were empty, but when the stores were open the streets would be jammed. For at least six blocks in every direction there were nothing but businesses, which meant traffic lights, office buildings. It would take too long to cover any distance.

I telephoned for another taxi and waited in a Standard gas station, and while I waited I checked the Yellow Pages Directory under "Diamonds", and "Jewelers—Retail". I could tell the approximate location of many addresses. One caught my eye: Gregory's. The name was as familiar as Van Cleef & Arpels, and the address was on Wilshire—but the number indicated it was east of the main section. On a hunch, I had the taxi drive down Wilshire and I looked out.

Gregory's had a private building, low and gleaming white, semi-colonial in design. I'd passed it countless times without ever previously noticing it. A brass signplate, brightly polished, was fastened beside the door. Gregory's, Fine Jewelers, it said, and nothing more. Across Wilshire was still the business district, but behind the jeweler's were streets of elegant apartment buildings and nice homes. Trees jutted over the sidewalks.

What I saw made me decide to come back and look further when I had the time. I leaned back in the taxi and fired a cigar. The evening still loomed empty. It was just getting dark. I decided to see Manny and soothe his ruffled feathers.

9

THE club had the usual Sunday evening slowness. Manny January was leaning against a cigarette machine in the back near the short corridor to the office, a flesh-colored Band-Aid pasted beside his right eye. When I came through the front door, he watched me apprehensively. Had I suddenly reached into a pocket he would have bolted in panic. Sight of his fear aroused a mild exultation, for if one has no other identity the ability to instill fear in others can satisfy a need.

It took ten minutes of assurances that I intended him no harm to get him to leave. We went for a ride in his automobile. When someone is terrified, the best way to allay that terror is to get in a position where you have the power to do them harm and, instead, treat them considerately. When Manny got the message, we were riding through dark residential streets. Only then did he show his smoldering resentment at being knocked down and made to crawl. This indignation was what I wanted expressed—for I didn't want it to become abscessed, growing larger and poisoning his mind. Fear, hate, resentment, none of these mattered if the person harboring them was at a safe distance. But Manny was within my circle, and secret venom could be a threat. A dime dropped in a pay telephone and a few whispered words to the police would get him full revenge.

Once he'd expressed his hurt feelings, I treated him as a child who's been naughty and punished, but who is still loved. I showed him where he'd failed to maintain his responsibilities, that he'd been wrong. I apologized for losing my temper, and yet made him understand where it was his own fault.

We stopped by his apartment, picked up a dozen joints and twice that many bennies. On the way back to the club, both of us high, he talked about his hopes, doubts, problems. I let him talk uninterruptedly, and when we got out and went in where the music played, he was more enamored of me than ever.

Somewhat later in the evening, perhaps near midnight, I found myself stoned on pot and pills and booze, in a booth with Abe, Manny, Angie, and two broads I'd never seen before. All Manny knew of the women was that they'd come separately to the club, and both had been there before during recent weeks. One girl was glitter without substance, hard and brittle and growing old. She seemed—from the haze of my intoxication—the kind to whom old age would be a special curse, for she lacked any reservoirs to sustain her when beauty was gone.

The other girl, Allison, sat across from me. Her pale blonde hair seemed colorless against the lacquered sheen of Angie and the other. On first glance she was just an average pretty girl in her mid-twenties, less flashy than most who frequented these places. On closer scrutiny I saw she required no flashy setting—she had high cheekbones and skin as smooth as a dove's breast, requiring no makeup to hide imperfections. Her eyes were colored somewhere between hazel and violet, and they looked directly into my stare without fluster. Except for the drugs in my system, I would have looked away, for to stare longer would have created a silent game of wills.

We said nothing to each other, and her few words to the others didn't reveal much about her personality. I noticed the faintest hint of southern accent in her voice. A popular folk singer-poet was mentioned, and she said, "Oh, isn't he good" with a stress on the last syllable that gave feeling to the simple sentence. Occasionally, when the music throbbed over the room, she rocked her head in rhythm. I now remember these things with more clarity than when they happened.

Everyone was going to a party, the girls leaving first. Abe and

Manny would show up after the club closed. Abe wanted me to go, but I turned the offer down. I'd slept three hours the previous night and had an appointment to commit a robbery in the morning.

Allison had an automobile, but it was parked on Sunset Boulevard at another club. Manny offered to drive her to pick it up, and then to take me home.

"Just drop me at the Carolina Pines. I'll get a sandwich and catch a cab," I said.

On the way, Manny brought out some more joints and we smoked them. I still had no opportunity to talk to the girl. If the robbery went right I'd get her phone number from Abe or Manny, if they had it. If not, I'd see her again, maybe.

I got out, watched the car pull away, and walked into the coffee shop, a vast, gleaming establishment of stainless steel and formica. The benzedrine sapped my appetite and I settled for coffee, being unable to get anything else down. It was also apparent that I'd never be able to sleep, much as I wanted to and much as I needed it.

Outside, I stood beneath the overhang of the coffee shop's roof, bathed in the light from the windows, and wondered what to do. Maybe go downtown. The underworld night people would be there, in the dingy Traveler's Café on Temple Street or Dixie's Waffle Shop on Broadway. I might even buy a balloon of heroin. The dope fiend whores would be there too. I could buy half a gram, pick one up and throw an orgy with her—an easy thing to do when one is full of benzedrine and heroin.

And if, by chance, I found no familiar faces, I could go to an all-night movie.

The thing that made me pause was that the downtown area at this postmidnight hour was heavily policed. They might stop me, and though my false identification was good the scene would be risky. Several hundred other fugitives were undoubtedly loose in Los Angeles, yet there was always a chance that some policeman would remember my picture.

A Yellow Cab deposited a customer at the curb. Without having decided my destination, only that I was going somewhere, I hailed it and started forward.

An automobile pulled to the curb beside me; I saw it in my peripheral vision. Reflexively, I looked over. Allison was alone behind the wheel of a sporty pale blue convertible. Its top was down and her hair was windblown; the sight of her sent delight shivering through me. Now that she appeared, I realized that in some chamber of my mind I had been expecting her, or at least hopefully waiting, having gotten some wordless communication to her during the exchange of looks at the club.

Her smile of greeting was whimsical, uncertain—as if she were afraid I'd rebuff her forwardness.

"What happened to the party?" I asked.

"I changed my mind."

"Uh huh. And you knew I needed a ride home? Right?"

"If that's where you want to go." She colored slightly, unsure of herself. It made me like her even more. I was standing beside the car, looking down at her exposed thighs; her short skirt had ridden upward as she sat to drive the automobile. They were very white thighs. She knew I was staring.

"Well, get in," she said.

She put her car in motion, heading toward Hollywood Boulevard.

"Well, what do you want to do?"

"Go fuck," was what I wanted to say—and yet that wasn't the whole of it. Something told me she was more than a quick lay. It was not the electricity of love, but something milder. She seemed to be someone who could ease the pangs of my loneliness. "We can blow a couple joints, drive around, and see if we really like each other."

"Groovy." She smiled with full warmth.

Soon, without being directed, she was driving where I would have gone—along the serpentine curves at the crest of the Hollywood Hills, an area of elegant houses on ledges and leveled hills. On a clear night it was possible to see southward for forty miles and north for thirty more miles—and every inch was city lights.

We parked at a vantage point. Allison turned on the car radio, softly, and we sat and talked. She'd asked Manny about me while they were going for her car. He'd told her that I'd just served ten years in prison. The information fascinated her. She'd never met anyone who'd spent a night in jail, much less a decade. I corrected the two-year error. "Oh," she said, "I've undoubtedly met someone, but I didn't know it."

What she said startled and entranced me—for it seemed that everybody I knew had been raised in jail.

She wanted to know what it was like—the violence, the absence of women—as if the prison world can be encapsuled in a night's conversation. I told her some truths and some lies, piquing her obvious desire to hear the romantic. Mainly I evaded and turned the conversation back to her, drawing her out, for I have a theory that if you allow anyone to talk about themselves for very long—especially about their feelings and problems—they will become attached to you.

Wryly, Allison described herself as a "swinging divorcee", though the divorce wasn't quite final. She'd been miserable, had broken free to find herself, to feel life—even its pain. She was the only daughter of a middle-class Kentucky family. Her father published a newspaper in a town of twenty thousand. She'd spent two years in a Baptist women's college. Her life had been dull, though she'd never realized it, never having another frame of reference. What joys she'd found had been in reading, but books had not instilled any desires, at least not conscious desires. A daring night had consisted of drinking beer and driving too fast on a country road, parking and heavy petting, and all of it filled with delicious guilt. She rebelled against Calvinist rectitude without gainsaying its validity.

Her husband was from Baltimore, an engineer fifteen years older than herself. She met him when he was in the army, stationed at a small base near the town. He was soon to be discharged and was going to California, where his training would ensure a career in the aerospace industry. He'd seemed the most sophisticated and worldly man imaginable, and California seemed the promised land, milk and honey and sunshine by the sea. She'd deliberately gotten pregnant and come west with him, a wedding band on her finger and expectations in her heart. She was nineteen.

Five years later she was on her hands and knees, scraping sludge from an oven in a neat tract home in suburbia. She threw down the steel wool and decided it was over. As she'd seen more of life and into herself, she'd grown disillusioned, discouraged, dissatisfied. She'd fought it by joining PTA, women's clubs, self-improvement groups; she'd had an affair and done social work. Dissatisfaction grew. And the man who'd seemed sophisticated in a small town was a slob in the city. She'd found herself watching the clock every afternoon with dread in her heart. All he worried about was that she had food on the table—and afterward he'd sprawl in a chair and stare at television until it was time for bed. Sex was joyless—though he reached for her daily. He went nowhere, wanted to go nowhere, and had read one book since their marriage: *The Carpetbaggers*.

She began going out alone at night to prowl the bars, and further despised him for the passive acceptance of her abuse. "He's so goddamned weak," she said, "and I was terrible for him. I drained what little manhood he had. And when I told him it was all over, he cried and threatened to kill himself. God, I loathed him—and felt like a dirty bitch. Yet I was suffocating. I had to get away, have something different, like my metabolism is geared to a different rhythm."

The child went with her parents in Kentucky and she'd moved into a hillside apartment and gotten a job in a lawyer's office. For six months she'd been exploring, meeting new people, trying new things. It had been a ball.

"What's the goal? What do you want?"

"I don't know, not yet. Until I shop around, how can I know? Right now I just want to see what's over the horizon. Maybe I just want excitement. I feel more living this way. Every morning when I wake up I wonder what's going to happen, what kind of adventure will come my way."

"What about love? Where does that stand in your scheme of things?"

"Yes, love . . . I wonder. It's wonderful to love, if you can—but to try and not be able to crucifies your soul. I think you should question it, make it prove itself. Don't seek it from hunger and delude yourself. What about you?"

"What do you want to know?"

"Do you hate society?"

"Sometimes. Sometimes more than at other times. I hate it more for what it made of me than what it did to me."

"Do you hate yourself?"

"No. I'm proud—in a way. I'm the freest man you ever met."

"Do you work?"

"Hell no!"

"What do you do?"

"Young lady, don't ask such questions. You're crossing a line into a prohibited area."

"I blabbed my soul and you won't say anything."

"We didn't make a deal—you tell me and I'll tell you."

"That isn't fair."

"Nothing is fair."

It was almost five o'clock. The horizon was brightening. "Want something to eat?" I asked.

"No, but if you're hungry I'll cook you something at my apartment. It's not very far, in a groovy canyon."

I said sure, and she started the car.

"You've only been out a few days?" she asked, the car moving around the curves.

"Uh huh."

"Had a woman yet?"

"No. I go for young boys."

Her face fell utterly blank, then turned to a consuming blush when I burst into laughter.

"I've got to pick up a car at a gas station in Hollywood at 8:30. Can you get me there?"

"I'll be late for work, but I can call in."

The building holding her apartment was older than most of those in the hillside canyons. It was a dark-yellow stucco with tile roof and wrought iron railings on the balcony, a Spanish-influenced design. A winding, curbless road led to it, and there was heavy shrubbery and trees around it. The door was heavy, dark wood in a thick wall. It had been built in an era of cheap labor and material—and before the Hollywood Hills had become fashionable. The high ceilings had wooden beams. A wide, deep fireplace covered most of one wall in the main room—a huge room for an apartment. The furniture was Mexican in style and color. I liked the deep reds, the blacks, the aura of rustic comfort. I dislike formica and stainless steel.

She scrambled eggs, fried potatoes and ham, made good coffee. I ate with gusto, and gulped down five more bennies with the coffee. I'd be on fire with alertness during the robbery.

We talked more while eating. I showered and shaved. She freshened herself. We did not make love, never mentioned it—both of us knew that the affair was just beginning and there was no necessity to rush. It would be better to wait until there was time rather than go to bed with one eye on the clock. Also, the delay would increase anticipation, make it better when the time came.

On the way into Hollywood, Allison asked when I'd call. I told her that it would be soon, perhaps later in the day, perhaps tomorrow, that I had some business and didn't know how long it would take. She didn't ask what I was going to do, instinctively recognizing that such questions were out of bounds. I wouldn't have told her—wouldn't tell her even if we were living together. Too many criminals trust their women with their business. I rigorously followed the rule of never confiding in anyone if it wasn't absolutely necessary. And it was unnecessary unless the person was directly involved. The most trustworthy person in the world today may become untrustworthy tomorrow—or next week, or next month—and the statute of limitations runs for several years. One wife put the finger on her husband for a murder ten years after it happened.

10

It was 9:45 A.M. We pulled into the parking lot behind the market. A refrigerated meat truck was at a loading dock a considerable distance from the rear entrance. It could be ignored. There were only a few cars, most of them probably those of employees.

"How do you feel?" I asked.

"Okay. Just hope we get some luck."

"We'll keep pulling until we get something or the string breaks."

"Or something breaks our asses."

The old Plymouth rested in line with the glass doors twenty yards away. I deliberately left the key in the ignition. If things got wild and we had to move in panic it would be an unnecessary hassle to dig through a pocket for a key.

We watched. Jerry raised the shopping bag containing the sawed-off shotgun, put it on the seat between us. He adjusted the .38 in his waistband beneath his sweater so the butt was hidden and it was comfortable. His hands were steady, his manner deliberate. His composure increased my own.

"Get any bad vibrations?" he asked, wanting to know if I sensed anything amiss—sensed not with regular faculties but with some primordial instinct that is highly developed in thieves. There was always a remote possibility that the police were waiting in ambush— a stake out. Stake outs for robbers are invariably announced by the flatulent roar of a shotgun rather than a demand to surrender. Police aren't giving up the chance to shoot first, nor would I in their position. As Jerry and myself were the only persons aware of the robbery, the odds of a stake out were very small. Yet someone else might have been ripping things off in the area.

A fat woman, looking obscene in pink stretch pants and scarf over hair curlers, came out pushing a cart with one hand and dragging a child with the other. Waiting police would never allow them to exit through a possible line of fire. The market was safe.

The manager hadn't appeared. We waited.

"Did you see that guy you belted in the chops?" Jerry asked.

"Last night. I cooled him off."

"Good. Especially if you hang around that spot."

"He knows he fucked up. He's not treacherous."

"Being sure of people gets us busted. Somebody you don't trust can't get next to you."

I nodded agreement, staring at the doors ahead.

"I'll check that spot in Beverly Hills tomorrow," Jerry said.

"We need to get a bank first. It's quicker."

"I'll look for one of them, too."

The manager's lean figure appeared, turned up the stairs.

"That's him," I said.

"Let's not keep him waiting."

I took the shopping bag with the shotgun. As we crossed the parking lot, my senses had special keenness, drawing into focus usually unnoticed background sounds and sights. I could feel the sun soaking through my shirt, the roughness of asphalt through my soles, could hear the whirring of automobiles on the freeway a hundred yards away. A carpenter's hammer was pounding a melody through the morning. The pungent odor of shrubbery was clear, though none was in sight. I could see globules of sunlight glistening from pebbles in the pavement.

Jerry carefully used a shoulder to push through the glass doors, leaving no fingerprints. Nobody in the front of the market glanced our way. We turned up the stairs, taking two at a time, yet treading silently. On the first landing we paused, donning rubber gloves and masks. Jerry's muscles twitched as they disappeared behind the nylon. My heart was pounding from the benzedrine and the excitement.

I drew the shotgun, flattened the shopping bag and stuffed it in my windbreaker. Jerry patted my shoulder with the revolver and pointed upstairs. I went first, the sawed-off shotgun in both hands.

At the top of the stairs, I stopped. The door was closed. Jerry bumped into me. I wondered whether we should rush the door or knock. If it was unlocked, rushing would gain us complete surprise. But to charge a locked door could create problems. Before deciding, a matter of three seconds, I saw a flicker of movement in an alcove ten feet away to my side. The manager was standing with an eye pressed to a peephole; he was looking for shoplifters in the store below.

I almost laughed, then moved. The manager jumped at the touch on his shoulder; it was the shotgun six inches from his chin. He looked into the twin barrels and neither blinked nor changed expression, except for going pale. I expected him to ask, "May I help you, sir?"

Jerry had slipped behind him, prodding his spine with the revolver. The man opened his mouth. No sound issued. His blankness was the paralysis of utter terror. I grabbed his sleeve with my left hand, holding the shotgun as a pistol. "Let's go open the safe, please." He followed my leading hand toward the office as if he was blind. We went inside.

"Open the safe," Jerry said.

"It's open," he gulped.

Locking the office door, I looked for something to use as a brace. Nothing fitted the purpose. I forgot it. The manager had swung open the safe door and was being led to a corner by Jerry.

"I've got a family," the manager said. "I won't give you any trouble. Don't hurt me."

"Wouldn't hurt you for the world," Jerry said. "We want money, not blood. Lie down on your side. Gotta tie you up."

Confident that Jerry would handle the victim, I kneeled at the open safe, filled the shopping bag with bundles of currency, dug through compartments, scattering what I didn't want onto the floor. Some money was high on the shelves; a canvas bag was on the bottom.

When I finished, Jerry was taping the man's wrists behind him. We'd been in the room three minutes. "How's it look?" Jerry asked.

"Fair score. What about the change?"

"It spends as good as green."

Coins in brown wrappers were dumped into the bag.

Jerry pasted strips of tape across the man's mouth. "Face the wall and don't look around," he ordered.

I'd removed my gloves and was reaching for my mask when someone knocked on the door. "Mr Ecklund," a muffled voice said.

Jerry crouched, unmoving, beside the prone figure. I was calm but my mind was racing. I picked up the shotgun from the floor and gestured Jerry to open the door.

The knock came again.

Jerry slipped along the wall. I stood directly before the door and raised the shotgun. The weapon made me confident I'd control whoever was outside. Jerry flipped the latch and threw the door open, instantly springing back from the possible line of fire. His pistol was ready.

A teenager in Levi's and a butcher's smock stood framed in the doorway. He swayed and nearly fainted at the sight of the masked man and the twin shotgun barrels.

Jerry leaped forward, grabbed the youth's arm, jerked him inside, half-dragged him to the manager and shoved him down. "Just stay there. Don't move a fuckin' inch."

"Tape him up," I said.

"No more tape. I'll just blow his brains out if he moves." Jerry was deliberately instilling fear. We were moving toward the door. Bounding down the stairs three at a time, we stripped off the masks and gloves, stuffing them in pockets. The shotgun went in with the money. We looked like exiting shoppers as we pushed through the glass doors into the sunlight—except close inspection would have shown us breathing heavily.

I forced myself to walk, not run, to the car. The scene was peaceful—early autumn morning in suburbia. I went to the driver's side and got in, dropping the sack on the floor. Jerry waited beside the passenger door, hand under his sweater, eyes on the market door. He waited until I had the motor started and came in, drawing the revolver to his lap, watching the door as I pulled toward the driveway. I drove with careful deliberation, conscious of every shift of gears, carefully balancing the necessity for speed against arousing unnecessary attention. At the end of the driveway, I paused; two cars went by. I turned in behind them. We passed directly in front of the market's windows. Everything within was peaceful; nobody was yet rushing about like beheaded chickens.

"The kid must've waited to untie the manager," Jerry said. "Otherwise they'd be frantic."

I braked at the first stop sign, coming to a more complete halt than under normal circumstances. The elation of success was beginning to surge. I eased through the underpass beneath the freeway, halted for the second stop sign, studied the traffic behind us. I grinned, thinking that they'd never expect us to go this way, halting twice within a hundred yards of the score. I eased off the brake, pressed the gas, meticulously flicking the turn indicator and also giving an arm signal.

"Bastard!" Jerry said. "I forgot his wallet."

"Man, don't do that. I thought you saw fuzz—and we can't outrun a motor scooter."

Now the sun was fragmented by trees overhanging the residential street. The speed limit was twenty-five, but I crept it up to forty—not too fast, but moving. The rear view mirror remained blank. Two minutes later we were in sight of Mary's address. There sat Jerry's car, baking in the sun.

Joey Gambesi was fidgeting with his bicycle in the driveway. He looked up when the horn bleated and moved the bicycle aside as we pulled in. I drove behind the front house, pulled into the carport and shut off the motor, leaning back with a sigh. "Home free, baby," I said.

"Like takin' candy from a baby."

Mary had heard the automobile. The curtains flickered. Moments later she came around the bungalow from the kitchen door, shaking her head and waving her finger in censure—but she was not angry; she was pressing her lips down to keep from smiling.

"Where have you been?" she asked. "New York? Miami?"

"The car broke down."

"The telephone, too? You've had me stranded here for a week."

Elated by our success (we were as safe as if we'd never done it) and certain my glee would be infectious, I got out and playfully pinched her cheek. "I've got something to pay you for your trouble."

She grabbed my wrist, her face somber. "Come over here. Let me talk a minute."

"About the car?"

"No. About Lisa."

"Can Jerry go inside?"

"Of course."

I motioned him. "Take the shopping bag. We'll be there in a minute."

"Don't pay any attention to the mess," Mary said. "There's coffee on the stove."

Jerry thanked her and went around the bungalow carrying the heavy shopping bag. When he was beyond hearing, Mary told me that Lisa was gone for the day, was just beginning to relax around her, and it would be best if she didn't see me for a while. She'd never turn me away, but she knew I'd understand. I agreed.

Joey came up the driveway, trundling the bicycle, grinning at me. He poked playful fun at his mother, reminding her how angry she'd been over the automobile and what she'd sworn to tell me when I showed up. He made her blush and ruffle his hair. I wished he was my son.

Yet it was best to send Joey away for fifteen or twenty minutes. There was stolen money to count, the license plate to remove. I sent him to buy a morning newspaper and a box of cigars. When he pedalled down the driveway, Mary started for the bungalow and I held back. She stopped, waited for me.

"Fuck it," I muttered, walked to the back of the car and tore off the taped license plate, bending it in half.

Mary saw what I'd done, understood the meaning. "My car!"

"Hard times make hard people. I was up against the wall."

"Why my car?"

"It was what I had available."

She shook her head, resigned rather than angry. When we entered the kitchen, Jerry was at the table with a cup of coffee.

"Let us use the bedroom," I said to Mary.

She didn't ask what we were going to do; she didn't want to know. She advised us, however, to pull down the shades. "There's a neighbor who peeks in windows."

When we were in the bedroom, shades lowered, Jerry nodded toward the kitchen. "Seems like a good broad."

"She's a thoroughbred all right. I could bust in here on fire from a murder and she'd hide me. She ain't evil either—no tramp."

Jerry dumped the shopping bag on the bed. We separated the shotgun and robbery paraphernalia from the money, which lay scattered over the bedspread. Each of us began counting a separate pile.

"Twenty-six forty," Jerry said.

"I've got twenty-eight hundred."

"What about the change?"

"It's about a hundred. Let's give it to the broad?"

"That's fair."

Mary interrupted us with a rap on the door. "Joey's here," she said. "You guys hurry up."

I pushed the rolls of change up under the pillow and put the shotgun back in the shopping bag.

When we went into the kitchen, Joey delivered my newspaper

and cigars. I gave him a five-dollar bill and told him I wanted to talk to his mother. He shrugged—the price was right—and went outdoors.

"There's a pile of change under the pillow for you. Get rid of the wrappers."

She looked at me and shook her head wryly.

"Don't you want it?"

"Sure. Do you think I'm crazy?"

We'd planned to stay at Mary's until noon when lunch traffic would give us additional cover. It was really unnecessary when we were traveling on boulevards that carried a thousand vehicles an hour and could be on any of a dozen roads and would be in a different automobile. Both of us fidgeted, anxious to be on our way, and so we left half an hour later.

Riding the freeway, the vinyl seat warm from the sun, a wisp of breeze spinning through the wind-wing, I closed my eyes and relaxed. The moves of the robbery went through my mind as a chess player might review a completed game. All in all, we'd moved with precision and teamwork. Recalling the face of the teenager confronted with the shotgun made me smile—but we should have brought extra tape. It hadn't caused a problem, but it could have. We might have had several persons in the office—and we should have considered someone walking in unexpectedly. Our margin of safety could have been shortened by several minutes if the boy had run down the stairs yelling.

Yet the robbery had been profitable in several ways. The money was the most important gain, but it had also been a good test. Jerry and I worked well together; he was a good criminal because he lacked the particular type of imagination which is subject to panic. Images of consequences would never make him shatter in a crucial moment. One thing was certain: we'd need better preparation hereafter. Everything has an unforeseen X factor, but in crime it must be reduced to the minimum. Winning almost every time is no good; a single loss cancels all the earlier victories. Boldness, all other things being equal, was usually an asset—but even the audacious had to be calculated with fine precision so that what appeared foolhardy was not really so.

"Where do you want to go?" Jerry asked.

"See a redheaded old pervert up on a hill. He can stash these guns and give me a ride. I'm going to buy a car this afternoon and send a telegram. I'm going for that dude up north. Where'll you be?"

"At home with Carol."

"I'll give you a ring tonight. Man, I need some fuckin' sleep. This fuckin' benzedrine is killing me. I need rest and it won't let me."

The Soto Street off-ramp was ahead. "Get in the right lane and go north on Soto. That's the quickest way to Red's."

"I'll leave the .38 with you. I don't want Carol to see it."

"I'll take it with me. Red can bury the shotgun until we need it."

Cars whirred by us as Jerry slowed and eased up the ramp. It wasn't quite noon.

11

L&L RED had sold the merchandise from the pawn shop for seven hundred dollars and was overjoyed when I told him to keep half. He was willing to drive me to Miami, much less to look for an automobile. He buried the shotgun.

The car I bought was a black GTO, four years old, but cared for with devotion by a young man who'd been drafted, sent to Vietnam, and blinded by a booby trap. His parents were almost in tears when they sold the car, for it reminded them too vividly of the tragedy. I paid cash, got the owner's registration in hand, and never sent it in to the Department of Motor Vehicles. If something happened it would be another obstacle in tracing me.

It was late afternoon when I got the car and left L&L Red. I was totally enervated. I went back to the motel—stopping to send Aaron the telegram—and fell asleep fully clothed.

After midnight I awoke, went out to eat, and then, impulsively, turned the powerful automobile toward the highway north. There was a joy in driving it, feeling the force I commanded, seeing only blackness surrounding me and the white line racing before the headlights. I turned to a classical music station and let the sounds blow with wild volume.

By dawn the hills of San Francisco appeared. I was not sleepy, but I checked into the Fairmont Hotel, choosing it because it was the best in town—and reflecting that only the criminal can be in a two-dollar flophouse one night and a forty-dollar suite the next.

I napped for an hour and then went shopping, waiting while alterations were made. It wasn't the complete wardrobe I wanted, but it was a major improvement. I bought clothes for Aaron, too—and boxes of ammunition for the .380 and .38.

The GTO crossed the Golden Gate into Marin during the commuter rush; everything moved with excruciating slowness. Soon, however, the river of automobiles began draining away as the highway passed through the outlying Bay communities. The freeway opened, traffic flying, and I hurtled along. The towns became farther apart, with rural landscape between them, and roadside billboards announced the virtues of Reno and Lake Tahoe hundreds of miles away. Near dusk I turned off the superhighway into a state highway. The yellowed farmland became foothills and woods, greenery. The last pink glow left the sky at the same time that the back highway was swallowed into the immense forests of northeastern California. I stopped in a small town for a hamburger. Soon there were no more small towns, or billboards. The pine forest was an endless, motionless wall of blackness, melancholy and mysterious. The headlights illuminated bushes that seemed like hostile shapes rushing to meet the automobile—until the highway inevitably curved away and they fell back into the maw of darkness.

The map had told me the route and the distance, but not the road conditions. I'd expected a more tortuous drive than was the reality and reached the destination an hour ahead of time. The headlights sprayed over the public campground, deserted except for the sign; there was the leveled ground, the cinder block bathroom facility, a barbecue, and a litter of trash. I backed out and continued up the highway, driving slowly. The side road of dirt with the sign designating Calif. Dept. Forestry Camp, two miles, was a mile from the campground. It meant Aaron would have to run three miles through the forest.

I swung the car around and went back to wait. Instead of sitting in the automobile, I took both pistols, the ammunition, and a blanket, and moved thirty yards to the concealment of the forest. If Aaron was wrong about when he'd be missed he might be hiking through the woods while the authorities sped down the road. They'd certainly stop to examine an automobile, and question its occupant, forty miles from the nearest town. It was colder in the forest, but safer. I could remain unseen, millions of acres of sanctuary at my back.

Settling on the blanket and leaning against the rough bole of a tree, I fired a cigar and began waiting. Above the high boughs of the trees, which rustled every so often from a vagrant breeze, a quarter moon cast just enough silver light to give some shape to objects. The sweeping majesty of the night overwhelmed me with a sense of lonely insignificance. I had the utterly senseless urge to fire the pistols into the forest, watch them spit inches of fire into the indifferent night—an act of defiance. Sad thoughts came into mind, Carol in the hospital, Mary in poverty, my father in a grubby furnished room without a friend, and Aaron somewhere nearby in the forest, running from the hounds, running for the hope of freedom.

I finished the cigar and tossed the butt. It described a red parabola and landed in a mat of dry pine needles. They began to crackle and spark. Would it start a million-dollar forest fire? What did I care if the forest, or the whole world, became ashes?

The question of what I'd do became moot when the cigar butt went dead without igniting a flame.

Half an hour went by. I was wondering how long I should wait before deciding he wouldn't arrive. Just then he called my name, his voice coming from somewhere in the line of trees. He was calling to the parked car, its shape visible in the middle of the empty campground. He appeared twenty yards away.

A minute later the automobile's tires were squealing on the curves as we stormed down the road. Aaron slapped me on the back and squeezed my neck in a headlock of joy. It was by far the most effusive I'd ever seen him. Of course it was the first time I'd ever seen him outside prison walls, which could have had something to do with it. It isn't every day that a man serving a life term manages to escape.

"Say, man," I said, "lighten up or you'll wrap our asses around a tree. Take this biscuit"—I handed him the .38—"and there's some clothes in the back seat."

He accepted the pistol and scrambled to the rear to rid himself of the prison denim. "I knew I could count on you. Yet when I was running through the trees I wondered what I'd do if you weren't there."

"There's ulterior motives. I'm talking you into bank robbery."

"Bank robbery! You'd better talk cogently."

"I'll talk shit."

"That's cogency."

Twin white-yellow orbs of headlights appeared ahead. Aaron crouched down, though it was impossible for anyone in the other car to see more than outlines. First there was the headlight glare, and the buffet of wind as the car passed. I watched the rear view mirror to see if the car began to turn. The GTO might outrun a highway patrol car especially when I was willing to take more chances for my freedom than they would for their pay, but it was impossible to outrun the two-way radio. If it was the highway patrol and they turned, I'd take a curve, slam on the brakes, and Aaron could dive into the brush. They were seeking a Negro. My identification could withstand on the spot examination.

The other car kept going, making the plan unnecessary. Yet I watched until we'd covered another twenty miles and turned on the superhighway—eight lanes—toward the south.

Aaron already knew from the grapevine that I was a fugitive. Rosenthal, or some other parole officer, might have told a parolee in jail—maybe trying to get information about me. The parolee went back to prison. The first few days he'd spend telling stories and answering questions: "I saw so and so; guy's doin' good." Or, "So and so's old lady is hooked to the cunt." Or, "So and so is out there snitching." Or, "Max Dembo belted his parole officer and lammed." Some other convict, going to camp, knew Aaron was my friend and told him.

"What happened to your good intentions?" Aaron asked.

"I was bullshitting myself. That's not me."

"That's essentially true, but there's more to it. What happened?"

I told him in detail, the image of Rosenthal in mind, adding venom to the story. Self-pity crept in too; I told him the awful tension and endless fear that went with being a fugitive. "It's a bad way to live."

"It's better to be fugitive from a cage than already in it."

I then realized that I was complaining to a man who was taking his sole chance for freedom. If caught, it would be twenty years before he had another chance. And in the recess of mind that stores opinions without examining them, I believed he'd be caught—sooner or later. Eighty percent of the escapees are caught within a week; less than 3 percent last a year. I could think of only two who'd been gone five years or more. One was an Australian, who'd travelled extensively around the world before his imprisonment and so was uniquely equipped to get away. The second, though still officially missing, had been dead and secretly buried within three months of his escape. He'd become deranged, paranoid, a threat to his friends, and one of them had shot him in the head and buried him in the wilderness. The story was common knowledge in the big yard, and undoubtedly the authorities knew it too; but there was nothing they could do.

My own chances of remaining free were just slightly better than Aaron's. Yet being hunted was better than being caught. Death is also inevitable, but one runs from it, too.

The speedometer rested at seventy for hours. There were almost no automobiles. A ninety-mile-per-hour speed would have been safe, but some rural policeman might pull us over for speeding, and would be suspicious of a black and white man being together, especially so late at night. Aaron lacked identification. It could turn into something ugly.

Aaron had things on his mind. He'd anticipated that I'd have a place for him to hide, that I'd provide help beyond taxi service to town. He hadn't expected as much help as I was able to give— money, clothes, identification—and he hadn't thought of robbery, but he did need enough money to flee the country. He spoke excellent Spanish, and from his years of working in the prison's dental department (convicts drilled, filled, cleaned, did inlays) he'd become a sufficiently qualified dentist to be in demand in many backward parts of the world. His knowledge of electronics was also an asset (one I wanted for us). He was thinking of Central or South America. First he needed a passport and money.

In the background of my own thoughts had been the idea to leave the United States, though definite plans—even the decision—had to wait until I had enough money to live comfortably. As a destination I was inclined toward Spain or somewhere else in the Mediterranean, preferably a country too poor to have a superefficient police force, or which was less than zealous in investigating foreigners with money.

Even now, as Aaron recounted his plans, mine were fuzzy about tomorrow. The Big Score was the dream, and who thinks beyond a dream?

At 3:00 A.M., fifty miles north of Bakersfield, I started to doze at the wheel. Aaron took over while I slept in the back seat.

In San Fernando, sun and morning traffic rising simultaneously, I was thrown off the seat when Aaron slammed on the brakes and swerved to miss a milk truck. He hadn't driven an automobile in a decade and needed practice before trying the Los Angeles freeways.

We found him a furnished room in a large Victorian house. The room was quite spacious, on the second floor. A huge window overlooked the front lawn and tree-shaded street. It was on the northwestern fringe of the black ghetto. And it was a ghetto only in the sense that all who lived there were black. It was middle-class. The homes were old, but had been fashionable less than a decade earlier. Aaron would be inconspicuous in the neighborhood, and it was ten minutes driving time from Hollywood. I wouldn't have to drive through hostile country to visit him.

I'd planned to spend the day with him, getting a photo for a false driver's license, buying clothes. But driving a thousand miles in thirty hours, and the pell-mell pace, including the robbery, suddenly caught up with me. Absolute exhaustion came all at once, as if some giant suction force drained me. I was staggering with the need for sleep.

"Take a nap here," Aaron said. "I can call my mother at work, let her know I'm all right. They've probably contacted her already and she thinks I'm wandering around the Sierras with rattlesnakes and bears."

"No, brother. I've got a broad. I'll go sleep at her place. A highborn southern gal."

"I'd like to stick my dick into something wet, but there's more important things first."

I gave him the telephone numbers to Abe's club and Allison's apartment. I was leaving the motel, so that number was unnecessary. "If anything comes up, call me. There's a shopping center three blocks from here. You can walk there and get yourself some rags." I left him three hundred dollars and the .38. I promised to come back for him in the evening; then we could make some decisions.

He walked me out to the car. The landlady, a chunky black woman whose husband was retired from the services and working at Hughes Aircraft, was watering a flower bed beside the house. Each plant had different-colored blossoms—yellows and reds as bright as I'd ever seen, eye-penetrating. Aaron had already charmed the woman when we looked at the room, for his education, his manners, his intelligence were obvious. Now he commented on the zinnias, complimenting her touch with them, and the woman was captivated—so much so that I doubted if she would call the police even if she knew the truth.

"Get me that robin down from the tree," I whispered when we went on to the car. We shook hands before I got in.

"Thanks, brother," he said. "I appreciate what you're doing."

"Man, fuck you! You got your issue. Friends are to be used, though not misused, so everybody gets stronger. Nobody can stand alone. I need you too."

"Quit running at the jaws like you're on speed. Get going."

"I'll be back around nine. I might bring my partner so you can get to know each other."

As I drove away, I hoped Jerry and Aaron would get along, respect each other as I respected both of them. If I could bind them together—as a cohesive factor, not as a leader—no score was too big to think about.

It was false to tell Aaron that a woman was "waiting". Allison was at work when I parked on the hill road, my clothes piled in the rear of the automobile. I was too tired to go any further. I broke a window, unlatched it, and climbed in. When she came home I was sleeping in her bed, wearing only shorts. She was surprised, but not angry. On the contrary, my unshaven jaws and general haggardness aroused feminine solicitude. I mumbled a story of having driven a thousand miles back and forth in Mexico. She didn't question me; I liked that.

It was getting dark outside. She was seated on the edge of the bed. It was time for us to make love. I knew it both from the yearning in her body and the silent waiting in her eyes. I reached for her.

Minutes later, already disheveled, blouse unfastened, skirt twisted, she got up and slowly took off her clothes. When she was naked, her body dappled by the dying sunlight filtered through a tree outside the window, she stood posing, breasts in profile. She was suntanned and they were strikingly light compared to her belly and shoulders and legs. "I like to make it delicious and slow," she said, coming onto the bed with one knee, reaching a hand between my legs, bringing her mouth to my belly button, darting her tongue into it.

We took a long, long time, sometimes becoming clumsy because we were unaccustomed to each other, and we did all the things with mouth and hands that uninhibited lovers do. We began gently, worked up to ferocity, and rested in between, delaying exhaustion. She delighted in being alternately coy and vulgar, and liked having me whisper crudisms into her ear. Her skin had a velvet texture, and she was lithe; at one point her legs were wrapped around me and she stroked my thighs with her soles. As we made love, now in darkness, I felt her warmth and caresses and all the splintered, harried facets of my days were drawn in and given repose.

Afterward, I went to sleep. When I woke up two hours later she was grilling hamburgers, wearing only sheer blue panties and slippers.

"How was I?" she asked.

"I thought you were going to suck my brains out for a minute."

She laughed, blushed—not used to such crudeness but liking it.

"I live here now, huh?"

"Sure do. That's what you had in mind, wasn't it?"

"Precisely. But we're going someplace, so get some clothes on."

"Where are we going."

"To pick up a friend of mine, take him to eat."

"Are we going anywhere special?"

"Put on anything ... Jeans are okay. But we're supposed to be there now, so hurry."

Aaron was gone when we arrived. He'd left a note with the land-lady saying that he was meeting his mother, that he'd tried to tele-phone me but had been unable to get through. He'd be back at midnight and, if I had to be somewhere else then, would call me in the morning.

"Your friend's a Negro?" Allison asked when we were driving away.

"Didn't I mention it?"

"No."

"Does it make any difference?"

"None whatsoever. I just asked a question."

"He's a man—by anybody's standards."

"Don't get defensive."

"I'm sorry. I didn't intend to sound that way."

She moved closer to me, rested a hand on my knee. We drove that way, and I didn't mind that Aaron had been gone. "What should we do?"

"Let's go back to bed and fuck," she said.

"Brilliant idea, baby. First, let's stop by the club. I want to see Manny January."

Before we were seated, Manny came through the crowd and excitedly beckoned me aside. The M16 was in the trunk of his car; that, and four hundred rounds of ammunition for it. The automatic rifle was precisely what I'd wanted to see him about, never believing there was a possibility he'd already have it. He'd even paid for it from his own money and said I could repay him when I tore something off—not knowing I had already made a move. I gave him back what he'd invested, and put my arm around his shoulder to show he'd made full amends for his earlier failure. It was what he wanted and he glowed in response.

When it was time to leave (one drink), I drove around to the alley, Manny went out the back, and when I braked he put a long flower box into the back seat.

"What's that?" Allison asked.

"None of your business," I said, but patted her cheek to soften the rebuke.

"I'm sorry," she said. "I'll learn. I'm just a curious bitch."

"Remember what happened to Pandora."

"Whatever you're doing, please be careful." She wrapped her hands around my biceps in possessive affection.

We were in bed before midnight. A television set at the foot of the bed was showing the late movie; we were too busy to watch. The second lovemaking was even better than the first, less awkward, and again the chaos of my life was washed away in lovemaking. There was only the hour of joy, the room, her body, and hands.

"Come for me, daddy . . . come for me," she chanted, her breath hot in my ear.

In the morning I found that I had $407.00 left from the market robbery. The pressure wouldn't let up for very long. Now, however, I had what it took to get money: two good crime partners and an automatic weapon.

12

CHRONOLOGICALLY, the events of the next ten days are difficult to recall. They were hectic, but no more than is usual in a thief's unregulated life. I know what happened, but not in precisely what sequence, nor do I remember many details. The utter clarity of memory that existed when I was first released now disappeared in the warp of life. Jerry and Aaron sniffed warily at each other during the first two meetings, but respect grew between them. Neither of them became as close with each other as each was with me. I was not the "leader" of the gang, but I was the unifying factor, the cohesion.

Aaron never met Carol, for Jerry wanted to avoid flaunting anything that might upset her. Allison and Carol, however, met during an afternoon visit and immediately became friends. They began phoning each other daily, and Allison visited her at least two or three times a week, taking her shopping or to the beauty parlor. Allison thought Carol looked only slightly ill, but Allison had never known her before onslaught of the disease. To me, Carol looked frightening. Her face had become dreadfully sallow, bloated from fluids, especially around the eyes. This was from the medicine rather than the disease, according to Jerry.

Once we tried going out to dinner together, but the night out was unsuccessful because Carol became totally exhausted. Her weekly transfusion of blood—and energy—had been given five days before. The disease had already consumed it and she had no strength. "It makes me feel like Dracula's daughter," Carol said, but the levity fell like lead; she was the only one who managed to chuckle.

Allison had given two weeks' notice to her employer, but was still going to work in the morning, so Jerry, Aaron, and I usually met at the hillside apartment. Aaron was usually there anyway, especially during the day. The furnished room, though much nicer than usual for the genre, was still unbearably confining and dreary. Aaron had good identification, identifying him as a dentist. It was his policy to be indoors before midnight, but other than that he moved freely, using my car as if it was his own, especially in the evenings when Allison's was available to me. He'd go off into the world of blackness. He met his family, but in out-of-the-way places. He knew the police would concentrate on watching the family and known associates of any seriously wanted fugitive. He'd found an ex-girlfriend—though time had atrophied whatever romance might have existed. She was merely a receptacle for sexual hunger. He mentioned her, gave me her telephone number in case I needed to contact him, but he foreclosed any meeting, and vetoed Allison's idea of a double date. The veto, I sensed, had something to do with race; maybe on the girl's part. No matter how sincere our friendship, something would inevitably stir up the issue of race. It was an ineradicable fact.

And while these things were going on, we were looking for a bank to rob. It would appear at first glance that finding a bank would be a simple matter, considering that Southern California has several hundred of them in its sprawl. We were interested entirely in Bank of America branches because in prison I'd been given information about their security procedures. The information was of untested reliability, but it was something to start with. The first fact proved true: there were no armed security guards. Not that a security guard, per se, makes any difference. He's generally an old man, and even if he's Wyatt Earp, what can he do with a holstered revolver when an automatic rifle is pointed at his chest?

Bank of America's main defense was the movie camera, which

brought havoc to barefaced bandits who handed notes to tellers and appeared in living color on television that evening. Cameras would be harmless to men with hoods and high gloves. According to my information, employees were not supposed to try setting off an alarm until it was absolutely safe. The bank frowned on a gun battle. True or not, we worked on the assumption that an alarm would be sounding the moment we started the robbery. Speed was our counter weapon—get in and out within a matter of minutes. We wouldn't have time to get the vault. That left the tellers and what was lying around loose. The bad part was that the average teller has no more than a thousand dollars or so, hardly worthwhile, especially when some of it would be "bait" money, bills with recorded numbers kept specifically for being mixed with other money when a bandit called.

Some branches, however, had a special teller for commercial accounts. This teller was usually in a semiprivate location, but with no more real protection than any other—and commercial tellers have between fifteen and twenty thousand minimum, a nice cornerstone for a robbery. It was what we were looking for, the problem being that most branches with such tellers were in metropolitan areas unsuitable for a robbery—too crowded on the getaway.

I looked for such a bank every day, but not with an unrelenting diligence. Rather, I was like a tourist exploring Southern California— and looking at banks incidental to lounging in dim cocktail lounges, bullshitting with ex-convicts and whores, or wandering through parks in outlying communities. Sometimes Aaron went with me. Jerry was doing the same in the northern and western regions of the megalopolis.

Aaron and I stopped on the way to Pomona, at Willy Darin's. Aaron wanted a ten-dollar balloon of heroin and I wanted a pound of marijuana. Willy was home watching the boys when we arrived. Selma was working in a toy company. Willy had been fired from his job and had devastated his car on a telephone pole when the brakes went out. From the wreck he'd also gotten a traffic summons for driving without a license. When he went to court it would come out that his license was revoked.

Willy was unruffled by his predicament. He'd used his personal miracle drug to erase concern. I gave him a hundred dollars to buy another junk automobile so he would have transportation. It left me with less than a hundred and made me more diligent in looking for a bank to rob.

The one we decided upon was part of a colossal shopping center in Anaheim. There were two department stores, an immense drug-store, a supermarket the size of a warehouse, and many large retail businesses. The shopping center and its acres of parking covered a square mile. It was so new that construction crews were steam-rolling blacktop on its fringes, and some stores had yet to open for business.

The bank was on one end, low-slung, ultra-modern. Its façade was designed to allow the maximum of light while surrendering the minimum of privacy. It had a commercial teller, isolated from the others. I got in line to ask a question and confirmed that there were stacks of hundred dollar bills in a drawer literally filled with green currency.

There were two entrances, one on the side, opening onto the wide parking lot. The side door was small, set into an alcove. Someone would have to cover that door, which was out of sight from the front door. It meant that all three of us would have to go in, leaving nobody at the wheel. One of us would step inside the front door, move to the side and wheel out the M16. All of us would have full hoods over our faces. The second man would vault the rail and start cleaning the commercial teller. If he got that done quickly he could clean the others, too. The third man would wait near the side entrance. We figured two minutes inside gave us plenty of leeway. A man can scoop a lot of money in two minutes.

The man by the side door would leave first, be in the car as we came out. We'd throw a smoke bomb for greater cover. A stolen car would carry us down a semirural road for one mile, and a private dirt road through orange groves to where we changed cars. We'd come out of the private road (which wouldn't be on street maps) on a major boulevard five hundred yards from a freeway entrance. The police would never anticipate us being in that position from the direction we'd been using.

Once we'd found the right bank, the robbery went quickly. We visited the bank for three days, drew straws for our roles—I got the M16 and Jerry was to go over the rail. Aaron would watch the second door and drive the car. On the next afternoon, at 1:55, we heisted it, using pillowslips with eyeholes for masks. Half the employees were gone for lunch, and half of those who remained weren't aware that a robbery was in progress until it was practically over—when Jerry came over the rail carrying a sack of money and someone yelled at him. Jerry pointed a pistol at the man and the yell was stifled. We were in the bank for two minutes and forty-one seconds.

At 2:45 we were squatting on the floor of the hillside apartment, hurrying to finish counting and dividing the loot before Allison came home. Piles of money and discarded bank wrappers covered the floor. The total was thirty-two thousand, which was ten thousand more than I'd expected. All of us were jubilant and relieved.

"We could've got more if we'd knocked out the alarm," Jerry said, stating a fact rather than a complaint.

"We'll have that next time," I said, meanwhile stacking my share in a shoebox—as good a place as any.

"This might be enough for me," Aaron said.

"Motherfucker," Jerry said, throwing a playful headlock around Aaron's neck, "you can't quit now. Get a few nickels and fold, huh? This is the easiest shit in the world—money from home."

"We'll talk about it tomorrow," I said. "We're not hurting. We can take time to decide what to do. Remember there's bait money in there, so don't spend any big chunks in one spot. Change it over first."

"Man, I know all that," Jerry said.

"I worry about you, fool."

"And I love you, jive ass motherfucker."

We were indeed very happy.

13

In the weeks after the bank robbery, countless things happened, some good, some bad, some exhilarating, others depressing or infuriating. But now, distilling them, I see that it totalled the most nearly happy period of my life, tainted solely by awareness of how precarious it was. The nexus of this happiness was Allison. My enjoyments were more fulfilled because we shared them, and the unpleasant, ugly things were soothed by her presence. Love was never mentioned. The feeling was not one of fiery passion. It burned softly. We were comfortable together. It was an end to loneliness.

Allison never knew of the bank robbery, though the sudden upswing of fortune was impossible to hide, especially when I'd bitched and grumbled about lack of money. By simply neglecting to mention the money I hid it for a few days, and this was long enough to cover its origin. One day's coverage was all a bank robbery got—on an inside page of the *Los Angeles Times* and thirty seconds on the 10:00 P.M. television news. If Allison saw either, the information passed through one ear and out the other. She first realized that I had some money on Saturday, the morning following her last day of work. I went to buy myself clothes, and she went along to give me advice and counsel, for she knew styles better than I did. When she saw what I was spending she arched an eyebrow and made a wry comment that I must have visited a Mexican gold mine. She thought I was involved in narcotics traffic, but limited her curiosity to that single oblique comment. She'd so thoroughly and so quickly learned to ask no questions that I might have confided in her—if I'd been alone. I had no right to entrust Jerry and Aaron's well-being to her, which is what I'd have been doing if I confided.

Thereafter, we fell into a life that was a long vacation.

It was the summer's end and we spent many afternoons at the beach. She was deeply tanned, golden with flecks of freckles, especially around the shoulders. She lay soaked in oil, basking with transistor radio and book. I'd bought her *Siddhartha* and she was entranced by Herman Hesse, though some of what he said depressed her. I never understood how she could read with acid rock belching from the nearby radio. My pallor burned, peeled, and finally darkened to a respectable Southern California hue. On Allison's advice—plus looking around—I let my hair grow longer than at any time since early teens and zoot suits, and wore more colorful clothes. She talked me out of growing a beard.

Days and nights were leisured. We browsed in musty bookstores and silent museums, or sat in parks smoking grass and watching children romp on carpets of sunny lawn. My anger at life and society never went out, but it dimmed. When I thought of how fragile this interlude was, how doomed (I was still a wanted man, still committed to further crimes), it hurt. The pangs came swift and unexpected, leaping to mind at Santa Anita when my horse won with fifty on his nose and I should have been exuberant. It came while we were laughing in Disneyland, and while we were in a discotheque being bombarded with mind-swarming sound.

Despite the spasms of foreboding, life was good. A Las Vegas weekend stretched into six relaxed days because we were enjoying ourselves and nothing required that we leave. I won eight hundred dollars at the dice table the first night; it was the only night we gambled. The way I lived was enough of a gamble to satiate that craving. The town was overflowing with entertainers and floor shows we wanted to see, and during the day we went horseback riding into the desert, or speedboating on Lake Mead. Jerry and Carol joined us for the last two days. Carol was losing weight and Jerry whispered in drunken, frightened confidence that the doctors were considering slicing off her breasts. I phoned Aaron and invited him to fly over. He declined without giving a reason, but lily-white Las Vegas is hardly the safest town for an escaped Negro lifer.

When we returned to Los Angeles, I mailed half a dozen bright picture postcards of the casino-hotels to friends in prison, knowing the token of remembrance would be appreciated.

Occasionally, when I was driving alone, I resented being happy, resented having found things that I cared about. I was enjoying life too much, was making things too precious, especially when it had to end. Had I lawfully reached my situation, a nice automobile (but not new), a decent wardrobe (but not a closet of silk suits and alligator shoes), a comfortable dwelling (but not a penthouse), and a woman whom I liked, nothing in the world could have induced me to risk losing it by committing a crime. I would have worked my ass off. Of course that was wishful thinking in the face of reality. And when it came down to truth—I didn't know how to do anything but steal.

I resented thinking about such things, for the only way I could cease being a fugitive was to become a prisoner, a Hobson's choice if there ever was one. Like everyone else, I could squirm and move around the boundaries of destiny prepared for me—and by me—but I could never go beyond.

"I've got to tear off another score," Jerry said. "Whether it's that jewel sting or another jug . . . with you dudes or Single O. It takes a millionaire to keep paying for blood transfusions."

Aaron shook his head slowly, refuting Jerry's desperate twang. Aaron soothed without condescension. "Cool it, brother. I'll loan you a couple rather than have you run wild into something."

Jerry looked down, abashed. He shook his head. "I don't need it right now. But if we don't crank something up in the next few weeks I'll be hurting. I'm gonna fail Carol, no matter what."

"They're not going to quit giving her blood and let her die. Run up a bill."

"They'll want credit references, all that bullshit. Blood we can get in the county hospital, and if I can't show them money or where it's coming from, that's where they'll wanna send her."

"Yeah, you damn sure can't show them where it's coming from. But we'll have something, don't worry. My bankroll's getting thin too."

It was true. Just two months ago we'd rushed from the bank with a shopping bag full of money. I had twelve hundred dollars left. Aaron probably had half his money, for being a fugitive required that he live in inconspicuous frugality. Actually, Jerry probably had more, too, but his expenditures were unavoidable and ongoing, whereas I could pull back from high living and not be forced into a caper for months. Desperation crimes, however, are bad business, for desperation blinds judgment. From my view as well as Jerry's it was best to pull a heist soon. Aaron and Jerry knew about Gregory's, and during the week we'd each looked at it separately. I'd gone in with Allison, ostensibly to price engagement rings, but really to look the place over. I'd also checked the manager out. His name was Jules Neissen. He was married, lived in Topanga Canyon, had a wife and an eight-year-old daughter.

Now we were conferring in a plush, dim steakhouse on the coast highway. A steakhouse with beamed ceilings and walls paneled in rich dark wood. I'd reserved a choice table beside a huge window that overlooked the ocean surf as it pounded jutting rocks. The restaurant had been a favorite place of mine before prison. It had changed very little. We talked over filet and lobster. Though the conversation sometimes wandered to include the recent World Series and the looming elections, our real interest was another robbery. We got serious about it over coffee and pie.

"Are you sure you can nail the alarm?" Jerry asked Aaron.

"I won't know for sure until I try, but it looks like I can, given the right equipment. Silent alarms work off telephone lines. That's how the alarm is transmitted. Somewhere in the area, on a telephone pole or, in this case, in a manhole, there's a junction box where a whole bunch of lines come together. I cut into them one at a time until I find the right line, then jump it so when the alarm is set off it doesn't go through—kind of like holding the ringer on a bell. I'll need a device to measure . . . Anyway, I think I can do it."

Jerry grunted, turned to me. "You say we might get half a mil in ice. Can you dump it? If that fence goes kaput we can't take it to a pawn shop."

"The fence says he can handle it. I haven't got any reason to doubt him."

"If you can trust him."

"I checked him out. If he wants to burn us, he's going to give up everything, wife, kids, business. It's a lot of dough and maybe that's what he wants. Maybe he owes a hundred thou and has a hot cock mistress and is looking for a way out. We can't run that through R&I. But I don't think he plans to tear up his whole life. He might get slick with the count, short us some money—and he might come apart like wet toilet paper if the fuzz gets him. But why should they get him? Nobody knows but us. Believe me, 60 percent of the whole-sale price is george."

"We get 20 percent apiece for risking our asses," Jerry grumbled. "He gets 40 per cent. I wish I had that hustle."

"You didn't have the foresight to get in his position," Aaron said. "He took twenty years getting ready."

"The only foresight I had was the walls in Canyon City. Okay, he gets 40 percent. What's to stop him from flying to New York and make an anonymous phone call to the heat? He could get us pinched and keep everything."

"That would be super-Machiavellian," Aaron said. "But even without knowing him I'd doubt that he was psychologically capable of that risk. It would take a desperate man to try threading that needle. He can't be sure we wouldn't spill our guts. Furthermore, he doesn't know anybody but Max—and doesn't even know where Max lives. He'd have to figure that if any of us was free there'd be revenge, and a fool would see that if we've got enough nerve to run into a Beverly Hills jeweler's with a machine gun we'd have no qualms about killing him."

"I trust Max's judgment about the guy," Jerry said. "I'm just playing the devil's advocate."

"If it was up to me . . . ," I began.

"It is as far as I'm concerned," Aaron said; Jerry nodded.

"I'd trust him," I finished. "It's a whole lot easier to steal a quarter or half million in diamonds than cash. Once they're out of their settings there's almost no way to trace them. Bank money—some of it—can always be traced. Say we jam that alarm. We can root around in there for fifteen or twenty minutes. Fix the alarm and we've got a cinch."

"I wouldn't say that," Aaron said, smiling crookedly. "It looks good, real good, if I can disengage the alarm, but if there were any quarter-million-dollar cinches in crime we'd be overrun with competitors. To me the gain seems worth the risk."

"I'm with both of you assholes all the way to the gas chamber," Jerry said, "if we gotta go that far. But I'm going to look around for another jug in case this doesn't get together."

"It's agreed," Aaron said; then to me: "I'll need somewhere to work on the equipment."

"How's a garage?" I was thinking of Willy Darin's.

"If there's tools a garage will be fine. It'll take half an hour or so—mostly just adapting components."

"I've got tools in my workroom," Jerry said. "But you can't do it there. Carol. I'll give you what you need. When do you want it?"

"The quicker we get it done the quicker I'll be able to see if it works."

"I'll get what you need from Jerry tomorrow," I said. "I'll pick you up."

"Good enough. I've got to buy an oscillator and get a portable telephone like repairmen use to cut into lines and dial."

"We can find one somewhere," I said. "We'll get on it early in the morning."

"Have you got a plan worked out?" Jerry asked.

"Simplicity is the keynote if Aaron can do his thing."

"I had some thoughts," Aaron said. "There won't be many people to handle. One of us with the M16 can cover, the other one can sack it up. The problem is the getaway. I think one of us should stay outside. We can buy a walkie-talkie cheap, and attach a little transistorized receiver that'll fit in the ear. We can get a radio that picks up police frequency, too. The guy waiting to drive getaway can keep lookout. The store's blind once you're inside . . . can't know what's happening on the boulevard."

What Aaron said was true. The plan was simple and direct. Yet having an automobile at the curb directly outside or in the parking lot was questionable. Either place would require turning east or south, or going a block and turning left across the flow of traffic. East would jam us up in heavy traffic along Wilshire's Miracle Mile—department stores, skyscrapers. South would take us two blocks through residential streets, which was good, but then we'd run into the heavy traffic on Olympic Boulevard. South was the direction the police would probably anticipate. Parking the getaway vehicle across the boulevard would make it more difficult to reach (but not on Saturday when traffic was thinner), but after we got to it a quick right turn would carry us north through wide, deeply shaded residential streets, miles of them. In minutes we could be in the hills, or switch cars. We could be going dozens of routes. Aaron was speaking again and I withheld my ideas, wanting to go over the territory more thoroughly.

"I can use overalls with Pacific Telephone on back," Aaron said. "Put my tools on a belt and use a plain car or a panel truck . . . maybe the truck because we'll need to steal one of those wooden barricades with 'Men at Work' on it. Wouldn't want some fool running his car halfway down a manhole while I'm gimmicking the thing."

The conversation trailed off. We'd finished the dessert and the waiter, seeing us, came over and asked if there was anything else.

Aaron ordered brandy and brought forth a long green cigar. "Just like white folks," he said, causing the waiter to blush.

I ordered Scotch and water and took one of Aaron's cigars. Jerry glanced at his wristwatch and furrowed his brow. He was thinking of Carol. She was demanding more and more of his diligent solicitude. Terrified by the nearness of death, her moods were erratic—one moment melancholy or suicidal, more often petulant, quick with tears. Tomorrow she was going back to the hospital for a bone marrow biopsy. Although it was a routine, safe operation, she was terrified. Jerry had lied to her about where he was going this evening, and he'd promised to be home early.

Aaron voiced my own thoughts. "Get on, Jerry. We know what's happening."

"How're you gonna get back to town?"

"Taxis run out here."

"I'll drive him home," I said. "I'll be over about 9:00 for those tools."

Jerry got up, shook his head. "I'd go to hell with either one of you dudes. You know that."

"Man, don't get maudlin," Aaron said. When Jerry was gone, Aaron added: "Poor Jerry. He's giving all of himself to something he's got to lose."

"So does everybody . . . sooner or later."

"Freeze on that."

"On what?"

"On all that heavy philosophy bullshit. I'm talking about here and now and everyday important things that people live by. If you extrapolate everything—nothing matters."

We were silent. I recalled our talks in prison, missing them. In the turmoil of these days we'd had little chance for idle conversation.

The waiter brought the check and Aaron picked it up. We started out between the crowded tables, the hum of voices punctuated by the clink of silver and glassware or laughter. The night outside was warm and our shoes crunched on sand filtered up from the beach to the parking lot. The ocean was oily calm just beyond the line of surf. A path of moonlight was painted on the water and it looked as if one could walk across it to the white disc low on the horizon.

"You don't have to drive me," Aaron said. "Drop me in Santa Monica and I'll catch a cab. My pad is twenty miles out of your way—and I know your old lady's waiting."

"She's schooled to my ways. Whenever I get there is good enough. We haven't had a chance to talk since we walked the yard—not serious conversation."

"We don't have any need for it. The only enjoyment we got there was vicarious, from books and conversation. Now we've got reality, so why talk about it? Or read about it, for that matter?

"I read five books a week in the joint. Now I sometimes look through the Sunday paper. The first couple days I was out, I bought some secondhand paperbacks, juicy shit I'd really wanted to read. I've still got them, haven't finished one. I've got some weed in the car. Let's take a stroll down the beach and blow a couple joints—unless you've got someplace to be."

"My woman's schooled, too."

I took the joints from the glove compartment. A dirt path led down to the beach from the parking lot. The tide was out and there was a wide strip of damp sand firm enough to walk upon without sinking. A bonfire blazed half a mile away; against its flames were silhouetted figures. We each fired a joint and walked toward the beach party, a destination as good as any.

The marijuana came on quickly. It was less intense than when I first got out of prison because I was again accustomed to smoking it regularly. Still it was good, and increased perception.

"So where's it gonna end, good brother?" I asked, apropos of nothing.

"Damn, you're soul-searching tonight. That's not your style. What's to it?"

"Who knows? The question was rhetorical—but everybody asks

it, to himself, out loud. We all die. That's the end. But say we make fifty thou apiece on this thing. What'll I do next? I can't rationalize to keep robbing when I don't need the bread. With fifty g's I'm a criminal success, except for being a fugitive from parole. A sensible idea would be like going back east and buying a bar, pay somebody off to keep from being extradited. That'd be easy. A parole violation ain't nothing. It'd be sensible, too. Somehow it doesn't grab me."

"Blow the money on high living and justify another crime."

"That's what I might do—but I can't plan it that way. That'd be deliberately thinking like a fool."

"Have you thought about going away, taking Allison? Mexico? South America?"

"It goes through my mind, but then I see that I'm bullshitting myself. Allison's good for easing loneliness, and we get along together, in the sack and out of it—but she doesn't light my fire the way love is supposed to."

"That's love among the very young. Nobody can do that for you anymore. It's more delusion than love. What you've got with that broad is what can last."

"You're some kind of romantic."

"Not hardly. You're the romantic, not accepting what's real because it doesn't meet the romantic ideal of love."

"Anyway, we're talking crazy. It's about something that's purely academic—to both of us. Love is way down the list of my needs. A whole lot of things come first."

"True. It's irrelevant to our position. It might even be a handicap. Look at Jerry. My first concern is how to avoid being caught and spending the rest of my life in a cell. I'm going to make a move out of the country right after this score. I should've done it after the bank, but I didn't have anything worked out."

"Do you now?"

"I've got a fraudulent dental degree, a Mexican tourist visa, and I've been writing to a town in the Yucatan. I speak Spanish and that's

225

where I'm going to build a new life. I couldn't get away with impersonating a dentist over here, but down there the folks are still riding burros and they care about getting rid of toothaches, not paperwork."

"The Yucatan is jungle. It's primitive. Is that all you want from life?"

"What I want isn't the question. What I need is what counts. I found out in a prison cell—and that's primitive—that I need very little."

"What about revenge? Don't you hate them—the system, society?"

"I burned with hate for a couple years—and then burned out. It might be sweet to get revenge, but it wouldn't be worth the risk. I still care about myself . . . not like you."

"What's that mean?"

"Your philosophy is 'fuck it'. You don't care. Look at yourself."

"I do look at myself, all the time. I like risk, but I care."

"Not enough, I think, not enough."

We walked on in silence, listening to the whoosh and hiss of the surf's hypnotic rhythm. Shadows from the fire began licking out across the sand toward us. Figures assumed identity. Teenagers having a ball. Beer bottles glinted in the firelight. We stopped some distance away, watching the flames and moving people with mild fascination. Rock and roll music blared from a transistor radio.

A fifteen-foot embankment sloped up from the beach. Over its rim a pair of headlights grew bright, probed out over the crest, slicing the night to the surf. A narrower beam of spotlight lanced down, moved around the beach. A red light on top of the automobile began flashing madly. Bonfires on the beach and beer-drinking teenagers were still illegal. The law was about to be enforced. A pair of dark figures in white helmets skidded down the embankment. Many of the figures around the fire bolted into the darkness.

"Man, let's blow," Aaron said, tugging my arm. The advice was unnecessary. We faded back. A walk on the beach had become dangerous.

*   *   *

When I telephoned Willy Darin before noon, he hesitated about letting us use his garage. Selma was giving him trouble, had learned that he was using heroin again. She hadn't gone to work and he was afraid that my presence would aggravate her. His fear collapsed when I assured him that we'd stay outside—and that he'd get a couple of twenty-dollar bills for the rent.

Willy heard the automobile turn into the driveway. He came out of the house just as we stopped. He wore greasy khakis and shower thongs; his burly torso, with hair sprouting thick from his shoulders, was pasty white. His face, forearms, and wrists were sundarked—the tan of the laborer. As always, he needed a shave. His sons, also shirtless and barefoot, came onto the porch and stopped to watch from a distance. They retreated behind large eyes, staring in wonder at Aaron. A Negro was obviously something new in their world. Without looking at the weed-infested yard, the flaking paint on the house, or Willy's junk automobile parked in front of us, I was profoundly struck by the slovenliness of poverty—and mine and Aaron's sleek tailoring in comparison. Willy's life was cruel and restricted and ridiculous. The moguls of society would proclaim that he would be wrong to rip something off them—meanwhile they had everything and he had nothing. That was ridiculous.

This interior dialogue went through my mind in the few seconds it took for Willy to reach the car. I expected him to note my clothes and purse his mouth in approval and envy. But he took no notice that my slacks were cashmere and my shirt was silk. Such things were immaterial to him. He dreamed about quick-money schemes, but any conception of money or what it bought (beyond subsistence and a fix) was unreal to him. His schemes always aborted against his psychological truncation; he was too lazy to work and too scared to steal.

He was solemn, worried.

"She's steaming," he said, jerking his head toward the house.

"Selma? About us?"

"About every fuckin' thing. Come over here." He glanced at Aaron standing on the other side of the car and led me a few paces away. "Man, I didn't know you were bringing him. I mean it was okay when I was here by myself, but with Selma . . . She's down on you in front—but she's death on spooks. It'll raise a shit storm if you bring him in the pad."

"Fuck the pad. I told you we'd stay outside. Fuck her, too."

"Man, don't run warm at me. It's her. I can't say I love 'em, but this dude's cool . . . and I treat everybody individually."

"If she sticks her nose out, you put it back in. We'll get done and be gone as quick as we can."

"Groovy. What're you gonna do?"

"Fix some gear to beat a silent alarm. There'll be no joy in Beverly Hills when we're through."

"Man, you're gonna fuck around and get busted again."

"Don't sweat it."

"Just sayin' what I think. How long will you be here?"

"Half an hour."

"If you're gonna give me that bread, why don't you loan me your car for a few minutes. I'll get back before you're finished."

I hesitated, knowing that he wanted to go buy some heroin. Reluctantly, I handed him the car keys. "Don't hang me up, motherfucker! Get back here so we can blow."

"Twenty minutes. I called the connection after I talked to you on the phone. He's waiting for me in a bar about twenty blocks from here." Willy sniffled. His nose was runny. I saw that his pupils were enlarged and there was a film of perspiration on his upper lip. He was suffering beginning withdrawal and I could sympathize with him. Nothing compares with the combination of mental and physical craving and torment. A sick dope fiend would rather have a fix than salvation.

Willy helped us carry the box of tools, electronics equipment, wire, and meters to the garage. Then he got into my car and backed out. I saw that his car's front tires were both flat—and had been for several days according to the leaves piling against them.

While Aaron tested and modified the equipment, he explained (as I understand it) that he'd measure the force of the particular electrical impulses going through the alarm line, cut through and feed the same impulses to the alarm company office. The alarm, if sounded, would run into a dead end. The normal impulses, from a different source (he had a device that would use another line), would keep the warning board at the company office dark. He explained that when he cut in on the line there'd be a momentary flicker on the board, but nobody would pay attention because it would be gone in a second. Cats, mice, rats—many things caused such a flicker.

Aaron finished in twenty minutes. He then put on gray coveralls with Pacific Telephone blazoned in red on the back. With a tool belt around his waist he looked as if he were a telephone company lineman.

"I'll cover you on the trial run," I said.

"We'll just open the manhole and you drop it closed after me. No use using the barricades for that. About five in the morning should be the best time for that."

Willy was still gone when the box was again full and Aaron was in his street clothes. We waited in the shade of the garage doorway. After fifteen minutes of watching vehicles speed past the driveway without Willy pulling in, I was smoldering. Aaron asked where Willy had gone.

"To buy some dope, the jive ass is undependable . . . I knew he'd fuck around."

"He might be busted. I've got to be in town by two."

"Let's go call you a taxi. There's no telling when that asshole will get here."

Uncaring about Selma's possible attitude, I led Aaron into the house through the kitchen door. The room smelled of boiled cabbage and the sink was stacked with unwashed dishes.

Our entrance brought the two boys to the doorway arch, one peering over the shoulder of the other. Moments later Selma loomed behind them, brushing them out of the way and glaring at me. In her anger, her gauntness was more apparent. She was as worn as a sharecropper's wife in the great depression. She refused to look at Aaron. He might as well have been invisible. He seemed amused. Before she could speak, I did.

"Willy's got my car and I need to use the phone to call a taxi for my friend."

Her teeth clicked shut. She wished to refuse—but wished more urgently to rid her house of our unwelcome presence. She pointed out the phone.

Twenty minutes later, Aaron departed—and Willy hadn't returned. I was furious. I thought about punching him in the mouth, but knew that in a brawl he was capable of breaking me in pieces. When he whipped me, I'd be forced to kill him. It was my fault for having given him the keys. I'd talk bad to him and let it go.

Willy drove up almost three hours late, grinning as he turned off the motor and got out. "Man, I got hung up. Where's your partner?"

"He's gone. And where the fuck did you go? Tijuana?"

"I'm sorry, man, but my connection didn't have anything on him and wanted a ride to East L.A. to see his connection . . . and he got hung up for an hour. You know how that shit goes."

Willy wasn't high. He was more sick than when he left. This phenomenon blunted my anger by arousing curiosity, for a junky will fix with the police kicking in the door, especially if he's sick.

"I gotta wait. Nalline today. But I'm ready when I get done." He brought forth a condom swollen with beige powder, its open end tied into a knot. "An ounce."

"You didn't get a piece with forty pesos."

"He gave me a little credit for the ride. He knows I'll pay him . . . and pull the rent money, too." Willy was happy, feeling that he had something going. "Hey, why don't you give me a lift to the nalline center? My short is fucked up and I don't wanna borrow Mary's wheels."

230

"I'll drop you off but I'm not driving you back. You're on your own there."

"Well, can you wait until I get through and drop me at the bus depot downtown?"

"How long will you be?"

"Twenty minutes."

"Yeah, like the twenty minutes with the car."

"Man . . ."

"Fuck all that 'man' shit. Put that box in the trunk and get in."

Willy wrestled the heavy box to the automobile and set it inside. "What's the portable telephone for?" he asked.

"I told you we're gonna jam an alarm and rip off a spot in Beverly Hills."

"Good luck." He slammed the trunk lid down. "Wait a minute while I stash this junk and tell Selma where I'm going."

The "minute" became fifteen minutes. I pumped the automobile's horn. Willy rushed out, buttoning a shirt.

"That broad was making a bad scene. She doesn't dig you."

"I don't dig her either."

Twenty minutes after leaving the house we were on the dingy street with the featureless building where Rosenthal had taken me. Willy got out half a block away. I told him to wait on the same corner when he was through; I'd come back by in half an hour. I didn't want to wait too close to the repulsive building. I drove several blocks away and ate chili and salt crackers at a greasy-spoon café in a neighborhood of scrap yards and industry.

Before going back for Willy, I telephoned Allison. She'd gone to the beach alone, her usual activity on days when I was busy. She'd expected me home by this hour—but my lateness didn't disturb her. She was happy, as if it was a pleasant surprise, as if she hadn't seen me six hours earlier and wasn't expecting me for days. Her radiance increased my good feelings. She'd planned a surprise, a super fancy supper, and wanted me to hurry because she was already cooking. "But don't ask me what it is."

"An hour more."

"Oh! There's my schedule down the drain."

"I'll make up for it with bonbons and flowers."

I started to say goodbye.

"Wait . . . wait. Bring some avocados with you. Just a couple."

"Okay, baby."

Willy wasn't on the corner when I drove by. I circled several blocks and came back. The corner was still empty. Two Mexicans were coming down the sidewalk; one was vaguely familiar. I pulled to the curb, assuming that they'd just come from nalline, and called them. Neither knew Willy by name, but when I described him they told me that he'd been held in custody, locked in the cage at the end of the corridor. I confirmed what they said by telephoning the testing center and passing myself off as an attorney. The parole officer who answered was evasive; when dealing with the poor the parole department was unaccustomed to answering questions; it was also unaccustomed to lawyers asking the questions. He finally put his supervisor on the line. The supervisor reluctantly and with a note of challenge told me that Willy was in custody as a parole violator—but the supervisor refused to say why. It wasn't really necessary. I knew Willy's pupils had grown larger instead of smaller. He'd failed to run the gauntlet.

Before starting home, and with trepidation, I called Selma, gave her the news in a couple of sentences, and hung up before she could burst into recrimination and self-pity. Tomorrow I'd drive Allison to the jail to visit him with clean socks, underwear, and cigarette money. As a fugitive I was going no closer to the jail than the parking lot. After the visit I'd give Selma some money to help tide her over until welfare checks began. It was the right thing to do, by the thief's code.

If Willy was lucky, if the prison system had enough bodies on hand to justify its budget to the legislature, some anonymous bureaucrat or committee would order him a "dry out", thirty to sixty days in jail. If he was unlucky he'd be sent back to the rehabilitation center for another year or more of group therapy. I felt no great sympathy. He'd been a fool to go in for the test in the first place, for he'd certainly known the likelihood that he'd fail to pass it.

"Like a fuckin' fly to flypaper," I muttered.

Afternoon shadows were stretching themselves on the jail's parking lot when Allison and I arrived. We'd overslept because after going to a drive-in movie we'd driven through the hills, following the curves of Mulholland Drive from its origins in Hollywood past expensive homes to beyond Beverly Hills, where except for a few palatial homes the countryside became almost empty. We ran out of gas in an isolated spot, but thought it was the fuel pump because the gas gauge showed a quarter tank. It took two hours to find a house, telephone for a truck, and be towed twenty miles to an all-night garage in the San Fernando Valley. Only after a new fuel pump had been installed and failed to work was a stick probed into the gas tank. The float in the tank had stuck and told the gauge a lie. When the tank was full the gauge still registered a quarter tank.

As we trudged upstairs to the apartment, Allison hanging on my arm and trilling laughter at how our sentimental night had fizzled, it was so near dawn that baby sparrows in the dark shadows of trees were calling out for food.

So we slept until noon and then rushed, missing breakfast, buying socks and underwear on the way. I told Allison to inform Willy that on the next visit the border on the three one-dollar bills would be saturated with the clear solution of cooked heroin.

"How do you do that?" Allison asked.

"Just cook it like a fix, and then use the eyedropper. It soaks into the paper like it was cotton. You waste two-thirds of it, but Willy can slice off the rim, put it in a spoon with some water and, wham, he'll get fixed."

"What about the ... hypo kit? Where does he get that?"

"Believe me, there's one in there he can get hold of."

233

I parked at the farthest corner of the lot from the building, beneath a stripling tree. Other cars had been parked close to the building to shorten walking distance. No car was closer than thirty yards. Nobody could sneak up on me. If something did happen, which was unlikely, I could drive through a flower bed and over the curb into the street. I also had the Browning pistol on the floor boards between my feet. Coming here where hundreds of deputies worked, and where every law enforcement agency brought prisoners, aroused tension that was cousin to what I felt going on a caper. I watched closely from the moment we arrived.

Allison came back in ten minutes. The bag of socks and underwear was still in her hand. Her quick return and the bag indicated that she hadn't gotten in, but she walked too leisurely for anything serious to have gone wrong. I pulled the car across the lot to meet her halfway. She'd been refused the visit because Willy was allowed one visitor per day and someone had already been there. Obviously it was Selma, and I should have anticipated that she'd rush to the jail as soon as possible to vilify him for his failures.

I felt compelled to drive out and give her some money, unpleasant a task as it would be. There was no reason to confront Allison with Selma's acrimony, so I dropped her at the nearby Union train depot where she could take a taxi. I promised to be home in two hours and to call if something came up.

When I reached Willy's home, Selma was gone. Willy's automobile was still leaning on its flat tire in the driveway.

I drove to Mary's, wondering if she had any news and to leave the money for Selma with her. Willy's two boys were there. Actually, they were somewhere in the neighborhood with Joey. Selma had left them and borrowed Mary's car. She was expected back at any time. I gave Mary a hundred dollars for Selma, glad to have missed her. I left quickly, not only to avoid Selma, but because Lisa was in the kitchen. The girl said nothing, and would hardly meet my eyes, except furtively. The vibes were bad.

*　　*　　*

Two days later I again drove Allison to the jail. Again she was turned away, this time because Willy was gone; he'd been released that very morning. It was a pleasant surprise. I hadn't anticipated his quick reinstatement on parole. I telephoned him to see what had brought about the miracle. Nobody answered. I planned to phone again later, but the momentum toward the jewel robbery was increasing and I was caught up in that, and so forgot Willy. That night, Jerry, Aaron, and I rehearsed and timed everything except the action with Gregory's. Aaron would drive, let us out, jump the alarm and pull around to wait and drive getaway. The alarm had to be fixed minutes before the robbery, because once it was done the phone in Gregory's would go dead. He'd wait across Wilshire with a radio tuned to police calls and the walkie-talkie—and he'd have the motor running when we came out. A huge market six blocks away had a block-long parking lot in its rear, an ideal place to switch cars. There were no traffic lights between the market and the jeweler's. After switching cars, it was two more minutes of slow driving until we reached the teeming traffic of Sunset Boulevard. We could follow it, hidden by the multitude, into Hollywood, or swing through the hills. Nobody in Gregory's would see a Negro among the robbers, so Aaron would be behind the wheel while Jerry and I lay on the floorboards. By the time the police got the description of the original getaway vehicle—panel truck or plain sedan—we'd be at least eight or nine miles away in an entirely different (and differently described) automobile.

Enthusiasm began pulsing through our conversation. Jerry was no longer hesitant as he drove me home, meanwhile looking over the route through the hills. We decided there was no use waiting. We'd all spent many hours casing the score. Saturday morning we'd make our move—the day when Wilshire's traffic was lightest. Gregory's opened at 9:30. We hoped to shorten its business day, drastically so.

As Jerry parked before the apartment, I invited my partners to a home-cooked meal on Friday night. I hadn't consulted Allison, but I knew she liked both of them. They liked the idea.

When I entered the apartment Allison was cross-legged on the floor, sketching something in charcoal and watching the election returns on television. The California polls were just closed, but CBS Election Central was declaring Lyndon Baines Johnson a landslide winner. Allison waved a greeting but said nothing until I came back from the kitchen with a cup of coffee and sat behind her.

"You're early."

"The guy hung me up. I'll see him Saturday morning. If it's a nice day you can go to the beach. You're losing color, and you know how I dig licking on that suntan." I wanted her gone while we used the apartment to examine the loot.

"'Lick a suntan'. You're not coy, not even subtle."

"You dig it. That's your fetish. Want to go somewhere?"

"Let's stay here for once. Take the TV in the bedroom and watch a movie."

"I invited Jerry and Aaron for dinner Friday night. Okay?"

"It's got to be okay, doesn't it? I can't say no. It'll be fun anyway. Is Carol coming?"

"No. It's sort of a business dinner."

Allison smiled and shook her head. "Monkey business."

I carried the television set into the bedroom and we watched it and made love at the same time.

Part Three

Do not go gentle into that good night.
Rage, rage against the dying of the light.
Dylan Thomas

1

THE morning of the robbery was bright. Mild rain through the night had washed away both smog and November's grayness. The yellow sun was mellow warm, and in the sky, tendrils of cumulus basked in lazy turnings.

Jerry led in his station wagon over the hill road that divided the San Fernando Valley from Beverly Hills. Aaron, wearing gray zip coveralls, drove a stolen panel truck a hundred yards behind. I sat on the floor in the back of the truck, holding onto the yellow and black wooden barricade (also stolen) with the Men at Work sign, and a lantern. On this much-traveled road motorcycle policemen frequently hid behind curves and bushes. The sight of a black man and a white man riding together would register sufficiently in his mind to be recalled in a few minutes when the robbery alert crackled over his radio.

The automobiles wound past houses cantilevered over precipice and sky. At the summit of the hills, I saw the momentary sparkle of the sea in the distance. Allison was there, lying on the beach, soaking up a last good day of sun. Tonight her body would contain a residual warmth.

Aaron was humming as he drove, one elbow propped casually on the window frame. He was showing no fear. Confidence in my henchmen relaxed me. Despite the robbery's size, I was less keyed up than usual, almost detached in my confidence. Once more I visualized what we were going to do—each step flashed through—and once more the X factor appeared reduced to the absolute minimum. The very simplicity of the plan left little that could go wrong.

Now the panel truck was on level ground. Over Aaron's shoulder I could see the rear of the station wagon, its brake lights flashing as Jerry halted for Sunset Boulevard's traffic light. We slowed, the light flashed green, and Jerry crossed the intersection and kept going straight. Aaron turned left, mingling in the flow of eastbound traffic. At the first corner, Aaron turned right, now going parallel to Jerry's course, but a block away. We went three blocks and turned into a long parking lot that ran the entire length of a shopping district. Aaron went through very slowly, stopped at the far end, and Jerry was waiting. He swung into the front seat with scarcely a pause. I passed him the long flower box with the M16. None of the Saturday morning shoppers gave the nondescript truck a second glance.

"My short's right where we planned," Jerry said. "Last row next to the curb. Keys under the floormat."

We were a block from Wilshire. I slipped into the suit coat, straightened my necktie, jacked a shell into the chamber of the Browning automatic—thirteen shots of Remington hollow point ammunition—and stuck it in my waistband at the rear. The tiny receiver (earplug) went into place, and the hat with the mask inside went on my head.

From the front seat there was a sharp clack of steel. Jerry was checking the automatic rifle. Between the divided seats I watched him lower it back into the flower box and pat his pockets to make sure the gloves and mask were in place.

Aaron's pistol was covered by a folded newspaper on the floorboards. His belt of tools and equipment was on top of it.

The truck pulled to the curb twenty feet from the intersection, across which sat Gregory's, gleaming sedately white, hinting of the riches within. A Mercedes roadster was pulling from the parking lot, and an old woman was waddling toward the side entrance.

Wilshire Boulevard's traffic was even lighter than we'd anticipated.

"Smell anything?" Aaron asked.

"Money," Jerry said.

The stop, the look, the conversation, took only seconds. Jerry opened the door and stepped out. Right behind him, I moved the seat forward and followed, careful to touch nothing with my bare fingertips.

"See you in fifteen minutes," I said to Aaron.

"Or on the handball court in Folsom."

"Or in the morgue."

"Let's settle for fifteen minutes."

"Right on."

The truck crossed the boulevard, moved pertly down the street between shops and offices.

"I'm gone," Jerry said, moving left. He would saunter down the sidewalk, cross over at the next corner, and double back to Gregory's front entrance. His stroll was relaxed. The flower box under his arm appeared natural.

From my vantage point, I could see both Jerry and the truck. Aaron went a block and a half and pulled to the curb, the line of parked cars hiding him from sight. Through the earplug, I heard him, "Here I go, brother." Down the street he appeared, carrying the barricade in one hand and lantern in the other. He placed them to detour traffic, kneeled beside the manhole cover, and pulled it up with a tool. Who'd pay attention to a Negro in coveralls with a tool kit strapped around his waist?

Minutes ticked away. He took longer than expected. Jerry was lounging at the next corner and I was beginning to fret, puffing a cigar that had no taste because my mouth was dry.

Aaron raised himself out of the manhole, replaced the cover, removed the barricade and went out of sight. I was already moving across the boulevard in anticipation of his signal. It came seconds later. "Everything's cool. Make your move. I'm pulling around to my spot."

Jerry had seen me cross the street and he was moving toward

the front entrance. I turned into the parking lot, tension sucking at my stomach. I wanted to piss and the thought made me smile. My movements felt jerky.

As I came near the doors, the old woman came out. I stopped, turned my head and bent over, as if examining something stuck to the heel of my shoe—actually hiding my face from later identification.

The automatic doors opened as I stepped on the rubber mat. Cool air conditioning made me aware of my sweaty face. The thick carpet was silent underfoot.

A young couple, accompanied by an older man, were examining a tray of rings placed before them by a salesman. No other customers were in sight. The second salesman was talking with a secretary; she held a sheaf of papers in hand.

The scene was ideal; nobody even looked toward me.

Jerry's silhouette darkened the front door. It started to swing inward. I turned my back, raised the hat and pulled down the mask, adjusting it with one hand while I pulled the automatic with the other, slipping off the safety catch with my thumb. Its weight and the checkered butt were comforting, filling me with a sense of power. I turned back.

Jerry looked frightening in the Frankenstein mask. More frightening was the awesome weapon he held. He hadn't been seen.

"This is a robbery!" he bellowed. "Don't nobody move!" He swung the automatic rifle in an arc that swept over everyone, threatening each one with instant death. He stepped to the side of the door. Nobody on the sidewalk could see him without entering.

While he yelled, while their agape faces were registering awareness, I was running from the side behind the counter, my pistol extended at full arm's length. "Turn around," I snapped at the salesman who'd been talking to the young secretary, arriving next to him as I spoke. I spun him around. The girl had been walking away, was near the office door. She'd frozen momentarily, hand outstretched. She wanted to duck through the door, slam it, and give warning. The idea was etched in her face.

I came up behind her as she was about to touch the knob. She heard me—she'd only seen Jerry until that moment—and turned her head as I grabbed her arm. The mask startled her, but it was less than real fear. My fingers squeezed viciously into her arm, deliberately hurting her. Those who lack experience with violence are unafraid of its threat—but they shatter completely when hurt by its reality. "Be a nice girl and you won't get hurt," I said.

Jerry was herding the others into a corner, ordering them to sit down with their hands over their heads. It was going smoothly.

I shoved the girl through the door. Jules Neissen was seated at his desk; he started to jump up as the girl stumbled across the carpet. He stopped and turned pale as I pointed the pistol at his chest from eight feet away. One squeeze would blow him through the wall—and he knew it.

"Hold it, right there, baby," I said. "Keep your hands in sight."

"Don't give him anything," the girl said. Before the words had crossed the room I backhanded her full force across the cheek and dropped her to her knees. The manager's color, such as it was, flooded back to his cheeks. He gathered his courage, shook his head with the stubbornness of a child. "Go jump," he said.

It was ludicrous, the words of refusal were prissy.

"You'll open that vault, punk! Don't be a dead hero. The insurance company pays, not you. They don't give a fuck about a dead fool."

"You won't get it by shooting me—and I'm not going to open it."

Five minutes would change his mind—and a bullet through his kneecap would certainly do it. But there was a better way. I pressed the pistol to the girl's ear. "I'm not killing you—not first. But her brains are going to fuck up the wallpaper." The threat was a bluff. I wouldn't kill the girl—but if it failed to work I was certainly going to kill him, or at least cripple him.

The girl was limp, eyes glazed. The true horror of the situation had seeped through. She believed herself about to die if the manager failed to coóperate. She began to whimper. I wondered if her panties were wet.

Neissen started to speak, but no words issued. He nodded. The resistance had lasted twenty seconds. "Get moving," I said, ushering them toward the door, still holding the girl, the pistol at Neissen's back.

Jerry had everyone gathered along one wall. Another couple had straggled in from the street and been captured. I shoved the girl toward the others. "Watch this one," I yelled to Jerry.

Neissen was moving reluctantly. I rammed the gun barrel into his spine, bringing a gasp of pain. "Hurry up, motherfucker." I shoved him toward the vault. As he opened it, I told him I wanted unset diamonds first; then diamond brooches (because they had multiple jewels), and finally diamond rings.

The vast steel door swung open. A steel-barred grill gate was opened with a key. "You've got sixty seconds to fill this," I said, handing him a shopping bag. "One . . . two . . . three . . ."

It took precious seconds for the meaning of the threat to penetrate; then he whispered in terror and became a man possessed as he dumped diamonds from trays, scraping them as if they were garbage on dishes. When a brooch stuck in a tray, he became frantic. Each motion of his hand was several thousand dollars. "Twenty . . . twenty-one . . . twenty-two . . ."

The earplug receiver crackled with Aaron's voice. "We've got heat. Prowl car's making a turn."

I was already running, having ripped the bag from Neissen's hand. Aaron's voice continued calmly: "They went by, looked me over, made a U turn—probably want to know about a colored man in Beverly Hills."

Aaron was calm—calmer than me. I tripped over a chair behind the display cases, stumbled, and kept going. "Cover the door," I called to Jerry. "Aaron's got steam."

Jerry flipped the M16 to full automatic fire and kneeled, facing the door from an angle.

Aaron's voice came again. "There's a robbery call on the radio for this address, Code Three."

The M16 calmed me. There'd never been fear, just a moment's confusion. I'd gone beyond fear; my commitment included the possibility of dying, and after accepting that there is nothing to be afraid of.

The hostages began to swivel their heads, whispered in fright, bunched together like chickens. They were a thousand times more frightened than I was. "Get down on your stomachs," I yelled, wanting to shoot over their heads for emphasis—but that would have surrendered surprise in the street.

I crouched beside Jerry. "They know there's a heist going down, but there's only two. Get ready. We're going out."

"Cocksucker!" Jerry whispered.

"They haven't got a chance against that thing," I said.

I'd already thought of using the prisoners as hostages and rejected the idea. The police would surround us and wait. The M16 would shred a police car. We had the firepower to get away—or create carnage in the attempt.

My shoulder was against the door. "When I kick it open, break to the left and run right across the street. I'll cover the right."

From outside there were two gunshots, the sound muffled by the doors, but clear nonetheless. "Two more cars coming," Aaron said. "I'm going to split, draw them off you."

"Wait, goddammit," I called—but there was no transmitter for my words. I pulled Jerry back from the door. "Out the side," I said, grabbing his sleeve.

A shotgun went off outside. A siren wailed. Another shotgun blast. Pistol shots.

We sprinted for the side entrance. As Jerry burst through the door there was a fusillade of shots from the boulevard; then the screech of tires and the rip of metal. I knew Aaron wasn't getting away.

I ran bent over through the sunlit parking lot, using the few cars for cover. I had the pistol in one hand the sack of jewelry in the other. Jerry was on my heels. Moments before the odds were in our favor; now they were a hundred to one against us.

I dropped to one knee behind a car, Jerry next to me. The gunfight on the boulevard had kept the police from even glancing elsewhere. We hadn't been seen so far. But ahead was a three-foot box hedge, and the sidewalk to the sidestreet. Automobiles went by, none realizing that they traversed a battlefield. Across the street was a medical building. We couldn't cross; we'd certainly be seen. The only way to run was down this side of the street, turning in at the first opening. We'd be exposed to anyone looking down from Wilshire, but we had no choice in the matter.

From around a tire, I saw a prowl car, red light spinning wildly, hurtle across the intersection and swerve into the parking lot behind us. Another swung in and stopped behind the first. Four policemen in black uniforms and white helmets bailed out, crouching behind their cars, pistols raised. They were covering Gregory's side door, believing we were still inside. Their backs were to us.

Jerry tore off his mask and threw it under the parked car. "Where can I put this?" he asked, gesturing with the automatic rifle.

"Hold the motherfucker. We might need it." I rolled the bag into a bundle and tucked it beneath my arm like a football. "Follow me."

I sucked in a breath, hurdled the hedge, and started running. The empty sidewalk stretched before me. Jerry began one step behind, but I quickly pulled away. There was no outcry, no shots from behind us. We were near the middle of the block.

I reached the driveway at the same moment that a black and white prowl car turned the corner ahead. I leaped through, feet skidding from beneath me as I hit gravel. I crashed on hip and elbow without dropping anything, came back on my feet scarcely losing a stride. The siren's scream spurred me onward.

The driveway opened into a loading yard. Behind me brakes were screeching as the police car turned in. I leaped left. Crates and boxes were filed against the walls. I looked for a drainpipe to climb to the roof. No time. I drove into the recess of a door, crouched behind a steel drum filled with trash. As I faced out, pistol raised, Jerry appeared. He ran blindly in a line toward a vine-covered storm fence twenty feet away.

The car braked, skidded, and threw up a billow of dust, but only the grill protruded beyond the building.

Jerry had thrown the M16 over the fence, had sprung to the top, one leg hooked over, fingers dug into the wire.

"Hold it!" a voice yelled—the body was hidden by the building.

Jerry stopped, remained hanging—captured. Seconds ticked away.

The policeman's shot made me jump. Jerry dropped, arching in a convulsion, his spine shattered. He lay writhing in the dirt like a dog with a broken back. I was sick to my stomach, waiting for the command to surrender, tensing to charge out shooting. "Chip time," I muttered.

The unbelievable happened. The policeman sauntered from the alleyway, pistol dangling beside his hip, a twisted smile on his face. He walked toward the wriggling body. He'd seen only Jerry. He didn't know there were two of us.

The black uniform had white sergeant's chevrons. The short-cropped blond hair shone in the sunlight. He was fifteen feet away. Dire necessity guided my actions, but there was joy, too, and joy of hate expressed.

He went down, leg blown out from under him. Blood darkened over hip and thigh. I leaped forward looking for his service revolver. It was in the dust five feet away. His trim uniform became filthy the moment he landed. Pain and shock marred the boyish face. He would beg, plead for mercy, mention wife and children. Policemen never admit begging for mercy, but they do it more often than criminals. Begging would make no difference. Even if he hadn't shot Jerry he was going to die.

He didn't beg. He glared. "You haven't got the guts," he said. "They'll get you and you know it."

It was amazing to view a man confronting mortality who believed that retribution is divinely ordained, that righteousness would protect him. "It doesn't make any difference to you," I said. I put my foot on his neck, forced him down, and put two bullets through his heart. The hollow-point ammunition blew his life out his back. In the last instant, already dead, his eyes registered that he saw the truth.

Jerry still flopped weakly, like a fish expiring on a ship's deck. His eyes were sightless and glassy. Formless sounds mingled with blood from his mouth. Dark arterial blood thickened the dust, turned it into a rich mud. I thought of dragging him to the prowl car and using it for a getaway. I thought of putting him out of his misery.

I could do neither.

Sirens screamed. Cars were careening nearby like a nest of aroused hornets. I pitched the bag of diamonds over the fence and leaped after it. In three seconds I was gathering the sack in one hand and the M16 in the other.

I ran through a back yard of flower beds and trees and a wrought iron bird bath. I had to get off the block before it was surrounded, had to cross one street in seconds. Existence was reduced to that of the beast fleeing blindly before the baying hounds. The future ended seconds away.

As I ran, my eyes scanned the house, looking for a fluttered curtain or other movement indicating that someone had been aroused by the shots, was looking out. All remained still as I tramped through a flower bed, skirted a garage, hurtled pell-mell down a driveway, hitting the street full stride, and pounded across and up another driveway. I hurdled a wooden gate on the run, one that I would have had to scramble over under other conditions—and might not have been able to encumbered by rifle and shopping bag. I was in another back yard. A small dog scampered beside me, yipping and nipping at my heels until I went over another fence.

I was in an alley, confronting a giant concrete wall: the side of a movie theater. The wall forced me to detour to the right, away from Wilshire. At the end of the wall was a narrow passageway.

I ducked into it, slowed down, my lungs on fire. Suddenly I stopped, realizing the mask was still on my face and the rifle was dangling in my hand. Anyone who saw me would know what I was. For the first time the paralysis of fear crept into me. My pants were frayed and dusty from where I'd skidded on the gravel, my face was drenched with sweat beneath the mask. It was miraculous that I'd come this far without being spotted. Yet I couldn't stay here for many seconds. Any moment a police car would cruise down the alley behind or the street ahead and the battle would be on.

I moved forward. The fence had a gate and the gate was unlocked. I slipped through into an incinerator and trash area in the back yard of a large, expensive home. The area where I stood was separated from trees and lawn and rosebushes by a lattice fence. A garage wall was ahead of me. Stacked against it were boxes of cans and bottles. I shut the gate and flopped behind the incinerator, out of sight of the house.

The sound of an automobile going down the alley rose and receded. Was it a police car?

I couldn't stay where I was for more than a few seconds. I thought of hiding, going to earth like a fox. It has proven successful in other chases—but none were like this was going to be. They knew I was on foot. Fifty police cars would be in the area in a few minutes. Hundreds of policemen would begin searching.

My only hope was to get away before they collected themselves— if they hadn't already. They'd draw a demarcation line on Wilshire Boulevard because they knew I was south of there. If I could cross it the Saturday crowds would give me some cover.

I dragged a trash box behind the incinerator and dumped it on the ground. I dropped the rifle in, put the shopping bag of diamonds on top. I tore off my dirty coat and tie, stuffed them in. The Browning was too big to hide in my clothes. I dropped it on top and refilled the box with trash.

Refusing to think of the danger, I went out the gate, walked along the passageway and turned up the sidewalk toward Wilshire. It was forty yards away. I began sprinting. An automobile motor sounded behind me. I expected a hail of bullets. The vehicle passed.

Near the end of the building I slowed down, trying to gauge the traffic light so that I would arrive as it changed to green. I'd walk across Wilshire—and for thirty seconds I'd be in sight from the sidewalk outside Gregory's.

The light turned green. I stepped toward the curb. To the left a wonderful sight appeared: a bus was pulling up ten feet away, doors whooshing open—doors of escape. I went to it, momentarily able to glimpse down the sidewalk two blocks away where half a dozen figures were bunched in front of Gregory's. The bus blocked the other side of the street where the panel truck was wrecked. I waited while a graying Negro woman climbed off, grunting and holding dearly to the handrail.

From the top step, as I stood beside the driver getting change, I could look through the front window. A police car cut around the bus, turned down the street I'd just vacated. If I'd not gotten on the bus we would have met in the middle of Wilshire Boulevard.

The bus pulled away from the curb. Police cars were going the other way, three of them with red lights flashing.

When I sat down I was stupefied. Thoughts spun too fast to focus. I began trembling. My mind knew that only danger's beginning had passed. The hounds were still sniffing for scent. When they had it the baying would begin.

I had to get to the apartment, get the .32—the only pistol remaining. I had to pick up my car, clothes, get moving. There figured to be at least several hours, perhaps days, before they got there. All I needed was twenty minutes. I was still oozing sweat, still trembling, and the enormity of the situation was held at bay by shock.

2

THE winding, curbless streets near the apartment were silent except for buzzing insects in the foliage and chirping birds. Going up the stairs (I'd left the taxi a quarter mile away) I wondered if my enemies were crouched in ambush, hidden inside the apartment. It was unlikely, and I didn't really care. Sometimes one is too tired for even life to be so utterly precious.

The apartment was silent, dim, cool, a sanctuary. I left the lights out. The sights were familiar: Allison's unfinished paintings, her flower arrangements, the record albums lying disordered on the sofa. The shell around my emotions was cracked by seeing these things. The first quick ache of sadness shot through me. My life had been a wasteland, but until today I might have turned back, done penance, and been forgiven.

I throttled down the feelings. The game had to be played. My role was hunted cop killer, vicious, unrepentant.

I changed clothes, throwing aside those I'd been wearing. The small revolver was in a hip pocket. My clothes were thrown on a bedspread, the bedspread tied into a bundle. I took the half pound of pot and half jar of bennies; might as well be high while being hunted.

The license plates on my car needed changing. Doing it here was impossible—some neighbor could too easily look out the window and see what was going on. L&L Red's hilltop seemed the best place for that—and to pause while I collected myself and decided what to do. Driving there would be safe. For a few hours, at least, I'd be in the eye of the storm.

An automobile was coming up the hill. Its motor grew louder, faded temporarily as it rounded curves. Suddenly, it was close and recognizable. Allison! She was three hours early.

Footsteps tapped swiftly up the stairs. What could I say to her? "Baby, I just offed a pig and I gotta blow."

The key turned, the door bounced against the night chain. She rattled the door. "Max! Max! Let me in."

I peered from a window, revolver in hand. She was apparently alone. I flipped the chain loose and she rushed inside, resetting the latch. She was visibly upset. She knew something. That was frightening.

"They're looking for you," she said.

"Where'd you hear that?"

"The radio."

"The radio! You heard my name?"

"A special bulletin."

Panic swelled up. It was 1:00 P.M. Unless Aaron had talked there was no way for them to know my name so soon. Even if they'd gotten fingerprints it would take hours to telephoto them to Washington. Wherever it came from, it meant they were closer on my heels than I'd thought. The apartment was no longer even temporary sanctuary. It was a trap.

"I couldn't believe my ears," she said. "I started home and it came on another station."

"How long ago?"

"Twenty minutes. I rushed back here so fast I left my towel and glasses. Did you kill a policeman? They've got two men, one isn't expected to live."

"I know."

"Aaron and Jerry."

I was at the window, peering down the hill. Nothing stirred.

"Was it Aaron and Jerry?" she repeated.

"Yeah. Jerry's shot."

"Poor Carol."

"Shit! Poor Jerry." I wasn't really talking to her. I had to think, make decisions. The first thing was to get away from here; then think. I wondered if it made any difference. It would be the same in the end anyway. It would conclude the same way if I smoked some pot, got drunk, and went to bed. The world still swung around the sun, Fingers of despair clutched at my mind. Where had yesterday gone? Fuck yesterday.

"Get your ass out of here. In twenty minutes you can come back. I'll be gone. If they pick you up, demand a lawyer, keep demanding one even when they ask your name. Don't say one word except you want a lawyer."

"I'm not leaving. I came to help you."

"Help me! You asinine, stupid bitch! You're outta your fuckin' mind, cunt. This ain't a nit-shit game or a B movie. The best you'll get is a jolt in prison with me, and you might get your head shot off. When they run up on me it's court in the street. I don't give a fuck if I'm standing in a kindergarten. I'm not going to surrender."

"I'll take my chances."

"No! No! Split! Stupid cunt!"

Tears puffed her eyes, but she was undaunted. Unable to speak, she shook her head in defiance. "I love you."

"Oh God! That's all I need. Love! I'm a cop killer."

"You need someone to help you. How can you buy food, go anywhere, rent a place to hide? Please . . ."

She spoke the truth. She'd be useful—at least for a few days, if I lasted a few days. I'd tried so hard to drive her off because I wanted her so badly. I didn't want to die alone. I pressed a forefinger to her lips to silence her pleas. "Okay, okay. You bought yourself some misery. You've got ten minutes to get everything you're taking with you. Just throw them in a blanket and tie up the ends. I'll be back to help."

I ran downstairs and pitched the bedspread of clothes into the GTO, then raced back to help Allison.

The automobile was stuffy from sitting outdoors, and I opened the windows to let in a breeze. On the way down the hill, my panic diminished. While in the apartment I'd had one thought: get moving, flee the trap. Now there was even a kernel of excitement, almost pleasurable, the anticipation of a journey. I'd always wanted to drive around the country, see things, and now fate was giving me the chance, probably the last chance, but for the moment it didn't matter.

Through the rear view mirror I could see Allison following in her car. I began thinking. Two cars were a handicap. One had to be sold, and it was Allison's. It was registered in her right name, and if we kept it and had to abandon it, the police would be able to trace her identity. Mine would soon be on the hot list, but with bogus license plates it would serve for a few days.

Griffith Park was nearby—in a line to L&L Red's—and I needed to tell Allison what to do. I pulled into the park, following the zoo road, and swung to the curb beside a golf course. Allison pulled up behind me.

I told her to sell the car for cash. Knowing she would never find Red's Cabin—which had no address—I gave her Mary Gambesi's address and told her to meet me there. And to wait if I wasn't there. Allison listened to my instructions. Her face was flushed. She nodded understanding. The new game excited her. She would do what I said, but something in her demeanor indicated she was playing a role, perhaps unconsciously; she didn't understand the true gravity of the situation.

"When you get to that address, just tell the woman I told you to meet me there. Don't tell her anything. She might not know what's happened. If I'm not there, just sit tight."

"You won't leave me, will you?"

"Don't act simple. Nine chances out of ten I'll be there first."

While I drove to Red's, taking a circuitous route to stay on freeways and out of the slums as much as possible (in the slums one was more likely to meet police cars), the realization grew of just how completely my world had been blown asunder. If I managed to retrieve the diamonds, it was impossible to sell them through Eric Warren, or any other fence. If I could flee the country with them, they'd be marketable in small amounts somewhere else, but not in the United States.

An inkling of just how alone I was came, too. The gunshots in the dirt-loading yard had destroyed every relationship. Everyone had to be treated as if an informer. As for Allison, circumstances forced me to trust her. There could be no prearranged meetings. I knew human perversity, realized the motives behind someone dialing a telephone: reward in money, tacit permission to deal drugs, dismissal of a criminal charge, pure maliciousness, or fear of being involved in something too serious. I couldn't afford to trust criminals. They might be trustworthy, but I couldn't take the chance.

I refused to examine the odds; truth might bring despair. I knew, however, that in the computer era, with everyone on file, it was impossible to disappear. Perhaps in India, or deepest Africa, but never in the United States. Everything went into the computers— car purchases, getting a job, renting a dwelling. My fingerprints could be checked in Washington in thirty minutes from anywhere in the country. I couldn't even pay taxes, for that would ring bells in the computer.

Hope consisted entirely of getting out of the country, off the North American continent, out of the Western hemisphere. I needed a passport—and had no idea of how to get one.

I shut off these thoughts. First things first. Get to Red's, get the shotgun, go back for the diamonds. It wasn't a long future to plan, but it was longer than I'd had running through back yards and alleys.

Red was getting out of his car when I came up. He saw me and waited. From the look on his face it was obvious that he knew about the murder. His first words confirmed it: "Man, you can't stay here!"

The terror-stricken words were not unexpected (once I thought about it), but they made me both queasy and angry. Red was a coward. I'd known that all along. Yet I'd been good to him, a friend, and on the basis of friendship he should screw up his nerve. I felt the flame of despair—and then fury jetted red to my brain. I wrenched the door open and sprang out, drawing the revolver. "Cocksucker!"

"Man! Max," he yelped, stepping backward, throwing up his hands as if they could ward off a bullet.

"I don't want to stay here, motherfucker!"

Red's heel caught on a large rock, causing him to sit down in the dirt. His hands remained up, stretched toward me. "I didn't mean it that way," he said. "I meant they'll be here looking for you."

I lowered the gun. "Don't sweat it, Red. I just came for my shotgun."

"I'll get it." He scrambled to his feet and went toward the shack. I followed him. "Johnny Taormina called me," Red said. "I was at the pool hall. That's how I found out. Too many people know we're partners. Somebody'll send 'em here—no shit!"

"Yeah, okay." What he said was true, but it would be quite some time before they got this lead.

Red yanked the crippled sofa aside, wrenched up a floorboard, and brought out the shotgun wrapped in a towel. He reached down again and came up with the extra ammunition.

"Goddam, Max, I'm sorry if you thought wrong. I love you like a brother. If I wasn't certain they'd be here . . ."

"Forget it."

"What happened? What went wrong?" He was following me outdoors.

"The fuckin' wheels came off."

"Jesus, it's shitty . . . just when you were starting to roll."

"Yeah." I was in the car.

"Man, if you need me, call the pool hall. I wouldn't come up here without warning."

"I'll do that."

When I drove down the hill, L&L Red was busy with a rake, effacing my tire marks from the dirt. It made me smile. Red was indeed a survivor.

I hadn't changed license plates. It wouldn't be safe to trust Red to know them. But I had gotten the shotgun, it was under a sweater on the seat beside me.

Minutes later I was on the freeway heading toward Mary's, wondering what kind of reception I'd get. If necessary, I'd hold her and her children hostage until Allison came. If her attitude was like Red's there'd be no choice.

Halfway to El Monte, I spotted two highway patrolmen on motorcycles behind me. They were closing fast, weaving through the heavy traffic. They weren't using their red lights. I restrained the impulse to stomp the accelerator. I'd never outrun them in this traffic, and they didn't seem to be after me. Yet I checked the shotgun and eased the small revolver to the seat directly behind my rump. They were splitting apart to pass on each side. If they tried anything I'd ram into one, crush him against the divider fence—then shoot the other one.

They zoomed by without looking toward me, the rumps of their motorcycles saucily upflung. I rubbed sweaty palms dry against the seat, one at a time, and realized that for the rest of my life every policeman I saw would arouse the same dread and consternation.

Fifteen minutes later I was in the driveway, pulling to the rear where the bungalows faced each other. Between them were clothes lines and a dozen yards of parched lawn. Mary was there, gathering laundry. She was barefoot, in faded jeans and a man's unpressed white shirt tied at the bottom and rolled above the sleeves. Another woman in faded print dress was in the small yard, waiting with a large basket of laundry and a pair of toddlers.

Mary's radiant smile declared that she was unaware of the news. "Howdy, stranger. Where you been?"

"Busy." I nodded at the woman and smiled. She smiled back, a gesture without significance. "Where's Joey and Lisa?"

"The Lord knows. Go on inside. There's coffee on the stove. I'll be there in a minute."

As I went around the bungalow I could see over fences into other back yards. The afternoon was absolutely silent. The hushing scene made me pause at the doorway. Clouds drifted overhead, edges dissolving like smoke. In my mind I could visualize the city's swarm, each going about his business. No more than a handful would care about the killings or the hunt. My friends in prison would talk for a while about my predicament, but it would be no big thing, a few minutes passing conversation and, because it was November, they'd become more involved with the point spreads on football games. Some policemen would be enraged, but when it got down to it my crime and fate meant virtually nothing except to my little ego—the ego that refused to believe the center of the universe was anywhere else, a very human belief.

I was sitting down with the coffee when Mary came in, the large basket held in front of her. She smiled at me in further greeting.

"You need a clothes dryer," I said.

"They cost money . . . and if I had money there are other things a lot more important than a dryer." Mary put down the dried clothes and got herself a cup of coffee. She sat down to talk with me, chattering gaily, asking me nothing, glad to see someone beyond the circle of her children and the Darins. She mentioned getting a letter from Joe that sent his regards to me, and told of how Lisa was getting boy crazy.

When she finished the coffee she excused herself, saying that she had to start dinner. While she began getting out pots and pans, taking things from the refrigerator and slicing string beans, I sat stupefied at the table. A quagmire of exhaustion engulfed me. It was beyond mere physical tiredness. It was the mind demanding escape from reality. It wasn't a new experience. Whenever I had been arrested and knew they had the goods, I felt this same overpowering need for sleep. The moment they locked me in a cell I went to sleep, avoiding the situation.

I almost went to sleep at the table. Mary spotted me, eyes twinkling. "You're wiped out," she said. "What happened, your girl toss you out?"

"No. She's on an errand for me right now. She's supposed to meet me here."

"Why don't you take a nap? Use Joey's bed."

I went into the bedroom, giving her a hug of affection on the way. The small revolver went in a shoe beside the bed. If the police sneaked in while I slept and it was under the pillow I'd never get a chance to use it. The shoe was just as quick to get at, and if they got into the room I might be able to reach for my shoes without getting blasted.

Sleep came instantly, without dreams.

Allison shook my shoulder, though for several seconds my mind resisted coming awake. Her scent was my first recognition, followed by my whereabouts. Then full recollection of everything exploded into focus. Her face was shadowed softly, for the windows were curtained with the darkness outside and light came solely from the doorway.

"It's seven o'clock," she said.

"How long have you been here?"

"Two hours, talking to Mary. I let you sleep."

"Does she know anything yet?"

"No. And the kids are watching a rock show on TV. I was ready to ask them to put something else on if they turned on the news."

"You're a pretty slick broad."

"I got eighteen hundred dollars for the car," she said, reaching into her handbag for the money. "Where do you want it?"

"Keep it for now." I moved over so she could sit down. I put a hand at the small of her back and reached down behind the tight waist of her stretch pants, feeling the soft panties and flesh. "You got rid of the bathing suit."

259

"In a gas station." She reached back and took my hand away. "Max, this isn't the time for that. You make me nervous."

"I'm just affectionate."

"It's just not the time. I called Carol. Jerry's dead. The police were there and she told me to call back."

"You shouldn't have called. Don't do it again."

"She's my friend. Imagine what she feels like."

"The phone might be bugged. I'll send her some money in a few days. In fact, don't get in touch with anybody that we know."

"Now what do we do? We've got the money."

"Let's take Mary and the kids to a movie."

"You're not serious."

"Yes I am."

Allison was silent, upset, unable to understand.

A shadow fell across the threshold. It was Joey, "I want my jacket, Max. I'm going to visit a friend of mine."

"Why don't we go to a movie instead?"

"I don't know if Mom'll let me."

"All of us are going. Where's Lisa?"

"She's washing dishes."

I swung off the bed, started to reach for my shoes and remembered the pistol. It was better if Joey didn't see it. "Go tell your mother to come here for a minute."

While the boy was gone I slipped the revolver into a hip pocket and put on my shoes. I was combing my hair when Mary came in. "What's this about movies?"

"Yeah, on me. Tomorrow's Sunday and you can sleep late. I'll throw in hamburgers and malts. The kids need a night out. So do you."

"It'll take a while to get ready."

"Hurry up, okay?"

Nobody questioned driving across town to a movie, nor did they ask what they were going to see. It was just as well, for I would have been unable to answer. I knew the whereabouts of the drive-in theater, three miles from Beverly Hills. I thought about taking a taxi from the theater, but rejected the idea. The last three miles was where I really needed the cover. Two women and two children in an automobile would quell suspicion if the police were still watching the area.

Allison carried the conversation during the journey, talking to Mary. Joey kept his nose out the rear window, like a puppy loving the wind. Lisa sat quietly beside him. Her withdrawn, almost sulky manner indicated that she hadn't wanted to come. She'd never forget our first meeting. I felt sorry for her—not because of what had happened but because of her life and future. She was pretty, with more than the natural prettiness of all young girls. A budding rose, but doomed to wilt prematurely. Alternatives in her life were so few that it was depressing to contemplate. Without knowing any better, hoping to escape drudgery, she would marry some neighborhood boy too soon—simply because he was available. The fresh beauty would disappear, for she would never learn the tricks of keeping it. Her slim body would lose its comeliness from too many babies too quickly, for on the level of society where the pill was really needed it remained unused through false shame and ignorance. I wondered if she dreamed, and decided that if she did it was of small fancy. She lacked the articulateness of big dreams.

My whimsical concern was more than altruism; it was simultaneous with realization of her young, nubile beauty. Notwithstanding the sexual implications, I was indignant at the unfairness of her life—an unfairness starkly illustrated by her being fifteen years old and riding in a car as cover for a murderer.

I had changed freeways downtown, using the Santa Monica Freeway rather than the Hollywood. The detour took us south of where the surveillance for me would be most intense. The movie was ten blocks north of where I got off.

One car was ahead of us at the ticket booth. The marquee blazoned *The Great Escape* and *Dillinger Days*. Mary nudged me and shook her head ruefully, believing I'd deliberately sought out the gangster film. The fact was that I didn't even see what was on the screen, and sitting through the films was like sitting through eternity.

I turned the automobile right on Wilshire Boulevard instead of going straight ahead to the freeway.

"Where are we going?" Allison asked.

"I've got some business. It'll take a couple minutes."

She said nothing more, but I knew from her sudden, absolute silence that she understood, at least partly, that there'd been a reason for the movie, Nobody else said a word. They were happy for the evening away from the bungalow.

The stores and shops on Wilshire Boulevard were closed, but the display windows remained cunningly lighted, showing everything from mink to Rolls Royces. A police car went by us in the opposite direction with only a glance from the driver.

"Why don't you put the radio on?" Lisa asked.

"It's got a short or something. After a couple minutes it starts smoking. I'll get it fixed tomorrow."

I saw the theater with the passageway behind it. The marquee lights were extinguished. My stomach felt hollow. The enclosed yard could be a deadly trap. If I was alone I'd have come from the other direction, starting a block away and moving in an inch at a time. If the police were waiting they'd be keyed in on the passageway and the gate. By coming up behind them, by waiting, I'd know if they were there. Because of the carload of people I lacked the time for this.

I turned down the street beside the theater. "When I park right now," I said to Allison, "get behind the wheel and drive around for ten minutes. Then come back."

Everyone in the automobile now knew I was up to something. It made no difference. I had control of the situation.

"What are you going to do, Max?" Mary asked.

The car was stopping. I didn't bother to answer her. I got out and went around the rear of the car, darted into the passage, halted just long enough to see the automobile start moving. I tiptoed through the darkness. Vague, darker shadows were all that designated objects. The tiny crunch of my steps sounded loud. I had the revolver out, the hammer cocked. I had an intense urge to urinate—but every sense was keyed to the surroundings. If the police were in ambush they'd be on top of the garage. To cut off escape they'd certainly be waiting behind the theater's emergency exits.

"Fuck it," I said. "If you're there let's get the shit down." I walked forward and turned through the gate, pausing not to see if anyone was there but to adjust my eyes. Joy swelled through me. The jewels and M16 were still there; if the police had found the stash they'd know I was coming back. I pissed against the fence, uncocked the revolver, and returned it to a pocket.

Heedless of the sound or the mess, I turned the box on its side. A dog yipped in another yard. I grabbed the bag, opened it, stuffed in my coat and the Browning. I had no way to hide the M16. "Fuck that, too," I said, thinking that I'd carry it next to the bag to partially disguise what it was. If I moved quickly into the car and put it on the floorboards the children might not see it. One thing was certain: I wasn't going to leave it. I'd rather have left half the diamonds.

I waited in the gate until I saw the car pull up, then hurried forward. As I went around the rear of the automobile to the driver's seat, I kept the sack and rifle down low in one hand, and shoved them to the floor as I slid behind the wheel. Allison and Mary saw what I'd done, but the children didn't know what they saw.

"That wasn't long, was it?"

Nobody answered.

"There's a good drive-in on Crenshaw and Wilshire. Anybody for a hamburger?"

"No," Mary said. "Take us home."

"Mom! I'm hungry," Joey said.

"I'll fix you something."

"That isn't the same thing."

"Be quiet."

"Gee, Mom . . ."

"Don't argue with Mother," Lisa said.

Joe flopped back, sulking, arms folded over his chest.

I turned south toward the Santa Monica Freeway.

3

NOBODY said a word during the drive back to El Monte. Mary and Allison seethed, and Joey pouted at his mother. Between my feet the bag swayed with the motion of the car, a rustling sound, gold and diamonds caressing each other. The freeway went through the downtown civic center. Among the tall buildings was the Hall of Justice, its top floors housing the old county jail. The lights up there shone out dimly from being filtered through steel bars and mesh wire. I recalled that from up there Los Angeles looked like a smoky and sullen bed of hot coals.

When the headlights swung across the driveway and sprayed the bungalow, I told Joey and Lisa to go inside, that I wanted to talk to their mother for a minute. They ducked into the bungalow, the lights inside flashing on.

"What'd you do, Max?" Mary asked, holding tight rein on her anger.

"I picked up something that I had stashed."

"Why'd you take us with you? It was a plan all along."

"I thought the fuzz might be looking for me in the neighborhood. They think I chilled a cop this afternoon. It's on the news."

"Oh God!" Mary gasped; then said nothing more for a long time. Finally, "What shall I tell the kids? They'll hear about it tomorrow. Probably the police will be here."

"I don't know what you should tell them. That's up to you."

"It's not your problem, right?"

"I've got worse problems. I can't think about anybody but myself."

"What would've happened if the police had been back there?"

"They weren't."

"What if . . . ?"

"You know what would've happened."

"You're a bastard, Max." Again she was silent, thinking. "I don't know what to do. I don't want to call the police, but what are they going to do when they question Joey and Lisa and find out the truth?"

"Do whatever you think is best. If I were you, I'd wait until ten or eleven tomorrow morning and call them. Tell them you just found out I was wanted and tell what happened. It won't make things any worse for me." I took the wad of money from Allison's handbag, opened the car door for light, and counted out five hundred dollars. "Take it and forget where you got it."

"I'll take it because we need it, but it doesn't make right what you did."

"It helps my conscience."

"Conscience!"

"We've got to split, Mary. I'll probably never see you again—but I want you to know that I'm sorry, for whatever it's worth."

Mary left the car, closed the door, and leaned in the window. "I still like you," she said. "I don't know what else to say." Then to Allison, "Look after him."

Ten minutes later, when we were back on the freeway, Allison spoke for the first time in half an hour. "You're the dirtiest sonofabitch I ever met. Using those children . . ."

"Hard times make hard people. I've told you that before."

At the top of the Southland news . . . law enforcement authorities are continuing the search for Maxwell Dembo, an ex-convict wanted as a suspect in the murder of a Beverly Hills police officer during a daring daylight robbery of a jewel firm. Also slain during the holdup was Gerald Francis Shue, one of the holdup men. Captured at the scene was Aaron Billings. The loot, an estimated five hundred thousand dollars in diamonds, has not been recovered . . .

"Nothing new," I said. We were on the Long Beach Freeway, swinging onto the Santa Ana. As long as we broke no traffic laws the freeways were safe. Similarly, the seven million population of greater Los Angeles was large enough to get lost in temporarily, until I changed my appearance and got another automobile. The fifty-mile sprawl of the megalopolis was useful to a fugitive. The hunt would center in Hollywood, downtown Los Angeles, and the northwestern suburbs. As long as I stayed away from those areas it was practically like leaving the state. Tomorrow, after questioning Mary and her children, the police would have a description of the automobile and Allison, but they wouldn't have her name or a photograph. Everyone whose name appeared anywhere in my records would be questioned and watched.

Orange County was part of Los Angeles in the sense that a marker was all that separated them. Anyone who missed the sign would never know that he'd crossed from one city to another. The police there would have the call, would be quickly getting mug photos, but they would never really be expecting me. Hundreds of motels were around Disneyland. I remembered one where the bungalows had carports and separate entrances so nobody would see me slip inside. I'd hide on the floorboards while Allison went into the office.

Before she turned on the bungalow lights, I slipped through the door. I quickly examined each room, peered out the windows at the surroundings, mentally planning possible escape routes. I unlatched two windows and opened them a few inches, making sure they slid easily. A trailer park was behind the motel. It had gravel walks, trees, and manicured shrubbery. From another window I could see the motel's driveway and office. Nobody could sneak in that way if I was watching.

Allison had been bringing our things from the car while I was examining the suite. "You look like an old tomcat prowling around," she said.

"I feel like a cat with kerosene dabbed on his ass."

"We're safe here."

"I'm not safe anywhere."

"You know something, I'm hungry."

I'd been ignoring a dull headache. When she spoke I realized it was from hunger. "Yeah. Even a killer has to eat."

"Don't say that word. It's too depressing."

"I'm trying to get used to a depressing reality. You should do the same." I glanced at my watch. "We passed an all-night market a mile back. Get something to eat—but get back here quick."

"Don't you trust me?"

"If I didn't trust you, you wouldn't be here. But as soon as you're gone more than fifteen or twenty minutes I'll figure something happened to you."

On my directions, Allison turned the lights off as she stepped out of the door, giving the impression that the suite was empty. I watched from a window as she drove away, the taillights flaming momentarily as she braked at the end of the driveway. When she was gone, I kept watching for another ten minutes, meanwhile thinking of things to be done: clean and reload the Browning, check the M16, wrench the diamonds loose from their settings, sort out and repack our belongings, which had been thrown into tangled bundles in our haste to flee the apartment.

Suddenly, I remembered the 1:00 A.M. news on KTTV. It was a few minutes after 1:00.

Newsreel clips of the Vietnam war were on the screen, youthful American officers leading South Vietnamese patrols through knee-deep muddy water in rice paddies. The announcer came on, read the week's casualty figures—theirs and ours—and the number of bombing sorties. The figures were read as if they were football scores.

A commercial for terrazzo patios was next, followed by commercials for a detergent, auto insurance, and the American Cancer

Society. A different newscaster appeared with news of the Southland. The slaying of the police officer and the bandit and the missing five hundred thousand dollars in jewelry was the big news. There were photos of the façade, then the interior, of Gregory's, and a few seconds of film showing the panel truck being towed away, it's front raised in the air; then a longer film of a sheet-covered body being loaded into an ambulance. The account of what had happened within Gregory's was supplemented by brief interviews with the secretary and Neissen. There was a photo of the slain police officer, young, blond, smiling. He'd left a widow and a six-year-old daughter. A grizzled police captain named me as the chief suspect, an ex-convict suspected of several other robberies in recent months. He said they'd known I was operating in the area and had been on the lookout, had spotted "Billings" outside. While he spoke, I recalled Aaron's words, the sequence. They had seen him, turned and sent out an immediate robbery alarm—without questioning him.

The announcer gave my description, flashed a ten-year-old L.A.P.D. mug photo. I scarcely listened. Things were jumping through my mind. They'd known in advance; that meant one thing. Someone had fingered us, someone with partial information. Just one person had any information: Willy Darin.

He'd gotten a hint about "Beverly Hills" when we were in his garage. He'd known a black man was involved. He'd been taken into custody on the nalline test. He'd bartered what he knew for his freedom—probably proved he wasn't bullshitting by giving details of the market robbery. Now it was obvious why he'd gotten out in three days.

It was my fault, too. I'd boasted. So far it had cost Jerry his life; it would certainly cost Aaron the same—and almost equally certain was mine. (At that moment I didn't think of the policeman's life.) And I'd known that Willy was weak; I had seen him display weakness many times, especially when he'd run out on me so long ago.

I recalled the gifts I'd made him, the failures I'd forgiven, the friendship. Memories were fuel to my fury. He had to die. I'd take him somewhere in the wilderness, murder him, and bury the body. The police would know what had happened, but they'd never be able to prove it. Not that it mattered. The old cliché of murderers was true: they could only make me pay for one killing. After killing the policeman all the other killings were free.

Headlights bounced from the walls. I turned off the television and hurried to the window. Allison was turning into the carport. I unlatched the door and waited.

She came in quickly, carrying styrofoam cups of coffee and a white bag stained with grease.

"You did okay," I said.

"The market was closed," she said. "I found a café. There was a policeman there. He looked me over. I don't know if he was giving me the eye or was suspicious."

"Did he say anything?"

"No, he just stared."

"On the way back, did you drive down any dark streets to see if you were being followed?"

She was silent; that was full answer. I checked the Browning and started for the side door.

"Where are you going?" Allison asked.

"To look around."

"Your sandwich'll get cold."

There was no answer to that. I slipped outdoors, hugging the shadows as I moved around the bungalow and through a hole in the bushes to the trailer park. There were neat gravel paths between the rows of mobile homes. I walked casually toward the front. A thick barrier of bushes hid the trailer park from the highway. I ducked in, holding an arm over my face, and found a niche where I could peer out by lying down. The highway was visible for a mile in each direction. A few automobiles went by—even a highway patrol car. I was watching for milk trucks, telephone company trucks, inconspicuous vehicles. That was how they sneaked up to spring a trap. I saw none of these.

I wondered how long I could remain keyed to the paranoia necessary for survival. I'd known three men who'd killed police officers during crimes. Two of the three were killers by nature, unlike murderers, who generally are cowards. These killers were enraged, bitter, vicious. They awaited doom with the fury of wounded tigers, preferring death to capture. They'd been taken without resistance. One of the three had been executed; the other two were awaiting execution, lingering on appeal. I'd wondered how they'd allowed themselves to be taken alive. In my own case I saw a danger that I would arrive at a paralysis of despair through having too vivid an imagination. They hadn't had imaginative natures.

As I lay staring out at the highway, I realized what had happened. The mental preparation to die is not something that can be maintained every moment. One can key oneself up—as in a battle or on a caper—but the visceral readiness to throw life away disappears when one is relaxed or exhausted. I needed to stay mentally ready so they didn't come upon me when I was unprepared for death.

For a few seconds I imagined finding a police station and rushing in with the automatic rifle and cutting loose. I recognized the idea as fantasy while thinking of it. It was suicide and I wanted to live.

Half an hour later I went back to the motel bungalow. Allison had removed her stretch pants and sweater. She was wearing a half slip pulled up over her breasts as a shift. Lace panties peeked out beneath the hem, a provocative ensemble. She was sorting out our belongings on the bed, folding the clothes neatly.

"Where'd you go?" she asked.

"To make sure nobody followed you."

"You had me scared to death. Please tell me when you're doing things . . . what you're doing. I'm with you all the way, but I'm scared to death. The sandwiches are getting cold—they are cold—and the coffee too."

"Okay, I'll try not to scare you after this."

The meal was on the nightstand, set carefully with napkins. She'd also turned down the bed and set out my shaving gear.

"I don't know what I'd do without you," I said. I went up behind her, held her close, pressed my face in her hair. She started to cuddle back. The pistol in my waistband jammed into her hip. "Ouch," she said, and laughed. "That's always between us, isn't it?"

While I finished gulping down the sandwich she finished arranging the clothes. "We must get some luggage," she said.

"Tomorrow . . . Lots of things tomorrow. What's on TV?"

"A terrible movie."

"Turn it on, unless you're sleepy."

"Aren't you kind of . . . blasé or domestic . . . under the circumstances?"

"What else should I do? Rip my clothes and beat my head on the floor?"

"No . . . but . . . it just seems we should be acting differently."

"Look around. There's a machine gun next to the window and a half-a-million in stolen diamonds on the chair—which we aren't even paying attention to. And I've got a pistol on me every moment. You eat and shit and breathe even when you've dusted a copper. Maybe not for very long, but for a while."

"Do you have a chance to get away?"

"Nobody gets away. We all just get postponements."

"That isn't the answer I want."

"I really expect them to find me and kill me. If I last ninety days it'll be a minor miracle."

Allison's brows drew down. "Whatever we have, we'll do the best we can. A dozen times today I've wondered how I got involved. Not doubt . . . not recriminations of you, darling"—she puckered her mouth in a silent kiss to show her feelings—"but to find something wrong in me, some flaw, some evil. I don't feel anything wrong. I know what society says, what they'll do to me for being with you. I feel more righteous in being loyal to you than anything I've ever done. My feelings aren't confused, but there's confusion in how I came to feel this way." She smiled impishly. "Fuck it, huh?"

She made me laugh.

We watched the movie, a Japanese-made saga of giant sea monsters, atom-created mutants rising up to destroy cities. One thing led to another and we made love. It was especially tender and fulfilling, as if precariousness made us more aware of sharing warmth.

Allison went to sleep, but I stayed awake. Although my body was enervated, my mind refused to yield its exaggerated churnings. More than anything, I dwelt on being alive and the feel of life, the sensation of the air-conditioned coolness washing my bare torso, the taste and scent of my cigar, the pulse of heartbeat, the ache of tired muscles, and the endless working of my stomach. Once I stroked Allison's bare shoulder, wanting to feel other life. Life was precious. Life was all that mattered. Yet it meant nothing if you weren't living as you wanted.

There'd been many prison nights when I dwelt on death, trying to conceive it, feel the mystery, and for a solitary moment had imagined nothing, a terrifying moment, a sudden terror that one cannot look at for longer than one can look directly at the sun.

Now I'd killed another human being. He was a symbol of those whom I hated—though in truth I'd met policemen and guards who were decent human beings, whom I'd respected and liked. They were rare, however, individuals whom I thought of separately from those who'd fucked over me year after year. I felt nothing, certainly no remorse, for having killed him—though I didn't think about his wife and child. He'd murdered Jerry, more cold-bloodedly than my killing of him.

Actually, it wasn't unexpected that I'd kill. Many times in my life I'd decided to kill, locked my mind and refused to think of meaning or consequences. Once or twice I'd tried in an explosion of temper, but either there'd been no weapons available or the person got away. I'd never had qualms about killing. My system of values came from the jungle of reform school and prison. I'd never heard anyone denounce killing on moral grounds. Violence was deemed by some to be "uncool" or "stupid", but never evil or wrong.

And tomorrow night I was going to kill Willy Darin, my bosom friend; Willy the Rat. I fell asleep meditating on how to do it.

4

WE woke to knocking. Even while springing from the bed naked, pistol in hand, I realized the police would have crashed through the door without knocking, or surrounded the motel and bellowed from bullhorns. My reflexive action showed that a hunted man learns to sleep like a beast, keyed to escape from it instantly.

The manager was outside. He told Allison through the door that it was almost noon. Coached by my whisper, she replied that she was staying another night.

The noon television news had reduced me to one line; the manhunt throughout Southern California was continuing for the suspected killer of the policeman.

During the rainy afternoon, using pliers borrowed from the motel's office, we wrenched diamonds from their settings. It was like shucking peas, and they became a glittering pile on the bedspread. The mangled gold was thrown on a newspaper, chaff to be buried. I counted them as if they were marbles—400 diamonds and two dozen rubies, emeralds, and pearls. Most of them went into Allison's purse. I took forty small diamonds in an envelope and put them in my pocket. If we were separated, if anything went wrong, I'd have running money—and if they got me they wouldn't get everything back.

We went through the classified ads in a Santa Ana newspaper, checking five-and six-year-old automobiles for sale by private parties. Allison began telephoning. When she was ready to leave, I told her that after she bought the automobile, she was to come back and move our belongings and drive to San Diego and register at the El Cortez hotel, that I would meet her there in the morning.

"Where are you going?" she asked.

"I've got some business."

When she was gone (it was now dusk), I shaved my head in front and top, leaving the sides full. I grayed them and applied tanning lotion to the newly exposed flesh. Now I looked baldheaded. I put on glasses. The changes added twenty years to my appearance.

I took both the Browning and the .32 revolver. The smaller weapon would make less noise. By 10:30 I was driving past Willy's house, the first time quickly, checking the surroundings to see if the house was being watched. The second time I went by slowly, looking at the dwelling. The lights were on. Willy's car was in its usual place in the driveway.

Circling the block, I parked on the street behind Willy's. I crossed through a vacant lot toward Willy's back yard. Ankle-high grass was wet with the rain which had stopped but still threatened. I scrambled over a waist-high, sagging wire fence and stopped beneath a tree. Willy's house was twenty feet away. The night was cold and dark. Clouds blotted out illumination from the sky. Occasionally the sound of a passing vehicle wafted back from the road.

I waited motionless for several minutes, acclimating my senses, shivering with the chill. Doubts flickered to mind. It might seem unlikely that merely a cold night could dissuade a sincere murderer, but I was uncomfortable and nothing but my own decision was forcing me. Who'd know that I'd changed my mind? Who'd blame me? I erased the doubt by remembering Jerry's blood in the dirt, by imagining Aaron in a cell. Willy had caused all of it.

I was waiting for him to come out to the room beside the garage to pick up his outfit. All dope fiends take a fix before going to bed. If he failed to come out, I'd stalk through the back door, throw on the bedroom light, and shoot him down while he was in bed. It would be a gory scene, with Selma screaming, but if it was the only way . . .

275

Waiting in the cold was foolish. I moved along the fence, keeping low to present no silhouette, and ducked into the dark room. The outfit was in the same place. I waited beside a window, watching the back door.

It was after midnight when Willy came out, the sound of the back door slamming shut loud and hollow in the wet stillness. He didn't come toward the room but went around the house to the driveway.

Quickly I went after him. It wasn't until I'd turned the corner and was exposed in the driveway that I thought of the possibility that the house was under surveillance. It was too late to turn back.

Willy heard my footsteps and turned, startled. In the darkness it was impossible to see his face. I had the Browning out, but held low so he couldn't see it.

"Who's that?" he asked, tense, poised between flight and struggle.

"Shh," I said. I hurried forward, wanting to get close to him.

"Max!" His voice was laden with consternation.

"Be quiet," I snapped. "Take it easy. I need help."

The words made him pause. I could see the confusion in his mind. He was thinking that I didn't know what he'd done. It was what I wanted him to think.

"Man, you're burning up. You shouldn't be here."

"Where else can I go for help?"

"Jesus! They were at Mary's for hours this afternoon."

"Did they question you?"

"No, but I've damn sure been expecting 'em."

"I thought they might know we're friends. Come on. Let's get out of here. I don't want your kids around if they show up and there's shooting."

"Man, I don't want to get involved. I'm no gangster. I can't handle this kind of weight."

"Yeah," I said, feigning indignation and hiding my real fury, "you're a friend when I'm throwing the party. You're a jivin' motherfucker."

"For Christ sake, I've got an old lady and crumb snatchers. I'm just a raggedy ass dope fiend."

"Look, asshole, I just want you to go with me to the Salton Sea and dump my car somewhere else. I've got a friend I can hole up with."

"Man, I'm scared shitless."

"I'll give you five bills."

"I'm still scared. You're on the news every fuckin' hour."

"Motherfucker, you're comin' with me, and you're going to drive my car back here and dump it." I raised the pistol.

"Max! Man, don't go crazy. I'll go with you."

"C'mon then."

We started back around the house. "Let me get my outfit. I'll need a geez before I get back."

"Go ahead."

I waited in the doorway while he fished up the outfit, and stayed behind him while he went over the fence. We moved back through the wet weeds to where my car was parked.

"You drive," I said.

"Yeah, but put the fuckin' pistol away, you insane mother—"

As we got in the car his manner lost its edge of panic. Fear was still evident, but it was different in texture. At first it had been terror. Now he was afraid but he believed me unaware of his infamy. This present fear was that my desperation would get him in trouble.

"I'll keep it out in case I need it." I kept the pistol in my lap, leaned casually back against the door—so I could watch him.

For the first few miles he stayed on back roads. It was slower but safer. Nearing the freeway entrance, it was necessary to swing out onto a boulevard and cross a heavily traveled intersection with a traffic light. It was unlikely that Willy knew he was going to his execution, but if he did this was where he would try to save his life. With automobiles and people on the sidewalk, he could dive out and run for it, his last best chance. After that he'd be going too fast. It was what I would try in the same situation. I decided that I'd start shooting if he reached for the door, though I wouldn't chase him if he got any distance. Revenge wasn't worth being killed or captured.

When we came upon the intersection, I began talking, wanting to soothe his fears.

"I got the big one," I said, "but bad luck got me."

"I just hope the shit doesn't go down tonight."

"We'll be all right tonight," I said.

"That was a helluva sting—half a million."

"If I get to spend it."

"Man, too bad you had to waste that cop. And your partners . . . I'm glad they didn't get you."

"It's still early."

"What went wrong?"

"They just ran down on us. Bad luck, like you said."

Willy was quiet, slowing for the traffic as we moved with the traffic toward the light. Just before we came to a halt it turned green and he punched the gas. It made me relax. He signaled and turned up the ramp to the freeway, the car gathering momentum.

"Does that guy know you're coming?"

"Yeah, I called him this afternoon."

"I started to knock the old lady down last night. She knew about the scene before I did. I found out when I got home last night. She was gloating. I was so fuckin' mad—but she's a hateful bitch. I sure talked bad to her." Willy's tone of concern was sincere. He did care for me, and yet he'd fingered me. Something other than malice had made him an informer. It was simple weakness. He was the kind who would feel remorse when he heard what he'd caused—a remorse now forgotten when he believed I was unaware of his perfidy.

The miles flew away, cars became fewer, the lights beyond the fence farther apart. I pretended to listen to the car radio, to songs that reduced life to simplicity. I had stirrings of sorrow for what I was going to do. He was a worthless wretch (but so was I by society's standards), and my killing him would hurt others—Mary, his children,

Selma, though I had no real concern about her. They would never understand the law of my world, which was all I had to live by.

The nascent compassion contained a wish to doubt his guilt. I had no real evidence—except by the process of elimination. Yet that was a fact that could not be reconciled with any other theory: he'd been the only person other than Jerry, Aaron, and myself who'd known. Allison had known nothing. And if Jerry had told Carol, she certainly didn't want anything to happen. The police had known just what Willy knew, nothing more.

I'd kill him. The decision was unwavering—but first I'd make him confess, remove any trace of doubt.

The desert began southeast of Riverside, though the freeway continued. I had no memory of the freeway going this far. I'd counted on a narrow highway, from which a certain side road turned off toward the San Jacinto Mountains. Up the side road was a dirt road and absolute privacy, nothing for miles.

The headlights flashed on a sign: Palm Springs, 25 Miles. I had no idea where we were in relation to the side road, and it was absurd to have him drive around looking for his place to be murdered. He could keep going toward the Salton Sea, for somewhere in the vastness was the right kind of place.

The freeway ended beyond Palm Springs. The automobile followed the broken ribbon of white. A single automobile, lights flashing in our eyes, passed from the other direction. Once we pulled around a diesel truck. All else was emptiness. We hurtled onward too fast for our headlights to pick up unforeseen objects, but there were none. A pregnant full moon gave silver form and shadow to the desolate land's bizarre beauty, highlighted the weird shapes of sagebrush and cactus.

Another problem came to mind. No shovel. And the earth was hard. What if they did find the body? It was better that they didn't, but not so much better as to make a difference. If I hauled him a few hundred yards from the road it would be weeks or months—more than enough time for me to be safely away or caught.

The reflections went on silently. Now I steeled my mind. I opened the glove compartment. Its patch of light was bright in the surrounding darkness.

"Pull over," I said. "I want to check something."

"What if the highway patrol comes by?"

"We haven't seen a car in forty minutes. And we can see one for ten miles. Stop the short. I want to fix this pistol."

"Man, you can do that when we get there."

"Stop the fuckin' short." I jerked the clip from the Browning. It was intended to soothe his fears. He pulled to the side of the road, the car bouncing on the soft shoulder.

"What's wrong with it?" Willy asked.

I switched off the dashboard radio. "The spring in the clip is fucking up."

"You can fix it later."

"I never know when I'll need it. I might have to dust somebody, some jiving motherfucker." I let the words hang, sink in, and at the same time took the cartridges from the clip, one by one. I watched Willy from the corner of my eye. The atmosphere was full of threat. He might jump me now that he saw the unloaded gun. It would confess his guilt. It would also be a massacre. I had an elbow on the doorlatch. As he moved, I'd slide out and bring the .32 from my hip pocket. I could almost smell his fear.

"Fuck it," I said, throwing the unloaded Browning in the glove compartment and slamming it closed. My hidden right hand was on the revolver. "Why'd you put the finger on us?" I asked.

Willy jerked, backed toward the other door, ready to leap out. "Man, what're you saying?"

"I know why, cocksucker. To save your funky ass."

"Man, you're nuts!"

Thoughts and sensations gusted through me, none waiting long enough to be formed. It was important that this scene be a morality play, have meaning. It had to be justice and I had to make it so. Yet there was nothing to say. I pulled the revolver, quickly jammed it against his kneecap and pulled the trigger, the butt snapping back against my hand and the sound in the closed space smacking against my eardrums. The bullet smashed through bone and cartilage and somehow ricocheted up through the window, leaving a hole and tiny cracks as it flew into the night.

Willy screamed, grabbed his knee in both hands, and doubled forward, his face smacking into the steering wheel.

"Rat!" I said. My stomach was queasy, but I forced everything but rage from my mind. It is easier to kill in fury than coldbloodedly.

"Please, Max, please!" he cried, eyes white in the darkness.

Leaping from the car, I rushed around the rear, opened the driver's door and dragged him out by his jacket. He tried to stand, but his shattered kneecap gave away and he crumpled to the road. He chanted, "Oh Jesus . . . Oh Jesus," over and over, as if the void would hear.

The windless night was icy chill. Silence and emptiness were absolute. The headlight beams shone out toward infinity. We might as well have been the only living beings in existence. Momentarily, I started to kill him out of hand, but remembered the confession. If the police could make him talk, so could I. Their lever was freedom; mine was life itself.

I leaned into the car and doused the headlights. Moonglow was enough to give shape and shadow, though colors were reduced to black and silver.

Willy struggled to a sitting position while I was turned, his fractured leg extended to the side in an unnatural curve. He held the sitting posture by a hand spread on the asphalt for a brace. Whimpers beseeching mercy came from his mouth, and garbled protests of his innocence.

"I know you did it," I said. "And you're going to die unless you tell me why . . . unless you give me a reason not to kill you."

"Max! Max! I didn't . . . I love you like my brother. I'm weak . . . but I ain't a rat."

The lies enraged me so I was dizzy with it. My eye caught on the splayed hand he was using for a brace. It was pressed wide and flat. I shot through it—flash, hole, and then the scream as he flopped outstretched, rolling around. I thought the movement was purely from pain, but suddenly he was crawling under the automobile, trying to hide. It was ludicrous—and horrible.

I began to laugh in frenzy. Murder, too, can have comical aspects. I was transcending life by destroying it. I was God the Judge and Executioner. "Peekaboo, I see you," I said to the formless shadow.

"Sweet mother of Jesus, help me. I didn't, Max . . . I didn't."

"Yes you did, Willy boy. Tell the truth."

"I swear on my mother I didn't."

"Don't treat Mom like that. Tell me, make me understand. I want to understand, so I can forgive you. It was because of your boys, and Selma, wasn't it? You didn't want to hurt me but you owed them a responsibility."

"No, Max . . . not me!"

I pulled the trigger, the explosion drowning his words. I fired the bullet into the ground deliberately. "Tell the truth."

Willy's answer was sobs, not tears but the long moans of an animal in agony.

"Are you sorry?"

"I'm sorry, Max! I'm sorry."

"You told them what I told you in the garage, right?"

"Yes . . . yes."

I shot him three times, each one bringing a gasp. In the blackness there was no telling where the bullets went in. He was motionless.

I leaped in the car and eased it forward. When I looked back there was no body. For an awful moment I thought he'd disappeared, or had managed to get off the road into the desert. Then I realized he was still beneath the automobile, clutching at something for refuge. I shot forward, slammed into reverse and spun back, reaching for the headlights. He lay in their beams, trying to crawl away. There was one bullet left in the small revolver. I got out of the car, pressed the muzzle to his head, and blew his skull apart. He died without a whimper, shook for a few seconds and stopped.

I dragged him by the feet (his upper body was too gory) several hundred yards from the road. The desert rolled slightly, hard dry earth with rocks and dry brush. The body left no trail. It was thirty miles to the nearest house. In a few months or years someone would stumble on the skeleton. By then my own fate would have been decided, and I'd probably be as dead as Willy.

My last gesture before leaving was to piss on his body. It was the sacrament a stool pigeon deserved.

5

DAWN in San Diego, misty rain polishing the streets and the sky gray with misery. I abandoned the automobile at the airport. Whenever it was found the authorities would believe I'd fled by airplane—or so I hoped.

A block from the hotel I got out of the taxi and telephoned ahead, waking Allison. She hadn't been out of the room since arriving, but she thought it was safe: the bellhop had tried to flirt with her late in the evening when she sent for a sandwich. "I don't think he'd have been so relaxed if they were waiting for you," she said. "And he'd have to know."

"You're getting pretty perceptive, baby."

Minutes later, after letting me in, she threw her arms around my neck, her eyes wet. "I've been worried sick."

Her emotion washed over me without arousing a response. The horror of the last murder, the imprint of the human head coming apart, was too vivid in memory for anything else to penetrate.

Allison saw the coldness and stepped back. "What's wrong? Did I do something?"

The simple and sincere question touched a chord that tears and hugs missed. With a lump in my throat, I shook my head. "No, you're beautiful. It's just . . . things on my mind and no time. Go back to bed."

"You'd better get some sleep, too."

"I'm too keyed up."

Unable to rest, I spent the day pacing the hotel suite, fighting off the sensation that this was sanctuary. It was merely respite and the moment the situation crystallized I had to move. Moving now would be useless, for I had no plan. I spent hours staring from the window, watching people and vehicles moving despondently through the wetness nine stories below. Neither newspapers nor television news mentioned Allison in describing the manhunt, but I was certain that they knew I was accompanied by a woman. A federal fugitive warrant charging unlawful flight to avoid prosecution for murder had been filed, which brought in the FBI. Nothing unexpected.

In odd moments when I wasn't trying to think of what to do, or when I wasn't thinking of something specific, recollection of the carnage instantly filled the vacuum. I understood why men seek oblivion in alcohol. I saw Jerry writhing in the mud of his blood, the policeman's eyes, Willy's head bouncing on the desert, sightless eyes flashing in the moonlight. The images were sharper than when they happened, for then my sensibilities had been blunted by fear and rage. There was no remorse. I tried to feel that and couldn't. But I felt the kind of nausea one feels seeing the butcher slice the hog's throat.

By nightfall, still bothered by the images, still unable to decide what to do next, I was cursing inwardly. Allison's feelings were hurt by my withdrawal. She was also under the strain of being hunted, and nothing in her background had prepared her for it. Her romantic fantasies were fraying at the edges.

When we went to bed early, for now I was drained of energy, I also had the need for touch and warmth and reached for her. She whimpered and we made love. Afterward, her head resting on my chest, her leg wrapped around mine, her finger dawdled with the hair on my stomach.

"What would happen if you gave yourself up?" she asked.

"If I got to jail alive they'd give me due process of law, and after a few years of getting fat on the row I'd get cyanide socked to me."

"How can they prove it was you? You wore a mask."

"Oh, they'll get witnesses. Aaron might turn over if they offer him his life. Maybe Carol wants revenge. Maybe even Mary. What about her kids? They can testify to that trip. Even you might be on the witness stand. If they can't do it any other way, they might use perjury. They do that too."

"Do you really think I'd turn against you?" She was angry.

"You wouldn't want to . . . but you've never spent a single night in jail, so there's no way to say what you'd do after three months, especially if they offered you immunity on one hand and five years in prison on the other."

"Would you surrender if they agreed not to give you the death penalty?"

"I could've done that before I started shooting." I chucked her under the chin. "I'd accept probation. That's all." Suicide crossed my mind—surrender never.

"But they'll get you, won't they?"

"Yeah, most likely . . . but they won't get you. I don't think they know who you are. I'm sending you home to Kentucky in a few days. You're going to forget you ever saw L.A. If the heat should find you, don't say a fucking thing, not one word. Do what I said before, keep asking for a lawyer. Don't even try to lie. You don't have to prove a thing. They have to prove you helped me, and that you knew."

"Why can't I come with you?"

"Because I'm going to get caught. Anyway, I don't even know where I'm going."

"If you get away will you send for me?"

"Sure, baby." I sugarcoated the lie by gently cupping a bare breast and then kissing the nipple.

"Are we going across the border?"

"At Tijuana! They'll be using my picture for wallpaper there."

"I'm trying to help. I want to help."

"Shhh. Go to sleep."

"I really . . ."

"Shhh."

She was quiet, closed her eyes. Perhaps she slept. I knew my only chance was to escape the continent, reach somewhere still unclaimed by computers. My destination had to be thousands of miles farther than Mexico. How to get wherever I was going was another question. That was what gnawed at me. Still without a plan, I fell into a dreamless sleep.

Allison wakened me, her eyes wide, cheeks pale, mouth quivering with emotion. "They found the man in the desert," she said. The abhorrence in her voice had physical impact. My stomach sagged. I started to ask "What man?" as a reflexive lie to collect my thoughts.

Instead I asked, "Where'd you hear the news?"

"On television. It's over now."

"When was it?"

"They found him yesterday—but they didn't know who he was right away."

It was unbelievable. Nobody would wander from the highway at such a desolate spot—not so soon. Six months was more reasonable than six hours.

Allison sensed my thoughts, or wanted to add to the horror: "The buzzards . . ."

The picture came instantly vivid—the usually solitary scavenger birds gathering from miles, soaring in circles. They flocked that way when something big had died, a cow or a horse. A motorist's curiosity had been aroused.

Allison had moved away from me. Despite my confusion as I digested the revelation, I could feel her loathing toward me. "What else did the news say?"

"That you killed him to get revenge on his wife."

"His wife!" Another revelation, the lightning realization that it was Selma, not Willy, who'd told the police. I saw it now. Willy had gone back in the house, had been gone for several minutes, and he'd confided in his wife, probably in response to her querulous questions. When he was taken in for the nalline testing, it was Selma

287

who'd gone and bargained. "But he confessed," I muttered. It was no balm to conscience. I'd forced the confession, a false confession.

"What are you?" Allison whispered huskily. "My God!"

"Dummy up and get off my back," I said. "I've gotta think."

"You must kill without feeling anything, like an animal. You'd just done that when you . . ."

"Shut the fuck up, bitch . . . And get the fuck outta here." Her accusations were meaningless as the flapping wings of a captured dove. When she started to say something else, I snarled a curse and stood up, raising a hand threateningly. She cowered and kept quiet, then slipped from the room.

Beyond the window the storm had broken and the city was again in the sun, though wind danced with cloud remnants and pools glistened on flat rooftops. The crystalline beauty increased my desperation and rage. Gone were my friends, one wrongly by my own hand. Allison was no longer to be trusted. Behind was the wasteland; ahead lay oblivion. Riotous imagination conjured images of the hunters closing on me, lurking behind automobiles, creeping down the hallway to the suite. The image hypnotized, and if I wallowed in fear too long I'd be unable to act. I felt helpless and lonely.

Pacing the room, I shook off the moribund mood, brought my thoughts back to pragmatic thoughts of what to do and what the situation was, on how to make the odds better that I'd live a little longer.

The body would tell them I'd been in the desert, and San Diego was a logical place to search for me. Soon they'd find the automobile, and though they'd speculate that I'd flown out of town, they'd be diligent in checking motels and hotels. They might be in the lobby now.

Mexico was out of the question. There'd be someone at the border stations doing nothing else but watching for me. Highways east crossed the desert, highways so empty that an automobile stood out like a cockroach on a porcelain bathtub. West was the Pacific

Ocean. The only way to go was north along the coast toward Los Angeles, which would have me going back toward where I'd fled from, running in circles. I disliked it but had no choice. The highway along the coast had towns every few miles, and beach houses between them. It was heavily traveled. The evening rush hour was the time to leave.

What about Allison? She was in the bathroom. I could hear the shower running. Her attitude was understandable. The veil had been torn from her eyes. She'd created an image of me instead of seeing the truth. It wasn't my fault. I hadn't confided in her, but I hadn't lied and deceived her either. The buzzards eating Willy had rudely given her a new perspective. Now she saw me as an unmitigated monster.

My attitude toward her had changed the moment hers toward me had changed. Was she a threat? Was she thinking of doing the "decent" thing? Suddenly, as if a knife was plunged through my brain, I saw that in the background of my speculations I was considering another murder. Revulsion came up. Killing her if she was really against me was a matter of survival, but to kill her because she might be against me was a madman's action. To do that would be to lose respect for myself in my own eyes. She wasn't overjoyed about murder, but I couldn't expect her to reach my view where killing was easy.

Danger or not, ally or captive, she was a handicap—and she had to go with me. I couldn't leave her behind. How long could I keep someone untrustworthy near me?

I began preparations to leave the hotel.

Speeding up the coast highway through orange dusk and heavy traffic, the thought came that my whole life was spent either being locked in a tiny cell or rushing headlong to nowhere.

Allison refused to speak except in monosyllables, so the ride was silent. It was just as well, for I had nothing to say that she could possibly understand—or accept. What sustained me in my own eyes could be understood only by another criminal. She did notice that I was watching her closely when we walked out to the car. She knew she was as much a captive as an accomplice.

By 9:00 P.M. the car was speeding through Santa Ana. Downtown Los Angeles was fifteen minutes away. The hourly bulletin on the manhunt changed. The search was now concentrated in San Diego and Tijuana, and the Mexican authorities were cooperating. No mention was made of the abandoned car, but it was unnecessary. I knew they'd found it. I grinned, knowing I'd made the right move at the right moment and could call my enemies fools. Allison understood my smile.

"They can make a thousand goofs," she said. "You can't make one."

"I thought you wanted me to get away."

She shrugged apathetically, curled her legs beneath her, rested her head on the doorframe and closed her eyes.

Energized by forty grains of benzedrine, I was alert, keyed up. We swung through the interchange ramps and turned east toward U.S. 66. By dawn, if nothing went wrong, we'd be out of California. As long as I closed my mind to anything but driving and the sensation of speed and power I felt actually good, full of a drug-induced glow. I didn't think of destination. Speed and distance were all that mattered now. If I got a thousand miles from California I could look at the chessboard and make a decision.

Dawn, Flagstaff, Arizona, and the need for gas all arrived about the same time. The sky was overcast. The desert's flamboyant colors were dulled to pewter. It was cold as a refrigerator. Nipping tendrils of icy air seeped through cracks and struggled with the heater.

Allison was still silent, arms folded across her chest, and hands tucked into armpits. Her face was puffed from the uncomfortable sleep. A crease of red was along her right cheek from the doorframe. Her clothes—stretch pants and rough sweater, chosen for hard wear—still looked presentable. I wanted her to put on makeup.

The way she looked might arouse curious glances somewhere along the line.

"I'm stopping for gas. Go to the women's room and fix yourself up."

"Yes, Lord."

"You can get an asskicking, if that's what you want—and you're asking for it with that sarcasm. You bought a hand in this. I tried to run you off. Now keep your mouth shut . . . or at least off me."

"You didn't used to talk like that."

"Times change . . . People change."

She flushed and was silent.

A gas station appeared and I swerved into its driveway too swiftly, tires skidding. It was an old station, yellow and faded orange, gravel worn to ruts around the pumps. A huge pile of used tires was along a fence and there was an overflowing garage with a stepdown pit rather than a hydraulic lift. I'd turned into it without looking it over. I slipped the safety off the Browning and moved it from the seat to my waistband, zipping my windbreaker over the butt.

The man who came from the office, carefully shutting the door to preserve the warmth, was a caricature of a cowboy. He wore faded jeans, an old sheepskin coat, worn cowboy boots. The lean six-and-a-half-foot figure was topped by a wide-brimmed Stetson dappled with sweatstains. He was in his forties.

The freezing cold hit me as I got out. My breath turned to vapor.

"Fill up?" the man asked.

"Yeah . . . and check everything. We've got a long haul."

"Comin' from Californy ya'll be needin' anta freeze."

"Put it in. Where's your restrooms? My wife needs to freshen up."

"'Roun' thar. Man's side is kinda raunchy. If ya'll gotta loose your bladder better wait'n use the lady's."

While the cowboy pumped gas, I got Allison from the car. "Go round back and straighten yourself up."

She gathered her cosmetic case. "Aren't you coming to watch me? Make sure I don't run away?"

"You'll have to run across an open field. It's a hundred yards. I can blow a hole in your ass."

"You'd do it, too, wouldn't you?"

Shaking my head in disgust, I waved her away. As she went behind the building, the cowboy, who was bent over the open hood, glanced over his shoulder at her swaying backside in the tight pants. It did look good—but I was thinking of kicking her in it. She'd turned into a quarrelsome bitch.

"Dry as a bone," the cowboy said, waving the dip stick.

"Shit! Just had an oil change yesterday."

"Damn sure dry now." He kneeled and peered beneath the car; then crooked a finger. I squatted and looked. Oil was dripping to the ground slowly but steadily. The underframe was coated with it.

"Looks like a broke seal."

"I can't wait to get it fixed."

"Looks like you're throwin' a quart ever' hunnerd or so. Ya'll might take a case of cheap stuff and pour in a quart ever' so often. At'll get ya where yar goin'."

"Good idea. Put it in the back seat."

He poured the antifreeze and got the oil. Allison had bought a lemon. I stamped my feet and watched the building for her, vaguely worried that she might try to sneak away. If she did—and went to the authorities—I'd be trapped in open desert.

"Boy, you're lucky," the cowboy said, cocking his Stetson for emphasis. He was squatted beside the left rear wheel, pointing a finger at a bulge the width of a fist. "Bad retread," he said. "Ready to blow out any second. Got a spare?"

The spare was in the trunk, and beside it was the M16. "I got one but I'd rather have a new tire on that wheel. How long will it take?"

"Fifteen, twenty minutes if ah don't get customers. Ah ain't figurin' on none this time a mornin'."

"Okay."

"Recap or new?"

"Recap. I'm not keeping this lemon very long."

The cowboy wheeled forth an axle jack and raised the car. Allison came back while he was working. She stood shivering. He was fitting the wheel back on the car when he asked: "Ya'll from 'roun' here? Seems ah seen you afore."

"I used to push a rig through here, stop for gas and eats."

"Naw, ah jus' came to work here. Been in the service?"

"No." I decided to go on the offensive. "When were you in?"

"Korea."

"Where were you stationed in the States?"

"Fort Benning . . . Fort Ord."

"When you were in Ord, did you go to 'Frisco?"

"Hell yes! Ain' nowhere else to go."

"What bars you water at?"

"Buccaneer, mostly."

"Hell, that's it. I was tendin' bar there. I remember you now. In there every payday. Big as you are, how could I forget?"

"Damn small world." He grinned as if he'd found a buddy.

Ten minutes later we were back on the highway. Miles and hours rolled away. The threatened storm fell behind and the sun was a fiery disc thrown against a white sky. Allison remained quiet. Despite the fresh makeup, the burning daylight showed the effects on her face of recent days—hollow cheeks, lines where dimples should have been. Her hand trembled when she reached for the cigarette lighter. Gone was open loathing and anger; now the silence was from exhaustion.

As dusk approached, we were in New Mexico. Billboards proclaiming Albuquerque's countless motels sprang up. The city was an hour away.

Dusk came to the eroded land with unbelievable color, the lowlands turning oily purple, the mesas a blackish-green at their base, but their summits glinted burning pink, vermilion, and gold. An awesome, sudden change to darkness. And with the darkness came a chill wind. The benzedrine was going out of me and exhaustion was rising. I'd been twenty-four hours behind the wheel.

We ate boxed chicken and French fries while seeking a motel. I selected one that was older, less occupied. When the door was locked behind us, Allison sank to the bed without undressing, legs drawn high and hands thrust between them. She was like a captive who has lost the will to resist and has surrendered to despair. She waited for me to direct her. I told her to go to bed. She did what she was told, letting her clothes fall unheeded to the floor.

I shaved the fuzz and renewed my false baldness with lotion and watched the 10:00 P.M. news. The killings received no mention in New Mexico. While getting ready for bed, I looked at Allison asleep and knew how to get rid of her without killing her. It would have to wait until tomorrow night. This was the wrong place.

6

IT was noon when we finished breakfast and turned back onto the endless highway. Allison was quiet and submissive, though not from fear. Nobody can remain enraged or terrified for very long. Allison was drained of the adrenalin needed for these feelings, and when I opened the restaurant door she gave me a wan smile—but sincere. None of this meant that the chasm in our relationship was bridged. We both knew without further words that whatever had been was no longer, and could never be anymore. We'd become strangers, but strangers without hostility for each other.

And the car raced across the flat plains of the Texas and Oklahoma Panhandle, dripping oil, so that every half hour I stopped and poured in another quart. The utter flatness of the land was broken only by sagebrush and an occasional gas station with café annexed, pulsing neon on a gray day in nowhere.

The turning wheels and growing distance from the crimes reduced the gut fear that pervaded me. They say time will heal, but distance is also a balm. I hadn't recognized how complete the fear was, for it mostly remained below the threshold of consciousness, erupting at odd moments.

That night, in Tulsa, Oklahoma, we checked into another motel. I waited until Allison was asleep and then brought her clothes in from the car without waking her. I left eight hundred dollars and a dozen diamonds and a note:

Everything comes to an end. The time has come, girl, for us to go separate ways. I hope someday you'll think more kindly of me than you do now—but then everyone wants to be thought of kindly. Whatever I am, I tried to be right with you. Think about it.

Do whatever you feel is right.

Max.

Minutes later I was following the white dashes on the highway. Within the hour flurries of light snow driven by gusty wind appeared in the headlights. I could feel wind tugging the steering wheel, and the highway was snaking through the Ozarks. I'd planned to push through to Chicago, but the radio warned that the storm would be severe, and so I pulled into Joplin, Missouri, checking into a second-rate hotel over a bowling alley. The room was twin to my first residence on leaving prison, including chipped enamel on the dresser and a window facing a brick wall. A steam radiator thunked and clanked but fulfilled its duties, while outside there was a blizzard.

In the small bowling alley, where a single game was in progress, I telephoned back to the motel where I'd left Allison. She'd left in a taxi an hour earlier.

I went back upstairs to wait out the storm, deciding that if she'd taken a taxi it was unlikely she'd have gone to the police. The normal move would be to call them, and they'd have come for her. Actually, she'd be more likely to contact them after she'd reached home. She might confide in her family—and wild horses wouldn't keep them from contacting the police.

For me, for now, all I could do was stay in the room. I had no chains for the car, nor even clothes suitable for the freezing temperatures. I took twenty large diamonds, divided them into four batches, and put them into toy balloons, tying off the ends. These I slipped up my rectum, a valuable suppository. If anything happened, I'd have them with me no matter what.

The next day the storm abated somewhat, though not enough

to travel. I bought fur-lined gloves and a mackinaw and a cap with ear flaps. Around the corner from the hotel was a Mom and Pop café. Beyond its vapor-fogged window moved shapes of persons and the aura of warmth. I went in as much for these things as from hunger. I wanted to be around people, and yet when I sat down, watching and listening (there were only a few, and they knew each other), my sense of aloneness swelled. Their warmth failed to warm me. I missed Allison intensely. I wished I'd kept her with me—even being hated is better than being lonely.

But I shook off the longing, and by the time I stepped outside into the icy afternoon I had the stoicism of accepted hopelessness, even glorying in it. The wind was needles against my cheeks, and I thrust my hands deep in the mackinaw, one clutching the pistol, my magic wand. The hunger for chaos, for my life as it was, swelled to swallow loneliness. I walked the dismal street aware of my freedom, a leopard among domesticated housecats. I felt contempt for the hunched, bundled creatures, all gray and colorless, hurrying desperately toward warmth and safety.

Two days later the snowplows cleared the roads and I took to the highway, having stolen another set of license plates for the car. The countryside was coated white, spotted with the barren skeletons of trees.

Memory of Chicago is more an impressionist watercolor, all blurred detail and color, than the clear image of a photograph. The city's tangle of red, green, and silver neon on wet streets was brilliance daubed on bleakness. In the day the winter light made a glare and wind shivered the sooty slush of melted snow. Chicago was cold and dirty.

The room I rented was in a neighborhood of blue movies, pawn shops, and honky tonks, a high risk area for a fugitive, but it was where the city's underworld surfaced and was visible—street hustlers, hookers, con men, boot and shoe junkies. Lines connected this milieu, the lowest stratum of criminal, with all the others. I claimed to be a bail jumper from San Francisco trying to get a passport. The money I spread around (and my criminal argot) overcame suspicion—but after three days it became evident that passports weren't on the underworld market. It was just that nobody ever wanted one. In time, no doubt, something could be set up. I couldn't wait. A black pimp told me that I might have better luck in New York, something I'd already decided. If nothing else, New York was closer to the ocean I wished to cross. I might even find a foreign ship's captain who'd carry me without a passport—if the money was right. And in New York I could probably sell off a few diamonds.

On the outskirts of Chicago, I stopped for a hitchhiker, a young man in fringed buckskin pants, brogans, and army surplus overcoat. He had a sleeping bag on his shoulder, long hair, a downy beard, and a funny round hat (an Indian hat?) with a feather in it. Actually, when I pulled over for him, I thought it was an old man, not recognizing that he was about twenty years old until he was in the car.

At first he was quiet, nervous, and unduly respectful, adding "sir" and such when he did speak. But there were also words and phrases common to the drug idiom. On a humorous and actually imprudent whim, I nonchalantly took out a joint of marijuana and began uncapping the twisted end with a thumbnail. The young man's eyes went wide in amazement. He actually blinked and shook his head, as if clearing his vision. I busted out laughing.

"Here . . . fire this up," I said, handing him the joint.

He still disbelieved until he lighted the cigarette and inhaled the smoke. "Wow, man, you're a groovy old dude," he said, sucking and gulping again.

Old! I'll be a motherfucker . . . Then I remembered the bald head, the eyeglasses—and I had to laugh again.

By the time we reached South Bend, Indiana, we were both bent, full of weed and pills. The youth's reserve was demolished. Problems were gnawing at him, and it is easy to pour out problems to the ear of a sympathetic stranger, someone who will never be seen again. He was running from the draft, not because he was afraid to fight but because he believed the war was senseless, wrong, certainly not a cause worth the risking of his life. He was on his way to Canada where organizations for draft dodgers were coming into existence. He'd never return to the United States, and if things got bad in Canada he could get a Canadian passport and go somewhere else. I began questioning him about how. In Montreal, he said, it was the easiest thing in the world to get a passport. Canadian regulations made it as simple as going to the supermarket—even under another name. When I pressed for details (veiling the intensity of interest), he was unable to give them, but he was certain that it was as easy as he said. A friend who'd gotten a Canadian passport said so.

The hitchhiker got off in Toledo, to lay over with a maiden aunt until he got in touch with friends in Canada.

I stayed on the superhighway heading toward the state of New York, but not toward New York City. The young man's information was vague, but it was something. My road atlas was marked with the route to Niagara Falls, for I felt the safest way to cross the border was among a crowd of tourists. Undoubtedly there were safer places, but I was from California and didn't know them. Nor was it something I could ask: "Hey, buddy, the police are looking for me and I want to know the safest way to leave the country."

I would store the car for a month—long enough so it would go undiscovered until I was long gone over the sea or at a dead end.

Montreal occupies an island on the St Lawrence River, a fact that surprised me when I arrived. Montreal in late November is also unbelievably cold. By comparison, Chicago in winter is the Bahamas.

In Chicago the circumstances had demanded boldness. Hope of getting a passport had been concentrated in the underworld, forcing me into an underworld neighborhood. Montreal was different, and I moved with paranoid caution, entirely avoiding any tenderloin areas, never going out after dark, keeping the pistol with me every moment, though this was as much to force them to kill (if they came) as for me to kill anyone else.

For two days I lived in a good hotel—vast and gleaming new—on the Place Bonaventure, then rented a room in a French district on the eastern part of the island. The couple, though born and raised in Canada, had a mellifluous fleck of French accent, and everyone was bilingual. The woman was gone when I knocked on the door, holding the classified ad in hand, and the man was obviously ill: his clothes were hanging on his emaciated frame, his hair was gone at the side—which was from cobalt treatment of Hodgkin's disease, I later learned. The room they wanted to rent had been added to the house for their son, now married. The wife had gone to work at the onset of his sickness, and they needed money. I looked at the room—big and well-furnished—and took it immediately, sensing that with such problems as they had this family would not be snoopy or curious. I was right. The woman came to see me that night—she told me about the sickness—but after that we scarcely saw one another. The room had a private walk and entrance, and the sub-zero weather foreclosed backyard conversations. We sometimes passed each other on the sidewalk, nodding courteously, and once rode the bus together. Sometimes the sound of their television came through the wall. I was more than content to be ignored. I rented a portable television (watching only football games) and bought many books to pass the evenings: the perfect tenant, quiet, no visitors, stable in my habits.

Every morning I took the bus downtown, as if going to work. I spent two days in the library, studying Canadian laws. They proved my hitchhiker right; Canada had such liberal passport laws that the United States, by comparison, was Auschwitz.

I needed an identity to borrow—a Canadian citizen unlikely to want a passport. From the city's records I copied several dozen names with birthdates near my own and checked these names in the telephone directory, for most persons spend their lives near where they were born, even in the age of mobility. I began making telephone calls, passing myself off as part of a survey team. Almost everyone answered readily about Vietnam, trade relations with Communist China, the United Nations—and background information.

To get a passport there was no need even to show a birth certificate. All I needed was someone to swear that they knew me. By the end of the first week in December, I cleaned up a wino, gave him strength with bourbon and benzedrine (slipped surreptitiously into his coffee), and he went with me to a notary. He swore that I was Ronald Lynn St Clair, born 12th April, 1934, in the city of Montreal. I swore to the same statement. It was all I needed for the passport office. When I finished with the forms and handed over the passport photos, the girl assured me with a smile that it would be in the mail by Christmas.

While concentrating on the passport, as while scheming on a robbery, other concerns were shouldered aside. Sometimes they swarmed up into awareness, a flash of horror—though never remorse—but subsided when I worked on here and now.

When the waiting began, especially in night's solitude, a galaxy of ugly memories spun through my mind—Jerry on the ground, the pistol jumping in my hand as the policeman fell, Carol's bitter warnings, Mary with the boys, Willy with his sons. He hadn't been much, but they'd adored him. I could imagine Aaron in the jail cell, and going to court draped in chains, a choke collar around his neck. I saw the twining thread of my responsibility in all of these things—and still I could feel no remorse.

The Los Angeles newspapers no longer mentioned the murders and hunt. Aaron's court appearances were recounted in short paragraphs on inside pages. It would still be months until the actual trial began.

Every morning I went downtown on a bus, maintaining the pretense of a job. I went to movies and sometimes wandered the docks in the gray days, watching the motionless ships at anchor, for during the winter the harbor was closed. Now and then I sat in the library, losing myself in a book.

The color of Christmas season blossomed. Suddenly the city was decked in cotton, tinsel, colored lights on silver trees in department store windows, and in the front windows of houses. Crowds grew, the mood of Christmas growing in them. When they bumped into each other, they smiled and excused themselves instead of staring angrily.

On Christmas Eve, the wife knocked on my door and invited me to Christmas dinner with them; their son and his wife and their grandchild would be there. She'd noticed, please excuse her, that I had no visitors or mail. I declined, told a lie that I was going to a friend's for Christmas dinner. I didn't want to be close to anyone, despite my loneliness—and I didn't want to see the death in her husband's eyes, for it would remind me of my predicament.

So on Christmas morning, to maintain the lie, I went downtown. On Christmas Eve the streets had been full of people. Now they were empty. Humanity had gathered into families. From a Salvation Army rescue mission came the voices of derelicts raised in song. They, too, had gathered together. I wanted to go in, merely to be among people, but my clothes were too nice, marking me as an outsider.

Knowing it was taking a foolish risk, I entered a hotel lobby, found a telephone booth, and called Allison. Her mother called her to the phone, not asking who was on the line. I could hear Allison approaching. "Who is it, mother?"

"I have no idea."

The receiver was picked up. "Hello." The familiar voice wrenched at me.

"Hi, baby!"

"Max!" A gasp; a pause. "Where are you?"

"Long ago and far away. Anybody been there?" I asked the question, though I knew from her mother's casual manner that nobody had.

"Not yet. I expect them every day. Every time a car pulls down the street. You didn't have to sneak away from me."

"I thought I did . . . then, anyway. How've you been?"

"Fine . . . I feel . . . well, I always despised this place. Now I'm grateful for the peace. I don't miss the bright lights at all. And you gave me enough excitement for a lifetime."

"I miss you."

Another pause. "Do you, really? It's hard to think you'd really miss anyone."

"I'm leaving the country in a few days. If I find a safe place and send for you, will you come?"

"I . . . I don't think so. Not now. What I was living wasn't really me."

"Okay . . . but don't decide now . . . think about it." I despised the plaintive twang that crept into my voice and stopped speaking.

"Max, I feel like I woke up from a dream. I'm not sure if it was wonderful or a nightmare. I have to sort out my life. I wanted to go anywhere with you, 'one brief hour of madness and joy.' I read that line by Whitman the other day. He says that should be enough. It was all I wanted. Now . . ." She stopped for a moment, changed her thoughts. "I don't judge you, or condemn you—but I don't understand you, either." Again she was silent, her thoughts going beyond her articulateness. Across the hundreds of miles of telephone line we both knew it was over between us. I'd already known it, but being alone in a strange city on Christmas day had made me reach out.

"How's your boy?" I asked.

"Wonderful. I feel guilty for having left him alone."

"Do you need money?"

"No, I haven't even sold any of the diamonds. They're buried under the house. I'm working, too, in the only lawyer's office in town."

"Okay. Look, I might call you in six months or a year. If . . ."

"Oh, Max! We could've been happy. I could've made you happy. If only . . ."

"If nothing . . . It comes down to if I was someone else."

She had no answer.

"Don't forget me," I said.

"Don't be ridiculous," she laughed—but it was nearly tears.

"Merry Christmas."

"Merry Christmas."

"Goodbye, Baby."

"Goodbye, Max."

The passport arrived on the morning of New Year's Eve. Until that moment I really expected the police. My fingers trembled as I looked at it and carefully put it back in the envelope. My ticket to freedom.

Using the landlord's automobile, I drove off the island and found a lonely stretch of woods beyond the suburbs. The M16 was packed in grease, wrapped in many layers of rubber and plastic, and buried inside a steel box. The chances that I'd return for it were almost nil, but I neither wanted to destroy it nor discard it. I'd already sold a few diamonds, enough so I could send a thousand dollars to Aaron's mother and the same to Carol. Later I would send them several thousand apiece, but I'd taken a risk selling any of the diamonds in North America.

The travel agency rushed through my reservation to a flight to Lisbon, via London. On New Year's day I walked aboard a silver airliner, greeted by the warm smile of a young stewardess. It was really quite simple.

Epilogue

Four years have passed since the buzzards eating Willy's body raised outcry to frenzy. The newspapers long ago stopped the story, though it was resurrected for a few days when an outgoing governor of California commuted Aaron's death sentence to life without possibility of parole.

I remain free. One may intellectually accept the idea that a murderer might escape justice, but viscerally (down there where faith resides) it is hard. Even the murderer finds it difficult, though history shows a plethora of unpunished murderers.

Until the airliner was high over the Atlantic Ocean I believed that man's vengeance would get me, that I'd die in police gunfire, by cyanide gas or in prison. It was a deeper belief than realistic appraisal of the odds against me, awesome as they were. It was as if at the inner core I'd believed that something higher than man assured my capture. My highest hope was to finish the game without flinching at the ultimate moment.

But four years have assured me that there is no reason above man that will help him. And there is no vengeance except man's.

For a year I wandered Western Europe and the Middle East, seeing the falling-down edifices of history. Now I have a house I've leased on a ledge beside an ocean cove. By American standards the house is small and uncomfortable, though exquisite in setting. Four rooms and no toilet, so it's chamber pot or out-house, depending on the hour, the temperature, and the need. It's no inconvenience;

too many prison cells have only a hole in the floor. I do have electricity and hot water, at least most of the time—provided by a generator left by the German Army two and a half decades ago. I have transoceanic radio, but there's no need for a television set, the nearest station is two hundred miles away. The floor is clay, hard as concrete. Thick, whitewashed walls sparkle in the sunlight, hold out summer heat and winter cold, though the seasons here are gentle. Twelve steps hewn into the ledge go down to the cove's protected beach of egg-sized rocks worn smooth by the water.

Overlooking the cove and the sea beyond are louvered windows. The view is panoramic. I frequently watch the sea's moods. Its depths are usually transparent as a fishbowl, and it lies motionless beyond any simile for stillness, as if the sea itself is sleeping in the sun. Sometimes a warm breeze stirs it awake and billowing waves roll over one another in a race to shore, white foam bursting like laughter as they pause on the beach before turning back. Occasionally the sea is angered by winter's nipping wind and it gnashes white teeth, writhes, becomes black in the face, and furiously backhands the shore.

When the infrequent storms are over, I walk the shoreline, for curious things are cast up; a strikingly formed piece of driftwood for the mantel, amethyst-colored shells torn from their beds, seaweed molded into arabesques of blackish-green, an injured seagull crying raucously to others overhead, who are frightened by the cry and circle endlessly without landing.

The surrounding country, except for a line that follows the jagged coast, is sparsely populated. Fresh water is short, the land mountainous and barren except for a scrub forest of pine. The sea gives life to the country.

My life is not that of a recluse. Boats are often in the cove, and children come to skip stones along the smooth water. Beyond the ridge a paved highway follows the coastline to towns and villages every few miles. In the nearest town, which I visit several times a week, several persons speak some English, and I've learned enough of the local language to be understood, albeit with smiles.

I'm as safe as I'll ever be anywhere in the world. When I arrived here with money and false credentials, it was the end of the rainbow, the faraway place in the sun that is one of the dreams of everyone. It was all I wanted for the rest of my life—simplicity, a seashore, peace.

Peace became boring and lonely. So I began this memoir, which became grinding labor, especially when it fell short of absolute truth. The lack is not through deceit, but because truth is difficult. Fools think truth is a simple thing, but I've found that it is hard. The facts I've written are real, but facts and truth are cousins, not brothers. I've imposed a rationality rather than exposed truth. Being alone, reading voraciously, writing this memoir, I've done a lot of thinking, and I believe the constant, underlying thought of all men who think must be of their own death, no matter what the surface thought might be. When they think of living, they are also thinking of death, for the two are mingled.

And thinking is a curse.

I'm leaving this idyllic place. After selling the diamonds and sending ten thousand dollars to both Aaron's mother and Carol, I had a hundred and seventy thousand left—and a tenth of that remains. I'm also tired of peace, but the shortage of funds gives me an excuse. My stomach is nervous with anticipation of playing the game again. I'll fly to Mexico City, cross the border at El Paso. They might get me this time.

Fuck it!

To find out more about Eddie Bunker you should read,

Mr Blue:
Memoirs of a Renegade,

his autobiography, but followed here is an article by
Crime Time's Charles Waring, the master of the retro-
spective, on a life like no other . . .

BORN UNDER A BAD SIGN—
THE LIFE OF EDWARD BUNKER

Charles Waring

Inauspicious Beginnings

Despite assurances from scientists about the nature of earthquakes, supernatural beliefs regarding the significance of seismic land-upheavals still persist in some parts of the world. Of course, in ancient times, natural disasters were often perceived as punishment from an angry deity. Although now, in the late twentieth century, we live in the epoch of the global village and at a time when science is regarded as an infallible avatar, superstitious notions are still harboured by many of the world's inhabitants. One such person who didn't accept earthquakes at face value was Edward Bunker's mother, Sarah.

A sense of profound foreboding (call it superstition if you will) affected the troubled mind of this young woman who, during the 1930s, had worked in vaudeville theatre and been a chorus girl in Busby Berkeley's extravagant Hollywood musicals. She sensed some portentous event had occurred at the moment of her son's conception. That was March, 1933, in Southern California. A major earthquake—resulting in fatalities and extensive damage to buildings—terrorised Los Angeles's inhabitants. It also mortified Bunker's parents, who were coupling at the exact moment the first tremors of the earthquake struck. To make matters worse for Bunker, at the time he made his unpropitious entry into the world (at Hollywood's Cedar Of Lebanon Hospital on December 31st, 1933), Los Angeles was in the grip of a torrential downpour of almost Biblical proportions with trees and even houses being swept away by dangerous currents. The alarming synchronicity of both cataclysmic events confirmed in his mother's mind that Edward would be trouble. For her, there was no denying that Bunker Junior was born under a bad sign, and sadly, she instilled this belief into him when he was an impressionable youngster.

Formative Years

Well, for young Edward and his parents, it was not long before the seeds of that pair of bad omens seemed to bear substantial fruit. At the age of two, Edward wandered off from a family picnic in a local park but was eventually located after a search-party of two hundred men had combed the area. Then he accidentally set fire to a neighbour's garage! On the face of it, young Ed may have seemed the toddler from hell but it's more likely that these incidents resulted from his parents' abject lack of supervision rather than any innate inclination on his part to do harm. Indeed, Bunker's abiding memories from this period focus on the deteriorating relationship of his parents, who fought and argued with an intensity that resulted in the police frequently being called out to intervene. Bunker's father, incidentally, Edward Snr, like his wife, worked in Hollywood. Principally he was a stage-hand although occasionally he worked as a grip (a specialised technician who builds film sets). He was almost fifty when his only son, Edward Junior was born. As the marriage became increasingly acrimonious (fuelled in part by alcoholism), so young Ed was left to his own devices.

Fight and Flight

Bunker was only five when his parents' troubled marriage was finally dissolved. A consequence of the divorce proceedings was that he was sent to a boarding/foster home. Profoundly unhappy, he ran away for the first time and found himself roaming the city streets at night. For this, the foster home rejected him and Bunker then went through a succession of draconian institutions which attempted to curb his defiant, rebellious nature with harsh discipline and sadistic, often brutal practices. He attended a military school for a couple of months (where, through peer pressure, he took to theft). He ran way from here, boarded a train and found himself four-hundred miles away in a hobo camp. The authorities were alerted and Bunker was accosted but this chaotic, peripatetic lifestyle persisted throughout his formative years. Shoplifting and the theft of ration coupons eventually landed Bunker in a heap of big trouble and he was sent to an institution known as a Juvenile Hall, a kind of borstal or reform school. Here, Bunker became acquainted with hardened young criminals and quickly realised that if he wanted to survive this experience or at least avoid being somebody's punk (being sodomised) he had to learn the rules of the jungle. Although younger and smaller than most of his fellow inmates, Bunker was smart (his IQ had been estimated at 152), highly literate, streetwise and recalcitrant. He soon became fearless and inured to the dog-eat-dog brutality of the place. After a fight with a fellow inmate, Bunker was sent to a state hospital for observation from which he soon escaped, living rough on the streets. He was caught by the cops after a car he hot-wired crashed. He was then sent to an insane asylum to be assessed and was almost beaten to death by an attendant. Fortunately, Bunker was declared sane, and was allowed to leave with his life just about intact. It was not long before he escaped reform school and was back roughing it on the streets. Three months later, he was apprehended by the cops living in an a old car in someone's backyard. He was then shunted on to the Preston School of Industry which was designated for older teenagers. Bunker was still only fourteen. Eventually, he was paroled to his aunt. By this time his estranged mother had remarried and his father (now sixty-two) languished in a rest home because of premature senility. While with his aunt, Bunker continued to keep bad company and late hours. It was only a matter of time before he fell foul of the law again, this time for an outstanding parole violation. But Bunker's reputation as a troublemaker had catapulted him beyond the remit of California's Youth Authority. Despite his age, he was in the big league now. This time it was serious. This time it was prison.

Crime and Punishment

While most teenagers were still at high school, Edward Bunker was a veteran of California's stern custodial institutions for young offenders. From his earliest days, his life had been hurtling on a relentless trajectory towards a life in crime that would ultimately lead to lengthy incarceration in prison. And that's where he found himself at sixteen years-of-age. But it didn't chasten him one iota. To the proud, hardened Bunker, prison was an underground university of life. He gained the acquaintance of some of America's most notorious criminals and from this experience gleaned knowledge which not only helped him to survive on the inside but inspired schemes and scams when he was back on the outside.

But back on the inside, Bunker was hard and vicious and proud of it. He stabbed a mass murderer in the showers while at L.A.'s notorious County Jail. He was feared and he was respected (some regarded Bunker as a little crazy but in *Mr Blue*, he stated it was a protective mechanism on his part so that people would leave him alone). The last vestiges of civilisation's thin veneer had been scraped away in prison, leaving the inner core of one's being. In prison, men reverted back to animalistic behaviour: the predator and the prey. In spite of his youth, Bunker made it patently clear he was not in the latter category. If anyone messed with him, they'd find themselves either dead or in hospital (in truth, Bunker was not a cold-blooded killer but would not hesitate to ruthlessly defend himself). Furthermore, he knew the consequences of his lifestyle, heedful of the old prison adage "if you do the crime you do the time." It was a simple equation that Bunker understood implicitly and accepted without question.

Hollywood's Helping Hand

During his rampant teenage years, Bunker made an important acquaintance with an affluent fifty-something woman who was to help him change his life. She was Louise Fazenda Wallis, wife of the legendary Hollywood movie producer, Hal B. Wallis, the mogul behind such cinematic classics as *Little Caesar*, *Casablanca* and *Gunfight At The OK Corral*. Louise Wallis had been a movie star herself in the 1920s, a slapstick comedienne starring in some of Max Sennett's riotous silent reels. In the 1950s, when she met Edward Bunker, she was involved in helping out those less fortunate than herself. When Bunker left L.A. County Jail she gave him work. Initially, Bunker was perplexed by Mrs. Wallis's interest in him and was under the impression that her motives were less than honourable: he imagined she might want a teenage gigolo or else wanted to hire him to kill her husband. But Bunker's suspicions were soon allayed by Louise Wallis's warm, ingenuous nature and zany sense of humour. She really did want to help him and gave strong words of encouragement without reproaching him for his past. Bunker was more fortunate than many of his peers in having such a magnanimous benefactress. He spent many pleasurable hours in her company, not only doing chores for her but also lounging in the swimming pool at her mansion. He also met many of that period's celebrities, including the boxer Jack Dempsey, the writers Aldous Huxley and Tennessee Williams and even the media magnate, William Randolph Hearst (the inspiration for Orson Welles' *Citizen Kane*). By this time, Hearst was infirm and wheel-chair bound. Bunker actually was taken to Hearst's palatial residence at San Simeon and was there, dipping in the old man's swimming pool, the day the mogul died.

But apart from his friendship with Louise Wallis, Bunker continued to hang-out with low lifes: pimps, whores, dope-addicts and boosters. He tried heroin and then began selling crudely-harvested marijuana. While out on a delivery a police car pulled up alongside him, indicating him to stop. Bunker drove off but crashed into a car and a mail truck. Apprehended by the law, he was sent to L.A. county jail. Fortunately, Bunker didn't have the proverbial book thrown at him (he was charged with violating parole and put on probation) and ended up at a parole centre from which he escaped, returning to drug-selling. He was eventually caught again and was charged with assault with a deadly weapon. It was 1951 and Bunker was seventeen. The exasperated authorities finally sent him to his destiny: the notorious San Quentin prison.

San Quentin—Blood and Books

At that time, in 1951, seventeen-year-old Edward Bunker had the dubious honour of being San Quentin's youngest ever inmate. While banged up in solitary (aka "the hole"), Bunker could hear the incessant clicking of a typewriter. It came from the cell of death-row inmate, Caryl Chessman. Chessman, known as L.A.'s notorious "red light bandit", had written a thinly-disguised autobiographical novel about prison life called *Cell 2455 Death Row*. Bunker already knew Chessman from an earlier meeting. Chessman sent over to Bunker's cell (via a sympathetic guard) a copy of *Argosy* Magazine in which the first chapter of his book appeared. Bunker was inspired by Chessman's example. He also identified with the writers Cervantes and Dostoyevsky, both of whom had written while incarcerated. Later, Louise Wallis (who kept Bunker on her mailing and visiting list) procured him a typewriter. Learning the fundamental mechanics of writing as he went along, over the course of the next eighteen months Bunker would eventually produce a novel which was smuggled out to Wallis who showed it her friends and declared that although it was unpublishable, Bunker evinced a nascent writing talent. But it would take a further seventeen years before a book of Bunker's reached publication (that book, *No Beast So Fierce*, would actually be his sixth completed novel). Bunker, who had a voracious appetite for reading books since a child, spent much of his time acquainting himself with the contents of the prison library, accruing, as a result, a vast and encyclopaedic knowledge. Louise Wallis (who by this time Bunker addressed in his correspondence as "Mom") gave him a subscription to the *New York Times Book Review*. Bunker even sold his blood to pay postage costs and the fees for a university correspondence course.

Cars and bars

Bunker was twenty-two when he was finally paroled. It was 1956. He had served almost five years inside San Quentin. The important thing was that he had survived (and without becoming anyone's punk!). But survival on the outside was a different matter. In fact, it seemed a far harder task to do it by honest endeavour, despite the many doors that Louise Wallis opened for him with her altruism. She wanted to assist Bunker in helping himself and pointed him in the right direction by finding him work and accommodation. But Bunker, as a former con, felt ostracised by a society which never truly felt comfortable with convicted criminals in its midst. And besides, after his being banged up for half a decade, the temptations were just too overwhelming.

For a time, Bunker stayed clear of trouble. However, his benefactor, Louise Wallis, evinced increasingly erratic behaviour and seemed at the point of recklessly giving all her wealth away. Although she bought him a car and kitted him out in expensive clothes, Bunker never tried to take advantage of her good nature. After a drunken outburst at her home, Louise Wallis was diagnosed as having a nervous breakdown and while she went to hospital to recuperate, her husband Hal Wallis alienated her network of old friends and acquaintances, including Bunker. He had harboured ambitions of becoming a screenplay writer but overnight had become a persona non gratis in the Wallis household (Louise Wallis would die not long after, in 1962). So he tried his hand at selling used cars for a short time and then worked as a salesman at a small garage owned by an English ex-patriot. It wasn't long, though, before he descended into L.A.'s seamy underworld and returned to crime to make ends meet: orchestrating robberies (though not actually taking part himself, he took a percentage for the planning), forging cheques and involving himself in extorting protection money from pimps.

Within a couple of years, Bunker found himself back on the inside again, having been found consorting with known felons (he happened to be travelling in a car owned by two burglars who had their tools in the boot of the vehicle). Details of Bunker's misdemeanours together with a damning report by his hard-ass probation officer conspired to give him a ninety day jail sentence which included being sent out on work detail to the county farm (where low risk prisoners were sent). Bunker escaped almost immediately by climbing over a poorly guarded fence. He was a fugitive from justice once again and stayed on the run for over a year, despite a couple of close shaves with the police. Robbed of his cash while staying in an hotel during a road trip to New York, Bunker resorted to armed robbery out of desperation for immediate funds.

Inevitably, the agents of justice caught up with Bunker, but not before a failed bank heist and a wild car chase had ensued.

Bunker tried to get out of going back to prison by pretending to be insane. He gave a convincing performance (faking suicide and declaring that the Catholic Church had inserted a radio inside his head!) and was declared criminally insane. Bunker was shunted back and forth between Atascadero State Hospital and the California Medical Facility at Vacaville (where he edited a prison newspaper). Although Bunker was eventually freed, he could not keep out of trouble. His notoriety as a criminal mastermind put him on the FBI's Ten Most Wanted list. In San Francisco in the early '70s, Bunker ran a profitable drug empire. He was eventually caught after the cops had put a tracking device on his vehicle and followed him to Los Angeles where he boosted a bank (in fact, the police couldn't believe their luck—they were under the erroneous impression that a drug deal was going down). With a helicopter and five cop cars on his trail, Bunker was apprehended after a car chase. He expected the book to be thrown at him for the robbery, anticipating at least a twenty-year sentence. Miraculously and largely due to the solicitations of influential friends and a lenient judge, he got only a five year custodial sentence.

Back in prison, Bunker focused on improving his writing skills. His perseverance (he produced six novels and fifty short stories between 1953 and '72) was rewarded by encouraging words from an genuinely interested literary agent. By 1972, Bunker had finally produced a novel, *No Beast So Fierce*, which, after some judicious pruning was accepted by the publisher, WW Norton. At the same time, Bunker's essay "War Behind Wall" about San Quentin's internecine race wars was published in the prestigious *Harper's* magazine.

Straight Time

When Eddie Bunker was released on parole in 1975, he had spent eighteen years of his life in prison institutions. Despite his new career as a writer, for a time, a life of crime still had its temptations, particularly when money got tight. But once Bunker was earning money from his writing and film appearances, he had no need to resort to crime to survive. His own view of his descent into criminal activity was that it was dictated solely by circumstances and necessity—once those circumstances changed for the better, the criminal impulse died in him.

A second published novel, *Animal Factory*, appeared in 1977 and articles followed in *The New Yorker* and both the *New York Times* and *LA Times*. Happily for the ex-convict, the actor, Dustin Hoffman, who had bought the film rights to *No Beast So Fierce*, in 1975, made a favourable deal with First Artists which allowed him not only to direct the movie but also supervise its all-important final cut. But taking on the mantle of director as well as starring in the main role as convict Max Dembo proved too much for Hoffman, who persuaded his old pal Ulu Grosbard to take over directorial duties. To Hoffman's dismay, First Artists reneged on their earlier decision to allow him the final cut and tampered with the film's editing in such a way that Hoffman sued for damages. Controversy aside and despite disappointing critical and commercial responses, *Straight Time* was a good movie and a faithful representation of life in the U.S. penal system. Bunker collaborated with Alvin Sargeant and Jeffrey Roam on the movie's screenplay. The film was also significant for Edward Bunker in that it represented his first acting part in a movie. It would be the first of many fleeting cameos that Bunker would play over the next two decades, including playing the part of a cop (Captain Holmes) in *Tango and Cash* (1988) and culminating with his famous role as Mr Blue in Tarantino's acclaimed *Reservoir Dogs*. Indeed, Bunker's minor thespian exertions even made him eligible for a Screen Actors Guild pension.

In 1979, Bunker claimed that he found true salvation in an attractive young lawyer, Jennifer, whom he married (despite a difference in age and background they are still together and have a young son, Brendan, born in 1994).

In 1981, Bunker produced a third novel, *Little Boy Blue*, which contained some of his most impressive and eloquent writing. In 1985, Bunker wrote part of the Academy Award-nominated screenplay to the film *Runaway Train*, starring Jon Voigt as a fugitive con (Bunker mainly wrote the opening half-hour of the movie depicting prison life).

In 1991, Bunker was cast by wunderkind director, Quentin Tarantino (at the suggestion of Chris Penn) in *Reservoir Dogs* as Mr Blue. Tarantino, in fact, had apparently studied the movie *Straight Time* while attending a course at Robert Redford's Sundance Institute for young film-makers. A couple of years later, in 1994, Bunker was hired as a consultant on the film *American Heart*, starring Jeff Bridges as the con Jack Kelson, who has just been released from the slammer and is hoping to go straight by cleaning windows. In Michael Mann's slick 1995 thriller, *Heat*, starring Al Pacino and Robert De Niro, some of the cast picked Bunker's brain about the nature of the criminal mind (Jon Voigt's character, in fact, was made to resemble Bunker in appearance).

In 1996, Bunker produced his fourth crime novel, the action-packed *Dog Eat Dog*, based upon a story a fellow con had related to him while in prison. His latest book, *Mr Blue*, a candid autobiography, has just been published with the possibility that one of his earlier, previously unpublished novels, a sort of Jim Thompson-esque, noir novel, will follow shortly afterwards.

Ironically, Edward Bunker continues to make a living from crime—but for the last quarter of a century, he's only been writing about it. After having begun life in somewhat unfortunate circumstances in Hollywood some sixty-six years ago, Edward Bunker has returned to whence he came to reside in tinsel town as a model citizen. No longer the human equivalent of an earthquake, Bunker (though still unrepentant about his criminal exploits), lives in relative serenity after many turbulent years evading the law.

Edward Bunker titles can be obtained from

NO EXIT PRESS

978-1-84243-264-8	Stark	£6.99
978-1-84243-266-2	No Beast So Fierce NE	**£9.99**
978-1-84243-267-9	Animal Factory NE	£7.99
978-1-84243-268-6	Little Boy Blue NE	£7.99
978-1-84243-269-3	Dog Eat Dog NE	£7.99
978-1-84243-270-0	Mr Blue NE	**£9.99**
978-1-84243-295-2	Death Row Breakout Stories NE	£7.99

Please send orders to;

HIGH STAKES BOOKSHOP
21 Great Ormond Street,
London WC1N 3JB

Add fifteen per cent P&P. Cheques payable to High Stakes in Sterling drawn on UK bank or pay by credit card (Visa, MasterCard, Maestro) quoting card number, expiry date, 3 digit security code and valid from date and issue number where appropriate

Tel 020 7430 1021
Fax 020 7430 0021

Or order online at www.noexit.co.uk/bunker